MARKING TERRITORY

BOOK 2 OF THE FREELANCE FAMILIARS SERIES

DANIEL POTTER

FALLEN KITTEN PRODUCTIONS

TO MY SPOUSE

Because I love them and to list all the reasons
would more than double the word count of this book.

1

I smiled at the waiter, and when he smiled back without flinching, my vision blurred. My third eyelids pushed away the excess moisture to wet the fur in the corners of my eyes. Mountain lions aren't made to suppress tears.

"Can I take your order, sir?" the waiter asked, his smile briefly fading. *Had he actually seen the tears?* The thought made it even harder to suppress the purr that desperately wanted to rumble out of my throat.

"I- uh-" I looked back down to the table where a thick leather board held a limited menu. I knew what I wanted. I looked to Noise across the table, her own smile broad with an edge of laughter as she watched me. Her usually amber eyes had faded to ice blue thanks to the new moon, and they glowed with delight. She wore a stunning sea green dress that accented her lithe frame. When she'd walked out of her bathroom with it on and her short hair styled with curls, I briefly thought she might have been kidnapped by an extreme makeover TV show. Never in my life had I imagined her looking so lovely.

I took a deep breath through my nostrils, pulling the

sweet scent of succulent beef up into my head, and my mouth flooded with anticipation for the meal.

Pity slipped into the waiter's eyes as I gathered my scattered thoughts. Really, I wanted to savor this moment for as long as I could. Thanks to the Veil that blinded mundanes to any magically-induced weirdness, he surely saw a miserable wretch of a man slumped in a wheelchair despite the snappy tuxedo. I didn't need pity, for this was a triumph! I sat at the table, instead of hiding under it like a pet. He couldn't see my smile filled with teeth designed to crush the windpipes of a deer or the huge paws that awkwardly pushed on the armrests of the wheelchair in which I perched. Nobody but Noise saw the nearly three-foot long tail that protruded from the space between the back and the seat of the wheelchair.

No one could comprehend a reason for a cougar to come into their restaurant dressed in a tuxedo sitting in a wheelchair. Therefore, logically, I must be a man. It was a trick I'd only been able to pull off on the internet or in a dark alley.

"We'll both have the prime rib, sixty-four ounces," I said.

The waiter only blinked once at that, his eyes flashing over to Noise's petite frame before returning to me. "Of course, sir. Will you be having anything to drink?"

I looked to Noise and bathed in her smile. This had been her idea, and gratitude flowed through me like a river flooding its banks. My body itched to press against her, feel her fingers rake through my fur. But jumping over the table for a petting session would definitely shatter the illusion. Instead, the low rumble of my purr became audible.

"I'll have red wine." Her smile dimpled her cheeks. "He can have water."

"Aww," I said.

"Remember last time?" She winked at me.

My ears started to burn before I drew up into a dignified pose and looked down at Noise over my muzzle. Perched on the seat of the wheelchair, my 200-pound feline frame towered over her. "Not at all," I said, even as the memory slammed into my mind, one filled with images of toilets and the taste of vomit on my tongue. Becoming a cougar hadn't done anything good for my alcohol tolerance.

"Lucky you." She rolled her eyes and laughed, shrugging off any effect of my newfound tallness.

"Very good!" the waiter announced. "I'll be right back." He spun on his heels and walked toward the double swinging doors that guarded the kitchen.

I took a moment to look over the Stockyard, the best steakhouse in Grantsville, which is saying something in ruralish Pennsylvania. The place had a rustic ambiance, brilliant white tablecloths draped over the simple lines of Amish-made furniture. Nobody came here to admire the interior design, though. The Stockyard was all about the scent of well-seasoned meat that flooded the room as our waiter pushed one of those doors aside.

I turned back to Noise. "Thank you," I told her. I wanted to follow up with the L word. But we'd both been avoiding that since the change. It sat on the back of my tongue, like a bullet in a loaded gun. There were reasons I couldn't pull that trigger.

"Happy Birthday." She reached forward, and I put my paw on the table, her fingertips touching it before retreating.

Aww, that's so sweet. The biggest of those reasons projected her thoughts into my head. Privacy is a difficult thing to come by when you're a familiar.

O'Meara! I thought-screeched at my magus. *Go away!*

Oops! Sorry! I didn't mean to! Just happened! I'm so bored with this show. My thoughts drifted...

O'Meara, it's my day off. Get out of my head. Unfortunately, the growl I accented the thought with might have been audible.

Going! I could still feel her squeeing as she pulled herself from behind my eyes. She slipped back though our mental link to her own crippled body and shut the door behind her. Lately the 'door' between us had become more like a gauzy see-through curtain than any substantial barrier. O'Meara's injuries had required that I allow her mind to be housed partially in my own brain for some months while hers recovered from saving my hide. But even after she'd moved out, she could slip back in without realizing it herself.

Noise's smile had vanished, her eyes gone stony and dull. The distinct sound of her teeth grinding together filled my ears. "Something wrong?" she asked.

"Nothing. I took care of it." At least O'Meara wasn't looking through my eyes. I could feel her on the other end of the link, noisily paying close attention to a pair of actors on the TV and hoping one of them would have their shirt ripped off soon.

"She was watching again, wasn't she?" Noise growled.

"I sent her home," I said.

Noise took a breath so deep it strained the fabric of her dress and squared her shoulders, placing her hands on the table as she did so. Had it not been a new moon, I suspected the tablecloth would have sustained some claw marks. "Six more months," she muttered to herself; the term I had told her that my contract was up with O'Meara, and a poorly thought out lie. Truth was the bond could be broken at any time I wished. I had my reasons, and the last thing I wanted to do was hurt O'Meara's brittle health, even for Noise.

Noise opened her mouth to say something, but the waiter appeared and her jaw snapped closed. He poured her wine and filled my goblet with water. Whatever she was going to say, she swallowed it down and managed a smile as the waiter departed.

She raised her glass as a mischievous gleam crept back into her eyes. I eyed her quizzically, and she nodded at my water glass. Apparently she wanted to move on from the interruption by testing how far the Veil would stretch tonight. While it had masked my appearance, it hadn't blessed me with actual hands. Still, I braced my thighs against the sides of my chair to avoid toppling onto the table before reaching out with both forepaws to grasp the glass. In these last six months, I'd learned how to do lots of things you wouldn't expect paws could do, but the glass trembled with the effort it took to hold it up from the table. The smooth glass threatened to shoot into the air like a banana escaping its peel. Droplets of water spilled over the rim and wet my leathery pads. I blinked away a sudden haze in my vision as I brought the glass up to clink against hers.

"To new beginnings," she said.

I momentarily racked my brain for something then said, "And happy endings."

She took an effortless sip.

I attempted to do the same, but the water fell out the sides of my mouth and dripped down my chin. I coughed and dropped the glass. Noise's hand shot forward and caught the glass before it had a chance to empty its contents all over the table. She chuckled. "No, you have to clench your lips before you sip. It's possible. I promise. If I can pound back a beer with a foot-long muzzle, you can sip from a glass with your itty bitty one." She leaned over the table and attacked me with a napkin.

A sudden haze pulsed and cracks of purple spidered across my vision. Not real purple, but the neon color of reality-buckling: magic. My heart dove for my stomach as I instinctively seized O'Meara's mind and slammed my vision into hers. I frantically twisted my head around, searching for the source. But there was none. The magic surrounded us like water pouring into a submarine.

Thomas? Aw crap. TRANSITION! O'Meara shouted in my head. *Spell now!*

My ears folded flat against my head. *A transition? Here? Now?* Transitions, a place and time where our reality passes through another and briefly blend, weren't entirely rare; one happened somewhere in North America every day. Yet I'd seen one happen in Grantsville two weeks ago! I didn't have the time to figure out the odds of that cosmic dart throw.

I pulled back from my body as the mental connection between us snapped into clarity and we formed a circuit with our minds. With our deep bond we didn't need a physical circle anymore.

Human magic extends not from rituals and odd hats but from the souls of the magus and her familiar. And real souls aren't little balls of ectoplasm that sit around looking pretty. They are connections to other realities. They stretch in a direction our minds have difficulty fathoming. Not up-down, left-right or forward and back, but another way separate from them all. And in that direction, yee-ward or yee-down, lie realities stacked on top of each other like an infinite sea of flapjacks. In one of those flapjacks is the other end of a magus' soul, their anchor, but it passes through hundreds of thousands of realities along the way. An experienced magus has mapped that pathway, knows what lies where, and can tap into any of those realities to bring their energies to bear. After a brief embrace, O'Meara's mind rocketed away from me, plunging into the thread of her soul. I likewise drifted yee-down into my own thread and braced my awareness, a stake in the ground to O'Meara's kite.

I felt the slightest tug as O'Meara came back through her tunnel. I pulled her back to me, reeling her in like a too-small fish on a line, the hook snagging occasionally on some pondweed. She gasped for breath as she stumbled into our mindspace and pressed a pearl of power to me. The glimmering white thing surged into my body and beyond it.

I opened my eyes to find myself in a crystalline bubble pushing away the purple of bending space around me. White, the color of Order, the universal color of raw magic. There had been no time to craft it into a useful spell, so instead O'Meara let it pour out of me, my body frozen as still as a statue. The Order would protect me from the surge of chaos. I could only watch Noise staring at me with concern as the purple light crept into her and everything around us.

"ThoOOOOOOMAS?" Noise's voice stretched out into an animal bay as everything around me twisted, including her! I couldn't turn my head away as black splotches appeared on her skin.

Her eyes, wide with shock, slid to the sides of her head, pushed there by the growth of a heavy muzzle. Horns erupted from either side of her skull, and her dress strained to contain the sudden bulk of her body and breasts. The glass she held shattered, crushed with the strength of a massive two-fingered hand.

Behind her the wall shimmered from plain white into roughhewn planks. The elegant table before us became a barrel covered with a red-checked tablecloth, and the silverware, wooden spoons and knives. The salt and pepper shakers blossomed into shallow bowls with piles of spice.

Noise held a hand up to each eye. Her mouth, a maw filled with blunt teeth and a black tongue, hung open like a dentist had used too much Novocain. She closed and opened it as if to speak, but all that came out was a loud, panicked MOOOOOO!

Noise clutched at her muzzle. The waiter, or what had been our waiter, appeared. He bleated a question at Noise as he effortlessly balanced on cloven feet, wearing nothing but his blue vest. Noise just stared at him, her huge blue eyes flicking up and down the man's goat-like body. Around us the mundanes, now blended with a reality that resembled a barnyard, continued with their meals, the Veil preventing them from noticing anything unusual had happened.

After a stricken silence, our goat waiter bounded away with an absurd spring in his step. Noise turned her head to regard me with one eye. She still sported human-like lips on the end of her cow's muzzle. She pressed them together and worked her bottom jaw back and forth, feeling out the newness of it. "Haaawmus," she tortured out my name.

Sorry, I couldn't grab enough power to get both of you. O'Meara's voice slid through my mind, the words heavy with exhaustion. A taste of her pain washed through the link. The scent of wrongness and rot rolled over me. She'd reopened that wound, AGAIN.

Yeah I did. It will heal. Always does. But at least you won't be chewing cud with your girl there. That'd be terribly embarrassing for a cat.

What about Noise?

It's a transition. She might have an echo or two, but they should fade in a few days. Next time wear your harness under the tux. She gave a long mental sigh, thought, *Goodnight,* and then slipped away into her exhaustion. Guilt flared up in my gut as I pictured my service dog harness sitting in the back seat of Noise's car where its protective enchantments were of no use to anyone. She'd just hurt herself to protect me once again, and for what? Saving me from looking odder than a talking cougar for a day or two. But I couldn't dwell on that with Noise here in front of me.

The waiter chose that moment to return with two huge slabs of beef.

Noise's nostrils flared and she gagged on the scent of the meat. She clutched at her throat and squeezed tearing eyes closed. Locked in the bubble of stasis, I could only imagine what the fragrance of cooked beef smelled like to a cow.

The purple light had filled everything, but something shifted within it, a shadow passing through everything as if something huge lurked beneath reality. The light flared as the change reversed itself. The bovine features left Noise as quickly as they'd come, and the charming barnyard cafe faded back into the upscale steakhouse, mostly. Small objects scattered throughout the restaurant hadn't made the trip back to our reality. A few wine glasses remained wooden cups, and my plate remained a wooden cutting board, all glimmering a dull gray in my sight and bursting with tass, the raw stuff of spells.

With the last of the purple haze winking out, air found my lungs and my body remembered to breathe. "Noise, are you okay?"

She wiped her mouth and glanced at her plate, her face instantly turning a shade of green. "Oh gods. No, definitely not. I'm sorry, but it smells like death in here. Check please!"

A confused waiter appeared. He looked human, except for the small horns protruding from his forehead. "Is there something wrong, miss?"

Noise stared at him for a moment, her hand flying to the back of her head where a set of horns had protruded moments before. Finding nothing but hair, her hands fluttered down her body, probing for lingering features. The waiter watched with furrowing brow.

I cleared my throat and pulled the waiter's attention to me. "My apologies, but could we have it to go? I'm having a slight health flare up."

Relief smoothed his features. "Uh- Of course, sir. I'm sorry you're not feeling well."

I eyed the glimmering cutting board with my succulent meal perched on top. If I had my guess, the tass it contained was worth several months' salary from O'Meara. "And the cutting board. It's charming."

2

After leaving the restaurant, it became clear that our evening together had come to an end. I needed to get back to check on O'Meara, and Noise grew increasingly disturbed by the fact that the best steak in town smelled like carrion to her. We stopped at her place to change out of our formal duds. Well, she changed into a t-shirt and jeans, and then carefully pulled me out of the custom tailored tux before strapping on my service dog harness. We stowed the cutting board in the tass bag that I keep in the side pocket of my harness, otherwise the tass would evaporate into the ether before too long.

"Are you sure there are no long-term effects?" Noise asked again on the way back to O'Meara's house on the edge of Grantsville.

"Hopefully your sniffer will be back to normal in a few days." I tried to hunker into the back seat. Noise had every reason to be scared, but there was nothing I could really do about it with O'Meara KO'd. "If I had felt like ransacking the restaurant, we could have gotten more tass. But other than that, I don't know much about transitions. I saw one happen at a distance a few weeks ago. If not for that I wouldn't even have had a word for them. And O'Meara hurt herself slamming me into stasis."

"Convenient," Noise growled. Even when fully human the sound was deep and threatening. I rolled my eyes. The two women's dislike for each other was a constant reminder that roses have thorns. To be fair, O'Meara did burn down her parent's home, and Noise's pack snapped our bond while doing their level best to kill me. So there were some acceptable reasons for their grudges. But still, my life would be a bit easier if the two of them would get along. "The waiter's horns didn't appear to be going anywhere," she noted.

He hadn't been the only one either. As we exited, there were more than a few patrons and staff of the Stockyard sporting mementos of their transition to the barnyard side. At least to my nose, Noise smelled completely human. "All those echoes should fade in a few days. We can get Ixey to check you out if you want to be sure."

"I'd rather not have your magi friends looking inside my head. Pa will have a fit if he catches their scents on me." The car turned onto the street that O'Meara lived on. The long wooded path cut through a thick secondary growth forest, with plenty of trees growing between each home. I decided not to point out that it would probably be just as bad for him to catch MY scent on her, and my scent got much deeper in her fur.

We lapsed into silence.

Noise broke it as the car made its final approach to O'Meara's. "I guess I'm fine. Sorry about your birthday."

"It was fun!" My tail tip twitched happily as I remembered actually speaking to a mundane without him asking if I was a good boy. "We have to do that again."

"Well that tux isn't a rental," she said as we pulled into

O'Meara's driveway. It was a perfectly normal two-story white colonial that looked to my eyes like it was decorated with Christmas lights powered with halogen bulbs. Those lights would be the wards. O'Meara had mostly lived in her office before she got injured. The house had been a fallback position, a safe house so heavily warded that even an Archmagus would lose more than his eyebrows burrowing through its protections.

The car stopped and Noise handed back the white bag that contained our dinners. "You sure you don't want one?" I asked.

She shuddered. " No. You enjoy them."

The scent of the meat drifted up and made my stomach growl. Reawakened and ravenous after the adrenaline of the transition had cold-cocked it, my appetite insisted on making up for lost time.

"Good night, Thomas," Noise said, leaning the driver seat way back, allowing me to rub my muzzle against her cheek. She pulled me into an embrace, wrapping her arms around my neck and squeezing me to her chest. A hand found my ear, and we lay there for a long moment, enjoying each other's warmth.

The moment passed and I pulled away. "Night Noise," I replied, taking the bag in my teeth. When I popped the back door open, her hand gently caught my tail on the way out and let it run through her fingers as I exited. I gave her a smile before trotting up the walkway to the front door and pawing the doorbell.

The door had scarcely opened an inch when Tallow's voice greeted me. "Thomas, what the hell did you do this time?" She stood in my way, glaring down at me with steel eyes and thick arms crossed. Her dark brown, not-quite-black hair curled onto itself in a way that made one wonder if it was resentful of the person beneath it and if the feeling was mutual.

I flattened my ears and placed the doggy bag at my feet, readying for the storm.

"She passed out mid-sentence. You made her channel again, didn't you? She was doing so well this week!" Tallow boomed. I'd really hoped she hadn't noticed, but the werewolf matron missed nothing, not even with the new moon clouding her normally supernatural senses.

"Sorry. I got caught in the middle of a transition! I panicked and we did some sort of shield spell. It wasn't a big one. I thought she could handle it," I replied trying to keep the whine out of my voice. It was always my fault when O'Meara channeled.

Ixey chimed in from somewhere behind Tallow, high and slightly halting. "But she assembled it very quickly, no doubt."

"We didn't have much time." I glanced over my shoulder at the woods and the road; Noise's SUV was long gone. I felt exposed. "Could you guys yell at me inside?"

"You're doing nothing for her recovery," Tallow growled. "You do want her to get better, don't you? Because you've done nothing but hurt her lately!" The words closed around my heart like a vice. Tallow was a tower of muscle, particularly during the half moon, but her tongue tended to be even sharper than her teeth, and she wielded truths like morning stars. My ears drooped so low that I'm fairly sure they tried to hide under my chin.

"Let him in, Tallow," Ixey said.

With a grunt she moved aside to reveal Ixey, tiny as Tallow was large and with more than a foot of height difference between them. While the werewolf matron wore gray sweat pants and an oversized t-shirt, Ixey's tailored suit shimmered with silver and gold sequins, and her razor-cut hair was dyed bands of pink, green and red. On her shoulder sat her familiar, Garn, a golden gecko with glimmering gemstones festooning his tiny body. I kept my eyes on him as I padded into the foyer with my meal. He possessed the only eyeballs in the room that weren't casting disapproval in my direction.

The door swung shut, and I felt like a kid who'd broken his curfew under their combined gazes. I could have stopped her, sure. Perhaps I should have, but in that moment I'd been scared and hadn't thought about what it would cost O'Meara. I never think about costs in the heat of the moment and neither did my magus. Or worse, she knew the costs but paid them anyway. Not being able to channel ate at her as if a hungry hyena had been trapped in her rib cage. She seized on any danger I found myself in as a chance to do something, anything. That note of pride in her thoughts before she collapsed into sleep echoed in my head. "Like you would just stand there and not ask for help as the world melts around you," I said.

"Transitions are opportunities for tass, Thomas, not something to be afraid of. You did get some tass, right?" Ixey asked.

"Some," I conceded.

"Give it here then." She held out her hand. "I'll send it up the chain to the Inquisition office."

"Funny," I laughed, taking that for a joke despite knowing she wasn't. O'Meara, as an inquisitor, had to send found tass up the line to her headquarters.

Ixey's hand closed into a fist as her body gave a tremble that I knew to be a sign of frustration. "Thomas, it's not like we can hire someone like Lady Cavell to come and fix the problem! Which means we have to wait for headquarters to care about us again. Any tass up the chain will help."

"O'Meara and I aren't one and the same, Ixey. We've been over that. It's my day off and therefore my tass." I only had to surrender tass O'Meara and I found on official business. Besides, no amount of tass would buy O'Meara and therefore her assistant, Ixey, into the Inquisition's good graces after the incident with her former familiar.

Still, I saw no sympathy in the eyes of the magus or the werewolf, so I took my doggy bag in my mouth and pushed past the pair. If I was going to endure this, I wasn't going to do it on an empty stomach.

Ixey sighed. "I know it's hard, Thomas, but you and O'Meara need to get used to living without her magic."

Tallow's triplets bounced and giggled in their playpen as I passed by on my way to the kitchen. At least they were happy to see me. To my relief neither magus nor werewolf followed. I ate both steaks while chewing over a single question: who the hell was Lady Cavell?

Right off the kitchen was the recovery room. It'd been the dining room, but they'd found settling O'Meara in the first floor much easier than a room upstairs. It stank of sweat, mostly O'Meara's, and a bit of Tallow's. The scent of wolves permeated everything and nibbled at my brain whenever my thoughts drifted. A tiny part of me, even after six months of living with Tallow and her cubs, still hollered about the danger of living in close proximity to wolves. I had nothing to fear from Tallow's cubs other than the really disturbing way they made my stomach growl. Tallow herself, well, she used to respect me. After all, I had sorta helped her deliver the triplets.

O'Meara lay in a hospital bed in the center of the room where the dining table had been. The china cabinet and other furniture had been repurposed to hold her things. Her breaths came easy with a slight whistle as she inhaled. She'd been huge when I'd first met her, but the months of bed rest had withered her body, and the brain injury she'd sustained had destroyed her balance. A wheelchair parked in the corner was her only means of transport. Her bright red hair had grown back in an unruly mop that spilled around her pillow. One hand dangled over the railing, and I padded over to her, took her wrist in my mouth and placed the hand on her heart. I rubbed her cheek with mine.

It hurt every time I entered that room. I could still imagine her as that brash and passionate woman who'd from the moment I met her addressed me as a person and not some intelligent pet. Her injury was my fault. If I'd trusted her more, then perhaps together we could have defeated Sabrina without O'Meara burning herself from the inside out. And now I wasn't doing anything to help her get better.

She did not stir in response to my touch, but her mind flickered in recognition. I felt the presence of an eye on my back. Tallow stood in the doorway, a babe held to her breast. With a nod she moved into the house to tend the rest of her litter. I went to my bed: a supersized deluxe dog bed in the corner. I hated the thing, it reminded me of my dependence on all these people around me. Yet I pulled it alongside O'Meara's bed, like I did every night.

I'd wanted to maintain my own apartment. O'Meara paid me in both mundane money and a little tass, unlike any other familiar. But all the money in the world wouldn't give me back the hands I needed to live independently of my bond. That had to be earned in the magical world. And before I could do that, my conscience demanded I fix what I'd broken. Ixey and Tallow were right. I had to start being the solution to healing O'Meara and stop being an excuse for her to channel.

I lay down in my bed and watched O'Meara's dreams, the rise and fall of memories playing in slow motion across the ocean of her mind.

Sleep didn't come for me, but a certain squirrel did.

"Pssst. Thomas! You up?"

I'd actually watched the rodent peek his head around the doorway, pull a cashew that he'd probably nicked out of the kitchen from his cheek pouch and eat it before crossing the threshold. Despite that, my voice was still heavy with my own exhaustion. "Not up. But not sleeping. Isn't it a bit late for squirrels?"

Rudy shrugged. He was wearing what he called his travel suit, which was a tube of nylon mesh that held an iPhone to his back and a mini-zippo lighter, along with a few firecrackers, to his front. "Had a horror movie marathon and sleep ain't in the cards tonight. Whatcha up to? I texted ya."

My eyes drifted over to my iPad in the corner propped against the wall. I hadn't turned the thing on in a week. The most effective way to use the device was to prod the screen with my nose, which got tedious real fast. "I, uh, missed it."

"No kidding." He scampered over to the iPad, swiped at the dark screen and then rubbed the dust off his paws. "You know if you use it more, you'll get better at it."

"Hmpf." Easy for the squirrel to say. His paws didn't take up half the screen. "Hey Rudy, you ever hear of a magus named Lady Cavell?"

The squirrel paused, his hands reaching for the pad's power cord. "Cavell? Yeah, she's House Morganna. Pretty high on the rankings but generally not considered political enough to go anywhere else. She's almost local. Might even be part of O'Meara's protectorate." Rudy pulled the phone off his back, a motion that could have been awkward if it hadn't been so practiced. After a moment of dithering on it, he said, "Yeah, she's about two hours out of town. Why you —" He glanced up at O'Meara's slumbering form. "Oh oh-oh-oh! Dude, she's like way out of our league. Even if she can fix her, she'll want your first dozen sons, or something worse, like enough tass to swim in."

I hrrmed, "So she's a healer."

"Well yeah, but she doesn't do charity, and there's no Magus health insurance."

"The Inquisitors should cover it," I grumped.

The squirrel shrugged. "Should but won't. O'Meara got placed here in bumbletown for a reason."

"Maybe she's the sort that will take a down payment and a favor. You got her number?" I asked.

Rudy cocked his head. "You think I've got major magi on speed dial?"

"You've named dropped Archmagi before."

"Well she's just not important enough to make that list. Seriously, I've never met the gal, but she probably didn't get where she is by being warm and welcoming." His tail twitched behind him.

I stood. "Then we'll have to invite her for tea."

3

Rudy chittered with amusement when he understood my plan.

I shushed him as I nosed open the door to Ixey's room, which was the only room in the house that didn't stink of werewolf. Instead, pungent incense made my nose itch. On first impression, the room beyond was dark even to my eyes, the heavy curtains closed to a moonless night. Yet as I continued to stare, globes of colored light winked into existence. The magic lights didn't illuminate so much as they formed constellations of objects in the blackness of the room. A small circle of green lights to the left would be the bracelet that Ixey housed her spirit friends within. Nearby, I found the soft blue glow of Garn's aura, composed of thousands of tiny bits that combined into the shape of a gecko.

I thanked the vast unknowns that the pair were soundly asleep and turned my eyes to the other end of the room where a single green LED cast its feeble light and transformed the piles of books and equipment on the desk into monstrous forms. To the left of that sat a roughly rectangular constellation of shifting purple lights, our target and the most complex magical item in the entire house: a transdimensional fax machine of sorts. It teleported letters to wherever its fellows were. But first I needed to find the address.

I felt Rudy's weight shift as he hunkered down between my shoulder blades as I crept into the room, carefully testing the floor board in front of me for give before I applied my full weight. The tip of my tail twitched with every completely silent step. Some humans talk about getting a runner's high; we cats get a sneaky high. There's nothing quite like the thrill of being somewhere but not perceived as being there. I made it all the way to the desk without the slightest change in the pace of Ixey's heartbeat.

The click of Rudy's penlight sounded like thunder in the still room, and the light it cast burned like lightning on my straining eyes. "Alrighty! There's the ledger!" Rudy's whisper seemed to boom.

I shook my head to clear my vision, and Rudy hit the floor with a soft thump.

"What was that for?" he said, his voice a harsh whisper.

I hadn't really meant to dump him off my head, but I decided to own it. "Stop making noise," I said, unable to prevent the grin from spreading.

The glow of the LED from Ixey's desktop computer allowed me to see Rudy's tail waggle indignantly. He gave a small hrmpf. "Damn cats and their sense of humor," he grumbled before jumping onto the desk. The penlight's beam fell on Ixey's massive ledger. The golden symbol of the Inquisition glimmered as the narrow beam of light crossed its surface. The book itself was more than half Ixey's height, as wide as it was tall and as thick as a human arm. It stood in the center of Ixey's doublewide cubical desk on a wooden stand to hold it at a forty-five degree angle. It contained everything

O'Meara and Ixey deemed official business, such as tass accounting, visitor logs and official reports. Most importantly, it had a directory of all North American magi in the back.

As O'Meara was the local inquisitor, there should have been no trouble with me accessing the ledger and I was sneaking into Ixey's room unnecessarily. In the six months I'd lived with Ixey, I'd learned that when it came to mucking with her desk, forgiveness was far easier than permission. Besides, she'd tell O'Meara about the letter and O'Meara would certainly forbid me from sending it.

Rudy carefully set the white envelope he carried onto the desk and hopped onto the ledger. He undid the latch that held the book closed, and I pawed it open, careful not to tear the pages. The paper crinkled beneath my paws as I paged through accounting lists, official reports and a very empty appointment calendar. I kept an ear trained on Ixey, but her heartbeat never changed. I slowed as I leafed through the reports in particular; the history of both Grantsville and O'Meara lay in those pages. I'd seen fragments of her memories from those times, but it would be interesting to see how she viewed the events as they were happening without years of distortions. Alas, they were in Latin and therefore Greek to me.

Finally, we reached the back of the book, a list of names accompanied by their personal sigil. Several entries looked recently crossed out. Maddeningly, the names weren't in alphabetical order and listed only the magus' common name. As a rule, magi avoided addressing each other with anything other than a single name. O'Meara was Mistress O'Meara, not Samantha O'Meara. Most seemed to use their first name. Perhaps there had been a Samantha at the time O'Meara finished her apprenticeship? I mused over names as I randomly flipped between pages, trying to find some hint of organization to the list.

"There!" Rudy called out, triggering a spike of panic to race down my spine. "No! Back one!"

"Why don't you do your alarm clock impression while you're at it," I mumbled as I flipped back to the page. There in the middle of the page sat Lady Cavell of House Morganna. A detailed sigil composed of three snakes wrapped around a rod next to the name; similar to the caduceus logo of my old medical insurance company but with an additional snake. I'd always thought snakes were fitting for an insurance company, and the fact that her sigil incorporated more didn't exactly fill me with hope.

Rudy hissed. "Rotten peanuts. That's gonna be tough to draw. Here, hold this."

I tasted plastic as Rudy shoved the penlight into my mouth. He scrounged up a pen from one of the drawers and then stood, squinting at the sigil. He then pointed at the envelope he stood on until I directed the light there. Poking the tip of his tongue out of his mouth, he concentrated on drawing a lopsided circle. With a huff of frustration, he scribbled it out.

Behind us, Ixey's heartbeat rose and the shaman grunted. Rudy scooted over and started again. He got the circle right, then the T-like rod for the snakes to spiral up, but the snakes themselves quickly devolved into squiggles.

"Rudy!" I hissed, my paws kneading at the mat underneath Ixey's chair.

"It doesn't have to be perfect, but it's gotta be recognizable. Why couldn't you pick somebody like Joseph of Hermes? His symbol's a triangle inside a circle. That would be easy-peasy."

"I bet he gets all the spam mail," I whispered back despite my better judgment.

"Thomas? What are you doing?" The question had been delivered in a flat monotone of total concentration on each sound in the word. Only one person I knew spoke like that. I looked to the left right before I spotted the aura of the gecko directly above me on the ceiling.

"We're sending a letter, Garn," I whispered without looking up. I didn't need my eyes to watch his aura. I could see magic all around me, but I hadn't learned the trick to paying attention to everything at once yet. Rudy made a futile glance around him but I doubted his diurnal eyes saw much of anything beyond the pool of light he stood in.

"You're disturbing Ixey's things," Garn said as Rudy's pen scratched furiously.

"We just didn't want to wake her up, Garn. This is urgent business," I said, hoping beyond hope that Garn was a bit sleep-addled. I didn't know the elemental lizard much at all. He'd never been much of a conversationalist.

Ixey groaned. "Garn? What?"

"Got it!" Rudy cheered. "Wait, no! Planters Peanuts!" He crossed out the sigil and started again.

"Rudy!" I hissed.

"Thomas?" Ixey said and then cursed in a language I didn't understand. I turned to face her, accidentally shining the penlight into her eyes and inducing an "Augh!" as she threw up a hand to protect them.

"Hey! Hold the light!" Rudy demanded.

The lights in the room flicked on.

"That works!" Rudy's furious scribbling resumed.

"What are you two doing in my room in the middle of the night?" Ixey demanded. Garn's aura flared and I braced myself.

"Sending a letter. Didn't mean to wake you," I said in the most innocent tone I could manage.

Ixey winced as if she suffered a sudden pain. Her eyes flicked to Garn and then widened. "No!" She pointed at me and then at Rudy. "No! Whatever you are doing, stop it now!"

"Finished! A masterpiece!" Rudy cried.

Purple flared behind me as the magical fax activated. Ixey's eyes narrowed to slits. "You sent a letter to Lady Cavell, didn't you?"

I groomed my paw. I assume Rudy did the squirrel equivalent behind me, likely head banging and throwing horns. "Maybe," I said.

Ixey slapped her forehead and slowly dragged it down her face. "You are such a child, Thomas. Now everyone in House Morganna will know O'Meara's a cripple."

"So? Maybe this is the first step to her not being a cripple," I said.

"And in the meantime you'll crush whatever dignity she has left. You are a wonderful familiar," she said with enough sarcasm you could butter toast with it. "Now get out." She pointed to the door.

I left with my tail held high and my heart trying to burrow into my intestines.

4

Thomas! What did you do? was the first coherent thought O'Meara had on waking the next morning. Ixey's words had been bouncing around my head all night, stirring up anxiety and guilt into a hairball-producing cocktail. Fortunately, the downstairs toilet didn't clog easily or else I'd have earned the ire of all three women in the house within the span of twelve hours.

Regardless, the events of last night spilled from my mind into hers like a bursting fire hydrant. O'Meara was still for a long moment as she sorted through the thoughts. She didn't say anything until she finished, but the heat of her anger grew with every passing second. She finished and then gave me a look that if she had been channeling the barest iota of power probably would have melted the flesh from my bones. *That wasn't your decision to make, Thomas. This is my problem.*

Luckily I had been prepping for this conversation all night instead of sleeping. *Your injuries are my fault! Therefore, as your familiar, I have the right to explore other options since the Inquisition isn't lifting a finger to help you.*

We'd circled around who had been more pigheaded the night she'd been injured again and again. It was an argument I knew the contours of. We'd never agreed, but I knew how to end it. Today O'Meara didn't rise to that bait. *I cannot accept favors from a House, Thomas! They'd expect something in return. I'd be in their pocket.*

You're not an inquisitor at the moment. You passed your sword to Ixey. You expect that not to get out?

O'Meara's anger collapsed into a wave of sullen despair. Her eyes shifted from mine to the blank TV on the wall as she spoke."Lady Cavell's price will be too high, Thomas." She closed the link between us, but fear leaked through anyway.

"Can we make that determination after we hear what it is? Maybe it will make the Inquisition feel guilty and actually respond to your request for a healer. They haven't even sent someone to evaluate you!"

"Lady Cavell probably won't come either." O'Meara rolled over and closed her eyes, ending the conversation.

She was wrong.

A limo pulled up to the driveway at noon sharp and sent the household into a full-blown panic.

"Ixey! Why didn't you tell me we were having company?" Tallow bellowed when we heard the engine pull into the driveway.

"She's here?" Ixey answered, half cry half squeak. She'd spent the entire morning in her room magicing up a ward on her door that appeared to be tuned specifically to cougars and squirrels. The next time I wanted to send a letter I'd have to sneak through the window or tunnel through the attic.

Ixey nearly jumped down the entire flight of stairs and gawped at the state of the living room, which was a scattered mess of baby stuff. It actually looked far better than it had a week ago. Six-month-old humans were containable; six-month-old werewolves were not. With a wave of Ixey's hand, half a dozen balls of yellow energy were zipping around the living room, grabbing toys and baby items. Too bad the spirits seemed to have no idea where to go. After a brief moment of hovering in confusion, they started shoving things under the couch with frantic abandon. Tallow, returning from ushering her children upstairs to her bedroom, watched from midway up the stairway, her arms crossed and head shaking. No doubt she was imagining digging all that stuff out after the dignitary left.

Thomas! Help me get in my chair. O'Meara's thoughts cut short my viewing of the magically enhanced cleaning. I padded into the recovery room to find her struggling to pull herself out of bed. I hopped into her chair and piloted it to the side of her bed. O'Meara gritted her teeth as the room spun around her. My stomach churned as her vertigo over-flowed into my own head, and I stumbled out of her chair. O'Meara stood on her own two feet for a precious few seconds but began to wobble, fighting against the vertigo. I stood next to her and arced my back, offering myself as a handhold.

Is today the day? I thought at her encouragingly. She'd walked to the door last week, and then promptly vomited.

With a defeated sigh, she flung herself into the waiting chair. *Not today. I don't want to greet your guest stinking of vomit.* The dizziness subsided the instant her legs no longer bore her weight. She'd been making great progress from being nearly paralyzed when she first came out of her coma but had plateaued recently with this vertigo proving resis-tant to any healing energy Ixey could find.

I nosed under O'Meara's hand and enjoyed a few pets as

we listened to Ixey plead with Tallow to help her move some of the furniture around.

I'm not happy with you today, Thomas, O'Meara thought at me even as she scratched my ears hard enough that I couldn't help myself from leaning into the sensation. *Feels like you've shoved me into a carrier and whisked me off to the vet.*

Guilt burbled in my stomach as the doorbell rang, my entire body flinching at the sudden chime. We both folded our misgivings away. Showtime.

* * *

Lady Cavell looked like she'd walked off the stage of a country western show and through our front door. She had a finely sculpted body clad in skin-clinging jeans and a denim jacket with dangling fringe along the sleeves. Her hair spilled down her back in blond waves, while her ice-blue eyes scanned the room from a face that probably would be carded as long as the bartender remembered to look at her face instead of her chest. So blinded by this unmagi-y looking magi that I didn't even see the rattlesnake draped over her shoulders until he stuck out his forked tongue to sniff the air.

Well that's a new face for her, O'Meara commented.

Ixey blinked and gave the senior magus a half bow. "Welcome, Lady Cavell and Humphrey to the O'Meara Household. We are pleased that you answered our invitation so promptly."

Lady Cavell smirked. "Yes and I'm sure it was sent with your blessing and approval." Her eyes lingered on the sword slung behind Ixey's back. "Inquisitor. Interesting."

"Won't you come in?" Ixey smiled widely, showing the white of her teeth as she moved out of the way.

I resisted the urge to roll my eyes. Magi were worse than cats when it came to posturing.

Lady Cavell's high-heeled cowboy boots clomped as she walked across the beaten hardwood floor to where O'Meara and I waited. She looked down at O'Meara and shook her head. "You should have called on me sooner. How long have you been in that chair waiting for the Inquisition to send a medic?" Her voice flowed like a mother talking to a child.

O'Meara's anger bubbled, but she kept a straight face. "Won't you sit down, Cavell? Tea will be a moment." She gestured at the couch across from us.

"Coffee, if it's not too much trouble." Lady Cavell flung herself into the couch. It squeaked. After a moment of surprise, she dug out a squeaky bone from between the cushions. Humphrey flicked his tongue at it with interest before Tallow plucked it out of her hand and deposited a tray with two steaming cups on the table in a single motion.

"Coffee's going to take a bit of time. Tea's ready now," Tallow said, already walking away. Cavell's eyes followed her all the way back to the kitchen.

"It was good of you to respond to Thomas' message so quickly," O'Meara said. "I know House Morganna's troubles keep you busy."

"House Morganna's troubles have so far not resulted in actual injuries, so I've actually had plenty of time on my hands. I let the Crones handle the politics. And the letter was charming. The penmanship was almost as bad as Humphrey's." The rattler looked annoyed for a moment, but she mollified him with a scratch to his head. Her eyes went to my paws. "And this is the talk of the town then? Thomas the cougar? You refused to join the TAU?"

"That's me," I admitted. This was the first time I'd heard someone mention the Talking Animal Union in several months. I'd figured Oric had written me off as a lost cause. "I preferred finding my own bond."

The snake's eyes narrowed, and I felt a prickle on the back of my neck. "And your own unique way of bonding," he said.

I circled around the back of O'Meara's chair, trying to shake his gaze. "Hey, stop with the deep scry. Not on a first date." The less folks knew about Mr. Bitey, the multidimensional snake anchored at the base of my neck, the better.

There were reasons besides the state of my tass stores why I hadn't reached out to Cavell earlier, O'Meara chided. I could see a pile of reasons inside her head. Some of them good, some of them mere excuses.

The snake's eyes remained narrowed, and I could feel him probing. "We came because you mentioned that Archmagi Archibald had a direct hand in your awakening," Humphrey said. "Even left you a fey chain to avoid the TAU."

O'Meara stiffened in surprise and a bit of fear. "Archibald is dead. Thomas awakened due to his death shock." *Is that what they're after? Confirmation that Archibald's really gone?*

I couldn't help but think of the faint outline I'd seen after the dragon had left.

O'Meara stomped on that image with a mental army boot. *Thought you saw. It was the end of a long day and nobody was in their right mind.*

"He's dead. Definitely." O'Meara stared at the young-looking magus.

"You're sure?" Lady Cavell asked with the hint of a drawl. "The man is known for centuries of scheming."

"Archibald was over three hundred years old and his mind had begun to fail. He had gotten sloppy and it allowed

Sabrina to murder him in hope of taking his position on the council," O'Meara said.

Humphrey's tongue flicked out and in. "And you sustained your injuries defending Archibald?"

O'Meara guffawed. "HA! No!" She coughed. "Sabrina attempted to resist her incarceration for Archibald's murder."

"If she rid the world of that crazy bat, she should have been applauded!" Lady Cavell sniffed. "The man attempted to destroy the Veil and they didn't even fully strip away his council seat!"

O'Meara straightened. "And had Sabrina not attempted to kill me, she'd be able to make that case."

Lady Cavell smirked. "So she is dead. Not missing like the reports say."

One of O'Meara's hands had drifted to the back of my neck. It tightened at that moment. "You are very well informed. I have no body and there was no death shock. So she is officially missing."

"So you fought. The same night the two Archmagi disappeared? No one recorded their death shocks either."

I cut in. "I fail to see how this is all relevant to you helping O'Meara with her injuries. Which I hope is the real reason you came."

"In good time, Thomas. No one here is bleeding out. I want to make sure I don't wind up tangled in an Archmagus' scheme. I will not find myself entangled in another coup attempt by the fool of a man." Cavell spoke with the venom that I'm sure Humphrey possessed. I had to wonder if she hated Archibald so much, why did she live less than three hours away?

"Archibald is dead," O'Meara said. "Ixey and Garn will

vouch for that under the oaths. I did not have a familiar at the time."

"Did you have a familiar at the time you battled Sabrina?"

"No," O'Meara said. "We bonded shortly after." She patted my neck.

The pair blinked as one. Cavell furrowed her brows. "Now I am curious. I'll see what I can do for you. I'll need a circle."

O'Meara nodded. "We'll need to go down to the basement then. Tallow, if you could..."

5

Set into the concrete floor, a circle of silver shone under the light cast by a single bulb hanging from the ceiling. This was the house's third circle.

Cavell eyed the bulb with suspicion. "Well this won't do." She closed her eyes for a moment, Humphrey's rattle flicked to the tip of his nose, and I watched as a tiny spell wove between them. With a flick of her finger, the spell spread through the room, and the basement lit up. The light came from everywhere yet nowhere at once. Nobody had the faintest of shadows. "Much better."

Their bond isn't as deep as ours if Humphrey needs to circle his body like that, O'Meara observed with smug pride. She was still being carried down the stairs by Tallow in a folding chair.

I gave her a mental hug and asked the senior magus where O'Meara needed to be.

"Place her in the center, please."

Tallow did so and quickly retreated to a corner, as if invisible.

"Good. This might take some time." She stood on the

edge of the circle, eyes on O'Meara, and went still. For a several minutes the only movement on her person was Humphrey's tongue flicking in and out of his mouth. Slowly, Humphrey slid down from his perch and began to circle around O'Meara. He moved oddly, always keeping his eyes on O'Meara, who watched him until he circled beyond the range of her neck's ability to turn. I felt prickles along the edge of my mind as our link itself coiled. Usually the link felt like little more than a gateway, but certain situations made me aware of it. Like swallowing cold water on an empty stomach, the length of the link betrayed itself as it moved to avoid the gaze.

"That's not where the problem is," I said.

"But it is an answer to why she is not dead." Humphrey's gaze did not waver as he extended his head as high into the air as he could manage.

"Yes," I acknowledged. "We had to share space for a bit."

"The bond is wider than most who've shared a link for centuries."

"Our link is not the problem," O'Meara said.

"No. It is not. I see scars of extensive power burns all along your thread. Your body is recovering, but your thread-your soul-is infected. Can you channel at all?"

"Yes, but it knocks me out." O'Meara gave a deep sigh.

The snake nodded. "Every time you do you rip the soul equivalent to scar tissue open, and then the infection rushes into both your minds. Not healthy at all. We suggest you stop channeling or the thread itself risks snapping."

A bolt of shock passed through us both and we quickly buried it. "We're hoping you can do a bit more than tell us that. Ixey figured that much out," I said. Though Ixey hadn't mentioned the danger of O'Meara's soul actually snapping.

The snake reared back. "There are more advanced inter-

ventions. The walls of the thread were burned but still function. O'Meara can think and dream. We can weave a web to
support the thread and insert reinforcements in particular
weak points. It would restore your capacity to eighty percent
in a few weeks."

"Great! Let's do that," I said.

The snake rounded at me. His eyes narrowed. "It is not a
simple procedure. We could not attempt it without compen-
sation for both the resources and time."

"How much?" I looked the snake in the eyes.

He cocked his head and appeared to give the matter
thought. "One hundred groat."

I winced. I'd hoped medical expenses were cheaper on
this side of the Veil. No dice on that front. One groat was the
amount of tass due to a low ranking magus in a single
month. For a working class magus, that was about nine
years of wages. And I didn't have much to haggle with.

I told you this would be a waste, Thomas, O'Meara thought,
covering her eyes to blink away her blurring vision.

*Hey, these transitions keep happening and maybe we could
afford it. Lemme work this out.* That incident with Noise had
been the second transition I'd seen in as many weeks. If the
dragon I had freed had done something to make them occur
more frequently around here, then maybe, just maybe, I
could get that tass. "Hey, Tallow," I said. "Could you bring me
the little black bag from my harness?"

The woman nodded and hurried up the stairs.

"Would you take a down payment?" I asked Humphrey.

*Thomas! You are not allowed to spend your tass wages on
me! I thought you were saving that to get your thumbs back?*
O'Meara argued.

A shiver passed through both magus and snake as Lady
Cavell began to move. "That would depend on how much

This indoor/outdoor decal is reusable.
Apply to any clean dry surface.
It is not permanent and can be removed without residue.

there is," she said, bending her neck to the side so it made several sharp cracking noises.

Tallow returned, holding what would appear to a mundane as a black dice bag. She presented it to Lady Cavell as Humphrey spiraled up her body to reclaim his perch around her shoulders. She opened the bag and allowed him to peer in. I wasn't really sure how much groat was in the bag. It had everything I'd grabbed from the restaurant as Noise and I had made our exit, as well as my tass wages from O'Meara.

Lady Cavell's eyes widened slightly, but she shook her head. "I'm sorry, but five groat isn't nearly enough. I would like to help, but my own resources are very thin. I'm not attempting to gouge you, but I need a substantial portion of those resources to build the spells required for treatment. House Morganna can't forward anyone those resources on loan. Even inquisitors."

FIVE GROAT! Bloody ashes, Thomas! How the heck did you get that much tass? O'Meara stared at me before shaking herself and redirecting her attention to address Cavell. "I can double that," she said, her voice smooth, collected.

Humphrey made a soft hissing sound. "In normal times we could petition the Crones for the tass, but with the loss of the Mother Grove last year and the succession of the Council of Merlins in question every scrap of tass is precious to our House."

Cavell handed back the bag to Tallow, sadness in her eyes. "I'm very sorry. I've seen this happen before, and it's hard for familiars who find themselves in these situations." She turned to O'Meara. "All I can offer the both of you is to put a block on your thread so you can't damage yourself further. Some minor spells to aid the healing and perhaps a lesson or two to your apprentice on how to apply some soothing spells. It will help and speed physical recovery."

"But we are still talking decades." O'Meara bit her lips as bitter disappointment flowed out of her like a river. She'd allowed a kernel of hope to form when the healer had arrived, like a pearl in an oyster. Now that hope had been crushed. For other well-liked, well-appointed people, her illness could be healed, but it appeared she would be left in the bottom of the barrel to rot. Again.

I only had one bargaining chip. *Thomas don't. It's not worth it.*

I spoke as fast as I dared. "Look, you're right. Our bond isn't the usual type. I was one of the Archmagus' final projects. If you can help O'Meara now, I'd cooperate in helping you study it. That could be very valuable."

Cavell regarded me carefully. "And you wonder why I ask if the man is truly dead? Bonds aren't my interest nor my expertise. Now let me show you the little we can do. Please understand I would like to help you both."

I looked into her face and saw none of her earlier hostility, a hint of pain in her eyes and lines where there hadn't been any before. I understood perfectly. I understood I was going to need a hell of a lot more tass.

6

True to her word, Lady Cavell lingered for several more hours, doing what she could without using tass. She assured us with her new treatments O'Meara's vertigo would begin to ease within a month.

Once she left, I drifted toward the kitchen where I found Rudy perched on the rim of a Costco can of cashews that had somehow made it onto the kitchen counter.

"Where the hell have you been?" I asked.

"I mon't like moctors," he said with a cashew stuffed into a cheek pouch.

"Particularly doctors with snakes?" I popped my paws up onto the counter.

"Doctors who are also snakes actually. Worst kind."

I caught the gist. "Humphrey had been human before?"

He nibbled on a nut clutched between his paws. "Dats the rumor. From the age when doctors were as likely to kill you as heal you. Chances are he ain't that good of a doctor to begin with if he Awakened. So snake oil lady can fix O'Meara's mojo?"

I pried open the fridge and fished a thawed steak out of the crisper drawer. I tossed that on the counter next to Rudy before carefully removing a clean plate from the dish rack. The plate joined the steak on the counter with a slight clack of ceramic on marble. "You don't happen to know where a cougar can find a hundred groat lying around?"

Rudy dropped a half-eaten nut back into the can with a bark of laughter. "Gee, I dunno. Rob the Council or House Hermes?"

"Don't even think about it." O'Meara's chair whirred though the doorway that opened to her recovery room. "You two have been enough trouble for one day." She reached past me, grabbed the plate with the steak on it and whisked it off to the microwave.

Hey! I had that handled, I protested mentally.

She punched in a minute warming time while remembering the various times I'd broken dishes. "Don't give me that. Yes, you can do it, but you always make a mess."

I grumbled in annoyance, but the scent of the meat filling the air eased the losing of that battle. "I'm going to get that tass, O'Meara," I said.

"You're not, Thomas. Nobody in this house is ever going to see that much tass in one place. I'm not worth it," O'Meara said. She extracted the steak from the radiation box and wheeled toward me. "I'll be perfectly satisfied if I can walk again, magic or no magic." She smiled, but it didn't reach her eyes. "I'll have to be patient. I lived as a human for my first fifteen years. I will... adjust. Officially resign my commission. Hell, people have been wanting me to do that for years." As she talked, her gaze became distant, long, useless years spiraling out beyond her.

I called her back by placing a paw on her knee.

"O'Meara! It's not impossible. I mean, I got three groat of tass yesterday from that transition. And there was more there! Lots more."

O'Meara shook herself, pushing her imagination away. "That tass is a windfall that should, by rights, go up the chain to the Inquisition."

I reached out and plucked the plate from her lap, carefully deposited it on the counter and placed my head where it had been. O'Meara's fingers slid through my head fur. "Are you suggesting I do that?"

"No. But technically you're my familiar so you gathering it counts as me gathering it. You should spend it. That should be enough for Ixey to rig up a spell that would allow you to operate a microwave without ripping them open."

I would not be deterred, even by the temptation of thumbs. "How often do transitions happen?"

O'Meara's fingers quested for the spots that made thought difficult. I twisted, pressing my ears against her stomach. Denied them, O'Meara shifted to petting my neck and back. "They happen. Randomly. They're not good ways to acquire tass. They're impossible to predict, and the tass fades in less than an hour afterward. Most tass from the Houses come from shallowings, stable overlaps between realities."

Or grinding up live dragons, I thought.

That, as far as I know, is not a common practice. O'Meara fought back against a tide of memories from that night.

"So Thomas isn't even allowed to look for the scratch to help ya?" Rudy asked.

"He's my familiar. For legal purposes he's me. Normally, the Inquisition handles all the needs of their members. If they have a legitimate need for a quantity of tass, it will be provided," O'Meara said, unable to keep the bitterness from creeping into her voice. "And it generally works for members in good standing."

"Well, maybe I shouldn't be your familiar anymore." The thought and the words slipped out before I had the chance to consider them.

The petting stopped. Cold dread poured out of the link. *No. Please.*

Despite that, we could both see the truth. Initially the bond had saved O'Meara's life. But now Ixey and Tallow were right. As long as O'Meara and I were bonded, there would be a temptation to channel. If I stayed, there would be no magic and I'd have no purpose. I'd be an overgrown house pet, bored, listless and eventually resentful.

Thomas please, not yet. Wait until I can walk again. Both hands pressed down on me as she flipped through things she could offer, reasons for me not to go.

That was the second transition I had seen in a month, O'Meara. What-ifs spiraled through my head. What were the odds that the transition had something to do with Archibald's dragon? Maybe the hole in reality at Valentine Park was finally starting to heal? Could that cause an increase in transitions? I'd gotten three groat from one item at the restaurant. I had seen dozens of tass lights in there. A hundred groat might not be that hard. Excitement at the thought of it sent the tip of my tail twitching. And if that didn't work, I could find a new client, get better pay and get O'Meara up on her magical feet again in a few years at max. I could be useful.

Across the link, O'Meara's mind had become a storm of contradictory thoughts. *Balls of fire, Thomas! Stop being so enthusiastic!* Sadness rolled over the link, and I realized she had both arms around my neck and there was a creeping wetness on the top of my head where she had pressed her face. Thoughts and objections swarmed in her mind and faded. Things like *it will never work, I'd forget about her,* would surface and then be buried again.

It can work, I assured her.

The pressure of her arms became crushing. *I have only one reason for you not to leave me, and it's not enough to keep you.* Anger rumbled within her. *And it's really a reason to let you go.* She pulled away and I looked up into her green eyes that, although wet, had regained some of that spark. "I love you. If it were up to me, I'd never let you go." She laid her mindscape bare before me. I fell into her, our minds melting together for a moment, meshing together like a key and lock. She'd known and feared the echoes of her own thoughts. *I'm only letting you go because I want you back. Understand that,* she thought as we cradled each other.

We sorted through our brief time together, moments of bravery on both sides. I saw her, hair blazing with fire, again facing down Sabrina with searing beams bearing the heat of the sun, pouring everything she had into protecting me while I dealt with the dragon. Earlier in that moment I'd had a chance to reconnect our bond, but I hadn't taken it, leaving her to face that terrible woman with only her fire. It hadn't been enough. Had I trusted O'Meara, Sabrina might have been defeated without a desperate deal with a dragon, the consequences of which would surely fall on us all once the Council of Merlins finished politicking.

She scoffed at my depiction of her. *Facing Sabrina was my own decision. It's not something you need to fix, Thomas.*

Yes it is. I'm going to fix at least something in this world. You're a good place to start. With that I pulled myself away from her, although her arms squeezed me tighter as we sorted ourselves into our own heads. Both of us left pieces behind. I stirred the being in the back of my mind that was my link. Mr. Bitey sleepily answered and our deep connection slowly began to close.

We shared a last inhalation together and breathed out alone.

7

It didn't hurt. Yet at the same time it was unbearable. I reached out with my mental limb and found nothing. It's a piece of you that you either don't have until you have a link or is an undeveloped vestigial thing, like the muscles in your ears. Yet once you use it, once you depend on it, it's an arm, a hand, a tongue, an eye and a cell phone all rolled into one pseudopod. Now there was nothing but the tiny mind of Mr. Bitey. Focused and uncaring, the snake pulled itself from the fabric of our reality and re-spooled itself into three-dimensional space.

Rudy chittered as a cobra constructed of fine jewelry chain manifested in the air beside me, its tail rooted in my spine. Without a word or sound it slipped around my neck three times and disappeared in my thick fur.

I breathed and opened my eyes. I found O'Meara's face and licked away a tear.

"Ow! Cat tongue!" She pushed me away, only to trap me in a firm bear hug. "Seven," she said as she reluctantly let me go.

Seven. I was the seventh familiar she'd had. Most magi

have one for life and the oldest and unfortunate might have three. O'Meara had lost seven in her relatively short life. It was both unheard of and a deep shame. I'd been different. I never intended for our bond to be lifelong, but O'Meara had always hoped that I wouldn't be that special after all.

She forced the most pained smile I have ever seen on her face or anyone's. "It was a good run. Thank you."

A chunk of me wanted to say I had just made a huge mistake and reverse what I'd just done. The deal with the dragon had given me absolute power over a bond. Mine. I could rebind her with a thought. Then I wouldn't be cold and alone in my own head. I found myself pressing into her hands, rubbing my scent on her. "I'm going to make you better, O'Meara. I swear it," I thought, then whispered.

"You'll try, I know that. But you don't owe me anything," she whispered back and let me go.

I didn't want to argue the point anymore. I looked to Rudy, who immediately stuck his head in the cashew can. "Come on Rudy. Let's go."

Rudy popped back up with both cheek pouches stuffed for the road. "What? Ah okay. I'm about full anyway." With a graceful spring, he arced through the air and landed on my back.

We left out the back door. I didn't have the energy for any more goodbyes.

8

"Now you're free! Free to travel the world! See the sights, smell the femmes and mark your territory!" Rudy sang as soon as we got out of earshot of the house. We were traversing my usual path in the woods behind the homes and I'd turned toward town.

"I'm not free at all, Rudy. I gotta get that tass. A hundred groat," I huffed.

"That's a tall order, and we ain't talking human height. We're talking 500-year-old oak tree tall. You only get that tall after getting all gnarled and twisted," Rudy said between crunching on nuts.

I chuckled. "Someway, somehow."

"Wait on the highway and show some leg. We hitch a ride to Vegas. There's trouble there that's gonna need shooting."

"I'm still thinking local. I don't think the Veil would like us in Vegas." I stopped to rub an itchy shoulder against one of my favorite scratching trees.

"No seriously," Rudy said, "there's no Veil in Vegas. What happens in Vegas stays in Vegas. Anything magical happens and munds assume it was all a wild bender. Most magical city in the USA. If you want clients to get this whole freelance familiar thing happening, go there. I'll dig you up a fedora somewhere."

"I'll think about it," I said, itch now banished, and resuming my stroll.

Rudy beamed. "We could be partners! Troubleshooters in the wild world of magi. Be a great act. You with your chain snake and me with the... awesomeness. We take Vegas by storm!"

"I suppose your expertise with explosives doesn't get put on the business card?"

"OH OH! That's right! Fireworks are still legal in Vegas! Oh, I can get all the best stuff delivered if we go there!"

I had a mental image of a door bearing the words 'Thomas and Rudy, Freelance Familiar Agency' on a pane of smoked glass shattered by a swarm of bottle rockets. "You're not allowed to doctor fireworks in the office!"

"Who said anything about an office?" Rudy protested.

"Well, if I have a fedora, then I need an office for dangerous dames to come into and tell me their sad stories about how their no-good husbands are trying to frame them for murder," I said.

"No no no. That's New York. PI's in Vegas wear mirrored shades and Hawaiian shirts."

Rudy and I continued to debate the proper way to run a freelancing office in Las Vegas as I wandered through the forest. I'd originally set out with a destination in mind but got so involved in the conversation that I defaulted to patrolling my territory, enjoying, if just for a few hours, not having to be careful with my thoughts. I had no intention of moving to Vegas. Noise lived in Grantsville, and the only shot of getting that tass quickly would be here. Nevertheless, entertaining the idea without guilt was fun.

As the afternoon stretched I realized I'd been drifting toward Noise's place. She'd be happy to hear that I no longer had a magus looking over my shoulder. And she'd have a fridge full of meat.

Rudy and I had lapsed into silence after a surprisingly heated discussion on whose name goes first on the door to our hypothetical office when I saw it. A purple flash in the dark of my eyelids.

"TRANSITION!" I sprang to my feet so fast that Rudy cried out.

"Hey, what's the big idea? You nearly launched me into orbit!" Rudy chittered as I broke into a trot.

"There's a transition up there! Get my tass bag out!" I broke into a flat out run as I saw the outline of a large house emerge from the thinning trees. "You can hop off when we get close. My harness has a focus that should protect me from getting warped." The light of the magic shone ever brighter; if this transition was like the one with Noise, then I didn't have much time.

"Got it!" Rudy said as I reached a fence that guarded the backyard, a tall wooden job painted a dull brown. Standing on my hind legs, I peeked into a yard littered with colorful toys. A daycare center. Beyond it stood a ranch house that had been expanded into the backyard. I swore internally. Little kids wouldn't be able to read the letters on my harness that spelled out SERVICE DOG. They'd see a huge cat. If they all screamed 'Kitty!' then the adults might see a cat too.

Worse than that, the back door had a hated round knob on it. With a growl, I circled around to the front. Rudy leapt onto the fence and paused. "Hey Thomas," Rudy said.

"Stay there. I'll be right back." The front door had a

handle. I leapt over the front gate and batted it open with a paw.

The front door opened into a living room scattered with more toys. The scent of drool, tears and youth smacked me in the face. My brain sorted through the scents: seven kids hung in the air along with three-ish adults.

None were in sight, although I heard muffled voices and the sound of...chewing?

I blew a breath out of my nose to clear it and centered myself, willing my vision to find light that came from something other than photons. Tass was fairly dim, and it was hard to see the grayness of it against the purple suffusing every surface.

Yet I found a spot of it fairly quickly, if only because it was moving in my general direction, keeping to the sides of the walls. It crept closer, zipping between toy chests and bookcases. It paused for a moment beneath a small trashcan by the door.

Tiring of being stalked, I batted the can out of the way. There, crouched against the wall, was a fuzzy black and white lump of fur staring at me with beady black eyes: a guinea pig.

With a sudden squeal, the overgrown tribble leapt at me. It pounced on to my foreleg, and I recoiled before the sting of its tiny teeth registered. The guinea pig rocketed across the room, hitting the plush carpet, bouncing once and rolling to a stop. The bugger didn't pause for breath before beelining straight for me, screaming a war cry at the top of its tiny lungs.

I had no time for suicidal guinea pigs. I smashed it with a slap of my paw and popped his little skull. I waited a few more seconds for him to stop twitching before picking up the body with my teeth and twisting around to slide him into one of the side pouches in my harness.

Something about that pig didn't taste right, and I chewed at my tongue to try to scrape off the wrongness.

A voice screamed from deeper in the house. "FOOOD! MORE FOOD!"

Then a chorus of higher pitched voices. "FOOOOOD!"

I got a prickling feeling from the top of my neck to the tip of my tail, which lashed with my agitation. I could see dim dots of tass moving beyond the far wall of the room. The doorway led into an expansion in the back. Tass usually didn't collect in people. Were there more pets affected? Maybe more rodents in the walls?

Several different parts of my brain had come up with compelling reasons to turn tail and run away. Yet, O'Meara needed tass, and therefore I needed tass. Then my life would probably get complicated again, but for now I focused on that simple need. I should at least take a peek. And I might have been a bit curious as to what was happening to these people. I crept through the doorway and down the hall. It had doors on either side before opening into a larger area. The commotion was coming from the right. The dots of tass were in there, some in motion, some stationary.

"FOOD! FOOD!" The cry was repeated constantly. I cautiously poked my head around the doorway. The room was straight out of a daycare worker's nightmare, with kids swarming all over the kitchen like oversized insects. The contents of a double door refrigerator lay scattered over the floor as children crammed the contents into their mouths without bothering to rip open the packaging. Other children had climbed to the cabinets. The air was filled with the sounds of crunching and smacking of lips.

The sole adult stood in the corner; her arms filled with snack bags of Cheetos, which she was shoving into her mouth, swallowing, foil bag and all, her neck distending with each one.

The tass was in each person's stomach, centered on their rapidly distending bellies.

I didn't mean to stand there long. There was nothing I could do, and I wasn't about to harvest that tass at all. The scene, the bizarreness of it, emptied all thoughts out of my brain.

A kid finished her frozen pizza and its box, searched the room for her next target and found me. Her eyes widened with delight, black with no irises, bottomless pits. She grinned too wide, showing too many teeth crowded into her tiny mouth and all too jagged. "KITTY MEAT!" she squealed in sheer delight.

Then every eye in the room was on me. All black pits of hunger.

"FRESH MEAT!" they screamed, as if my body had been composed of ice cream.

Time to go. They charged. I ran.

Sprinting back down the hallway, I heard the beating of tiny hands and feet behind me. Four kids made it through the door, running after me on all fours, like demonic monkeys, faster than any tiny harbingers of death had any right to be. I mentally screamed out for O'Meara and slammed into the ironclad wall in my head as my body slammed into the door. The door didn't give because it opened inward! Of course it also had a smooth knob on this side! My teeth slipped off. Then the kids were on me and I had to dodge and weave around their gooey hands and tiny maws. Kicking one away, I fled along the side of the room. The purple tint to the world started to fade, the transition ebbing away. I just had to keep them at bay for maybe a minute more without hurting them.

I followed the same route the guinea pig had followed in reverse, adjusting for being thirty times its size. The kids might be possessed, but they were still rather clumsy. Shoving toys and chests and boxes into their path confounded them briefly.

The adult had no such trouble. She burst from the hallway with a bellowing roar of "MEAT!" The cleaver in her hand looking as hungry for my flesh as her distended mouth.

I shot down the hallway and juked left, slamming my body against a closed door. The old latch burst, and the door spilled me into a bathroom. Skidding to a stop, I reversed and slammed my body back into the door. The door reverberated with the thunk of the cleaver slamming into thin wood. I braced my legs on a cabinet below the sink and pressed all my weight against the door. The cleaver's impacts became hammer blows as the sitter attempted to chop down the door. Cries of "Kitty Meat!" became a chant.

Then the cry echoed from the direction of the tub. "Kitty Meat?"

Two black eyes popped over the rim of the tub followed by a body as a three-year-old stood up, her black hair matted and shiny. White foam ringed her mouth. She issued a belch and a swarm of bubbles floated out of her maw, a desperate bid for freedom.

"Nope," I told her. "Not meat. I'm made out of Brussels sprouts and lima beans. I taste awful." The wood above me splintered as the tip of the cleaver punctured the door.

"Hmmm vegetables." The kid tumbled out of the tub.

"Wouldn't you like some candy instead? I know where you can get some!" I lied.

There was no distracting her. She staggered toward me, arms out like a zombie with a grin of pure delight on her dimpled face. I extended a paw to her chest, trying to fend her off.

Her hands closed on my ankle like a steel trap, and her slimy mouth closed on my toes just as the last of the purple haze faded.

The kid froze and emitted a soft moan. "Ooooooooh oowwww."

Beyond the door I heard the sound of two adult knees hitting the floor and the moan of pain echoed by a dozen other voices.

Then the retching began.

I made my escape, weaving around nearly a dozen children vomiting in disturbing harmony. Outside, Rudy's grinning face waited for me.

"Oh good! You didn't get eaten!" he said as I shut the door behind myself.

"No thanks to you," I growled. "First carnivorous toddlers and then I'm dodging vomit. It's straight out of Dirty Jobs in there. Mike Rowe would have a field day."

"There's a reason why gathering tass is usually left to the junior magi." Rudy jumped onto my back. "As I was saying, that's a hunger plane. You won't be getting much tass from those. Black planes, they call them."

"You can tell what type of plane it is by hearing it?" I asked, standing beside the road and not sure where to go. Unlike felines, rodents didn't see magic. They heard it.

"You mean you can't tell by looking at it?" Rudy sniggered and then yawned. "Let's weather the night at my place. Then you come with me to my job interview tomorrow."

I had wanted to go to Noise's place but showing up stinking of vomit didn't seem like the greatest of ideas. With the adrenaline ebbing, I wanted another nap, then a bit of grooming. As I pondered what to do, Rudy's words finally burrowed into my brain, causing me to look to the squirrel in surprise. "Wait. You have a job interview?"

Rudy chittered, running up and down my back before answering, "Yeah, it involves a robot!"

9

Rudy's tree doesn't sport many amenities, but there was a pretty good sleeping tree nearby with a branch my size. After a decent amount of shuteye we headed into the center of town in search of employment.

The neighborhood technomagus, Jules, and his familiar, Jowls, ran what appeared to be a cheap electronics store with windows crammed with ancient cell phones in yellowing packaging. Yet if a mundane actually walked in to buy a cellphone they eventually threw up their hands in frustration as Jules did everything possible to convince them they actually didn't want to buy anything from him.

Had any mundane ever paid attention, they'd realize the store was a front. However, thanks to the Veil mucking with their heads, they never put two and two together. It was indeed a business, although legit wasn't a word O'Meara associated with it. Jules, as a technomagus, had no house and traded everything he could get his hands on. In order to fund his research into what he called the democratization of magic, aka magic without familiars, the store sold tass, information, and foci, and was a clearinghouse for getting anything you needed but really didn't want to know where it came from.

So I was pretty surprised to find the garish signage that usually graced the place had been removed. The blinds were drawn. It appeared Jules and Jowls had packed up and left town. Or something. Since the shop supposedly existed in three places at once, changing its location wouldn't require much in the way of movement at all.

Had I been alone, I might have backed off and watched the building for a bit before approaching. Yet, the way Rudy chittered with mirth from my shoulder blades as I crept closer indicated all was not as it seemed.

I peered through the glass door to see that any resemblance to a shop had been swept away. Instead the interior had been converted into a workshop of sorts. Two people stood at one end of a table in the middle of the shop. I recognized the thin frame of Jules, but the woman with a welding mask on her head I didn't recognize. On the other end of the table crouched Jowls, who, judging by the way every strand of fur stood on end so he more resembled a giant orange Koosh ball than a feline, was a wee bit upset.

"Looks like ol' magnanimous magnitude is having a bad day," Rudy said with a chuckle.

Whatever could so disturb the jovial Jowls had my whiskers tingling with curiosity. I pushed my head against the door and stuck my nose into the shop. "Hey! I'm in the market for a cellphone! You wouldn't happen to know where I can find one?"

"Oh Thomas! My Savior!" Jowls leapt from the table and charged my legs. No sooner had my ass entered the building did I have Jowls cowering behind it.

"Uh, what's going on? What's with the remodeling?" I asked, scanning the workshop.

Jowls pawed at my side, and I caught both Jules and the woman rolling their eyes. "It's terrible! Absolutely unnatural! They want to make me fly! These foul technomagi must be stopped at all costs! Will you be my brave knight? Please?"

I could see now what sat on the table. To my eyes it didn't appear to be anything magical at all. It looked like a cat-sized helicopter welded together from plumbing supplies. It featured a large blade and, instead of a single tail rotor, it had a quadcopter strapped to a three-foot pole extending out the back. While I didn't see any spells, it certainly looked like it needed a few. Jowls never approved of Jules' technomagic, and I couldn't really blame him for not wanting to get involved with this contraption.

"I can't say that looks particularly safe," I ventured.

"So? It's a freaking helicopter! It's awesome by definition!" Rudy chimed in.

"Why don't you fly it then, tender morsel?" Jowls hissed, backing away from me as he noticed my gray passenger. Why hadn't I figured out that Rudy was a Jowls repellent earlier?

"Hey, I got a name, Tubbs. I even got a friends-not-food song! Wanna hear it?" Rudy cleared his throat.

"NO!" I shouted. I'd already heard it. Too many times.

"Cats," Rudy grumped. "You guys are never any fun unless your tail's on fire."

Judging from the deepening of Jowls' glare, Rudy might have been referring to an actual incident. I hadn't seen Rudy's collection of vanquished cats, but apparently Jowls was a fellow member of that club.

"One day, my fluffy friend, you will know your proper place in the food chain. Mark my words. Just you wait." Jowls stuck his nose in the air and turned away.

Rudy leapt onto the windowsill and chittered, his hands grasping for an invisible acorn to throw. "Why you listen here, you gluttonous fuzzbutt—"

"HEY! HEY!" I cut in with a bit more volume than required. Both cat and squirrel flinched. "That's enough, both of you. We're not here for a fight. Now cut it out!"

They both gave me a sullen look but to my surprise they kept their mouths shut for the moment.

"So that leaves the question," Jules said, "why are you here? Acting as Ixey's errand dog today?"

I snorted. "Not today. And not for the foreseeable future."

A look of quasi-mock concern broke through his normally placid face. "Oh, what's happened? Did O'Meara kick her out for waving her sword around at everyone?"

I was fairly certain Jules would dislike anybody who happened to be the local Inquisitor on general principle. The man had warmed right up to me and O'Meara as soon as Ixey claimed the sword for her own. "No, nothing like that. I've parted ways with O'Meara. Judging from that contraption, you are in the market for extra eyes."

Jules blinked and snapped back to his poker face. Jowls, who wouldn't know a poker face if you branded his backside with one, sighed heavily. "Oooh, that's seven familiars. Poor dear. What'd she do to you, Thomas?"

I wasn't sure how much I could trust Jules and Jowls, and the woman hadn't said a word. "Nothing traumatic. Just time to move on. Fey chain, remember?" Mr. Bitey was no fey chain, which was an alternate way of creating a familiar bond that was far less permanent than the traditional link but also fragile. It was the only plausible cover story I had. I straightened. "Therefore I'm on the market." I looked at the woman, "Thomas Khatt, freelance familiar at your service."

The woman smiled with an amused twinkle in her

brown eyes. Then snorted as a familiar weight impacted the top of my head.

"Hey! No stepping on my tail, big guy! That's my client!" Rudy's claws dug into my ears as I tried to shake him loose.

Jules gave the woman a dubious glance. "You're hiring Rudy? For the golem?"

She nodded. "He's the perfect size and tells me he has experience driving things."

After herding Rudy back to his more usual perch in the small of my back with a paw, I approached her. "And you are?" I asked, looking into her round face set on her narrow, almost gangly frame. She appeared to be one of those people who forgot to eat with some regularity.

"Oh yes. Call me Sandra." She made no move to extend her gloved hand, but I didn't need her to be polite. I could smell her human funk layered with the tang of burning metal and motor oil from where I stood. Reminded me of an old car. Her eyes didn't quite meet mine.

"Sandra is a close friend and colleague, Thomas," Jules said. "Were there a house of technomagi, we would be members of the same cabal. She's a shaman." That answered the question as to why she hadn't inquired about bonding me. She couldn't. Shamans were essentially the same polarity as most familiars, with our soul threads anchored in realities that are complete worlds of their own instead of a more uniform plane that embodied a concept or energy. Shamans like Ixey summoned spirits into our world from their home planes to help out. In order to be a magus, shamans had to capture an animal that was bonded to one of those energy planes (rare to begin with) and give it part of their own intelligence, a painful and dangerous procedure, fundamentally altering the personality of the magi. According to Ixey, most shamans didn't go through with it.

"So are you saying you don't want my help to figure out where all these transitions are happening?" I asked.

Jules sucked in a breath. "I didn't say that. But then again, there are the issues with the TAU."

"Whom you notice haven't been around much." Oric and his cronies had been far too busy to pester me all that much lately since he thought I had been permanently bonded to O'Meara.

"Still, you're not formally trained."

"I can spot a transition from at least three miles away through trees and I've tracked a single magus who wasn't channeling through town. I think I have the training you need." I glanced at the helicopter. "And I'm not afraid of heights. One hundred fifty groat for a year of service."

The technomagus and Jowls were seized by a sudden hacking fit. "You think you're worth twelve Magi for a single year? Thomas, that's ludicrous," Jules replied when he had recovered.

My expression didn't waver. "I'd have fetched a lot more than that at an auction. But you guys are friends. I'd be happy to drop it to 120 groat as long as it's upfront." That would more than fix O'Meara, and a year of service would prevent me from bonding with her immediately. Large portions of me still wanted to run back and throw myself into her bed.

Shock blossomed on Jules' face as it dawned on him that I was serious.

"You fabulous bastard! You know something about these transitions?" Jowls exclaimed.

"Maybe," I conceded. I had a hunch.

"That's too much, Thomas," Jules said. "We don't have that sort of tass."

I doubted that. Tass was his main currency, but I could

imagine that was a dent in his reserves he didn't want to take. I could roll with it. "Then let's talk percentages. Twenty-five percent of all tass you gather while I'm working with you."

"You can't even use tass. Five percent," Jules countered.

"Keep in mind I could take my act to Vegas if I need to."

"Is that so?"

We haggled in a manner that my father would be proud of; fifteen percent would be my cut. Unfortunately, I did agree to take a ride in the helicopter. I really need to find someone who makes cougar-sized helmets.

10

The damn copter was noisy, rickety and generally an unsafe contraption once Sandra overhauled it to accommodate my bulk. Yet once we lifted off, I didn't care about any of that. The damn wind cut through my fur like dozens of icicle-laden buzzsaws. I actually started to shiver, which hadn't happened since I'd become a cougar. When you have as much fur as I do, you don't generally notice little things like the difference between sixty and thirty degrees. I mean, you're aware of the temperature change. I can see my breath just as well as anybody and stepping onto snow is cold, but I can't say I care unless I get wet. By the time we'd reached the extent of our 500-foot-long tether, I was resolving to add a four-legged flight suit to my contract.

I sat in the metal basket with a propeller on the top while Rudy perched on the edge. He seemed as impervious to the cold as he was to common sense, his paws on the twin joysticks of an expensive looking RC remote, minus the radio controlled part. Instead, Sandra had wired it into the copter. A plastic garbage bin lid was the only thing sepa-rating my tender ears from the whirling blade above us. The little quadcopter on the tail whined and wheezed trying to keep us steady.

I said I wasn't afraid of heights, but I might be afraid of heights from the inside of homemade helicopters. Besides the roaring wind and the quadcopter, the helicopter itself was quiet. There didn't appear to be anything resembling an engine in the craft. The propeller shaft instead extended from an industrial gas canister. To fit, I had to curl myself around it but did so without much prompting, as the tank radiated a pleasant heat.

"You see anything?" Rudy shouted over the wind.

"Not yet! Hold it steady!" I hadn't really been looking since I was too busy pondering if a fall from this height would kill me or whether or not the spinning blades less than a foot above my head would get me first.

A gust rocked us to the side, and Rudy banked the craft almost expertly. I bit back a question about how the hell a squirrel learns how to fly. I didn't want to know. Instead I closed my eyes and concentrated, searching for purple.

There, a flare of it. I opened my eyes and squinted to the east. The gray light of the day had grown dim, and it was difficult to pinpoint the source of the purple other than over there, in some trees. "Bring us a little higher!"

Rudy brought us up, and the floor moaned from the strain on the rope. A group of birds chattered at us overhead. "That's as far as she goes!"

It was enough. The white blotch near the purple had resolved into the peak of an old church, a wooden cross on it. I wasn't sure which one it was, but I'd bet Noise would ID it if I asked nicely.

The purple grew dim.

"Got one! East! Near a church. Maybe five miles?" I

needed to have the technomagus rig me up a head-mounted camera. And a helmet. Definitely a helmet.

"Okay! East, near church." Rudy turned to his left where his iPhone had been zip tied to the frame of the copter, typing this into the touch screen.

"Okay, they're on their way!"

"Won't be much left by the time they get there."

"Better than—"

The world went sideways as a wall of cold slammed into us, howling through my ears and whistling over the metal of our cage. I twisted, managing to get my forelegs around the central cylinder of the copter. Something within it screamed as the rotor shook under the force of the wind.

"EEEEEEEE!" Rudy cried into the wind. He clung to his phone with two paws, the rest of his body flapping like a manic windsock. Craning my neck, I reach up and bit down on his tail. He screamed, and then I felt needle-like teeth pierce my ear. Tiny claws dug at my scalp.

"OW! Rudy! Stop!"

He bit me again!

"Never touch my tail!" he hissed in my ear as he pulled his tail out of my mouth.

The copter bucked. No time to argue about tails and lifesaving.

"Rotting walnuts! The tether's gunna snap. Get me to the controls. We gotta get down!" Rudy shouted.

He crawled onto the underside of my jaw, and I shifted around the central cylinder. I stretched toward the controls, ignoring the two paws clinging to my lips. He let go with one paw and stretched it out beyond the tip of my nose to grab at a stick. We angled into the wind as the rope gave way. The ground shot out from under the helicopter as the wind carried us away like a barrel down a river. Distantly I saw a blaze of purple blossom.

I felt Rudy fumble, and two spots of sharp pain spiked my chin.

"I need two hands!"

I understood. "Get in my mouth!"

"What? You nuts!"

"Just remember that you taste terrible." I opened my mouth as if I was at a dentist's. "GUT IN!"

Rudy hesitated only a moment before I tasted him on my tongue. And everywhere he'd been today. I stilled a powerful urge to bite down hard on his squirmy, meaty body and carefully held him there, lifting him in reach of the controls. He pushed both sticks up, and the heat from the tank grew to an uncomfortable level as the craft started to climb.

The wind subsided.

Rudy pulled himself from between my jaws, only a little soggy. His little body shook from head to tail. "I-I Never w-want to do that again! Everevereverever!"

"Yeah." My eyes were on something else entirely. "Hey Rudy, what's about ten times brighter than a transition?"

"I dunno. You're the one who sees ma—" He stopped,

cocking his head to listen. "Holy caramel roasted nutbags! That's a shallowing!"

There, nearly obliterating my entire vision, was a bloom of purple so bright it could have been an alien sun shining from the plaza hill.

Rudy's hands were on the controls, and the copter tilted forward as we zoomed toward the Shallowing.

Closing my eyes made it worse. I discovered early on that my eyes had little to do with seeing magic. It was a function of my soul. Various folks had said that with training I could learn to shut it off. I'd yet to find that particular button in my brain. What I could do was look deeper, block out the real world and dive into the details of the magic. It cut down on the searing brightness of it.

As we hurtled toward the star of I found its center. A pulsating glob where everything around it swirled like a river. Rapid, churning and frothing. Two realities not phasing through each other, but mixing. Beneath it all, long shadows dived at the glob. They were like tentacles beneath the fabric of reality. I'd read about these. Shallowings were one of the few events that revealed the Veil for what it was, a creature that clung to our reality. Munds saw the results of magic perfectly fine until the Veil reached into their minds and changed them. I wondered how many times one of those tentacles had reached into my head and changed something before I had awakened. Those moments where I thought I saw something but it turned out to be a leaf blowing across the road? What had it actually been? In the six months I lived with Noise as a human, I had never noticed her slow shift into a wolf. But I'd wondered about before. How often had my life been touched by magic before my transformation?

According to those history books in O'Meara's house, the

Veil had been put there by something that magi as a whole were forced to forget. For lack of a better term, they called them the Fey. And the Veil was one of them. I could see it, its arms knitting the hole in our world back together as we shook and vibrated our way toward it. There'd be tass there. A steady supply of it.

The hole closed as we crossed over the last intersection between us and the plaza. It had been a messy patch. Realities still flowed together. I tried to picture it all as shadows of fourth-dimensional space the way the books and O'Meara had urged, imagining the shapes beyond this reality.

A tangle, a knot. The veil had patched the hole by tying the two realities together, and now they were bleeding into each other.

Someone was screaming far louder than either wind or the blades.

I opened my eyes and saw that in our reality, people were in deep doo-doo.

A man, or what had been a man, stood not a foot from where the rip had been. His entire body had been turned to ice so clear I could see the outline of the curb through him, and yet he still screamed. Jagged crystals a foot long pushed up from the ground around the portal, a carpet of icy spikes spread outward. The man clutched at his head, bowing in pain, his crystalline body swelling then becoming smoky white as the ice cracked.

A car, whose driver was totally oblivious to what was happening, pulled into a space across the parking island where the ice-man screamed. Its tires crunched on the ice, then popped with a bang as they were pierced. The munds couldn't see it. They had no idea. The sun was setting. People were doing their shopping after work. The Veil would probably keep more people from stumbling into the plaza, but for the hundreds who were already here? It wouldn't give a damn.

"Bring us down, Rudy!" I said as a woman stepped out of her car and skewered her foot with an ice spike. She didn't even get the chance to scream as purple light surged through her body. She frosted over as if she'd just been injected with liquid nitrogen.

"Where? I don't wanna be a popsicle!" Rudy stared at the frozen people below.

I squinted, looking for the border of the shallowing and trying to figure out how big an area the crystals could claim. Rudy could hear magic, but it wasn't enough at the moment.

I gestured. "There. No traces of purple in the first half of the parking lot."

"By the sign?" he asked.

The plaza sign was the highest thing in town, designed to be seen from the highway that ran behind the plaza. It had a huge Kmart logo on it but was built in an era before the proliferation of lit signs. Small spotlights below it provided illumination. "That will work."

As I'd found out months ago, the four-story tall sign was about my fall limit. So as Rudy brought the copter level with it, I leapt out. "Text Ixey!" I called to him as I vaulted over the edge of the basket.

I hit the hood of an unfortunate Ford with all four paws, the pain of four simultaneous high-fives shooting up my legs. A little girl and a mother pushing her in a red shopping cart stared at me in shock. I let loose an angry hiss. If the pedestrians couldn't see the ice-man yet, then I'd give them a mad dog falling from the sky to worry about.

"Excuse me! Sir!" came a new voice. "Could you please stop that moaning? Do you need an ambulance?"

I looked over to find that first frozen man now towered

over the rapidly frosting cars. He peeled his club-like hands away from his head to reveal a featureless face with two black holes for eyes and a round pit for a mouth. Those holes focused on a security officer who smartly stood some distance away from the ice giant and had parked his car so it stood between him and the new monster. I jumped up onto the hood of a SUV for a better view. The circle of ice spikes hadn't extended past the trunks of the parked cars, so the rent-a-cop wasn't about to be given a fatal cold foot.

The ice giant took a step forward, reaching for the man. The guard reached for his Taser. No time to think, I launched forward. I bounded onto the hood of some cheap car and stumbled as it gave beneath me with a POP! The guard swiveled and met my eyes as I crouched in preparation to tackle him out of the way. The ice giant's fingers were a foot from his head as I surged through the air. The Taser came up. My ears registered a discharge of air. Pain exploded through my chest, becoming my world. I couldn't see anything. My limbs disappeared.

A scream pierced my awareness and the pain stopped. I opened my eyes to see an ice statue of the rent-a-cop standing over me, the plastic of his Taser now nothing but ice. On his shoulder, like a father's hand on his son's shoulder, rested the ice giant's hand. It stared hungrily at me with two black eyes. *Shit.* Panic propelled me to my feet, and I ran before I knew what I was doing. The ice giant howled, and a blast of wind hit me so hard that I briefly ran on my front legs. I dashed around the side of a car as two more screams burst through the air and were cut short. That was five people. Five people dead or permanently changed. I poked my head around the corner. The giant had turned and now stalked toward a parked car with an older woman behind the wheel watching death approach with saucer-shaped eyes. Jagged crystals sprouted in the wake of his footfalls.

"NO!" A feral scream tore from my own throat, and my muscles tensed. I don't remember jumping, but my teeth were sinking into the back of his neck. Despite his appearances, the frozen flesh yielded like still-thawing meat. The cold bit back, sending root canal levels of icy pain rocketing along my teeth and jaws. I held on, my claws tearing at his back, ripping out chunks of slushy flesh. He reached a hand over his shoulder and clutched my back, wrenching me upward. Gravity fled as the world spun. Some sadistic part of my brain counted three rows of cars before I crashed onto the roof of another SUV.

The momentum tumbled me off the vehicle, and I fell to the asphalt with all the grace of a rag doll. My head spun as the worst ice cream headache I'd ever experienced lanced through my brain. Wind howled across the space between the two cars.

Oh good, I thought. *I pissed it off.*

I got to my feet and the world slanted. I had to use the door of the SUV for support as my tongue worked to massage some feeling back into my lips and gums.

Metal squealed and the sky went dark. I looked up to see the H symbol of a Honda coming down on me like a budget meteor. I hit the deck as a Honda Fit crashed into the much larger cars on either side of me. Glass rained down like bladed hail, and I covered my eyes with my paws. I backed out of the tunnel formed by the three cars, my adrenaline so amped that my third eyelids refused to retract. I could see the monster well enough as I poked my head over the trunk of a hatchback. "You gotta do better than that, you walking popsicle!" I shouted.

His response was to grab another compact, this one

partially frozen. A chorus of screams were starting to swell as shoppers realized that a live action Donkey Kong was being reenacted in the parking lot. The giant hurled a green VW bug into the air, but with my wits finally about me, I dodged it easily. The frozen bug crashed into the pavement and shattered like glass.

I had his focus, but the ice garden was still spreading. It had consumed eight hopefully-empty cars, but who knew how many people were cowering nearby. I had to—

"BANZAAAIII" a tiny voice screamed from overhead. I looked up to see the copter beelining at the giant. Rudy leapt out the back a moment before impact.

Searing heat blasted into my nose as a column of flame tore into the air as the copter exploded. The flame spiraled up and spread huge wings across the sky. A green shimmer rolled off it with the superheated air. An elemental, a colossal wyrm of fire. It bellowed hot rage into the sky as the green intensified. In a blink, the creature disappeared.

So had most of the ice giant. Just two legs stood, steam rising from where they had been attached to his hips before toppling over.

I breathed a sigh of relief, and then worry seized my heart. Rudy didn't have a transition charm, so if he'd touched a frozen shard, I'd have to store him in a freezer. "Rudy?"

"Yeah?" His tone was sullen. My ears zeroed in on the sound of his voice.

"Where are ya?" I asked.

"Down here. He got me, Thomas. He got me good."

Panicked, I poked my head beneath several cars before I found a shape crouched beneath the right one. Rudy sat, shoulders slumped as he clutched at something in his paws.

He didn't look frozen, nor did I see any ice crystals near him. Instead I caught the strong odor of burned fur.

"Frigging fire elementals. My beautiful tail!" Rudy lamented. My third eyelids drew back, and I saw details again. Rudy cradled his tail in his paws, brushing the remains of his blackened fur from its pink skin.

"Don't worry about it now. You need to get out of here. I don't want you getting iced," I said.

Rudy crossed his arms. "What, no thanks for blowing up the guy hucking cars at you? Literally sacrificing my beauty for the life of my friend!"

I growled.

The squirrel chuckled, and I knew the little bastard was just fine.

"Get on," I grumped, and he scrambled onto his usual spot as I padded cautiously toward the epicenter of the shallowing. Trying to get Rudy to leave the area would take more energy than I had, and with Mr. Frosty Freeze gone the squirrel should be safe enough. The harness' protective aura must extend a little bit around me, right?

I first checked the car that had contained the saucer-eyed woman. She appeared to have exited the car at some point. In the one next to it, with ice crystals starting to puncture its tires, I found a woman with horns and too-large ears staring at me from the back seat. Her arms clutched around two toddlers huddled to her chest. She flinched when I tried to open the door. It was locked, which would be wise except the ice would kill her and her kids anyway. I wished I still had my bond to O'Meara. We could have burned through the door or something. "Come on. Let me in, lady! Can't you see I'm a service animal?" Who knew what she saw in place of my face. I peered into the front seat. The car, an auto-

matic, was in park. That made sense. Terrible sense. "Ideas?"
I asked my companion.

"Well, if the fire hydrants stored fire instead of water,
we'd be all set," Rudy said.

Groaning, I went around the side of the sedan. Ice crystals were rapidly colonizing the car's bumper. I tried
knocking them off with a paw, but as they snapped off at the
base, new ones formed without a care. I hopped up on the
trunk. If I could shatter the window, maybe she'd run.

But how the hell was I gonna do that? I clawed at it
futilely. The woman shrank deeper into the car, pulling her
kids into the space behind the seat.

"NO! DRIVE DAMMIT! GET IN THE FRONT SEAT
AND DRIVE! DRIVE AWAY!" I screamed, but she just
stared at me with animalistic panic. Despite the horns, she
was still on the mundane side of the Veil. "COME ON, VEIL!
LET HER HEAR ME! LET HER UNDERSTAND!"

"Hey Thomas. Don't look now, but you might have to get
ready for round two," Rudy said.

"What?" I looked up from the stupid woman. The ice
folks weren't where I'd left them. The woman who'd stepped
out of her car and onto the ice, the second person claimed,
was less than four feet away. The crystal clear ice of her
body had clouded around her joints as she staggered toward
us, which emitted a symphony of pops as if you'd dumped a
truckful of ice cubes into a pool. "ARRRGH!" I threw up my
paws in frustration. "Stop right there! I've had enough of
this. Go away! Shoo!"

The car beneath me started to move. "Hey it's the Cavalry!" Rudy cheered.

I looked over my shoulder to see Jules standing in front
of a black van pointing a device that looked a bit like a sonic

screwdriver at the car. It emitted a diffused yellow beam of light at the car.

"Sorry for taking so long. Must be a holiday with all that traffic." Jowls smiled, his head sticking through the van's open window.

"Blow the windows! We gotta get her out of there before the car freezes," I said as I retreated from the roof.

Jules nodded, adjusted the dial on the bottom of his wand and pointed it back at the car. A yellow beam lanced out, shattering each window in the car one by one.

That did it. The woman leapt out of the back driver-side door and ran, a kid under each arm, directly toward the outstretched arms of the icy rent-a-cop. But she jigged around his fatal hug at the last moment.

"Cleanup on aisle five!" Jowls sing-songed.

"How many of these things are there?" Jules asked.

"At least five."

Jules used his wand to corral the ice zombies with cars, flipping them onto their sides to prevent them from climbing out. Meanwhile, I dragged or scared a few more people out of their cars. By the end of it, his wand was smoking. The ice continued to steadily creep across the parking lot. It had grown into a circle nearly forty feet wide by the time Ixey rolled up on her scooter, O'Meara's sword slung across her shoulder.

"A shallowing in Grantsville. That's amazing," were her first words after she pulled her rhinestone-studded helmet off her head.

Garn, perched on her shoulder, bobbed his head as he stared at the spreading ice. "The way the realities are bleeding into each other..."

My chest was heaving. "It could have picked a less populated location."

Ixey frowned when her eyes focused on me. "Not surprised to find either of you in the middle of this," she said, her voice flat.

I stood my ground. "Don't be mad at me. You and Tallow told me to leave the other day."

"We didn't tell you to leave, Thomas! We told—"

"To stop O'Meara from channeling. Well, she's not channeling now, is she? Despite the fact I could have really used her help a few moments ago!"

Ixey pondered that for a moment, surveying the scene before letting her posture slump. "Fine. I assume you're alright then? O'Meara will ask." She turned, pulled a bag of salt from the scooter's saddlebag and offered it to me. "If you can walk, make me a circle."

"I've had less violent days." Still, everything seemed to be working at least. Soreness blossomed everywhere.

"You're not going to let it reach its full size?" Jules asked, wandering over, Jowls at his heels.

"Jules, this is literally the center of town. I'll make it as large as I can," Ixey said.

Jules winced. Everyone knew wards weren't Ixey's strong point, but the technomagus didn't volunteer to help either.

Ixey gestured to the trapped ice zombies, which to my relief didn't seem to be getting any bigger. However, one had gotten his hand between two cars and was trying to widen the crack. "Are they?"

"Dead, I think. They don't seem to be intelligent anymore," Jules said. "They could just be starving for heat or whatever they consume now. We'll have to watch them."

"Right." Ixey turned to me, spinning her index finger in a circular manner. "Thomas, make it as big as you can, but I only have that one bag."

I nodded then ripped open one end of the bag and

proceeded with the circle making. Ixey needed to get the ward up before the SWAT team arrived looking for terrorists. After someone attacked a crowd of kids at Valentine Park with a barrage of fireworks, something I suspect Rudy had something to do with but wouldn't admit to, the Grantsville police had gotten their own APC and automatic shotguns. According to the twitters, so far all they'd swatted were a few teenagers who had the misfortune of possessing friends with twisted senses of humor. Once the ward was up, the entire circled area would be impossible for mundanes to perceive and those ice zombies would be trapped inside.

Rudy chattered as I walked the perimeter. "Man, I could go for some roasted chestnuts right now. My tail is freezing! And what the heck was with Jules' little toy?"

My mouth occupied, I let Rudy monolog as I trotted around the parking lot. My circle wasn't terribly circular, as I had to thread through the cars and go back a few times to fix the line. As I walked, I felt eyes on the back of my neck while I was out of sight of Ixey and Jules. I paused and looked about. The only visible bits of life were four crows hanging out on the arc of a street lamp; well, it wasn't a streetlight since it stood within a parking lot, but you get the picture. Two of them had a distinct aura about them. The telltale sign of a magus. I hurried to finish the circle and get back to the others.

Had anyone else noticed? I attempted to whisper the thoughts to O'Meara, futilely.

11

The crowd of crows had swelled by the time Ixey finished the avoidance ward, or as I called it the "Somebody else's problem" ward. Sadly, nobody got that joke.

Eight birds stared down at us as Ixey opened her eyes. One was no crow. You might mistake him for a giant raven, but the beak had a wicked curve to it, his talons vicious hooks. This was no scavenger. He was a black eagle, feathers darker than the others, given almost no shine by the glare of their lamppost perch. He hopped forward, gliding down toward us. A single crow followed his lead, her body bursting into a blue light and form blurring as she swooped beneath the eagle, landing as an elegant woman in a white dress. She wore a falconry glove, which the eagle alighted upon as the last of the blue light faded from a ring she wore.

Despite her sudden emergence from feathered kind, the woman might have walked straight off a fashion runway. Long and thin limbs accented her dark eyes. Raven black hair swirled around her head, held in place with two shining rods of silver that glimmered with the golden color of protective magic. The air around her rolled into my mouth and tasted like the stale air of a long forgotten attic. "Greetings from House Morganna." Her voice sounded honeyed like a spider inviting in a fly. "I am—"

To my surprise, a hiss from Jowls cut her off. "Oh, I know who you are, missy. You're a claim jumper and that's totally unfab- uncouth!" Jowls made a mewling spitting noise as Jules scooped him up and clapped a hand over Jowls' mouth.

"I apologize, Veronica," Jules said. "Jowls is jumping to conclusions." However, my own brain was on the case now. Wasn't House Morganna Lady Cavell's house?

The woman blinked, then smiled.

The eagle spoke. "We can hardly jump your claim if you are not qualified to make it. Which you are not, unless I am sorely mistaken. Have you joined a proper House? Even a minor House will do."

"What does that have to do with anything?" I asked.

The bird turned his huge eyes on me. "You should know that, being the familiar of the inquisitor."

My blood pulsed in my ears. Had Lady Cavell given me a huge price to heal O'Meara and then dispatched these birds to snatch away any chance I had to actually obtain it? A piece of me calculated that the bird was well within pouncing distance, and he probably had a fair bit of meat on those wings... I stomped on the instinct.

Ixey spoke up, placing a hand on my shoulder. "The Council has ruled that shallowings are too valuable to be kept by individuals. They must be maintained by Houses so their tass is properly accounted for."

The Eagle nodded. "So glad that someone around here is schooled."

"Now, now, Neelius, there's no need to be quite so confrontational," Veronica chided the bird. "I'm sure a healthy finder's fee can make everyone satisfied with the outcome. And avoid certain questions." She pointedly directed that sentence at me.

I huffed at the obvious good cop, bad cop routine.

Jules failed to contain the struggling Jowls, and the big tomcat kicked free. He landed with an un-catlike whump on the ground. "This is poppycock! You have no claim! You have no Dominion over this town! We've been here for ten years!"

Neelius sneered. "A co-located shop doesn't count as Dominion!"

"It counts more than a carpet bag!" Jowls spat. With his back arched, the round feline nearly looked dangerous.

"We have ties," Veronica said, gesturing to the rest of the flock. A pair of birds dismounted and flew down in that same burst of magic. As the two landed they became a dark skinned woman and a black lab with ears that inched into fennec fox territory. The woman wore a flowing green dress, and her hair was a nest of half-inch braids bedecked with golden rings. Several had the soft glow of foci, and as she stood to her full height, I saw it in the angles of her face.

"I'm Dorothy of House Morganna, and my familiar, Fee." She spoke with the trace of a southern accent. "Sabrina the elder is my great aunt."

"Blood is nothing," Jules said. "You can't use blood to tie yourself to a missing Magus."

"It is enough," Neelius stated.

I wasn't about to let this happen. A shallowing like the one behind me could produce tens of groats a month. If I could hold onto my fifteen percent, then I'd have the fee for O'Meara's health in several years, worst-case scenario. "I believe that House Technomagi has a stronger claim at this moment," I said. Adding a bit more bullshit to the pile couldn't hurt at this point.

Jules and Jowls each gave me a hard stare. Jules swallowed and Jowls' face broke into a grin.

Neelius fluffed himself up like a certain owl I knew. "That claim will never hold up in Council session!"

"Well, that does depend, doesn't it?" Jowls nearly sang. "Mostly on who is on the Council when it reconvenes. House Morganna might lose their seat this time, eh?"

"House Technomagi claims Dominion over Grantsville city limits, and we were at this scene first," Jules stated.

Jules and Jowls' eyes went to Ixey. As the possessor of the inquisitorial sword, her word would be law until a higher up said otherwise. She could let this farce move forward or dash it to the ground here and now. After a moment's pause, she stepped forward, cleared her throat and said, "The Inquisition recognizes the claim."

Veronica's nose climbed higher in the air as her lips pressed together so hard they turned white. Neelius looked back at her. I could almost see the thoughts flying back and forth between them. There was an edge to her eyes, something desperate as she stared at Ixey.

Ixey, for her part, glared back.

Neelius replied, "Well if that is the case, we can play this game of House with you."

Veronica stepped toward Jules. "I, Veronica of the Blackwings, challenge you to a contest of the Aegis and Sword for this shallowing."

Jowls bounced up and down with excitement.

"There's no need for us—" Jules began, but he was cut off by Jowls.

"We of the Runic Circuit, Prime Cabal of House Technomagi, accept your challenge!"

"Jowls!" Jules sputtered.

The cat grinned like a Cheshire.

Both Neelius and Veronica's heads rocked back, surprised. Their eyes hardened in the same instant. "To the Exhaustion then!" Veronica declared.

"To the Exhaustion," Jules said, a smile spreading across his lips.

Veronica smiled back nervously, her gaze flickering to Ixey. "Are you capable of officiating the duel?"

Ixey nodded. "In eighteen hours I will send you the location of the duel, and it will happen twenty-four hours from now."

"Very well," Veronica said. "We will reside at the Country Lodge on Main Street. Send your messenger there."

In a flurry of wings, all of the Blackwings departed.

12

Jowls entwined himself around my legs the instant the Blackwings were out of visual range. "That was fabu! Absolutely FABU! You're a genius, Thomas," he purred like a lawn mower pumped full of nitro.

Rudy laughed as I attempted and failed to extract myself from the amorous cat. "House Technomagi?" he said. "Couldn't have thought of a better name than that? Maybe House Albert or House Neeerd."

Jowls backed up just enough so he could fix Rudy with an unkind stare. "House names should be descriptive anyway. Traditionally they're named for the founder. So officially it should be House Jules!"

He bounded back to his bond, entire body jiggling, and circled around the magus' thin legs. Jules blinked as if he wasn't sure what to do. "Do you like the ring of that, my friend? My bond? My best pal!"

"Easy, Jowls." He looked to Ixey. "I really appreciate you supporting us, Ixey."

"We owe you." Ixey smiled warily. "And despite

O'Meara's grumblings, you've been mostly honest with us. We don't need House Morganna in Grantsville."

"Is House Morganna particularly bad?" I asked.

Both Ixey and Jules shook their heads. "House Morganna's been on their back foot for a decade now, so it's not that they're bad. They're desperate to get more leverage on the Council. This—" She gestured to where the ice zombies had wandered out of their pen and were milling about aimlessly "—would help their position. The Blackwings are their most junior Cabal. Besides Veronica, none of them are more than a decade out of their apprenticeships. Grabbing a shallowing would be a major feather in their cap."

"Which was why she was willing to try the dueling gambit," Jules said.

"But win or lose, we win!" Jowls purred.

"I don't understand," I said. "You already had the shallowing."

Jowls chuckled. "Cuz you're just a cub! It's all about the legalese. Standing."

"Standing?" I asked.

"Remember the whole bit where a House overrides a claim on the shallowing? Well, think about it." Jowls' tail lashed with impatience.

It clicked. "Oh, so by dueling you they'd recognize you as a House!"

"It's a really nice booby prize," Jowls said. "We're gonna found a House! We're gonna found a House," Jowls sung, bouncing around Jules' legs.

"Course, it will be better if you actually win the duel," I said.

Jules nodded. "I'll have to assemble—" He winced. "The Cabal of the Runic Circuit."

The cat laughed. "It sounded technomagical to me!"

Ixey departed soon afterward, muttering something about hitting the books and reading up on dueling rules. Rudy and I boarded Jules' van to retreat to his shop after spending a few minutes gathering pieces of the homemade helicopter.

Sandra's initial excitement about the shallowing quickly soured when she saw the pieces of her creation in Jules' arms.

"You lost my biggest elemental! That's a month's worth of work!" Her fury flitted between Jules, Rudy and me, like an angry hornet that couldn't decide who to sting.

Jules waved her off. "You'll trap another. You always do. We have bigger projects now. We've got twenty-four hours to make an aegis capable of defending against a black sword."

Sandra blinked. "You got yourself into a duel? Are you mad? The Council's outlawed dueling for decades."

"Council isn't here right now, Sandra. It could be years until the politicking around those three open seats ends," Jules replied.

"A shallowing is on the line," Jowls said with that manic grin of his.

Sandra's eyes went wide and continued to widen as the pair explained the situation involving the duel. Then cat, man and woman huddled, talking about force negation and arcane drains. I fell asleep fairly quickly.

* * *

"We don't have enough tass to do it." Sandra's raised voice pulled me out of my nap. The three of them hadn't moved, except Rudy was now perched on the table with the others.

"Then we need to get some more," Jules said. "This is a shallowing. We'll get back our investment."

"We didn't get enough data to figure out any pattern to the transitions. We have what we have," Sandra shot back. "Even with Tom, Dick and Harry coming in, we don't have the time to gather it and craft the aegis."

Hearing my name, sorta (I much prefer Thomas precisely because the world is full of Toms), I wandered over. "If you need a loan, I might be able to help."

"Do you have twenty groat floating around, Thomas?" Jules asked.

"I've got 5 and change," I informed them as I inspected what they'd all gathered around. The table was covered by a blueprint from the mind of a madman. It was filled with absolutely nonsensical patterns of wavy lines, but as I examined it, my perception shifted, went deeper. My stomach churned a bit as the lines went in directions that made my mind really uncomfortable, directions that should not be. It was a diagram of a spell, a complex spell, similar in complexity to the magic fax machine on Ixey's desk that teleported documents wholesale. I only understood the barest basics, but it was a focus with four separate nodes on it. Beyond that, my brain was lost in the bewildering connections.

I looked away and into the faces of Sandra and Jules as my brain threatened to overheat.

Sandra and Jules' eyebrows raised. I knew that Rudy had even more of his stash socked away somewhere. 'His rainy day fund,' he had called it. "Why are you after so much tass anyway, Thomas?"

"To pay to get O'Meara's anchor treated."

"You broke your bond to help her?" Sandra's voice held bewilderment.

"I owe her."

"Isn't he delicious!" Jowls said.

Everyone's eyes swiveled to him, and the cat suddenly focused on cleaning his paw.

I rolled my eyes. Jowls was harmless.

I knew where we could get some tass. A lot of tass even, but it would be no good for healing anyone. Yet, maybe as a weapon... I had a hunch about these transitions.

"Have you mapped out all the transitions you know about?" I asked.

"Yes," Sandra said. She grabbed a roll of paper from a nearby table and unrolled a simple map of the town in front of me. It had locations circled in red pen. With a sharpie she drew an X on the plaza. The shallowing we spotted from the helicopter was marked already. In my head I placed the other transitions I knew about: the stockyard, an apartment building with a bookcase that had emitted birds and a few locations Noise had talked about weird stuff her pack had found in the woods a few months ago, possibly leftovers from the transitions?

It didn't confirm my hunch, but there were more transitions closer to the site where the Archmagus had hidden his captured dragon: Valentine Park.

Rudy appeared to read my mind. "Aw come on, Thomas, you know that's bad mojo there!" Rudy whispered.

"Shallowing is fifteen percent mine if you hang onto it, right?" I looked up to Jules.

The Technomagus looked like he had a bad taste in his mouth. "Yeah. Fifteen percent."

I tapped Valentine Park. "You can get the tass you need here. It's not high quality, but it's tass. There's a spell there that you could break down for more."

"What do you mean by 'low quality?'"

"It's like elemental essence," Rudy chimed in. "It's pain

tainted. You don't want it. Anything you make with it isn't going to hold together long."

"I'm not in the position to be picky. We're not making something that has to last the ages," Jules said.

"What if they challenge us again?" Sandra asked.

"Then we'll at least have one shallowing," Jules said.

"This isn't a good idea, Thomas," Rudy said.

"You going to stay here then?" I asked.

"Oh hell no!"

Valentine Park had been closed with prejudice. I've never seen that many chains on a gate before. It gave the park an extra bit of foreboding. The sky's gray had given way to a starless blackness. Even I needed the van's headlights to see.

I didn't need to see magic to feel the wrongness of this place as we pulled into the parking lot. It prickled my whiskers and felt like something slimy was working up my spine. Six months ago I had rescued a dragon (or what magi termed a dragon; it was closer to the spawn of an elder god than a reptile) from a cage beneath the park. A cage equipped with spells that cut off pieces of the thing's multi-dimensional flesh and ground it up to pure tass. I had literally swum though the dragon's pain and agony to make contact. I'd assumed at the time that the tree the dragon had unleashed to break it out of prison would purify the area.

That had been wrong. I recognized the dragon's pain as soon as my paw touched down from the van. It seeped up and rang in my ears, heralding a migraine if I stayed too long. The grass pulsed with a subtle orange hue. The drag-on's pain had seeped into the place like a toxic chemical.

"Let's not stay long. This may have not been my best idea," I said as I made to climb back into the van.

"Tass is tass," Jules said, stepping out of the van and looking at me expectantly. "It's either this or I get my ass handed to me tomorrow. Losing a duel isn't good business."

Sighing, I padded over to the edge of the parking lot and looked down into the snow-covered field. Patches of grass poked through the week-old snowfall as autumn refused to go quietly in the night. Two soccer goals marked the borders of the soccer field to the left, while a backstop indicated the baseball diamond to the right. Or what had been a baseball diamond, as it appeared to have encountered a bulldozer recently.

In between the two structures was a pulsing blister of pain. If I stared through the glare of the magic, I could see a small depression in the ground, about a foot deep at its center. The statue had been destroyed by the dragon's escape, but crater it had left bubbled with sickly orange ichor. From the way the magic flowed, it called to mind pollution from eighties cartoon show.

Jowls stared at the open sore in reality. "The snack was right. That's some bad juju there."

"It looks worse than it is, I'm sure. What happened here, Thomas?" Jules asked.

"You could say it was an experiment of Archmagus Archibald. And I kinda broke it," I said.

"Is this where Sabrina died then?" Jowls asked, scanning across the field. If they could scry the past like O'Meara, then Jowls might be able to replay the entire scene. My own eyes drifted to the spot where O'Meara had fallen when her last ditch attack on the elder magus failed. In my ears I heard Sabrina's screech of pain as the dragon's spell speared her familiar through the heart. Sabrina had dived into the writhing mass of murderous roots without a single thought to her own safety.

I had killed them both, dealing with the dragon. I'd signed their lives away along with two Archmagi and their familiars. At least I knew Sabrina and Cornelius had every intention of murdering me. But the Archmagi? I doubted that their hands had been clean, but how was I to know that?

"Thomas!" Jowls sang through my memories. "You might want to get down. This might be messy." Jowls and Jules sat across from one another. Working together they had formed a circle around the awful blister. Jules opened a small black sack and placed it into the circle.

A golden ward sprung up between them, its runes bright and ordered like lines of code. A whisper of tass floated from the bag, curling on itself, forming a long tube that led back to the bag. With a swift motion, the tube pierced the bubble of the blister. It trembled but didn't burst. Then, slowly, the tainted magic flowed inside the tube. The abscess drained into the tass bag. As the thing deflated, I approached with a wary eye.

"Was that tass?" I asked

"You weren't kidding about this stuff not being all that useful." Jules looked up at me as Jowls stared into the ground. "It's tass but not dense. Magic gas."

"Dragon farts, and we're not talking the types that shit rainbows," Jowls said as he peered. "However, much of that will be useable."

I looked at the patch of ground Jowls stared at and gasped as my vision seemed to be ripped from my eyes. I fell into an abyss that hadn't been there. I recognized it, memories of pain, of awful twisting blades, spinning, biting, ripping flesh away. Drowning in the blood that filled in the chamber, the pain redoubling, echoing through my being.

"THOMAS!" The visions shattered. And I found Jules' face inches from my own, frowning with concern. With a screech I tore away, retreated to the safety of the parking lot and cowered behind the fence, my whole body trembling and my heart pounding so hard my entire being pulsed with each beat.

I coughed violently, and a twisted part of me surged up my throat. A space in my chest that hadn't been there before the dragon had taken me apart then put me together again. The spot in my soul where it had hidden the bomb that had ripped off the top of its prison. Why had the dragon left it's prison intact when it had made the Archmagus' entire house vanish? Why leave such a thing just sitting there?

Jowls still stared toward the hole, his green eyes wide with wonder. I opened my mouth for him to stop looking, to walk away, but my voice only gurgled in my throat. I sat my chin on a fence post and waited for my body to stop shaking. That memory of pain had been the dragon's, not mine. I focused on my breathing and tried to push the memory out of my head. It refused to slink away into whatever corner of my mind it had been hiding in.

Jules approached me, palms out, as if to show he carried no weapons. The questions danced on his face, warring between a demand to know and simple curiosity.

"The Archmagus made it. He compelled me to destroy it. Sabrina wanted it. I couldn't let her use it. You should finish the job. Break it down. Destroy it." The words babbled out of me, truth and lies all mixed together. They'd see the chain soon enough. If I could frame it as Archibald's last project, then they might not realize the dragon had built Mr. Bitey, and by the same token, me. Awareness of that compartment in my chest, that empty space faded no more than that terrible memory.

Jules knelt. "It's okay. It's just a complex spell. We can take it apart. Reuse some of the tass. What did he use it for?"

I wanted to shout at him for being so dense. Could he not see? The cutting tools, the grinding wheels. The memory recycled itself and I saw it again. My stomach rolled, rebelling at the wrong angles and impossible motion. A flash, in an instant, I saw down that hole, as the memory had overwhelmed me. But I had still seen it. Still, lifeless. Not moving and from one angle. The vision showed everything all at once. I remembered the dragon's complete perception. To Jowls and Jules, it was nothing more than a collection of angles, a spell of bewildering complexity and inscrutable design. They would have no more idea of its purpose than ants marching along a drill bit.

I searched for words. "Nothing good. A processor."

"Well, you were right. There is some denser tass in there. Jowls thinks we can extract it, but it's not good tass. It's almost as if it's decaying somehow."

A buzz. Jules pulled an iPhone from his pocket and answered it. "It's about time!" he said as he placed it against his ear. "What? I'm not at the shop." He listened for a moment, then glanced around nervously. "No, there aren't any munds around but—"

Three purple columns expanded up from the ground a few paces behind Jules. Space twisted a knot around each column, then untwisted. Three men stood where there had been none before.

Each of the three men wore a gray suit with a blue tie, but the similarities ended there. Each carried a toolbox of some type in their left hand, and the one on the left, a guy with a reluctant afro, had a huge lump of machinery slung over his back.

Jules whirled around. "Damn it! It's not wise to do that here!"

The three shrugged in absolute unison and spoke as one. "You said you had a familiar here with a fey chain! We must use him to test the LAPIS. It is essential!"

I sunk lower behind the fence. I was in no mental state to make a good first impression. The eyes of the guy to the right, the more rounded of the threesome, found me as soon as I moved, while the other two fixed their gaze on Jules.

Jules straightened. "Of course." He gestured to me. "This is Thomas. The freelance familiar I texted you about. Thomas, this is Tom, Dick and Harry." He pointed to the round one, the tall one and the dark one in sequence.

"I much prefer Richard these days," Dick said, alone.

"I know." The way Jules said it suggested a long familiarity with the trio.

Seeing as I wasn't going to be able to slink off to the van, I swept my own conflicts away and put them in the bin marked 'later' while slapping my best front desk face over my muzzle. The customer service muscles were a bit rusty from disuse, but they were still there.

"Hello, can I help you?" The customer service line slipped out like a creaky recording. Not really what I'd meant to say.

"Yes! You can!" Harry set down his toolbox and unslung the tube of machinery from his back. It pulsed with the light of several dozen foci embedded within the patchwork of circuitry, wires and a few vacuum tubes. "Can you enter a bond with a magus without disrupting another?"

I had no idea if I could. "I dunno. I'm willing to experiment." I smiled. "What does that do?"

"This is first portable detection device for reality anomalies. It is the first of its kind." All of their chests swelled with pride.

"It's an abomination," Jowls called from his place at the crater.

The three waved their hands dismissively in unison. "We are aware of your stance on the matter, Jowls, but please rant about how we are stealing the rightful place of familiars. Not all of us were fortunate enough to be born into a Major House and receive a stunning example of hard working dedication such as yourself."

Jowls sniffed and held up his nose high in the air. "The universe has its reasons!" Then he looked back down in the hole.

"Thomas, Tom, Dick and Harry were my mentors in technomagic. They're a collective of two channelers and a shaman. Together they are capable of spellcraft that rival those of magi twice their age." Jules' voice was level and polite, although he had that slightly distracted look to his eyes that probably meant Jowls and Jules were shouting at each other in their heads. Jules and Jowls had a rep as an argumentative odd couple, but from the last few hours it was clear to me it had been at least partially an act. Or at least they could put their differences aside once the chips were down.

I studied the trio. So if Harry was the shaman, he served as the familiar of the other two. But why two channelers? Still that meant, like Sandra, the three were blind to magic outside of a circle. Another magus could toss a spell at their heads and they'd never see it coming. "How are you all at healing?" I asked.

"It is not our area of expertise. We have been focusing on mitigating the limits of technomagic in general as of late.

Hence why we need to figure out the baseline we are aiming for. Please attempt the binding now. If it fails, we can reattempt under more controlled circumstances." Their voices combined in an eerie harmony.

"Here?" I looked around at the pulsing orange light and the blue auras of the magi. Out of the corner of my eye I caught a flicker of something moving in the trees. The Blackwings. Not Veronica, one of the others. They'd followed us. I suppose I shouldn't have been surprised.

"Yes here. Once we obtain a baseline for comparison." Harry wandered over to the fence and placed the LAPIS device on a post. He twiddled with some knobs. The device's glow trebled, one golden part flaring then expanding. A ward grew out of it like bubble gum enclosing dynamite, flinching as it passed through me, and encapsulating all of us within a barely visible dome about a hundred feet in diameter.

Harry squinted at the screen on one end of the device. His eyes lifted from the screen to where Jowls still sat. He had inched around the lip of the crater, looking at the Archmagus' device from all angles, I realized. I wanted to stop him, but there was no doubt the Blackwings would do the same thing as soon as we left. This cat was out of the bag and I wouldn't be putting it back in.

Harry panned the device to point at me, and the ward pulsed. A part of me shifted, sidestepping the ward.

"You have some foci in that harness?" they asked.

"Minor protective bit and bobs," I conceded. Mostly Ixey's work. The anti-transition charm, a minor heat ward in case of an accident with O'Meara and a kinetic shield that might stop a bullet or two before burning out.

They all grinned. "Now, please bind me." Richard

stepped forward, and I was glad. Binding a Tom to a Thomas would be way too confusing.

"Okay, stand still." I glanced at the tree line where I could see the tiny aura. No sense really in hiding this. Lady Cavell had seen my "fey" chain. Veronica was about to find out she'd been tricked a bit. With a mental poke, Mr. Bitey awoke from his slumber. The chain around my neck writhed as it unspooled from the dimensions it dwelled in. Tom, Dick and Harry's mouths fell as it pulled itself from the fur of my neck. Constructed of fine jewelry chain, the hood flared behind its head. I looked at Richard. *Bind him.*

"What is—" He didn't get the third word out.

Mr. Bitey struck with a shimmer of silver light, arching toward the magus' neck. The instant before impact, the snake split into a mass of chains, each encircling Richard's neck.

A flash of thought. The agreement Jules signed with me flicked between Richard's mind and I. Fifteen percent of all tass is mine. Termination of the bond at will. Agreement flared, not one mind, but three.

And it was done.

Flashes of a young man. The scent of paper and burned out electronics. Things moving through his street, unseen. Tall figures moving about, looking down but not seeing him. Isolation.

A big man grinning down. There are crumbs in his beard. A black cat with mismatched eyes perches on his shoulder. The joy of finally being seen. Harry and Tom, both young, all of them sitting at the table with the bearded man. The table is a circle, and they're all holding hands.

I pulled myself back. Just as I saw him, he had been seeing me. We breathed and slid away, feeling the shape of our bond. No gauzy curtain, this bond felt like a ship's porthole: big enough to look and stick a paw through but not at the same time. Wariness and a bit of fear on both sides constricted the divide. And that was fine with me. After nearly being a mental roommate with O'Meara, I could stand to work with someone a bit more distant.

I heard the distant echo of the other two voices. *Richard, you went dark for a moment.*

I know. Just finding out our familiar is a tough bastard, and I think he's dating a werewolf?

The other two squawked in surprise. I tried to avoid thinking about the dragon. *So you all want to see what magic looks like through the eyes of a familiar?*

Yes! The enthusiastic force of their thought nearly rocked me off my feet.

I showed them. Pulling Richard behind my eyeballs was easy, but then the other two of them pressed in as well, jockeying for space within the bond's narrow width. I had to meet them halfway, pushing my vision out to them. I directed my eyes toward them. Foci dotted their bodies like constellations.

You see every single one! They're colored! one of them exclaimed.

I spent a few minutes touring them around my vision, explaining the colors as far as I knew them. Richard mentally vibrated, Tom wailed at the beauty of it, and Harry had to be physically restrained by the other two from dashing the LAPIS on the asphalt of the parking lot.

"It's a useless piece of junk compared to this! Five years! Five full years! We have no color, no resolution. It's been a useless endeavor!" Harry shouted, guilt rolling with his cries. LAPIS had been his idea, clearly. Richard's thoughts filled in some blanks.

The two consoled Harry. I heard more than enough to

realize the trio were very close indeed. Not wanting to intrude on that, I shut the porthole.

They left the LAPIS itself unguarded. Curious. I drifted over and took a closer look at the complex mesh of its machinery. There was less magic involved than I'd guessed. Odd spells were scattered here and there, bound into blocks of shiny metal, as if the spells had been used in place of electronic chips.

"That will be enough," Jules' voice rung out. I turned to find him holding his tass bag out in front of him. It bulged and wiggled in his hand.

Jowls curled around his bond's legs, looking both sleepy and pleased.

"I hope you all had a good night's sleep. Because all of House Technomagi has a lot of work to do tonight," Jules declared.

13

Jules hadn't been lying. As soon as we got the corrupted tass through the door, I realized the Technomagi weren't messing around. Sandra wheeled carts of machinery to each of the three workbenches she'd set up while we'd been gone. One served as a metal working station, another as an electronics bench and the third had an ornate casting circle inscribed on its surface, far more compact than anything I'd seen O'Meara use.

Tom, Dick and Harry were overjoyed with the precision my vision provided them. It was nice to feel useful again, but I hadn't been in a spellcraft circle for anything more than an hour since O'Meara's injury. The trio never seemed to tire as they directed me to move around the circle for a better angle. I watched their threads expertly manipulate the spells they grafted into the parts that Sandra machined, layer by layer. Harry handled most of the summoning energies duties as I attempted not to blink.

The evening disappeared in a blur of movement and magic.

I found myself back in the van being talked at by a

chipper Rudy the following morning. I swore I would eat him, but I couldn't find the energy.

"What's the matter, Thomas? I thought you got along great with night owls," he quipped.

My groan of pain wasn't the only one in the van. "The next time I make a contract I'm building in a nap allotment. Most cats sleep eighteen hours a day you know."

Glad we dodged that bullet, Richard thought at me. *We barely got this thing done as it was.* He patted the metal disk in his lap. The shield's three spell nexi shone in my vision. Green, yellow and purple: Summoning, Kinetic energy and Space, respectively. I had no idea how the spells worked and only an inkling of what they did, but I knew the thing was a ticking time bomb. They attempted to use as little of the orange tass as possible, but the threads they spun with it frayed even as it was woven into a spell. The device wouldn't hold together long.

But it only had to last one duel.

I felt good about this little crew. Tom sprawled against Harry in the back of the van, his head resting on the smaller man's lap. Sandra sat in the passenger seat cleaning the controller that had been salvaged from the crashed cougar-copter. Her hands were completely unbothered by the bumpy road as we drove toward a picnic area in a state park on the edge of town. Notably, it was on the edge away from where Noise's pack lived. Jowls had curled up in a box between the two front seats, squeezed in so tight he looked like a cat muffin.

"Good to see they're taking us seriously," Jules muttered, jostling me from sleep a bit later.

In front of the van lay a sparsely snow-covered picnic area. A golden ward covered the majority of it (one of Ixey's) and several tables had been cleared of snow.

Dorothy stood atop one, a green Frisbee twirling around a finger. Two dogs and a wolf sat in front of her with rapt attention, the black lab I'd seen before along with a German Shepherd. She threw the disk, and the canines took off like a shot, barking like hounds on the hunt. The wolf leapt up, but a burst of yellow pushed the disk just out of the arc of his jaws. Dorothy continued to channel, using subtle bursts of energy to steer the disk away from the pack. They made feints and false grabs until the German Shepherd nabbed it by lunging off another picnic table.

Two other women applauded nearby. I only recognized them from their auras, but Richard gave me their names. Rinoa wore her hair in multicolored spikes, so sharp and perfect that it had to be either a magical effect or a wig. She wore a long dress that appeared to be the uniform for the Cabal but covered her top with a leather vest. I couldn't decide if the look was punk or simply awkward. The German Shepherd, called Tack, was her bond. The last woman, Naomi, appeared remarkably birdlike, rail thin in her black dress, with a prominent nose. Her hair was buzzed short, but her large smile made up for it. While the punky magus next to her seemed to be cloaked in dourness, this woman projected warmth like a summer's day. By process of elimination I assumed her familiar was the wolf chasing the Frisbee, Morie.

The rest of the figures gathered I knew. Veronica sat on another picnic table cross-legged with Neelius in her lap, their eyes closed. In a field back from the picnic tables crouched Ixey's small form, her jacket catching the already fading light. O'Meara peered down at her from her motorized wheelchair, no doubt backseat magicing her sort of apprentice.

All in all, it looked more like an obscure cosplayer picnic or pre-prom party than a gathering of magi.

I beelined for O'Meara as soon as somebody popped open the van's back door. She smelled tired, but her smile kindled some life into her eyes as I thrust myself into her hands. She only hesitated for a second before her fingers found my ears. Touch was wonderful, and I hadn't realized I'd been craving it.

I'm maintaining professional distance, Richard commented on that thought. *Do you need brushing or something?*

I waved his concerns away and focused on getting a large portion of myself in O'Meara's lap. I missed her already. Some independent apex predator I was. "How are you doing? What are you doing here?" I managed between purrs.

"Exhausted as always, and lonely, which is new. But I can't live through you anymore, so I figured I'd visit your little circus. After all, it's going to be a few decades before I can channel again." Her voice had a bit of strain in it.

"It's not gunna take that long, I promise."

"It's not your responsibly to heal my injuries, Thomas. I'll heal on my own time and dime."

This wasn't an argument I was going to have with her. Not until I had my harness bursting with the tass I needed. O'Meara's soul was a good one, and I wasn't about to see her sidelined for a decade or more.

"What's the meaning of this, Inquisitor!" Veronica said. I could see her clutching her pearls in my head before I turned around.

"Now look what you've done," O'Meara whispered as I pulled myself away to stand beside her. She patted my side. "Meaning of what, dear Veronica?"

"Can you not at least pretend to be neutral in this conflict? Understand that treating this place as your own fiefdom won't last forever. Sending your familiar to assist this...House will come back to you someday." Veronica strode toward us.

"Oh, but she *is* neutral," I said. "It's just that I'm not her familiar."

Veronica's eyes narrowed, and so did Neelius'. I felt the prickle of his gaze.

I opened the porthole in my head. *Trouble?* the trio asked.

Nope, I replied as the bird leaned forward, peering. My link shifted a bit. Apparently Lady Cavell hadn't told them everything she'd seen about my particular talent.

"I'm bonded to Tom, Dick and Harry for the moment."

"For the moment?" The bird fluffed his feathers, then smoothed. Veronica's stern expression didn't waver.

"Well, our contract's length is indeterminate at the moment. To be maintained as long as it's profitable." I smirked at their bewilderment. "Thomas Khatt, freelance familiar, at your service."

Veronica's jaw worked in such a way I could almost see the questions piling up on her tongue. Neelius was looking at me as if I'd offered him a rotting rat to eat.

"I'm still working on the business cards, but I offer fair rates if your House ever needs a substitute cougar." I pulled away from O'Meara with a long, languid stride.

Richard strolled casually in my direction from the picnic table where the technomagi were setting up camp. Rudy was sitting on Sandra's shoulder, and laughing at something, judging from the twitch of his tail.

"We thought you were O'Meara's bond at the shallowing," Neelius said.

"I wasn't bonded to anyone at the shallowing." Kinda a lie. I had a contract at the time. It occurred to me that I never had gotten that in writing, and while I was fairly sure the contract involving my bond would be honored or risk angering my link, I made a mental note to get all future employment outside of bonds in writing. A proper business required a paper trail. A reckoning with the dang Talking Animal Union would come at some point and I'd have to buy Oric's goodwill.

"An omitted fact," snapped Veronica.

I chuckled and walked around them. "Excuse me, but my client needs my attention."

I walked over to Richard with Veronica's eyes burning in my back and met him halfway, making sure to circle his legs in a gesture of affection. The trio mentally giggled. *Well, she is nervous.*

What, she's not usually an angry woman? I asked.

Usually that's Neelius' job, Richard thought.

You have unnerved her, Harry chimed in.

I paused. *She should know that we bonded. One of them was watching when we bonded at the park.*

But unless it was Neelius himself, they could only sniff the magic out. And there were plenty of other magics to be sniffed out, the trio commented.

"Not to mention your bonding is a bit different. I've never heard of a fey chain that anchored in one's body." Richard reached down and touched the place where the ethereal chain merged with my spinal column, and I shivered as if he had poked my very soul.

Don't touch that! I scolded them with a fiery sense of violation.

They apologized, but we lapsed into a mental silence as we joined the gaggle of technomagi and squirrel waiting for the appointed hour of the duel, just after sunset.

Ixey summoned forth several brilliant globes of light as

the sky dimmed. With a flick of her wrist a top hat appeared in her hand with a small explosion of green sparks. "Ladies and Gentlemen, Dogs and Cats. We are gathered here today to witness a legally binding duel. The first conducted in Grantsville in nearly fifty years!"

Both sides scoffed in offense, and Jowls bristled. "That's not how it's done!" two voices cried out. Voices belonging to both Jowls and Neelius. The two familiars glared at each other for a moment and then back at Ixey.

Ixey grinned impishly. "Nobody's ever interested in the local history. Now as the officiate of this duel I am required to ask both parties to consider working out your disagreement without a dangerous contest. Will you do so?"

"NO!" both Neelius and Jowls shouted back. Jules and Veronica's eyes met across the space of the picnic tables, and they nodded to each other.

"We decline," Veronica said.

"As do we," Jules said.

Ixey twirled theatrically. "Then the participants will declare their weapons and present them to me."

Jules stepped from his perch on the picnic table and with a heave of effort hoisted from the table the device we'd spent all night creating. He staggered over to Ixey and presented it to her. Tension circulated through the minds of the magi. If she saw the bits of tainted tass in the aegis' construction, then she could rule it as unfit for the duel. And without it, Jules would most assuredly lose. Tom, Dick and Harry had attempted to shield that flawed tass from view while the shield was inactive.

I held my breath while Garn stared at the aegis from Ixey's shoulder. With the shallowing, I was guaranteed to get the tass I needed in time. Without that, I lost a guarantee. His black garnet eyes shone in the harsh light of the globes.

Moments passed. I counted my breaths before his tiny head nodded.

Ixey looked to Veronica. "Do you have any foci to declare?"

"We do not need anything of the sort," Neelius replied as Veronica looked down her nose at Jules.

Richard thought, *Meaning: I thought this would be easy. She forgot that Jules grew up in House Hermes. The House that invented dueling.*

Ixey snapped her fingers. Behind her, blue flame leapt up from the lines of an intricate circle on the ground. "Then the duelists may enter the circle."

"Oh, this is going to be fabulous! I just know it!" Jowls bounded from his seat and skipped across the ground before impacting Jules' legs. He made two circles around them before Jules scooped him up and carried him into a smaller circle inside the dueling circle. The trio clapped for the pair as Jowls shot everyone a grin.

Veronica stood only after Jules had taken his place, striding to her position with Neelius perched on her arm. "Proceed."

Once the dueling magi entered the circle along with their familiars, Ixey deposited Garn on one side of the circle before walking the edge to her own station opposite Garn. The shine of a warming spell rendered him easy to find on the frozen grass. Veronica faced Jules with a small frown and a wrinkle in her brow. Jules' expression was stony, but Jowls grinned up at his opponents.

"Fellow magi! Friends and fellows!" Ixey's voice rang out across the park. "Bear witness. This is a contest to resolve the Dominion of a shallowing between House Technomagi and House Morganna." Both of the duelists stood a little straighter. "In the absence of the Council, these houses will abide by the results of this nonlethal duel. The first magus to falter will be declared the loser. Neither magus will stray from their appointed position. Should one die, they win the match."

So if you really want to win, you could commit suicide? I asked the trio.

Hey, if you believe in your case enough to die for it, you have to respect that, Tom thought as he pulled a beer out of his backpack.

I note that there was no mention of a familiar's death in there, I thought.

Well sure, killing a familiar is one way to exhaust a magus. He took a swig from his bottle and passed it to Harry.

This endeavor suddenly seemed like even less of a good idea.

After the opponents declared that they understood the rules and stakes, the golden bubble of a protective ward encircled them, guarding against outside intrusion.

Veronica and Jules faced off a good thirty feet away from the other. Jowls at Jules' feet, Neelius on Veronica's outstretched arm. Each stood within a smaller circle. The trio explained if that circle was breached, it inflicted a great amount of pain on the magi that stood within it.

"Ready your weapons!" Ixey called out.

Both magi closed their eyes in concentration as small circles in front of each of them glowed and twisted on themselves. Veronica's pulsed with blue light and then went dark in my vision. It rose into the air and coalesced into a curved blade, a crescent moon of blackness that seemed to eat the air around it. I had only the basics of the duel explained to me last night. The contest was supposed to test both the strength of the magus' channeling ability and their spellcraft.

That sword represented her anchor and the strength she could draw with her own will.

Veronica's anchor is entropic energy. Richard nodded at the sword.

Jules' sword meanwhile was nearly insubstantial, a tiny speck of a dagger no bigger than a pocket knife. A concept perhaps? The planes were infinite and not tied to things within the physical world. Just as O'Meara channeled fire, there were magi who channeled emotions like fear or awe or even concepts like math.

And that's why he didn't stay in House Hermes. A conceptual plane isn't acceptable for a House of Elementalist Fascists. Richard's thought dripped with acid as dark memories flittered though his mind far too fast for me to see.

"Aegis!" Ixey announced.

Jules smiled and thrust his shield through the wall of his personal circle. Its yellow nexus blossomed even before he let go. Had I been in the circle, I might have seen the workings of the spells on the object. Both Neelius and Veronica paused, the woman's lips pressing into a thin line. The effect of the spells was crystal clear. Green surged around the small plate as hundreds of tiny rocks swirled into existence.

The pebbles formed into a phalanx of stones swelling the small shield to the size of the door on O'Meara's van. The yellow stone flared as the rock fused into a single metal plane.

Jules allowed himself a smirk as Veronica's own shield, a shimmering circle of bent light no bigger than a hub cap, formed around a single purple nexus.

The smugness that flowed from the trio as they smiled was slightly nauseating.

"BEGIN!" Ixey started, and the clash exploded. Veronica's moon blade dashed at Jules like lightning, his shield moving just as fast to intercept it. Veronica's blade spun into the shield like a buzzsaw, sparking on the metal in a flurry of blows. The shield held and the sword retreated, its blackness no longer all-consuming, but a mere shadow in the fading sun. Veronica's shield covered her sword as it darkened. While she remained unfazed, I could smell the scent of her sweat mingling with her perfume on the breeze.

The shield bore wounds as well, creeping cracks, each one harboring shadows injected from Veronica's blade. The yellow nexus flared and all the summoned material shed in a flash of green light. The metal regrew just as it had before.

Veronica sputtered. "You built a custom aegis!" She didn't say the word cheating, but everyone could hear it in the pitch of her voice.

"Well, it's not like we had one just sitting around," Jowls said.

"It's a good one for general purposes, but I think you'll find it particularly a challenge to pierce." Jules smirked. "Would you like to concede before you break on this particular beach?"

"You've just stalemated. That little needle you call a sword can't get through our Aegis either." Veronica drew herself up to her full height.

Jowls hissed, "Girl, you picked the wrong magus to use a probability shield on." His tail was in full-on lash mode, as if he had a mouse in his sights.

Jules' pin of a sword darted forward. Veronica's aegis spun to intercept, and the needle bounced off it. There didn't seem to be any impact. It was more deflected. I only saw the tiniest wisp of blue in Jules' sword.

"Two-hundred-and-forty-nine blows and your Aegis will be extinguished," Jules announced. "I can land thirty-two in a minute, Veronica."

Jules' shield is self-repairing. Veronica's has no such feature, Richard commented.

Veronica narrowed her eyes. "Nice plan, but it's time to throw it out the window."

Her blade hurled itself at Jules and struck the shield with a thunderclap clang. It bounced off like a boomerang, whirling around Jules and Jowls to dash at them from a new angle. The huge aegis followed just as quickly, spinning through the air as if possessed by a ballerina, shedding and re-growing pieces of itself under each probing blow.

"Ha! Get her! Counter attack!" Rudy cried.

But he didn't. While Jules had no trouble intercepting any of the blows, his sword went after Veronica's own aegis like a methodical wasp. I could see it losing energy under the constant assault. The trio sat in rapt attention beside me, the scent of excitement and sweat wafting off them. Sandra sat back, calm as a cucumber.

Veronica tried several different patterns of attacks but to no avail. While I could see the techno-aegis' yellow nexus, the power source of its flight, dimming, it wasn't doing it nearly as fast as Veronica's own aegis. She began to sag from the effort of maintaining her blade. Sweat streamed down her face in bullets, and both her and Neelius' chests heaved under the strain. She hurled her own aegis against Jules and swatted his blade away with her own.

That worked momentarily. Jules charged with his own massive aegis, using it like a battering ram. The two shields clashed, and hers was driven back, nearly violating her circle until she forced it away with her blade.

Nearly at the threshold.

Too soon, Jules! Way too soon! Richard's thoughts echoed.

With a sweep of Veronica's arm, Neelius screamed into the battle, his talons and beak crackling with a black energy all his own. The battle changed instantly. Neelius swooped toward Jules and Jowls. When the shield interposed itself, he struck with both talons as the blade swooped around. The shield spun like a top and batted the bird away from it. As Neelius spun away, the shield jerked sideways but not before it nicked the circle. Jowls let out a yowl of pain and Jules winced. The shield struck the blade head on. White flared from its thus far unused nexus as Jules activated the shield's last trick. Energy from a plane of stasis blasted out, catching Veronica's blade head on. The black blade fell to the ground and simply dissipated.

"YES!" The trio cheered. "We've got you now!"

The Blackwings howled with indignation. "Dirty trick!"

"Simply accurate predictions of behavior," Sandra called back.

It's over now, the trio thought. *She won't risk her familiar to serve as the sword.*

Yet it wasn't over. Neelius scraped himself up from the ground and launched himself back into the air. He circled the interior of the arena, and Jules' shield shadowed his movements. Veronica, her dress soaked with sweat now, shook with effort as she drew on her anchor. Her aura moved oddly as she reached out, her attention divided. A smaller portion flowed into the circle, and the spot where she had formed her sword before grew bright. Jules cursed, the glow of the stasis nexus flaring in his shield as he turned it toward Veronica.

The second bolus of energy discharged as Neelius dived with the sudden speed of a gunshot slamming into the back of the shield. The stasis spell burst and the dark halo around Neelius shattered, but the bird himself was unfazed, clinging to the shield with his talons. With a grunt of effort, Jules sent the shield into a spin, trying to fling the bird off, but Neelius rode like a pro cowboy, his head hammering at the underside of the shield.

Jules' eyes bugged in panic as the life went out of the shield, and Neelius fell to the ground with a thud. Neelius stood on the shield, the yellow nexus clasped in his beak.

The black eagle's eyes beamed with pride.

The gem exploded.

14

Several things happened in rapid succession. Veronica screamed, the auras of other Blackwings and their dogs filled with power. Shock rang through the heads of Tom, Dick and Harry as if you'd slammed their heads together. O'Meara's wheelchair lurched into motion as Veronica fell to her knees, her eyes blank, jaw slack.

Jules and Jowls stared at Neelius' toppled form on the ground. A pool of blood spread from his headless neck.

All eyes were on him, his mangled form. There would be no coming back. All magi and familiars stood in shocked silence.

"The winner is... House Technomagi." Garn's small voice carried across the silence.

Then things moved all at once. A duet of growls rumbled through the air as Dorothy and Naomi erupted in a nimbus of blue light. The air around us howled to life, and Naomi's form shifted, dagger-sized talons growing from her fingers as black feathers sprouted across her skin. Rinoa, the youngest, ran toward Veronica, crossing the ward as it blinked out.

Dorothy and her companion took a threatening step toward us. Tom, Dick and Harry's minds replayed the scene, bouncing it among their consciousness like a pinball trapped between three bumpers.

"Murderers!" Naomi croaked. Her wolf crouched to leap, his teeth bared, feral with rage.

"Stop this NOW!" O'Meara shouted, heat enveloping my senses in a second before an inferno erupted between both sides. The wall of fire drove Naomi and Morie backward, their fur and feathers smoking from the heat. All the magi's blue nimbuses winked out, except for Dorothy's. The wind-mistress reached up into the air as if grabbing something and a ball of blue and yellow energy coalesced in the air.

O'Meara charged up to the young magus in her chair and delivered a vicious backhand. The force of the blow nearly lifted Dorothy from the ground. She spun to the side, barely catching herself on the picnic table. "WHAT DID I SAY!?" O'Meara bellowed. She stood on the footrests of her chair and towered over the two Blackwings. "You will be civilized while you are with my—" O'Meara gave a small grunt of effort, and her intimidating stance wobbled slightly "—jurisdiction!" she managed before falling back into her seat. "There has already... been too much." Human ears might have lost that last bit, as the consequences of that last spell continued to settle onto her body, her muscles clenching in such a way I knew she was in agony.

I looked to Ixey, but she appeared lost, staring at Neelius' headless body. My eyes went back to O'Meara and found her looking at me like a drowning woman on the verge of losing consciousness.

Richard, I need to take a small leave of absence, I thought at my bond.

What? Richard mentally sputtered, but I had no time to explain.

I broke my bond to Richard with a snap, the link withdrawing as suddenly as it had been made. The chain swirled into existence and hurled itself at O'Meara before Mr. Bitey's snake form could fully manifest. The chains wound about her wrists and neck. More eyes widened around me.

Oily orange sludge flooded O'Meara's mind, sticking to memories and thoughts, weighing it all down, drowning her under it all.

I strode into her mind even as she made a feeble attempt to bat me away. *You know you were supposed to do less magic, O'Meara,* I chided.

I don't need your help, O'Meara thought.

I call bullshit on that. I studied her thread. The block that Lady Cavell put in place had been blown wide open, and the wound flowed this sickly substance into her mind. Her insecurities were positively swimming in it. Negative emotions boiled up in her mind like a geyser of bile out of an upset stomach. They'd all been there before, but now, barely two days since I broke my bond with her, they were just as swollen and inflamed as the wound I leaned against.

Get out of my head, Thomas!

You invited me in, I told her as I pushed myself against her source, stanching the flow of nastiness.

You're supposed to be bonded to someone else! O'Meara protested.

Apparently the dragon rebuilt me to take advantage of shifting loyalties. I prattled on as I searched her mind. *You have to promise me you won't channel again until you're healed.*

I'll do what is required to keep the peace, she thought, and there I saw it, rising from the murk of guilt and pain. A black thing, a parasite on her sense of duty. I fell upon it with imagined teeth and claws. You can't kill a thought, but I did my level best, ripping it off her sense of duty. O'Meara's mind recoiled from the attack, shuddering and pushing, trying to close around me and push me out. I retreated from her consciousness and to the place in her mind I called the garden of regrets: A congress of the fragments of all the six familiars O'Meara had previously bonded to. Most were mere shadows. But not Sir Rex. The dead Great Dane guarded O'Meara's most traumatic memories. So strong was the shade that there had been times when I'd heard his voice streaming from O'Meara's head.

There was a new resident there. The sight of which had me skidding to a stop.

My own amber eyes looked back at me with a smug reassurance. He, or I, sat to the left of Sir Rex in the court. While Sir Rex still loomed, I was nearly half his size. The others barely reached his knee, or in the case of the house cat, his ankle.

"See?" the memory-me said. He had a cobra around his own neck. "I told you I'd come back."

I wondered if I'd have a court in my own head before too long.

Rex's eyes were dead things and did not focus as he glared down on me and growled. "You have hurt her, ripped something out, violated her trust."

"She just attempted to kill herself." I spat the death wish at his paw. It tried to scrabble away, but the Dog pinned it with a massive claw.

"There will be more of these. They breed like vermin. Feed on her loneliness," the dog's voice echoed.

"Rub it in why don't you," the memory-me said. "I've got to be free. It's the only life for me."

"I can't cure her while I'm bonded to her," I said.

"Without magic, she cannot serve her purpose. Without purpose, her darkness grows. A bond is a raft in the darkness. She will drown without you." The dog spoke as if he'd seen eternity.

"She'll drown with me as well! Just slower." I and the memory-me spoke as one.

Rex hrrmed, picked the death wish up by its tail and popped the squeaking thing into his mouth, swallowing it whole. "Do not come again unless you are ready to take my place."

My hackles rose. "O'Meara's my best friend, old dog. I plan on keeping her around for a long time."

"Then stay and help her!" O'Meara's own voice bled into his.

I wanted to. There was something about the trio I didn't like. Something I couldn't put a finger on. O'Meara's mind was different. Her hands felt like home. Yet I didn't trust that feeling either. The entire reason I'd fallen into this insane world was that I'd allowed myself to value comfort over everything else. "Because if I stay, I'd be a pet. That's something I can never allow for myself."

I strode back into O'Meara's consciousness.

She sagged from the exhaustion filling her mind, yet the anger still seethed around me. *What did you do to me? I felt you do something!*

I purred reassuringly. *I took out some garbage.* I retreated back to my own head, pulling the bulk of her exhaustion with me. Then, as quickly as I'd initiated it, I pulled Mr. Bitey back from her.

I caught O'Meara glowering before I collapsed into Richard's lap.

"You spineless half magi!" Dorothy spat as I struggled to keep one eye open. "You couldn't win on your own!" Her fists were balled at her sides, but she wasn't channeling now at least.

"Hey, remember, Veronica challenged us!" Sandra stalked forward.

"Indeed!" Harry and Tom said. "Duels are risky. You expected us to just fall over for you? To sit by and let you take our prize?"

"The risk was yours," Sandra said with a tone of grim finality.

Dorothy wasn't about to let her have the final word. "We are a House! You are a group of rats scheming in a basement!"

"ENOUGH!" O'Meara roared. "The next person who speaks across this divide will be banished from Grantsville. Go your own ways and cool off, all of you." Her gaze shifted to the arena. Veronica sat, her white dress stained red, Neelius' body cradled in her arms. Behind her Rinoa stood, tears streaming down her face, her hand hovering over Veronica's shoulder, trembling as if afraid to touch the other woman. Tack had paused outside the circle, one foot raised in uncertainty.

"You have more important things to attend to," O'Meara said in a softer voice.

Silence reigned. The animal features of Naomi's body were reabsorbed into her human form, and Dorothy's anger collapsed into a wince of pain. The wolf's teeth disappeared, and Fee gave a whine, each familiar immediately seeking the touch of their bonds.

Jules, with Jowls bundled in his arms, walked toward us stiffly. Ixey followed, biting her lip. As he walked past, O'Meara whispered, "If I find out that was not an accident, Jules, I will not be happy."

"Neither will I," Jules whispered back. Then to everyone else he said, "Let's go. You all need rest."

Richard's hand tensed on my neck. He'd been petting me, I realized belatedly. A tickle of adrenaline had been keeping my eyes open and now with the situation defused the exhaustion clawed at my mind with heavy pillows. My third eyelids slipped halfway over my eyes.

O'Meara and Ixey were speaking to each other. Ixey held the inquisitorial sword out to O'Meara but the older woman pushed it away with a shake of her head.

"What did you do?" Richard asked.

"Magic trick." I gave a little laugh and tried to lift my head. My body obeyed sluggishly as I forced myself back to my feet. "Could you all drop me off for a bit? I need to sleep this off."

"So, are you done with us?"

"No. I need the tass more than ever. And I need it quickly." *Unless you know a suicide ward that's willing to commit a fire magus,* I added mentally, glad that no one was in my head to hear it.

I had them drop me off at Noise's place.

15

Noise's place wasn't much. A one-bedroom, ground-floor apartment in a building hidden behind a hill just a mile from the main thoroughfare. A voice told me it wasn't the greatest idea to tell the technomagi where Noise lived, but it chimed in after we were en route.

Real werewolves didn't change at the sight of the full moon. Their humanity ebbed and flowed with the moon herself. During the new moon they were completely human and slowly added wolf until the half moon, then lost the human until they were entirely wolf at the full moon. The Veil had no room for such subtlety however, so mundanes saw them as human before the halfway point and wolves beyond it. Most werewolves lived outside of towns and cities their entire lives, but Noise had always wanted more humanity in her life, so she stayed in the city as long as she could, maintaining her own apartment on what she made on freelance coding jobs.

I pawed at the button that was her doorbell then stopped, noticing a ripple of motion. The front of the apartment featured a door and window off to the left. The simple two-paned sliding window stood half-open. This struck me as odd. The apartment had a draft in the best of times. Now it was two days after the new moon in the early winter, a few days before she had any fur to speak of. My muzzy brain and I decided to view it as an invitation. After pushing the window the rest of the way open, I slipped into her tiny kitchen and froze.

A deep sense of wrongness prickled from my nose and down the fur of my back. Had I gotten the wrong apartment? The kitchen, while not spotless (that would have been impossible for even a SWAT team of maids) was tidy. I'd stepped down from the window and into a sink that had no dirty dishes in it. Not a plate, not even a coffee mug. Worse, it smelled wrong, not just of the acid scent of Lysol that hung in the air, but due to Noise's diet the place always had the lingering scent of cooking meat.

My ears tracked breathing and a distant sound of music deeper in the apartment. The sound of typing, but it had no rhythm. The taps were hesitant, coming one at a time instead of the practiced babble of plastic on plastic I normally associated with Noise working.

Cautiously, I crept down onto the kitchen floor. The apartment resembled a storage container in layout. The kitchen was at the front with a hallway from the door that ran into a modest living room. Then two doors: one opening into her bedroom and the other to the bathroom. It was similar to the house we used to share but smaller. I peered around the corner and into the living room.

Noise's desk chair sat empty, but a figure hunched on the couch in front of the TV. It had her black and green high-performance gamer headset over her ears. I blinked. It was

Noise, but she was far too large. She usually didn't give up on the desk a mere three days after the new moon; normally at this point she resembled a werewolf from a wolfman movie, ears pointed and fuzzy, talons like nails (which she trimmed every few hours if she was trying to work), enlarged canines and a general wild look. A slight increase in bulk. Her shape was wrong. She'd slammed on a hundred pounds since I'd seen her last and not all of it muscle. Her scent had also shifted. The human scent was strong, the lupine faint and something else mingled with it.

"Noise?" I asked, padding closer and edging around the couch. On the coffee table was a platter of precut veggie sticks, more than half consumed. She made no reaction and continued pecking at the keyboard. "Noise?" I asked louder, knowing it was futile. She stared into the screen, not seeing anything else. I could hear the heavy metal screaming into her elongated ears, the tips rounded, not pointed.

I'd have to poke her, and it's never a good idea to surprise a werewolf. Wolves had a fear response to cats my size and that instinct came in as soon as the barest sliver of the pale mistress showed herself in the sky.

Gritting my teeth, I circled around Noise and sat in front of her. She didn't glance up. Carefully standing out of arms reach, I batted the top of her screen. She exploded with an animal bellow, jumping clear over the sofa. The black matte laptop flew up, tumbling toward me. The floor vibrated beneath my body as her feet slammed into the ground on the far side. I reared up, waited another half-second and caught the laptop between two paws, closing it the rest of the way with a click of the latch. I carefully took the thing in my teeth and set it on the coffee table.

Noise stood, her hands gripping the couch as if she were

moments away from picking it up and throwing it at me. The changes had subtly crept into her face as well, her features wider, her eyes rounder. She bared her fangs. I sat still, waiting, my tail wrapping around the front of my paws, my ears forward and friendly.

Abruptly the tension in her form eased. "You are such an ass, Thomas," she managed to growl and sigh at the same time. "What have I said about surprising me when I'm working?" She rolled over the back of the couch, which creaked in protest when her body impacted the cushions.

"Not to let your laptop hit the floor. Or bite through it while catching it. Don't accidentally spill ice cubes down your back or smack you with my tail. Well you didn't say that last one, but it was a fairly painful experience for me and you should feel guilty about it." She narrowed her eyes by degrees as the list continued. The tip of my tail started twitching.

I took a step forward, smiling to myself.

"You're insufferable," she told me even as she reached out and curled her hand around my neck, pulling me into her newly smothering chest. I leaned into her. This close, I could smell fear and nervousness soaking through her shirt.

"For your Christmas present I'm going to sew a cell-phone into your hide. Tallow had no idea where you'd gone. Said you broke your bond and abandoned O'Meara."

"I did not! Well, abandon her I mean," I protested.

"I figured. That witch has you wrapped around her broomstick." She slid her hand down the length of my spine and banished the last of my adrenal vigor, the only thing holding back the tide of exhaustion. It hit me like a locomotive constructed of couch cushions, and the tension left my body.

Even altered, her scent spoke of safety, and I let my head fall into her lap. "You should have mentioned the..." My words swam away from me. "Bigness."

"I don't need help from O'Mooora." She clapped her hand over her mouth and swore. I finally got a good look at her hand. The tips of her fingers had knitted together. She looked down at me. "You said this would fade," she said, her tone slightly accusatory.

I tried to respond, to snap something back, but I couldn't find the words. They were there somewhere in the haze of my mind. If I could just sleep for a bit. I closed my eyes.

"-omas! Thomas!" An earthquake shook my world. I peered up at Noise through the hazy film of my third eyelids. "What's wrong with you?"

"Tired," I managed before slipping back into the black.

I woke to the sound of running water and the wet scent of body wash. I started awake with far less grace than is usual for a cat, rolling off the couch and getting tangled in the blanket that'd been placed over me. I looked around, a bit dazed. Bright, natural light crept around the corner of the kitchen. *Dogs on pogo sticks, how long have I been sleeping?* I wondered. I usually woke up an hour before the crack of dawn. I nosed Noise's cellphone and the display, along with the chibi Tracer from Overwatch, read 9 AM.

The door to the bathroom opened to reveal Noise toweling herself off in a blast of steam. I whirled, and my eyes nearly popped out of my head. Every part of her had enlarged and rounded, from her hips to her arms, and nearly double for her chest. It was only a little outsized for her nearly six-and-a-half-foot frame but edging into cantaloupe range. She caught the angle of my eyes and raised a thick finger in warning. "You make one dairy joke and I'm going to lock you in the closet with an open bag of catnip for a day."

I wrenched my eyes away, wincing at the thought of the time I'd "tried" catnip. Noise only broke out that threat when she was being serious. "Sorry."

"Well, at least we know you're still a little human beneath that fur, despite the feline sense of humor. You going to tell me what happened to you?"

"What are you talking about?"

"You passed out so thoroughly that I painted your claws."

"What!" I looked down and flexed out my claws. Sure enough, the claws of my right paw had been painted hot pink and the left sported fluorescent green. "NOISE!" I pulled them into my paws so hard my muscle ached. I looked up into her huge impish grin. Her ears flicked with amusement.

"Do you want me to get the remover?" she offered, innocently.

My jaw fell open. "No!" If there was a scent worse than nail polish remover in the universe, I had yet to experience it. The barest whiff and I'd have an awful sneezing fit. "You are a cruel and sadistic person, Noise."

She cupped her breasts with two-fingered hands. "These are your fault. If I don't get this fixed, I'm going to be on my father's menu. I thought you might need a reminder of me when you're out gallivanting with your magi friends."

That struck me as unfair. "Noise, I don't cause the random overlaps of realities. That sort of thing requires a magus that doesn't faint every time she channels."

"I don't care, Thomas! I want you to fix it." She pulled her hair back so I could see the nub of a horn that had begun to poke out of the crown of her skull. "At this rate I'm going to be a slab of beef before the half moooooo—" Noise slammed her fist into the doorframe, cutting off the prey animal sound with a saw-toothed growl. She closed her eyes and took a deep breath before continuing. "If we don't fix it by the half moon," she said, clearly annunciating the word, like a hiker skirting the edge of a sinkhole, "then my family might decide to have me for dinner. Then you won't have me to crawl to after O'Meara does whatever the hell she did to you last night."

That got my hackles up. "She didn't do anything to me!"

"Her scent was all over your fur! And I've never seen you so out of it! And you had supposedly left her!" she growled. "Where the hell have you been?" Her voice cracked and a soft sound escaped her, neither cow or wolf nor human, but the hurt in it was crystal clear. She turned away and took a drawn out sniff that might have been the start of a sniffle.

My ears wilted as my mind broke out the clear-in-hind-sight-hammers. *Stupid, stupid, stupid.* I'd hurt her, again. I should have gone to her the night I'd walked away from O'Meara. I trotted over and encircled her legs. "Sorry. Just a lot of magus stuff is going down. There was a duel and O'Meara nearly killed herself. I had to re-bond her to stop that, and I wore myself out. That's all." Noise's gaze remained skeptical, so I continued to babble. "I broke it again once I was done."

That piqued her interest. She knelt, took my head in her massive hands and stared into my eyes. "Are you telling me you're not bonded to anyone right now? There's nobody in there with you?"

Well, there was Mr. Bitey, but he didn't kiss and tell. "Uh, no. I'm unbound." It finally dawned on me what she was saying.

A slow smile spread across her slight muzzle. "So we're really alone. After six months?" She slid her hands down my neck and sides in a decidedly non-platonic way. Heat rose into my ears, and into other places as our lips met, finally unhindered by the thoughts of another.

16

We rolled into the parking lot outside Jules' workshop around noon. Noise had developed a nervous grunting in her breath as we opened the door.

I'd expected stares and inquiries as we walked in. Instead, Jules and Jowls were huddled over one of the work tables, Jules frantically sketching on the paper before them. The rest of the crew snoozed on cots spaced out between the other tables. Tom, Dick and Harry slept on a large yoga mat piled on top of each other, a mass of wrinkled suits.

"You sure this is the spot, Thomas? Kinda looks more like a tech start up that's running out of funds," Noise commented after she walked through the door. Nobody even glanced up at the nearly seven-foot-tall werecow-wolfwoman.

I couldn't really disagree. "Jowls? Jules?"

Jules' gaze never wavered from the paper in front of him as he held up a hand. "Busy. Need a few more moments."

I padded close to the huddled men and poked at Richard's leg. The three snorted as one and each of their eyelids fluttered. Harry finally opened one eye. It lazily slid over to me, to Noise as she loomed over the Magi, and then it slowly traveled up her body. The other eye joined the party as they paused on her chest. Noise had broken out her largest bra, one usually reserved for the night of the half moon. Yet her new form was challenging the thing to the very margins of its design specs..

Harry muttered something that I didn't catch, peeling himself from the pile, which groaned. "Hello there." He rapidly wiped the sleep from his eyes and ran his fingers through his short, fizzled hair. He stood up and extended his hand. His head was precisely level with Noise's chest. He blinked.

"My name is Noise. I'm hoping you can help me." Noise took his hand with her massive two-fingered one. Harry jolted with shock as it engulfed his.

"Well that's awkward," Tom and Dick said, smiling from back on the mat as Harry tilted his head back to look at her face.

"I'm, uh... I'm Harry." He rubbed both eyes with his fingers to clear them of the remaining crusty sleep, then gestured back at the yoga mat. "The layabouts down there are Tom and Dick."

"Richard," muttered Richard.

Harry's eyes flicked down and back up to her face. "You're not a werewolf. What are you?" Fear flashed over his face as the other two men's eyes burst open.

I quickly interposed myself between Harry and Noise. The motion wasn't as successful as I'd hoped since my head only reached her waist. Harry stumbled back as he noticed me. "She is a werewolf," I said.

"I got stuck in a transition," Noise added.

Immediately, the other two of the trio were hauling themselves up, peering at Noise with curiosity. "I'm hoping you all will be willing to take a look at her and try to help us figure out what went wrong," I said.

"After you cut us off at the duel?" Tom said. "Why did you abandon us like that? Are you still bound to O'Meara? Did you tell her everything we are working on?"

A slight whine slipped out of my throat, but I centered myself and tried to look unfazed. "I thought it would be better for all parties if O'Meara hadn't lost consciousness at that moment. And to do that I needed to take her fatigue."

The three heads reeled a bit. "You can do that? You can sleep for her?"

"Is that why you fell asleep mid-sentence last night?" Noise stared down at me.

"It's something familiars can do sometimes, but it requires a very open bond," I said with as much authority as I could muster. Truthfully I had no idea. I'd done it without much thought months ago to enable O'Meara to spend a few hours awake at a time when she'd first come out of her coma. "But yes, if you wanted, I could sleep for the three of you." I unspooled Mr. Bitey. "Same deal as before."

"We require a bit more warning if you plan to break the bond," they said.

"A whole minute would be nice," Richard added.

"Deal." And we re-bonded without a fuss. Although the link seemed even smaller than before. A note of wariness flowed from the three magi.

"Miss, if you would stand on this table here." The three gestured at the workbench with the inscribed casting circle.

Richard then glanced up at the ceiling, which was about six inches above Noise's head. "Well, sitting within it might work better," he amended.

Noise nodded and levered herself onto the table. The wood creaked dangerously under her weight.

You realize we've never actually looked at a thread itself before, Thomas? the trio thought. *That's not something we can do easily without the sight.*

Harry's voice drifted over the other two's. *Not to mention it's the opposite of what we're trying to do with our current research with the LAPIS.*

I mentally kicked myself. Raking through my memories, I hoped I hadn't actually told Noise that these three could fix this.

How hard could it be? Let's take a looksee, Tom countered. *Go ahead, Thomas.*

Okay. Would this be a scrying spell then? I closed my eyes to Noise's knitted eyebrows and stared into the dark of my eyelids. I could make her out, a pale figure in the dark, slowly focusing as if I were watching a Polaroid develop. Her hand blurred up to her nose. "Stop moving!" I snapped and continued to stare into her. Interconnected lines of faint energy flowed through her like a web of rivers, a hidden circulatory system. Yet the energy appeared to have no source or outlet.

I felt Richard's eyes flutter open, broadcasting another image of Noise, fuzzier, shifted, less crisp but Noise all the same. Yet the lines of energy didn't line up, didn't connect. More images flowed from Tom and Harry.

Wow, the trio breathed.

What? What are you all seeing? I asked.

Hold all four viewpoints in your head at once, they instructed. *It's much easier that way.*

I did as instructed, trying to hold what I saw as well as what they saw in my mind's eye. It hurt, stretching parts of my brain that had not been used before.

Bob your head side to side a bit.

I did so, and the lines flowing within shifted as my viewpoint changed.

Suddenly I saw it, like something in my brain slipped out of alignment, and for an instant the lines knitted together.

There! You had it! Do that again!

Like probing your teeth to discover which one has the toothache, I concentrated on the feeling. I'll never forget that sensation. After several attempts, I found that white hot spot in my brain and pressed. Noise snapped into clarity in front of all of us, the thread of her soul a river looping through her body and out into the unknown. All the smaller rivulets broke apart and resealed again. Yet some of the flows appeared disturbed. A stream of something else ran through, tangled in the capillaries of her very being.

Following all the flows to their source took some doing. Threads braided together as they exited her body. Peering inside these threads, the vision of the full moon flashed through my mind, carrying with it a name, *Luna*. I pulled back with the speed of a reflex, but not before I felt a searing weight of perception slam down on me. Pale light began to fill the darkness between the realities.

Yet in that light, my eyes caught the glint of something else in the braid of Noise's soul. A thread clear as glass had invaded the braid. I peered closer and saw green fields within. It had actually pierced Noise's original thread and, as the pale energy flowed down the thread from the moon, bits of this invading thread came with it.

Merciful tides of Mercury! the trio exclaimed. *She's like a tiny shallowing! As the moon grows stronger it will push more and more of this plane, this reality down into her.*

With all that friction between planes, it's got to generate some tass! Harry thought, peering deeper at the connection.

Within it, a distorted image of a cow lay at the intersection point.

You could milk her for tass! Tom laughed.

I broadcast what she would likely do to someone who attempted that along with a growl of my own. *I'd like your help fixing this, not harvesting my girlfriend.*

A ripple of embarrassment went through the three men, along with a note of disappointment from Harry. As they thought on the problem, the three turned in on themselves, their thoughts becoming distant murmurs for a few moments.

We're no experts on werewolves Thomas. It's an interesting problem, and we have several ideas. She's got a corner of a universe lodged in her soul. It's wonderful as long as she survives it. Events like these are what create creatures of myth. Fixing this sort of thing usually isn't done.

She's a werewolf, not a science experiment. Give me options.

They grumbled about the waste. *With a lot of tass, you make a soul spider spell. It crawls up the thread and carefully pulls the thread apart, separates the strands and then weaves them back together. You'd need somebody good with souls, like Lady Cavell of House Morganna or Exploding Fox of House Hermes. What we could do with a bit of tass, a groat maybe, you trim off one corner of that plane with a blade of tass and give the soul a good shake. Should get it disentangled. Might snap though.*

Snap her soul? That didn't sound good.

Souls are neither immortal nor indestructible, Thomas, but they're tough and repair themselves. We'd probably need to wait and—

"Eureka!" A distant shout echoed through the shared mindspace as heard by four sets of ears.

"They did it?" the trio burbled excitedly and started pulling their attention out of the shared perceptions. While

Noise's condition was interesting, whatever Jules shouted about was capital-I important. I looked back at the tangle of Noise's soul, and the loss of the magi's perception made it look flat but I could still make out the invading energy. I traced it back into the void. The thread attached to a tangle of colors that twisted upon itself and bent around everywhere. It hurt to look at.

My vision flared to white, sending searing pain into my mind. I tore myself away and blinked. My mind felt sunburned as my vision started to clear.

"We did it!" Jowls said. "Oh, it's going to be fabulous! But we have to move quickly before the calculations decay!" I could hear the sound of the workbench creaking under Jowls' bouncing weight without seeing him.

"Thomas, why is she here?" Jules asked.

"Oh never mind her! She's clearly a friend! Aren't you, hun?" Jowls countered.

I smacked the side of my head with my paw, as if that would help get my eyes back online. The white had faded into blotches of runny colors and dim shapes that might be the table, but everything continued to be fuzzy.

"Yes, I'm Thomas' friend," Noise answered. I felt her eyes on me. "Thomas, are you okay?"

The fuzzy bits in my vision resolved into absurd shapes that could be reality. "Maybe?"

"I believe you broke the circle while he was still in deep scry mode. He'll be okay," Tom said.

"Oh my poor handsome Thomas!" Jowls cooed. A warm body pushed against my flank. "Do not worry. If you're blind, then I can guide you!"

Okay, that object in front of me was definitely a table. The thud of a pair of booted feet hit the ground next to me.

"Just what are you doing to my boyfriend, cat?" Noise growled at Jowls.

Oooooh. That's why you didn't rebind us! Richard thought. *A night with your lady.*

Jowls' weight promptly disappeared. "Oh ho ho! *That* sort of friend! Thomas, I'm so hurt!"

I looked toward him, an orangey blob. I'd never seen the purple bits of him before, however. At least twelve different foci ringed Jowls' collar, a multitude of colored nexi and more than half of them golden, wards of some type. I'd never noticed them before. I wondered if they were concealed.

The weight of Noise's hand on my head reminded me of the conversation. "Jowls, you're male."

"Of course! You're open to dating way outside your genus, but you're troubled by a little thing such as gender?" He sighed dramatically, pressing the back of his paw to his forehead. "It's alright. I'll gather up the pieces of my shattered heart and carry on. Somehow! Some way! I'll find a way to distract myself. Maybe a ton of tass will have to do for now."

A cheer went up from the trio. "Where is it?"

My vision had recovered enough that I could see the cat's sharp-toothed grin. "Barely two miles away. But we have to hurry! We have less than an hour to get there and setup.

"You're not leaving without us." Sandra had appeared in the corner of the room, her face flush with excitement. "It's finally ready."

"Oh no!" Jowls moaned and staggered.

"Oh yes, you little luddite! Behold progress! We'll gather more tass than the rest of you put together! Behold!"

The wall behind her slid into the floor and revealed a figure that might have clanked out of a Jules Vern novel. A heavy frame of shiny brass stood a foot taller than Sandra. It had great three-fingered pinchers for hands and a round belly that might have been salvaged from an ancient boiler. The belly exuded the bright glow of energy magics, but the rest of its frame was studded with silver valves that whistled as the thing moved through the opening with heavy, methodical steps. The metal man's head had been constructed from the bottom of an industrial gas cylinder. It had no mouth but two huge eyes, long and cartoonish, just cut into the metal and covered with a metal mesh.

The thing wobbled as it stopped beside the mechanically-minded shaman and teetered. Sandra put a hand out to steady it. "Stabilizers," she hissed out the side of her mouth.

"That's the green one, right?" a voice whispered back. One that I instantly recognized.

"Yes." The robot sank to its ankles with a mechanical thunk. She smiled at all of us. "May I present the Mark 7, Autonomous General Purpose Unit!"

A polite applause erupted from those that had hands.

"A bit less autonomous than the Mark 6, I'm guessing," Jowls needled.

"No! I am robot! I obey!" The voice from inside the metal head said, before erupting into a peal of laughter. With a hiss of escaping steam, the thing's head rose on a pair of pistons on each side of it, revealing Rudy surrounded by a mass of buttons and levers. A pair of familiar-looking joysticks were mounted on the front edge of the rodent-sized cockpit. They'd been salvaged from the copter-wreck. Rudy beamed at me.

"Check it out, Thomas! I got me a mecha!"

"It's not a mecha!" Sandra said in a tone that suggested they'd been over this definition a few dozen times.

"Then its a kaju! Point me at Godzilla! I can take him!" Rudy's left paw hit a lever, and the right pincher spun up with a whirr. "Drill punch!" Rudy shouted as the robot's arm swung upward. The mech pitched forward from the momentum and began to topple forward.

"Step right! Step right!" Sandra squeaked. Rudy cursed and the mech just barely managed to catch itself.

I laughed, "If that's a Kaju the only thing you're going to terrorize is mousyoko! Its totally a clank."

"It is a bipedal steam powered automaton." Sandra gave me an icy glare.

"Which goes clankity clank clank when it walks!" Rudy said, nodding his head in a approval.

Sandra covered her face and squeezed her temples as if suddenly experiencing a migraine. "Fine. At least the term origin isn't from children's TV."

"Oh the networks would love it Sandra," Jowls said. "A snack-driven robot would drive the kiddies wild."

Lightning quick, Sandra jabbed a button on the Robot's neck and the head slammed down on Rudy, cutting off his retort. "This way we can test all the mechanical structures and make sure those are sound before we move onto implanting it with intelligence."

"Excellent progress then, Sandra," Jules said. "Now let's hurry up and test it in the field. Everyone pile into the van."

Everyone nodded and moved out to the parking lot. Noise had one foot inside the van when she froze and emitted a small moo of distress. "Damn it, I'm herd following!" She whirled back to me. "Thomas, did you find out what's wrong with me? Can these people help?"

"Uh..." I began.

Tom stepped up. "Yes! And maybe! But right now we have to move!."

"Why don't you come with us, Noise? We can explain on the way," Richard said, gesturing into the van.

"Magi,"Noise muttered the word like a curse under her breath and crawled into the van. We piled in after her, the van proving a bit of a squeeze for six people, a robot and a cougar.

Jules pulled onto the road and headed north as I tried to explain what I'd seen. By the time I finished, Noise was grinding her teeth together.

"What happens if my soul snaps?" she asked Richard.

Richard grimaced. "If a magus' thread snaps, they usually die, and if they don't, it means no more magic. Ever. Also their personality tends to be fundamentally altered. You'd be human and a different person."

"So if I survive, I die too." Noise slumped.

"Now, that's hopefully not what would happen!" Richard said. "But we don't know! We're not experts on lunar energy. It's a really bizarre thing. To have an anchor to a specific plane be hereditary is a huge mystery to all magi, despite the considerable effort that's gone into trying to understand it. You draw energy from it, but you also send your humanity back along it as the moon waxes. It's like a conceptual ecosystem: wolf, human and change. Now you've got another plane between you and it."

Noise bowed her head for a moment, digesting that and looking down at her two-fingered hands. "So I risk dying or I become a monster."

Well, technically she was already a werewolf, but it didn't seem like the right time to split whiskers. I put a paw on her leg. "Look, just help us out for now. I'm sure we can figure something out."

She nodded minutely and slumped against the wall. At least Tom, Dick and Harry were having an animated discussion about the problem, even if the discussion mostly consisted of trading what-ifs.

After a few minutes, the muscles I'd been leaning against tensed and Noise stirred. "So, where are we going anyway?" she asked.

Jules regarded her in the rearview mirror. "Just a spot in the state forest. Nobody will be there."

"This is my pack's territory!" A note of panic crept into Noise's voice. "I can't help you raid my pack's territory."

"We're after tass, not game, Miss Noise. I doubt anyone in your pack will notice. Since they're all nearly human at the moment."

"What if you're wrong? My Pa could kill me!"

"Thomas, could you please have Miss Noise quiet down," Jules said, staring at me through his rearview mirror as if I was a misbehaving child in the back seat.

I shouldered myself onto Noise's lap, pinning her legs. "Noise, please don't antagonize my clients," I whispered. "I need them on our side if we want to have a shot at curing you."

Anger flared in her eyes. "I don't work for magi! I'm no spell dog!"

"Without help you're not going to be a werewolf either! You can stay in the van if you want and sulk, but that's not gonna help anybody. You might as well do this little thing!"

I got a close look at her teeth; all were wider than they should have been but plenty sharp. "That's how the damn cat got us. Little things, little favors, and before you knew it we were growling over which of us had the honor of being stepped on!"

"It's not like that, Noise! There's no mind control here! But there's no health insurance either! You gotta work while you still can!"

Noise snorted hot breath directly into my face. "Oh, so this is totally my problem now? Meanwhile you're scraping together all your pennies for O'Meara!"

"Hey g—" Rudy tried to interrupt.

"Not now!" I snapped at him before turning back to Noise. "Leave O'Meara out of this! You're not dying!"

"If I'm still tainted like this come the half-moon, then I might as well be dead! My pack will kick me out, Thomas! Don't you think that's a high priority?"

"Thomas!" I heard Rudy somewhere off to my left and ignored him.

I growled. "I owe O'Meara my life, Noise! That's a debt I have to repay! I have to heal her because nobody else is going to! You're a big girl! I can't fix everything! I'm only one guy!"

Noise opened her mouth to reply right before the words came out a squirrel attacked my nose. "THOMAS!" Rudy chittered at me, flinging his body across my muzzle and my vision. "Hey, listen!" I shook my head to dislodge the rodent, but he stubbornly held onto my face. "Thomas! Thomas! Thomas!"

"What, Rudy? What do you want? Get off my nose."

"Okay!" The squirrel sprang again. "Just needed to tell you guys that we've arrived." He smiled, and I realized everyone in the van was looking at me and Noise.

"Sooo awkward!" Rudy whispered.

Jowls smiled from his box. "Are you two going to be alright?"

Noise and I made the briefest of eye contact.

"We're fine!" we both spat.

"Good! Now let's get some tass!" Jowls crowed.

17

Noise avoided my gaze as the magi began their preparations, but she took a black tass bag from Jules as he passed them out. Once Sandra powered up the robot and got Rudy situated, Noise kept it between her and me. Trying to sort out the damage from that little spat would have to wait. I made sure Jules and Jowls crafted Noise a short-term protection charm so she didn't get any more echoes from whatever plane of existence was about to hurtle into ours. At least this one didn't threaten anyone in town.

Jules had parked the van in front of a perfectly normal looking patch of forest. The sun shined as a chilly wind whipped down the road.

"Here it comes!" Jules said, peering at his watch as I leapt onto the van's roof for a good view and threaded my vision back into the trio. I loved Noise, but I just couldn't fix her problem. Hell, it might actually be a good thing if she had to leave her pack. Her father, Walter, was the portrait of an asshole and was probably abusive to boot. Who knew, anyway? The problem could sort itself out. The trio seemed like a capable bunch. Hopefully they could figure out a solution that didn't have the whole chance of death thing attached.

Richard mentally prodded me to pay attention as a purple haze swept the forest in front of us. I waited for it to all transform into birds or crystal squids. Instead they began to melt. Their needles shrank into waxy nodes dripping like hot candle wax. The tree trunks started to sag, until the they were all bent like willows. A small bird attempted to flee its shelter but landed on the ground with a wet plop. It struggled before its wings melted away, leaving it a bean-shaped ball of gray wax with a beak.

A murmur came from among the magi, tones of disgust.

"This doesn't look too friendly," Rudy commented, his voice muffled from the confines of his cockpit.

"Double-check your warding charms," Jules instructed as white stars appeared among the branches of the sagging trees. "Get as much as you can but don't lose your footing." Jules took out the same wand he'd used to push the cars around while the trio, Rudy and Noise advanced toward the transition on foot.

Why don't you guys have something like that? I asked them.

Oh we do, but it's not safe to use kinetic magic in a transition. You never know what the transition will do to the physics, the trio said.

He'll risk it because he hates getting his hands dirty, Tom added.

A new star bloomed, bright blue, from deep in the forest, the light of an anchor being drawn upon. A savage gale howled out of the forest, answering the question of who before I identified the aura. It hit me like a torrent of pillows fired from a rail gun. My claws scrabbled on the van roof but found no purchase on the smooth metal. It swept me off and I fell head over tail, mewing in a most undignified way. The trio were bowled over where they stood. They were all attempting to shield their eyes from the hail of debris the wind was flinging at them. The wind picked up all manner of waxy droplets from the transition, and the stuff was turning back into stones, pine needles and bark as it whipped across the threshold. By the time I'd sat up, Jules, Jowls and Sandra had joined me on the far side of the van.

Jowls howled indignantly, "Those Blackwings! The nerve of them! I won the duel! It's not right, Thomas! Not right at all!"

"Well, nobody owns a transition, right?" I said as the trio turned the corner of the van and joined us, panting. "Where's Rudy and Noise?" I asked them.

When they jerked their thumbs back toward the transition, I threaded around them to stick my head around the corner. It was like sticking your face out the window while your buddy was driving a hundred miles an hour on the highway. Not that I've ever done that.

Noise and Rudy slogged across the transition's border, each sinking up to their ankles in the muck. Rudy's clank took another step and squished down nearly to the knee. Past them, that brilliant blue star continued to shine. I recognized the aura, streaks of red and green, as Dorothy. It could be no other. Then among the treetops more auras flickered. The remainder of the Blackwings flitted about in the form of crows, the howling wind ruffling not so much as a feather. Two pairs of them worked, one holding a tass bag while the other, the dogs most likely, dug the tass out of the trees with their beaks.

Were they immune to the wind? Or was Dorothy steering it around them somehow? And what the hell were Rudy and Noise doing? She couldn't see magic unless the moon was entirely full, and Rudy, well, he didn't look like he was going to make it very far at all.

The wind increased and hurled a glob of wax that elongated into a whirling stick of hurt that smacked me in the face with a crack. I retreated before I sustained additional head trauma. I turned to Richard. "Options? Can we block the wind?"

As if in answer, the wind around us became a deafening roar and the van began to tilt toward us. Only when Jules hit the side of the van with the beam from his wand did it slam back down onto four wheels. The grim faces surrounding me confirmed it: the Blackwings had won this round. All we could do was wait it out.

In five minutes the windy assault ended, along with the transition. Silence reigned for a brief moment before six raucous caws of victory split the air.

"Come back here, you moldy peanut brains!" Rudy cried out after them.

I waited for a similar invective from Noise, but one didn't come. I bolted around the van and ran into the forest. Rudy had made it another step or two and had sunk into the ground up to the robot's waist. "Noise?" I shouted.

"Here," came a quiet moan deeper in the trees.

She'd made it much farther, but the ground had solidified around her knees. She was plastered with detritus from the forest, pine needles clinging to every bit of clothing and skin.

"Are you alright? Did you get hurt?"

Instead of answering she extended her tass bag toward me. It was stuffed with pinecones, dirt and sticks. "Tell me this is tass."

I studied her and then the bag. I shook my head.

Her anger flared up out of nowhere. She slammed the

bag into the ground and let out a bellow of rage. "You mean I just did that for nothing? And let me guess, it was another mage?"

I stepped back, glad she was rooted in the ground for this moment. "They won this round. Next time we'll be ready."

"You never mentioned there were more magi out there! Don't you think that detail would have been helpful?"

"Noise!" I glanced back at the van.

"NO! I'm done! I never should have listened to that old man! Pa is right! Nothing good ever comes of getting mixed up with magi! Nothing!"

"Old man?" The words hit me like a sucker punch. "Do you mean the Archmagus?"

"You were supposed to be a wolf! You were supposed to be MY wolf! The bastard lied. Just like they all lie!" Tears blazed paths down her dirt-covered cheeks, making muddy rivers.

My heart thundered as my hackles rose. "You helped him? You helped him ruin my life!"

"You couldn't remember me! You bought me drinks three times! We went on dates, but as soon as the moon rose you forgot me! He offered to help."

"No no no!" I hissed. "You can't be involved! You're the reason I fought so hard to stay here, to avoid the TAU. To not be a familiar to some random magus!" I didn't want to believe it, but I could feel doors opening in my head. My heart beat so hard that it hurt, threatened to burst.

Yet she stared at me, eyes ablaze, totally defiant. "What are my options? I have a small pack. I can't leave to find a mate. Pa would fucking get himself killed and the pack will just die out. So I asked him to make you into a mate, a **suit**-

able mate. He gave me a powder to slip into your coffee or meals. You loved my cooking."

"SHUT UP!" I roared and lashed out. My claws caught her cheek and tore out three gashes on her face.

"Motherfucker!" Noise swore, clapping a hand over her cheek. Blood already ran down it in a solid stream.

"Why are you even telling me this? I didn't need to know! It's done! I can't go back! You, we, are the one part of my life that never asked for anything! I didn't have duty or a job or a fight with you. We could just be!" I could barely see now, my vision blurring.

Her growl rumbled like thunder from the sky. "You want revenge now? Well, you got it! I'm a freak among freaks! In a few days they'll just put me out to pasture!" She jerked her head upward, showing me her throat. It pulsated with the force of her frantic heart. "Go ahead. Rip it out! If you don't, my father will!"

Part of me wanted to. Part of me wanted to clamp my jaws down on that neck and taste the hot blood of the mate that betrayed me. The rest of me told that part to go jump in a cold lake.

I reared up and put my paws on her shoulders and whispered. "If your father kills you, then I'll personally see that he's sent to the very special hell reserved for fathers who kill their daughters. If it doesn't exist, then I'll create one for him." Noise's eyes widened as I pulled away. "I'm sorry about the cheek," I said, and then left her there.

18

On the way back I spent a lot of time staring at my paws. Useful things, deadly weapons and still painted green and purple. How had I been so stupid? It had been a physical struggle for us to date after the change. I'd ignored all the instinctual bullshit my body threw at me because I'd fought so hard to stay in Grantsville for her, defying everyone who hinted at shipping me off somewhere else. I'd killed three of them. Sabrina and Cornelius' deaths had been tangentially related, but I'd snapped Cyndi's neck because the damn cat wanted to sell me. That had been the cost I'd been willing to pay for her.

And when I'd found out she was a werewolf? Part of the same pack that had snapped my bond with O'Meara? Well, that hadn't been their fault. They'd been mind-controlled. Sunk costs. I made it work. She made it work too. Because of what? Did she feel guilty about what she'd done? Bitch.

I wanted to rip something, slash the upholstery and smash the windows. But to do that I'd have to unsheathe my still-painted claws and remember all the tiny details as to why the effort to stay with her had been worth it.

Women are trouble, a bother. The thought floated through my mind, uninvited and not mine.

I mentally cursed the trio. I'd never shut the link. I'd completely forgotten about them. *Sorry. I can sever the link while I put myself back together. I'm not in a... professional mindset right now.*

A burble among them, *That's not necessary.* A flow of amusement followed. *Maybe we could help?*

"I don't think three gay men are going to assist me in my love life."

"I'm not gay! I'm bi!" Harry protested.

A mental eyeroll from Tom and Richard. "We know."

Anyway, their mental voices remerged, *it is odd for familiars to date at all. Can you imagine the relationship models that would spider web through the houses?*

How would you know? You've never had a familiar before. Besides, I happened to know of a particular cat who was probably as prolific as availability allowed. I glanced toward the front of the van where Jowls squeezed into his shipping box. Jowls, to his credit, hadn't said anything to me, but the fuzzy Romeo was radiating smugness and seemed primed to explode in I-told-you-so's. The entire van had been silent thus far on the way back to the shop, everyone lost in their own heads, shared or otherwise.

You can do way better than a werewolf anyway, the trio thought with cheer.

If you want to stick to canines, we know a few lovely spell wolves in Las Vegas, Harry added.

I growled, drawing a look from Sandra and Rudy. Rudy for his part was sitting in the open cockpit of the mech and crunching on a bag of cashews he'd pulled from somewhere. "You okay, big guy?" he asked.

"No. But I'll live."

The squirrel nodded and to my complete surprise said nothing more, his own eyes distant.

"Too soon for a rebound then," Richard commented, not really to me.

Well, if she wants her problem resolved, that tangle probably isn't going to fix itself. She'll calm down and come back to you. Maybe apologize, Tom thought.

I slashed her face open. I think we're beyond apologies, I thought bitterly, trying to stamp on all the regrets that seemed to be bubbling to the surface of my mind.

They didn't have an answer for that. Well, Tom was about to ask something, but the others quickly cut him off.

"SO!" Jowls' voice boomed through the van, cutting off any more of my wallowing. "You are all technomagi. Give us an analysis."

"We got blown away!" Rudy chirped.

"That wind was a simple channeling, yes?" Sandra said, looking in no particular direction. "And we had no counter to it."

"Despite taking Veronica out of the game, the Black-wings still have us beat in terms of raw magical ability. They're major House magi. You need a strong anchor plane to get membership." Jules grimaced. "Versus technomagi, who as a rule have nearly useless anchors in terms of a fight."

"Hey, we can light a match with Richard's plane!" the trio interjected.

Sandra snorted. "Tom's plane is more useful in a pinch."

"What?" I asked.

"Yes, through the power of the conceptual plane of circuitry I can compel an unfortunate individual to have an overwhelming urge to draw or solder together useless circuitry for a few hours. It's very useful," Tom said without his companions, a bitter note in his voice.

"Now, now, gentlemen and lady," Jowls tsked. "Let's refocus on the problem. The rest of the Blackwings were untouched by the wind. They probably had foci to prevent it. There's no reason we can't construct the same, right?"

"Within the next four hours?" Jules inquired. "That's when the next transition is and it's going to be in town."

"If it's foci then they were probably created by Veronica. With her anchor plane she'll have no trouble creating spells that disrupt kinetic energy," the trio said.

Sandra nodded. "The rest of the Blackwings are kids. Freshly graduated apprentices. Their spellcraft will be poor. Counter their anchor planes and it will take them considerable effort to come up with a counter play."

"So you just need a wind shielding spell right? Just find the right plane and pull it into an object," I said, thinking of the time O'Meara pulled authority into a plastic cop badge.

"Kinetic energy needs to be handled precisely," Jules said. "First you need to find the right plane to use. Too strong and you won't be able to move, too weak and it will be ineffective."

"Harry and I," Tom said, "will work on creating an effective hurricane blocker, but it will take longer than the four-hour window. We suspect once we counter them they'll probably cycle Rinoa to the fore."

"Rinoa's plane can be countered with a pair of ear plugs." Jowls chuckled.

"Nevertheless, Jowls and I have a plan that's longer term and should remove them from the equation," Jules said.

That sent a bolt of anxiety through my intestines, and it must have shown on my face.

"Oh don't be such a worry wart, Thomas!" Jules said.

"This is a friendly turf scuffle, not a blood feud. Besides, the moment anyone does permanent damage, either the Inquisition or House Morganna will be on us like a ton of bricks"

"Neelius doesn't count?" My tail curled with doubt.

"His death will be laid directly at Veronica's feet. The elders will cluck their tongues and say, 'And this is why you should not duel, child,'" Jowls said, invoking a fair imitation of an elderly grandmother.

"They're not looking to kill us either. This is an ancient game that we're going to play in order to become a true House," the trio said.

The other magi nodded.

19

It quickly became apparent that the Blackwings knew this game much better than we did. The wind blockers were nowhere near ready when the next transition hit, so it was up to Richard, Rudy, Sandra and I to contest it. Fortunately, the plane that intercepted ours didn't make the ground completely impossible to travel on. None of the munds noticed when their high school basketball game of the local Grantsville Cougars versus the Clarkston Panthers became bulls versus goats. With the ball unable to bounce on the grass, they converted it into something more akin to rugby. The Grantsville Bulls flattened the much smaller Goats.

Apparently unwilling or too tired to flatten the entire gym with a localized hurricane, Dorothy tried to keep me distracted with focused whirls of air. I had to keep moving, weaving in and out of the crowd trying to spot the tass as it gathered, primarily in the pennant flags and noisemakers held by the crowd. The birds proved to be much quicker than us in grabbing those. The only major tass we managed to obtain was when Rudy charged the field, grabbed the ball and made for the goats' end zone. The engine of the clank screamed as he ran, the crowd exploding with moos of victory. As the transition faded and the game turned back into basketball, that ball alone proved to be worth three groats, but the Blackwings had snatched at least nine more from us.

Even at fifteen percent, this was beginning to look even less like the get rich quick scheme I'd imagined. At least Rudy was in high spirits with his play and chattered happily to us all on the way back to Jules' shop.

Once back, Richard and I tried to assist with the foci crafting, as the next transition wouldn't be until tomorrow, according to Jules and Jowls. The pair had once again entered a fugue state at their table, working on their "solution" to the Blackwings with a worrying fervor.

I learned more about technomagic than I really wanted to working on those devices. Compared to O'Meara, who always seemed to know where the right plane was for a certain magic she needed, Tom, Dick and Harry had no understanding of the realities that weren't near their anchor planes. They treated the universe as a giant bag with an infinite number of marbles in it. While they could reach in and feel around for the size, they had no idea of the color until they pulled it out. They'd built a spell into the device and then instead of filling it with the planar energy they would thread a strand of pure tass back to the plane, which draws a continuous amount of planar energy to the device. All so the focus could be used without the presence of a familiar. The process was quite expensive tass wise. The two anti-wind shields cost most of the three groat to craft. At this they celebrated the efficiency and thanked me for my help.

"Now this should take care of that windbag." Tom lofted the two foci into the air, a belt for him and a collar for me.

Their circuitry made a high-pitched hum as the devices activated.

"It will at least make them reveal their plan B," Jowls said. He and Jules were taking a break from their "solution."

Jules sipped a steaming paper cup of tea. "I've also invited a select few from the University to join us."

Sandra's head popped up from where she was working on the clank. "What! We've barely gotten any tass from this venture! And you want to invite more folk?"

"Indeed!" the trio chimed in. "We're at a net negative so far with the silvers it cost us to get here!"

I caught Jules smiling at his familiar as Jowls puffed out his chest. "If we're to be a House, we need at least two Cabals, do we not?"

"Yes, but that shallowing can produce, what? Ten groat a month? That's not enough for a Cabal, let alone two!"

Jules looked up. "Preliminary estimates are good! Twelve a month."

"We're technomagi! We need far more than six groat a month or we're hamstrung! Not to mention the familiar is going to be skimming fifteen percent of that all by himself under our deal."

I failed at not looking smug. "I might renegotiate after I have the sum I need."

Sandra sputtered. "A hundred and fifty! We'd have to collect over a thousand groat to do that!"

Jowls grinned and faced Sandra. "And we'll need even more than that!"

All the other magi laughed nervously. Jules stirred his tea with a wooden stirrer. "No one is going to take us seriously as a House unless we have the resources of one. The Council requires taxes to support the Inquisition, and to survive we'll need at least one Archmagus to support us. That will be expensive."

Tom, Richard, Harry and Sandra stared at Jules with open mouths.

Jowls bounced and jiggled, his eyes all but exploding into sparkles. "You see, these transitions will keep coming! We're witnessing a historic collision of the planes, similar to the one that led to the creation of House Hermes a thousand years before! Don't you all see? The transitions will get bigger, yield even more tass than all of us can collect. These skirmishes with the Blackwings are just mere practice for the larger battle! Thomas, my expensive friend, will get the groat he wants in a matter of weeks! Not to mention a few more shallowings are bound to happen! House Technomagi might not be a little House scraping by, but a major political force! It will be a new age! Our portraits will hang in the Great Council hallway! Wait and see!" Jowls stared off into the distance, no doubt imagining his face hanging in some hallway somewhere.

"Hey! Earth to Jowls!" Rudy barked. "The Blackwings are still getting most of the tass!"

"Well, stop losing to them, Snack!" Jowls put his nose in the air. "Speaking of which, you all should start moving. The next transition is in thirty minutes."

"A little more advanced warning would be appreciated, Jowls," I grumbled, rising from my position and stretching my back. The little circle workbench hadn't been made with large cats in mind.

"The predictions get more accurate the closer the transition gets," Jules said. "Get going! We'll text you the location once we have it precisely."

I note that they had more than an hour advance for the first shallowing, I thought to the trio.

So noted, t hey thought back.

Did Jules and Jowls suspect a leak among us? I wondered. We all piled into the van, Sandra driving. Jules and Jowls stayed behind to operate the "command center."

I'd curled up in the back for a quick nap as the van hurtled toward some unfortunate place when the van hit a pothole that damn near tossed me up to the roof. Instinct carried me back down, and I landed with an angry hiss, ears and eyes scanning for an attacker. I caught a dim blue flutter out of the corner of my eye.

"Sorry!" Sandra called back. Richard had scrabbled away from my scary teeth.

Ignoring them, I turned and faced the back of the van and concentrated. There, the steady blue pulse of a magus' aura. Distant enough that I'd miss it if I hadn't been actively looking.

"Thomas?" Richard asked. "You alright?"

"I'm fine, but we're being followed." I attempted to figure out which Blackwing it was. Then another joined it, this one definitely Dorothy, her aura bright from channeling. "Well, the good news is I don't think the Blackwings know how to predict the Transitions. They're tracking the van,"

"That's somewhat logical," Richard conceded after a few moments.

"That makes ditching them super simple!" Rudy added. "Quick, somebody make an invisibility ward. Scenting us won't work too well when they're flying."

The van's engine revved as Sandra accelerated. "Hey! Stop!" I cried. "Don't tip them off we spotted them."

"We're almost there. We gotta do something," Sandra said.

"I got some bottle rockets!" Rudy thumped the chest of the clank with his foot. "Even got a few... special ones."

I didn't know what Rudy meant by special, but I knew him well enough to know that I probably didn't want to know. I peered out the front of the van and spotted a bridge in the distance. "Sandra, keep it steady. Rudy and I will bail out and head for the transition," I said. "Richard, can we use the wind inhibitors to cushion the... sudden deceleration?"

"Not on that." Richard jerked his thumb at the contraption, which probably weighed half a ton. "I'll go."

"They'll notice you bailed eventually," Rudy said.

"All we need is a good head start. Dorothy can't blast in an elementary school," Richard said.

My eyes tried to pop out of their sockets. "The transition is at Grantsville Elementary! We can't!"

Sandra snorted. "Jules thought you might balk. But either we do it or the Blackwings will. The transition will happen if we're there or not. It's not something we can stop and collecting tass won't change anything."

She was right, of course, but it left a bad scent in my nose. I thought of the squiggling death wish in O'Meara's head. Maybe I couldn't do anything for the town, but I could save her at least. And Noise, a voice in my head reminded me.

They're munds, Thomas, Richard thought at me. *They'll carry on as they always do.*

"They're people, Richard," I nearly hissed back. "And I don't work with magi who view it otherwise."

"I know, I know. And we try not to hurt them, but we can't save them all either. If magic happens to them, it happens."

That mollified me a bit, but it didn't ease the fur on my neck back down either. Rudy's eyes whipped between Richard and I. "Hey, hey, you two, no fighting on the job!"

Richard nodded. "Shall we get ready to worry about

things we can do, Thomas? Like hurling ourselves out of a moving van?"

* * *

Technomagic foci are fragile things, and I heard something pop when I hit the asphalt with four feet. My vision flashed pure black. Then I stood on the side of the road under a bridge. By my side stood Richard, a nimbus of yellow and black energy flowing about his aura. All I had around me was a puff of gray smoke and the scent of burnt resistors.

"Damn it," Richard cursed.

We told you it's not designed for that! Tom and Harry thought distantly, muffled through Richard.

Worked well enough. I'm not a road pancake! Let's get this over with. It's a five-minute run to the school. A moment of concentration and I saw Dorothy and Rinoa's auras in the distance. The trick had worked for now, but with Dorothy the bird forms of the Blackwings could probably move at speeds approaching warp. I made for the school at a lope. Richard followed at a labored jog, still arguing with his fellows over the probabilities if the buffering spell could be repaired or if they'd have to rebuild it entirely.

Grantsville Elementary was a sprawling complex of flat-roofed, interconnected brick buildings with lots of windows. The screams and laughter of recess echoed over the walls. Three flags flew at half-mast in the center of a roundabout in front of the school. A lone bus was pulling out from the driveway, which burst with the chatter of even younger kids. A midday preschool or kindergarten perhaps?

A few stragglers sat under the supervision of a tired looking teacher or aid with a blotchy discoloration to her face. I wondered how old that echo was. Had she been at the basketball game yesterday? Or perhaps the Stockyard with Noise and I?

I didn't have much time to ponder it, as one of her charges pointed a pudgy finger at me and screamed, "KITTY!"

I froze, already imagining a tranquilizer dart materializing in my buttock. The girl's companion, another girl with curls so tight they could probably trap insects, turned to her, looking affronted. "DOGGY!"

"KITTY!" the first girl insisted.

"Sign say Dog!"

I just stood still as the teacher watched me with wary eyes. These kids were right at the border of when the Veil took hold, but a strange two-hundred-pound dog showing up in front of an elementary school would set adults on edge, service dog harness or no. The woman swallowed something down and smiled nervously. "Hi boy! Good doggy. Stay right there please."

I attempted to wag my tail but a slow lash is the only speed I managed.

"Sorry!" Richard called from behind me, puffing to catch up. A haze of purple had begun to rise in the school behind us by the time he clomped up beside me, the scent of his human sweat rolling off him like a thick cloud. "Sorry. Thomas here got ahead of me."

The woman regarded him with a serious frown. "Please keep him leashed at all times on the school grounds, sir."

"Of course." *Hey, Thomas, do you have a leash?*

Left pocket.

Richard withdrew the leash I kept there and clipped it to the harness, a cheap thing, easy for me to break should the need arise. I only used it when Noise and I went shopping; usually for clothes for her or meaty treats for us both.

Richard said, "Sorry, we're late for a show and tell. Come Thomas."

The woman frowned but didn't stop us from walking through the front door of the school. I already smelled a change in the air, thicker and dense with moisture. I prayed things didn't start melting as the purple glare of the place intensified. We walked down the hallways with purpose, observing the tiniest of details, from the water fountains to the lockers, all of which were lower than my head level and led to the general feeling that I'd entered the valley of the midgets.

The carpet grew thick and spongy beneath my paws, moisture soaking into my fur. The bell rang. Students and teacher surged into the hallways then slowed. Richard and I stopped as the students murmured in puzzlement when their feet refused to lift from the ground. The teacher, a young man with short cropped hair, made an odd squawking sound and attempted to shoo the children onward even as his face pushed out into a beak and his ears began to flap. The children made little noises of surprise and pain as their bodies continued to betray them, their flesh transmuting into wood, clothing into multicolor bark. The teacher's head took off from his shoulders and circled above his garden brood, their hair blossoming into green and the hair adornments of the little girls opened into a bewildering array of colorful flowers.

The ceiling opened and streams of bright sunlight fell onto the students, who made cooing noises as they shifted, widening their stances to soak up the light.

Richard and I had both taken several steps back from the spectacle. The teacher's body grew into a nursery tree, his roots tangled with the feet of his students as his head developed further into a roundish bird with facial features on the torso, like a peacock potato head.

"Well chop chop. Let gets the tass," Richard suggested, squaring his shoulders and sucking in a breath between his teeth. His unease mirrored my own.

Do it for O'Meara, I thought to myself and fervently hoped that the teacher's head found its way back to his body. Letting my eyes un-focus, the tiny points of light twinkled into existence. I breathed a sigh of relief as they gathered in the rapidly swelling fruits in the girls' hair and on the branches of their teacher tree. Richard readied a tass bag and hurried into the child garden to pluck the tass fruits and flowers. Nothing objected and we moved down the hallway to the next group and then another.

I did my best to ignore the children as we moved among them. Their blank wooden eyes with irises of green moss would only move when my back was turned on them.

The purple tint of the place began to fade after Richard's bag had become so laden with the tass fruits that he tied it to my harness and took out another one.

I was focused on the tass so closely that I never even saw the starburst of Dorothy's channeling until a gale of wind punched me into the air and tossed me down a hallway. I sailed through a door and crashed into several bush-like students. They made an odd whistling sound that could have been pain or laughter.

Dorothy stood in the doorway, her braided hair whipping around as her head had its own personal whirlwind. I attempted to disentangle myself, but the students seemed to be quite intent on petting me with their twig-like fingers. I feared if I moved too fast I'd break them. "That tass you have belongs to House Morganna, cat. Hand it over."

I regarded her coolly as I carefully extricated myself

from the children, while a chorus of birds squawked over-head. "Heh, no. This is fairly gathered and spoken for. If you hurry, you might be able to pick up a few scraps."

Thomas, where'd you go? Richard's thought had a frantic edge to it.

Windbag blew me down a hallway. She's got me cornered in a classroom, I responded, giving him the full view of her.

Which classroom?

Any possible room numbers were covered with the thick vines that had grown over the walls. *One with kids in it.*

The technomagi swore in frustration as he turned to retrace our steps. While we'd talked Fee had appeared, pushing around Dorothy's legs and showing me her white teeth.

"You should reconsider that!" Fee growled low and dangerous.

"Oh you're resorting to muggings now? How very high class!" I said. "We won. You lost this one. Now why don't you both step out of my way before my magus blasts you both in the back with a force wand?"

The pair startled and both flinched their heads to the left to glance behind them.

I leapt, striking Fee in the shoulder with a paw and slammed my body into Dorothy's midsection. "Oof!" she exhaled as she sailed into the foliage-covered wall.

As I sprinted down the hallway, Fee let loose a torrent of barks and scrabbled after me. The scent of blood filled my mouth as I bounded over a trio of de-woodifying third graders. They let out cries of surprise as Fee plowed into them like a jet-black bowling ball. *Idiots!* Couldn't these two decide to pick a fight in some transition that wasn't popu-lated with children? I hoped they hadn't hurt any kids with that windblast. I crossed the intersection where I'd be ambushed.

There! I see you. Richard's mind sagged with relief.

"Come back here!" Dorothy shouted from somewhere behind me. A whirl of yellow energy flickered to life ahead of me. I dropped out of my run, twisted my front paws and dug them into the still-moss-like floor. My momentum forced my entire body to pivot around to face Fee. I didn't have time to growl a warning. I lashed out with a paw and smacked her in the side of the head with the full force of my 200-pound frame. The much smaller dog pitched sideways and I caught her with a second paw, smacking her legs out from under her. A rush of violent air exploded behind me, interrupting my pounce and knocking me to all fours.

Fee rolled back to her feet and staggered as the wind tore at my fur while the lab's black coat was undisturbed. A focus on her leather collar shielded her from the storm. Beneath me the flooring rejected my claws as our reality emerged as the victor once again. I hunkered down as the battered dog backed up three steps before retreating to Dorothy's side.

Richard skidded into the intersection, his shoes squeaking on the tile. "Cease assaulting my familiar!" The dull yellow aura of the anti-wind shell pulsed around him.

"Liar! He's not yours! I don't know why you're trying to hide your connection to the Inquisition, but it stops now!" The wind behind me ceased, but Dorothy pulsed with so much energy that it drowned out Richard's aura almost entirely. If she unleashed it, that would be like loosing a tornado inside the school.

The entire trio was paying attention now. "Thomas is my familiar," Richard said, trying to project calm into his voice while the three of them feverishly calculated if the anti-wind spell could handle that much energy. The probabilities did not offer much hope. "And he has shown restraint so far in defending himself." I approached Richard and pushed up against the man's hip.

Fee spoke, "I smell only the barest whiff of a bond between you. It must be faked."

"It's a newer one," I said.

"No! I sniffed your true bond, cat! For a brief moment at the duel! Your cloaking spell on it failed. You're still bonded to her!"

A burble of confusion came from the trio. *Is that how it works?*

"If that's the real issue, you probably should have led with it instead of throwing me down a hallway." I chuckled. "You wanted my lunch money." The burbling of children drifted through the hallways, and I felt the cold prickle of the Veil on my neck. The hall monitor had returned. "Feel that? The Veil's back. You release all that wind you're holding onto and it might take some drastic measures. It's been having to work real hard with all these transitions lately, and I'm sure it's looking for an excuse to flatten a magus or two."

Dorothy narrowed her eyes, but her channeling ceased. "My cabal and I don't know what O'Meara is trying to pull here! But I'm going to find out what she did to my aunt."

"Again, you won't get very far with me if you lead with a punch. You attack me again like that and I'll use my claws. I don't like bullies, Magus Dorothy, and I didn't like your aunt for the same reason."

Dorothy flinched, ever so slightly, when compared to the elder magus.

Richard thought, *We believe she was attempting to get you*

to channel through O'Meara and reveal your nonexistent bond
with her.

Dorothy glowered. "You can't break a bond like Fee
scented between you and O'Meara! You'd both be dead!"

I shook my head. "And yet we breathe alone. Anything is
possible with enough tass, time and knowledge. The Archmagus had plenty of all three. Because of him, my bonds
work differently. That's all there is."

"That's not fair," she whispered more to herself than me.

"Let's go, Thomas," Richard said.

"Ask those three kids you and Fee bowled over trying to
get at me what's fair, Dorothy," I growled as I started to back
away.

Richard and I had made it around the corner when she
called out at us. "This isn't over!"

Damn right it wasn't.

20

Richard and I both expected to find a respite and a bit of decompression back at the workshop, but no sooner had we laid out my broken wind blocker in front of a clucking Tom and Harry did a pint-sized ball of shine and fury explode through the door.

"Who did it? Tell me now!" Ixey shouted.

"You know, Jules, since this is a House chamber now maybe it's time you start locking that door," Sandra said, not looking up from her workbench where she had several pieces of the clank laid out on the table.

Ixey focused the full force of her fury on the woman, crossing her arms and glaring. It was much more intimidating when O'Meara did it. Ixey lacked the bulk to suggest she could toss you through a window, magic or no magic. When Sandra refused to meet her eyes, she turned them on Jules, who blanched.

"Ixey—" Jules started.

"Inquisitor Ixey," she corrected him, jabbing a thumb toward the hilt of the sword slung over her back. Her clothing was unchanged from when we'd last seen her at the duel and looked it. The scent of days and paper lay over her like a thick musk and the circles under her eyes hinted that the shaman hadn't slept much if at all since the duel.

"Inquisitor, my mistake." Jules grimaced. "Perhaps you'd like to tell us what you're going on about?"

"You should know," Garn said in the loudest voice I'd ever heard from the lizard, "It's technomagic!"

"What is?" Jules insisted.

"If you don't know, then someone in this room does." She scanned the room and scowled, her eyes lingering on Sandra. "If it wasn't you, then the duel is doubly invalidated. Not only did someone cheat, but that person was outside the duel itself."

"WHAT!" Jowls finally looked up from his feigned nap on the corner of the workbench. "Madam! I assure you we conducted ourselves in the highest of honorable fashions. It was win-win for us, even if we lost."

"That's what I thought, which is why I allowed that barely held together aegis in the first place. But then I found this buried under my arena circle." Ixey pulled a plastic baggie from her pocket that contained something small and battery-powered. One of those computers on a tiny board. I crept forward to try to get a better look only to find it shoved in my face. "Recognize it, Thomas? See any of your new friends here working on it before the duel?"

The device had two layers, a printed circuit board studded with fairly large chips and a breadboard with a host of fried electronics centered round a broken silver ring. The plastic in the circle appeared to be worn, having a powdery coating.

I shook my head. "We were focused on building the aegis. Nobody worked on a side project as far as I can remember."

"And how much can you remember?"

None of us did it, the trio thought at me. *But any of us could have.*

"I can vouch for Richard," I said.

"As a good familiar would," Ixey said.

"Ixey, that's a very basic remotely detonated spell," Jules said.

She whirled back to Jules. "Nothing basic about it. The spell that went off consisted of entropic energy collected from a plane similar to Veronica's anchor. With her slinging around her entropic aegis the burst would have been a flicker against the background." She held up a finger, wading off interruption. "It was specifically tuned to degrade spell weaving. Not so strong that it would hurt a good spell, mind you, but a cobbled together thing like that aegis? Worked well. Brilliant way to manufacture an accident."

"Ixey! Please! Stop pretending you're O'Meara and jumping to conclusions!" Jules protested. "Anyone with a basic understanding of spellcraft and technomagic could have rigged that circuit."

Ixey drew herself up and regarded Jules with cold eyes. "If O'Meara was well then there wouldn't be a question of who had done it. But! I'm far more likely to delegate." She shook her wrist, which contained the gems that housed her spirits. I caught a flitter between them.

Jules regarded them. "Spirits generally can't see real magic any more than a human."

"Untrue," Ixey said. "But I'm not delegating the task to my friends. I'm delegating it to you, Jules."

"What?" Jules nearly squeaked. "You can't ask me to do that! I won't!"

"Why not? You clearly know more than I about the spell. It's perfectly understandable for a young Inquisitor to recruit local experts, and I know you have a shred of honesty when you're not bilking the local werewolves. You're the only technomagus I trust." Ixey's eyes shimmered like one of the sequins on her jacket.

"And if I... refuse?" Jules looked pained.

Ixey shrugged. "Then I'm clearly out of my depth. I'll be forced to call for a full Inquisition in the matter."

Sandra froze, along with everyone in the room. "That is a very, very wide hammer you are wielding, Miss Inquisitor."

"One that will hit all of us in many ways, I suspect, but if I can't trust my friends, then it will be worth the hit." She included me as she scanned the room.

Sandra spoke, "The Inquisitors will never bother coming. Grantsville is too small."

"Small places with a transition every three days? They'll be here faster than I can pop the popcorn." Her head snapped to Jules. "I want a signed confession within twenty-four hours."

Without waiting for an answer she and Garn strode out the door. The customer alarm binging once before the door eased closed, the piston at the top emitting a soft hiss. Jules stood, stalked to the door and locked it with the twist of his wrist. He paused, and I heard the soft thud of his forehead falling against the glass.

He picked his head up and let it fall one more time against the glass. I could see the grim outline of his face reflected in the glass. "I don't know who did this, but if they are in this room, then I suggest you never let me find out. The weaver weaves as she wills and all of our threads may have shortened today."

"I didn't expect you to have a melodramatic streak, Jules," I quipped, trying to break the tension.

I felt Richard reaching into my mind, searching for something. I pushed him away and gave him a stern look.

"You have no idea what a formal Inquisition means," the trio said, their voices synching together.

"If Ixey's right, then Neelius' death was no accident. And whoever's responsible has something to answer for." My tail gave a slow, dangerous lash as my muscles tensed. "Almost worse, it would mean Dorothy was right."

"You and your justice, Thomas!" Rudy's laugh bounced around the small room. "Forgive him, guys. Thomas watched a lot of Law and Order when he was a mund."

The joke hit the magi with an almost audible thud. Jowls chuckled a little as he lifted his head from his tightly curled body. "Are you showing your kitten teeth again, Thomas?"

Everyone else laughed then, high and nervous.

"We need to figure out House Technomagi's response," Sandra said. The other magi nodded.

"I agree, but it's best we do that without the hired help." Jules looked at me.

Rudy across the tables and onto his usual perch behind my neck. "Come on, Thomas, let's go menace a noodle dog or something!"

"Alright. Mind unlocking the door then?" I waved one large paw in Jules' direction, hopefully illustrating that deadbolts were beyond my ken. While I could do it with my teeth, the process was quite undignified.

Jules looked over to Richard, and the trio shifted nervously. "Unless you're willing to pledge yourself to House Technomagi's service for life, I'm going to ask you break your bond with Richard. Perhaps 'withdraw' would be a better term?"

I looked back to the other magi and found Jowls staring

at me with particular intensity. Scrying no doubt to see how I did it.

"You can re-bond me as soon as we're done," Richard assured me.

"Well, maybe I want a turn," Tom added.

I pondered making an effort of pledging client confidentially but decided I really didn't want to go down that rabbit hole. "That is no problem at all." I nodded, mentally nudging Mr. Bitey's mind to wakefulness. The snake read my intentions and snapped the link. The trio shivered and it was done. The fur around my neck stirred as Mr. Bitey's body slipped through it.

Jules blinked and opened the door for Rudy and me. I trotted into the parking lot. "Give us about six hours to discuss our options please. We'll text the squirrel when we finish."

"Great, I guess I'll just walk myself. You guys should think about getting a bigger pad," I said.

"Working on that," Jules said as he closed the door behind me. The click of the lock seemed to echo through the parking lot.

21

"Hey Thomas, you want to see a magic trick?" Rudy chittered from the branches above me.

Lacking a better idea, Rudy and I had retreated back to his abode. He lived in a huge misshapen tree with oak leaves that didn't smell right. The leaves had also completely refused to shed, making it the only tree outside of a granny's greenhouse that sported bright green leaves. Also rather suspicious was the tree-sized hole in the house that occupied the nearest lot. The squirrel had steadfastly refused to talk about it, and I decided that unless I caught the thing moving I really didn't need to know.

However, the "tree" was an ideal spot for Rudy. He had built a nest nearly four times the size of a basketball nestled between the two branches that reminded me of arms, with the nest itself being the tree's head.

I eyed the squirrel. "How about you tell me why the hell Jules doesn't want to find out who killed Neelius? Because I don't think he did. If he finds the perpetrator, he avoids this Inquisition."

Rudy made a disgusted sound. "Cause you wedged this

whole House idea into his head, and a House never ever gives the Inquisition a member unless ordered directly by the Council. He gives somebody up, and he invalidates his House before it's recognized."

It clicked. "And Ixey's pissed that somebody rained on her parade as an Inquisitor. That bomb was something a more experienced person might have caught."

"As punishment for screwing her, she's going to strangle House Technomagi in the crib with an Inquisition."

"O'Meara hasn't really filled me in on precisely what an Inquisition is other than bad."

"Well, their investigation techniques are inspired by the Spanish one, including the protections afforded by money. If you have a House, then they'll submit those under investigation to questions three."

"Just three?"

"Three that you gotta answer truthfully or the Inquisitor's seal burns out your eyes as a warning and burns one alive with the second lie or half-truth."

"And if no House?"

"They ask questions, you answer until all your secrets are lying there on the floor."

"That wouldn't be good." I thought about just how well the knowledge of my deal with the dragon would go over with the wide world of the magi. "Would the Inquisitors question O'Meara?"

"Oh yeah. They might go a little easy on her if they decided that ol' Archibald's death was too political to get involved in. Otherwise that whole thing with Sabrina's gunna become public domain. But we don't have to worry. Only magi get put to the question. Us familiars are too stupid to testify and too valuable since we so often nobly sacrifice ourselves to protect our beloved masters."

"So this wasn't a threat at me to figure out who killed Neelius then?"

"Ha! Detective Khatt is on the case?"

I rolled my eyes. "Is that so wrong to want to know?"

"Jules doesn't want to know. That will force the Inquisitors to question everyone."

"But that only works if they're a House? The Inquisitors would have to acknowledge the Technomagi as a House, right?"

Rudy nodded. "I bet that's what they're being hush-hush about now."

"I'm guessing declaring a House is a matter of gunboat diplomacy?"

Rudy shrugged. "Never seen it happen."

That perked my ears. I'd gotten that despite Rudy's bravado and energy, the squirrel was quite old. How old? I had no idea. If I could find out when the last House had been established, then I had an upper limit on his age. I filed that away for whenever I stumbled across a textbook on the Council of Merlins history, which if it existed was probably in Latin or worse.

"What do we do?" I asked.

He chuckled. "Dude, I'm going to keep driving that robot!"

"Is she paying you for that?"

"Eh, not much. You feel the ice between her and Ixey? Brrrr! They both think the other is missing screws."

"Sandra jealous of her? Ixey's a full magus. What does Sandra do exactly? She doesn't have a partner, familiar or otherwise that I see."

"In terms of magic, not much. She pulls elementals out of her anchor plane and puts them in the engines of stuff. She's still pretty sore that we lost that big one fighting the ice-man. Says Sir Clanks-a-lot would move double time if that big one was in the tank."

"So they're like smaller versions of the dragon?"

Rudy grimaced. "Yeah kinda, but... Giant robot!"

I let the matter drop. I had my paws full trying to remind the technomagi not to hurt people while we harvested tass. I'd have to worry about equal rights for elementals at a later date.

So we chilled for a bit. Rudy set up his iPhone on a root and we watched a movie, something with so many explosions that I tuned them out.

I woke up hungry. A chill had seeped into my bones as the sun began to set. I heard rhythmic crunching above me and found Rudy messily devouring a bag of peanuts. He had what I could only describe as an electric washcloth draped around his body, a power cord leading back into the mass of leaves that was his nest.

"No calls?" I asked.

"N-nut nada," he chattered.

"Shouldn't you be hibernating?"

"And miss out on four months every year? Ha, no! Just gotta keep the calories coming." He shoved a few more nuts into his cheek pouch. "So you ready to see my trick?"

"Sure, as long as it doesn't involve flames." Although I could do with a warm fire.

"How 'bout some off the books tass? Maybe, maybe!"

"I'm listening."

Rudy scuttled down to the base of the tree and tapped his iPhone to open the photo gallery. "Snapped these while everybody was working on stuff." He scrolled through the photos until he reached an overhead shot of the map Jowls and Jules had been using to track the transitions. The camera hadn't captured the depth of the paper, but a portion of it. Nonsensical ink lines dashed across its surface.

"Okay, that's kind of what I thought would happen if you took a picture of that paper. Tech and magic don't always mix well," I said.

"Wait, wait, wait." Rudy held up his paw. "I got an app for this." He opened up his options and selected depth of field. A slider appeared beneath the picture and as he slid it back and forth the lines on the paper slithered. Their movement stirred a memory in my mind. "See? See it yet?" He increased the speed, and I saw it! Each frame was a slice of the entire four-dimensional image of Jowls and Jules' map of the transitions!

It still didn't make much sense, a map of the town, twisted, as if someone had stabbed the earth with a fork and begun to twirl the map like a plate of spaghetti. Shadows played out over the town's surface. The placement of it all made my brain itch.

"Cool, right? Got it from a different technomagus. Multidimensional lens. Can do section imaging of 3D projections. It's entry level stuff, but it's the sort of thing that allows Sandra to do any magic at all." Rudy continued to talk, but I didn't hear him. Something about the angle of the map and the way the shadows had moved built like a pressure in my head, like a blister that refused to pop.

"Show me... Show me again." I could almost see it.

"Kaaaay. You alright?" He scrolled through the sequence. Still, whatever thought was growing inside my brain refused to come into the light. Instead, I saw something else. One of the shadows, a particularly dark one, hovered directly over Noise's apartment building. I focused on it and the pain and the thought retreated.

"Did you just take the one shot of this?" I asked.

"Yeah, I just thought it was neat. Wasn't really trying to spy. Unless you can read it! Is a transition gunna happen while they're all in their little war room?"

"How long does that charm last?"

"What charm?"

"The one that protected Noise from the goo transition."

"Eh, it sounded sloppy. Few hours. Why's it matter? You're not going to go crawling back to her, right? You forget what she said?"

I looked down at my paws, their distinct lack of thumbs and the chipped fluorescent paint on my claws. No, I hadn't forgotten about her, I'd been mentally tiptoeing around the giant sinkhole of hurt that yawned open in my mind; centering my thoughts on O'Meara's troubles instead of Noise. I had tried to convince myself that Noise's troubles were none of my business anymore. Despite that resolution my paws began to move in Noise's direction.

Rudy jumped on my back, chittering. "She's not going to want your help or even see you. Werewolves sulk violently!"

"We'll just swing by and warn her. That's all. We should be in the area anyway to collect the tass, right?"

"You're a fruitcake full of half-baked, cracked and mildewed chestnuts, Thomas."

"Yeah. I know," I said as I broke into a full out run.

I didn't notice my tail until I had nearly rounded the last bend on our way to Noise's apartment. And I don't mean the long furry one attached to my ass. This tail had feathers and four wings between the two of them. I couldn't be sure which Blackwing it was, but I didn't care. It wasn't Dorothy. That was good. So, options were: Naomi, who had turned into a fierce looking bird lady, and Rinoa, about whom I knew nearly nothing.

"You better bail, Rudy. In case this gets ugly," I said.

"What?" I felt Rudy stiffen on my neck. "Oh. Rinoa. I'll go hitch a ride and get backup."

"You know what her anchor is?"

"Either a musical conceptual plane, or literally a plane of sound. That guitar had too many foci in it for it to be a hobby. Good luck! I'll go grab the clank. Here they come!"

With that, two black shapes flitted ahead of me, landing thirty feet on the sidewalk directly in my way. Foci flared as their outlines blurred from birds to a woman and her German Shepherd. Rinoa held out her hand in the universal sign of STOP! "Hold up!" she barked.

I started to slow but as I did I caught the barest trace of purple in the corner of my vision. The transition had started already! The last thing Noise needed was to get stuck in another transition. "No time!" I growled, feinted right and bolted to their left. Tack made a half-hearted attempt to get in my way and managed to trip himself. I braced myself to dodge whatever Rinoa could throw at me.

To my surprise, the woman's aura didn't even flicker. She just spun on her heel and watched me sprint past, calling, "It's a black plane! Stop, you idiot!"

I'd really hoped the darkness of the plane on the map had been a generic mark for a transition. I had no time to imagine what that black plane at the daycare would do to a 300-pound werewolf. I redoubled my speed.

I thanked my lucky stars that the transition didn't appear to be in any hurry to impact reality. The purple stayed in the corner of my vision and pulsed, as if gathering strength. I hit Noise's front door at a dead run, making a thunderous bang.

"Noise! Open up!" I raked my claws across the wood, ripping spiraling shavings out of the cheap wood.

"Go away! We're done! We're over! You hate me!" a voice bellowed from inside.

"Noise! We can work that out later! There's a transition that's about to happen and I don't think it's a good one!" I checked the window, but it was closed tight.

"Oh, what will happen this time? Maybe I'll grow wings and start laying eggs in the bathtub."

The purple had finally gotten fed up with waiting and a haze descended into my vision proper. "Noise! Come on! We gotta go!" I dug my claws into the door, ripping out chunks of wood from its surface. The wood splintered easily, exposing a white Styrofoam core.

Too late. The purple surged into my vision and into
everything around me. Reality itself rippled and the haze
shifted, concentrating into a hulking figure huddled on the
other side of the doorway. The blur shifted and a hand
larger than my head ripped through the door as if it'd been
composed of wet newspaper.

Noise pushed through the doorway, her massive shoulders cracking the doorframe. I stepped away, my back
arching like a common house cat's. One of her short horns
caught on the top of the doorway and she ripped it off with
a casual twitch of her neck. It'd only been two days, but the
creature before me stood eight feet tall, more massive than
Noise had ever been. Thick, muscular, apelike arms hung
down to her knees. Her legs, as thick as my torso, ended in
an odd two-toed paw the size of a dinner plate. Bovine and
canine features had blended into a thick muzzle sporting a
huge leathery nose and a pair of tusk like canines that jutted
over her lower lip. She'd kept the black and rusty coloration
of her fur, but the colors now ran rampant over her body,
patterning themselves in the manner of a Holstein. She
wore a fuzzy robe that had been hastily converted into a
chest binding to contain her breasts and nothing else. A tail
with a tuft of black fur flicked back and forth, swatting at
nonexistent flies.

I'd been expecting some of this, but it was the look in her eyes that made me back up and hiss defensively to shout with every piece of body language I possessed, "I AM NOT PREY!"

There was nothing in those eyes but hunger.

"My meat," Noise growled, her lips peeling back to show a maw filled with newly predatory teeth.

I ran, my paws scrabbling at the pavement for a stroke before catching. Noise could have grabbed me right there and then and it would have been over. But she howled instead, letting loose a jagged song that spilled cold panic into my legs. I stumbled. Her thundering footsteps pounded after me as her call began to be echoed by other voices, human and otherwise.

Tearing down the sidewalk, I saw the doorways to the homes along it fling open as the occupants of the houses rushed to intercept me. The humans didn't concern me.

They staggered toward the road in an almost shambling manner, perhaps still warring against the alien hunger that had claimed them. Far more concerning were their pets. Through every door sprang at least one four-legged figure. All sizes, from a Saint Bernard that knocked his owner clear into the air, to a pack of dachshunds. They were all running toward me like a swarm of teeth-laden missiles. I zigged toward the nearest house and swatted away the lone terrier that barreled toward me. A jump and I was on the roof of the single story dwelling.

The houses were closer together here than out at O'Meara's, and I used it to my advantage as I leapt from roof to roof. I made four houses this way before I looked back. A pack of red-eyed rodents and cats were swarming up the walls. I could hear their claws scrabbling up the aluminum siding of the house I over the thundering of my own heart. I'd covered almost half a block. How large was this transition?

The next house was too far away to jump, so I scanned the ground for possible landing sites. Everywhere I saw shadows of movement. Indecision paralyzed me until dozens of eyes peeked over the gutters of the house I stood on. Having no choice, I moved, leaping out and over the hungry swarm. Something impacted my back legs, and biting pain lanced up my spine as needlelike teeth tore into my ankle. I landed and rolled, my teeth crushing the clinging rodent. A chorus of canine howls went up behind me, but I didn't pause. I simply ran as fast as I could, knowing it wouldn't be enough. I could see the edge of the transition, still a block away.

The barking behind me became a frenzy as the houses raced by. My chest felt as if it would burst, but I pressed on as a growing hope propelled me. I was going to make it. As if waiting for that exact thought, a sharp thing jabbed me, and then I felt a dozen more things, including the distinct flutter of wings. The sharp thing became a multitude of stings and pecks. I had to keep running.

In the distance I could see two figures in the middle of the road. Rinoa and Tack. They marked the edge of the transition. A sharp pain stabbed into my shoulder and I stumbled, the weight of the flock on my back growing with every step.

The dogs howled, and I knew that I'd lost my last gamble. The punky magus and her familiar were going to watch me die.

Yet as I stumbled a second time Rinoa's aura pulsed. A series of deep explosions rocked my ears. The weight of the birds on my back lifted with warbling cries of alarm.

Rinoa reached into her pocket and lobbed something square and pink at me. "Catch!" she commanded.

It landed far short of me, bouncing over the pavement, but I scooped it up a second later. It tasted of human hands: a smartphone encased in plastic armor. It began to emit an eerie warbling sound. Then a flash of golden light blinded me.

Thuds followed by several yelps sounded as my vision cleared to reveal the pulsating golden globe of a ward surrounding me: five feet in diameter and just tall enough for a person to stand up in. I whirled to see five large dogs of varying breeds picking themselves up from the ground. A sixth... Didn't. The phone in my mouth continued to warble, and the ward pulsed with its beat. I backed up to the far side of the globe, but it didn't come with me, and my tail brushed up against its vibrating surface.

"That might outlast the transition! It's my panic spell," Rinoa called. I looked back to see her channeling again.

CRACK-O-THOOM! Impossibly loud cracks of thunder staggered the approaching swarm, and the force of the shocks vibrated the ground beneath me. The smaller members of the swarm, the rodents and the cats, were blasted into the air while the humans were knocked off their feet.

One figure hadn't been affected at all. Noise strode toward me as the swarm broke apart under the assault. The explosions detonated around her, merely ruffling the slightly longer fur on the top of her horned head.

"Aw come on, Noise! Can't we try to go six months without you trying to kill me?" Maybe she heard me despite the concussive blasts, but she didn't give any sign. I looked back to see the magus slumped on her knees, obviously spent. The dog had lain down beside her. They were maybe 300 feet away.

An ear splitting crack sounded, assaulting my already tenderized ears. Whipping my head back to Noise, I found her hauling off for another punch. The golden surface buckled like a car door. Yet the ward held, almost returning to normal as she withdrew her hand for another attack. WHAM! WHAM! WHAM! On the third hit a spider webbing of cracks began to spread through the impact site. The reserves in the phone had been drained.

"Noise, come on, get control of yourself here. You don't want to eat me," I pleaded.

"I do! I want to rip the flesh from your bones and consume it. It's less complicated this way," she growled.

"I know you're upset! But eating people is never the solution! If you eat me, we'll never beat the next Fallout together! You'll have to play it all by yourself! With nobody to tell you when you've made poor dialog choices."

"I hate it when you do that!" She delivered a wild

haymaker that ripped straight through the spell wall, creating a jagged hole. I'd hoped that the entire structure to pop like a bubble and be able make a break for it. No dice. The thing had become a serving bowl for raw cougar. I hunkered down as far as I could get from her reaching hand. If Noise was going to grab me, she'd have to make a hole big enough for her and plenty big enough for me.

"Hyiiiiaaaaaaa!" a distant voice screamed, followed by the continual pounding of metal on the pavement. Rudy. How the hell had he gotten back so fast?

Noise's nostrils flared as her eyes tracked what I assumed to be a rapidly approaching metal man. She sneered, "He's my meat!" as she ripped a hole in the barrier, not with her hands, but her teeth. One bite, two bites and I smashed her in the nose with a paw. She neither flinched nor even slowed. She reached through the hole with a massive two fingered hand. I felt her dull talons brush over my ear and fumble at the scruff of my neck before I twisted away from her grasp.

"Hyiiiaaaaa!" Rudy screamed again, his voice like the whistle of an oncoming train.

Noise had shoved her head and one shoulder through the ward, her arm stretching into the bubble where I huddled against the far side of it, pressing my body into the quivering wall as much as possible. She snorted with annoyance, tracking the oncoming clank with her eyes. With a grunt of effort, my ex-girlfriend made a last bid to snatch me from my hidey-hole, forcing the magical field to bend around her body, cracking as the kinetic energy escaped as the sinews of her muscles strained. Her deformed hand reaching towards me...

...Her fingertips barely brushed the fur on my shoulder. A bellow of frustration erupted as she pulled back to meet the oncoming machine. The clank struck her with the monstrous ring of a bell. Noise met its outstretched pinchers with her own hands, her feet ripping furrows into the pavement as Rudy drove her back.

"Thomas! Get out of the transition!" Rudy cried as the pinchers spun, twisting them out of Noise's grip. Momentarily off balance, Noise tipped forward as Rudy slammed her chest with a double piston punch. Noise stumbled backwards, giving Rudy a precious few feet of space. The clank's pinchers came up into a fighting stance. Steam poured out of every port in in the clank's body, emitting a chorus of shrill whistles.

"I'll eat you too, Rodent! I'll eat EVERYTHING!" Noise swung out with a savage right hoof. Rudy stepped back, but it glanced off the head, the metal ringing like a gong. The clank staggered but warded off the next blow by slapping Noise's fist away.

"You and what army?" Rudy declared. "You're just gonna be another one for the photo album!" Rudy jeered as I slipped outside the remnants of the ward. Where had the swarm gone? Howls of hunger went up as soon as my paws set foot outside it.

The last house I'd leapt from had entirely disappeared beneath a mass of bodies, furred and otherwise. The swarm had fallen onto the house itself like a colony of caffeinated termites. A strange buzzing sound stopped as several hundred eyes fell on me at once, the madness within them scrabbling at my own mind.

I ran then.

"NO! He's MY MEAT!" Noise cried. Followed by a—

"Hey, no fair! Put me down!"

Metal screeched.

I kept my eyes on Rinoa and Tack, my finish line.

Rinoa looked pale but better than a few moments ago. Behind me I could sort out the pounding of Noise, hot on my heels, and behind that the metallic clomp of Rudy's robot and then the terrifying cacophony of the rest of the swarm.

"Rinoa! Can I ask you for one more salvo?" I shouted as I ran up to but didn't step through the transition's border yet.

She looked me up and down with wide eyes. "Yes. But only one more. You're going to owe me a favor at this point." She drew in a deep breath.

"Sure, yes. One favor. Just stop the swarm from catching up to the wolf-woman and the robot."

"Little late for the robot," Tack said.

Aw crud. Noise was running directly toward me. Behind her the dogs had caught up with Rudy. The massive Saint Bernard latched onto his shoulders and was gnawing on the head. Not that the dog was doing much damage, but Rudy clearly couldn't see where he was going. The clank's beeline pursuit of Noise shifted to more of a waggling line as more dogs latched on.

"I got the robot," Rinoa said, a smirking note in her voice as she stretched out her hand.

"Wait! It's not a—"

Too late. The metal man flashed yellow and rang with the force of many gongs. The metal skin rippled with the vibrations. The dogs slipped from him to the ground, stunned. To my surprise the clank continued running, veering off from Noise's vector at an angle.

Noise of course hadn't noticed. Her eyes were only fixed on one thing: me. Her jaws opened, her body tilted forward and with a final step she leapt with a snarl.

If there's one thing I don't miss about being human, it's gotta be the reaction time. Side-stepping Noise in an effortless motion, I watched her sail past, her body twisting, her jaws snapping in the air, the look of betrayal in her eyes.

Her momentum carried her beyond the transition. She started screaming before she hit the ground. Black swaths of energy burst from her skin, boiling out of her eyes and ears. Clawing at the ground, she attempted to crawl back into the transition, back to where that hunger could exist. She got up on her hands and knees before I hooked her ankles with my teeth and pulled them out from under her. I slammed her back to the ground, grabbing one of her wrists and forcing it behind her back. She screamed and cursed, slamming her free hand into the ground like a hammer until the last of the blackness boiled away and she sagged still.

I breathed a sigh of relief.

A laugh sounded behind me, followed by a clap. "You're pretty hardcore for a technomancer familiar," Rinoa said. She'd gotten to her feet, although she looked a bit wobbly.

"Thank you for the assist. I guess not all the Blackwings are raging assholes," I said.

Her grin grew wider. "Oh, I am a monstrous asshole, trust me. But I've got some karmic debt to work off. Sorry about your robot."

"My robot? Oh shit! Rudy!"

When I found it the clank had run into a tree and keeled over. Yet it still continued to walk forward. I ran up and pawed at the release button on its neck. It took a few smacks to hit it with the right amount of force, but the helmet hissed free, revealing a limp gray form tangled in the control sticks.

I nearly panicked, but there, before my own heart blotted out the world around me, I caught the note of his heartbeat, which sounded like a tiny turbo charged motor.

The fur below his ears was darkened with blood. I nosed him. "Rudy?"

The rodent groaned and then coughed. "Oh nuts, get it away! It's horrible!" He made weak pushing motions in my direction.

I huffed directly in his nose, and the squirrel coughed. "Gross! Meat breath!" His eyes opened a hair. "You're an awful nurse, Thomas, and a terrible friend! Yuck!"

"You okay then?" I asked.

He groaned and tried to push himself to his feet but quickly gave up the effort. "Feels like my head's been roasted on an open fire and cracked open."

I cursed internally. "I don't think the technomagi are big on mending spells."

He nodded weakly. "Particularly after what I do next."

"What do you mean?"

"There's a knob on the back of the robot, right where the ass crack would start. Open it, will ya?"

"If this thing farts on me, I'm going to eat you."

"That would at least stop the ringing. I think my meat ears are hamburgered." Rudy lifted his head, wobbled and set it back down.

I pulled the knob, and the back of the clank folded open. A meshwork of gears and electronics encased a metal cylinder that pulsed with heat, much like the one in the copter, a pressure tank of sorts.

"Open it. I promised it I'd let it go if it got me out here in time. It did."

That proved to be a bit dicey. The tank had an emergency release, a long handle connected to a valve, but it was so crowded by spinning gears and red hot mechanisms that I didn't want to get my nose anywhere near. A human hand would have no trouble extending a finger and hooking the tip of the lever. Too bad I was fresh out of those. I carefully hooked a claw around it and pulled the lever. The first one snapped, but the second try succeeded, and the bar began to give.

"Hey. Hey!" Rudy chittered. "Don't stand in front of the valve."

The valve had been staring me in the face. My ears burned. That could have been bad. Contorting myself to the side, I pulled that lever upward. Fire roared out of the nozzle in an epic spray of deadly heat. I pulled back my smoking paw with a yip of pain. The flame didn't vanish. It didn't spray out into nothing. It collected and hovered as a cloud, eyeless, but I could feel the flame thing's gaze sweep over me.

"Yup. We did it." Rudy gave the fire elemental a V for victory sign.

The fire elemental vanished into a pinprick of green light, returning to its own plane.

Noise coughed and sat up, blinking. Rinoa and Tack had apparently vanished. So I trotted over to Noise.

"How you feeling?"

"Better than those folks." Noise pointed to where three houses and all the vegetation on the lots had been devoured while I'd been mucking about with Rudy. All around were humans, dogs, cats and various other species on their backs with bulging stomachs. All moaning in pain.

A black plane indeed.

23

"Good news!" Richard smiled at Noise about an hour after Rudy, Noise and I came back to Jules' shop.

The technomagi's meeting had concluded shortly after the hunger plane had faded. Richard pushed off all questions about the outcome and the trio eagerly applied themselves to helping Noise after I rebonded Richard. I let it pass, not sure I wanted to know what they'd decided to do.

"You haven't gotten yourself tangled up with the hunger plane, although there is an echo, which explains..." Richard waved his hand over to the demolished pallet of foodstuffs they'd pulled from the back of the store. "Although the four stomachs account for some of the increased appetite."

"If that's the good news," Noise said, her now-baritone voice rumbling like thunder, "then what's the bad news?"

Richard deflated. "That whole mid-moon deadline you were talking about? It's not happening."

Noise grimaced, displaying her muzzle full of teeth that were nearly as long as Richard's arm. "Do you at least know what's going to happen to me then?"

"And that bounces us back to good news!" I interjected.

Noise gave me the "I am about to slap you very, very hard" look for a brief moment, then broke eye contact with a jerk of her head, ears sagging.

I dialed down the cheer. "We can pause the transformation where it is. Just stop it from going forward. Then when you get to the opposite point in the lunar cycle we can remove the tourniquet and hopefully the cow leaves with the wolf. Come the new moon, we might be able to snap the connection entirely."

"There were far too many If-Then statements in that sentence, Thomas. What's the chance of all that actually working?"

"Miss Noise, we're all technomagi here and we pride ourselves on being precise," Richard said, "but this is magic and the Lunar plane has been noted to be one that doesn't appreciate being mucked about with. So somewhere between zero and a hundred percent. You have no guarantees either way."

Noise studied her hands and let out a low moan of distress. I rose to go over to her but forced myself back to a sitting position.

"Do it," she said. "Not like I have a better option. I'll have to make peace with being an abomination."

Rudy peeked over the edge of a shoebox the trio had fashioned into a recovery nest. His ears had been stuffed with cotton while the first-aid spell knitted his eardrums back together. It looked like his white matter was escaping from his head. "What they talkin' about?" he whispered. Neither Rudy or I had a natural capacity to talk. Speech was granted to us via magical spells that mimick talking but are actually a sort of broadcast telepathy. As a result we can't talk through anything electronic but our voices don't require working ears either. I filled him in.

"You're not an abomination! You're a Moof," Rudy called to Noise once I explained the argument.

"What is a Moof?" Richard asked.

Rudy waited for a translation.

"It's a Mooo-Wolf," I volunteered.

Noise glared at me, again.

"Hey, he made it up!" I pointed my nose at Rudy.

"But you support it!"

"It's better than 'abomination'!" I paused. "And it's sort of cute."

Noise started to laugh and then caught herself, giving a forceful snort through her nostrils, ears flicking with frustration. She glared at me, and I held that gaze with my own. Anger and guilt simmered between us, I could almost see that scene in the forest replaying in her eyes. It hung between us, a barrier that neither of us wanted to address. It was no longer my place to call her cute.

She turned away. "So what happens to me in the meantime?" she asked, looking at Richard.

"Well, you definitely want to wear one of these." He held up a collar fitted with a transition defense focus; a real one that wouldn't burn out. "We don't know when another black transition will hit." He made to fasten it to Noise's wrist. She caught his arm, but Richard wasn't cowed. "It's either you wear this or you leave the state."

A moment and she relented, offering her wrist. "So in the meantime, I'm your hired muscle, is that it? Do you have a massive club for me to swing? Should I shout 'Moof Squish!' before I hit something?" Her tone was flat, but I noted a twitch in the corners of her lips.

"Careful, Noise, they might summon you a furry bikini to wear. Complete that barbarian look," The snark slipped out before I could restrain it and I braced for the angry retort.

Instead, she groaned and crossed her arms across her chest. "I'd go for any sort of support I can get right now. How the hell does Tallow hunt with cantaloupes on her chest?"

To be fair, everything about Noise was larger than Tallow at mid-moon. She probably had a hundred pounds on her father. If we'd let her go the two days to the half moon, she'd probably start breaking through the floorboards.

"Shall we clear the area? This is going to need a circle a bit bigger than the one on the table," Tom suggested.

We have to hurry, Richard thought at me.

What's the rush? I thought back as I settled myself out of the way. Noise and the trio needed to move the furniture.

Jules and Jowls want us to meet them back at the park in an hour. The solution is ready.

24

The solution looked a lot like a giant metal sausage. Taller than Jules by a foot, it curved up from the crater where the ruins of the dragon grinder rested. Its gunmetal gray surface was studded with doors, vents and breadboards filled with circuitry. In the interior of the structure pulsed a predominantly purple nexus of power interwoven with a rainbow of other colors that spun around the interior. Notably, I saw silver motes mingling with the purple, a color of magic I'd never even seen before. Sandra sat some distance away at a card table precariously perched in the snowy field. She fiddled with a control board that seemed to have been cobbled together from several sound mixers. It was all dials and sliders.

Jowls was strutting in rare form in front of the thing, his tail held high and waving. The trio, Noise and I peered down at them curiously from the hill. Rudy had insisted on coming along as well, he sprawled on my back. He had pulled the cotton out of his ears and seemed a lot more chipper.

"Gentlemen! Aaaaaaand Ladies!" Jowls called out with a

voice that rumbled with pride. "We welcome all to witness a historical event!" He looked off behind him. "And I welcome even House Morganna to this demonstration!" He chuckled. "Although I would advise against perching in that particular tree." He gestured to the monkey bars on the playground. "That would be far safer."

A small murder of crows flitted to the ground beside the magic sausage, becoming a cluster of women and canines. All except one unpaired crow, who perched unsteadily on Naomi's shoulder, the feathers in her tail sagging. Dorothy and Fee stood in front, their noses wrinkling as if they'd stepped in a moist cow pie. "You invited us. Do not treat us as interlopers."

"Then don't sulk about so." Jowls' voice became slightly muffled as he busied himself with a tangle of fur on his thigh.

"So you called us out to witness a miracle in a place rotten with the stench of spoiled tass? And prowl about as if you'd found a gold mine? What happened here?" she demanded.

Jowls sat up and curled his tail around his front paws, a sign of peace or concealing unsheathed claws digging into the ground. Possibly both at the same time. "I do believe that Thomas is the expert in what happened here." Eyes flicked in my direction before Jowls continued. "But we have found an opportunity for all of us in what it is today. Through a triumph of technologic magic, we have assembled the Aligner in a mere forty-eight hours. A feat that no Arch-magus could claim."

I cocked my head to the side and marveled at how much Jowls' tune had changed in the last week. When I'd first met Jowls, Jules had to bribe him with sushi-grade tuna to get him to do anything. Yet now the cat had such ambition I'd rarely caught him doing anything but work. I briefly pondered the possibility that he'd been replaced by some sort of transition doppelganger. Or perhaps I'd fallen into a mirror zone? I stared hard at the cat but saw the same aura I usually did.

"You sure it won't put us out of work?" I called down to the orange feline.

Jowls swiveled. "Thomas, this is not the time to fear wet paws! We are talking about something that has not been done in modern mystical memory!"

"Perhaps there's a reason for that," I heard Morie, the wolf, mutter.

Jowls stared at him for a half second before turning back toward the sausage. "We begin!" Sandra adjusted knobs, and the purple stars within the object spun, slowly twisting it into the ground.

In my head I heard the trio babbling about what the sausage was as they argued about the identification of the parts of the focus. They were excited but with an undertone of anger that rolled through them all. *Interchangeable foci! That's what he's been working on all these years! The bastard! The Genius!* All of them were imagining how much further they'd be on refining LAPIS if they'd had access to a bin of component foci, ready-made pieces of spells.

I didn't care to comment as I watched the sausage sink further into the ground and out of our reality. Jules stepped forward with a grin so wide it looked like it might escape the confines of his thin face. "What we stand before is not a mere spell but a wound in the fabric of our mother plane! One that appears to be untouched by the Veil!" He looked directly at me. "Whatever Archibald built here was a grand design sporting numerous ensnarement charms, which probably held something in place. Something very large and very dangerous. But now with the entire structure open, exposed to the winds of the planes, they haven't snared creatures but planes themselves!"

The device blossomed into a many-petaled flower, then folded in on itself surfaces rippling into stomach-curling, impossible angles, It shuddered briefly before shifting entirely out of our reality, leaving irregular circles of purple disturbances rippling toward us. The ground beneath me gave a lurch, as if it had just settled into place. The purple ripples, the bending of space itself reversed themselves. As they flowed back over me I felt a presence in the same way I feel the Veil work around me but utterly different in texture. The Veil is an unpleasant prickling, this machine seemed to roll thick rods of ice against my spine. The disturbance began to focus on the trees the Blackwings had perched in moments before. Their outlines bent and twisted as if their image had been printed on a piece of taffy that first melted then caught fire. Not just a leaf here and there, but as if you doused the whole tree with white phosphorus and subjected them to a desert heat. The fire had no origin point. Entire trees ignited like a matche head, twisting and blackening. Many fell, igniting their cousins, but one out of every six stood tall, gaining height, and refused to be consumed.

A transition, I thought at first, but then as I studied the way the space aligned and pulsed together too brightly. Finally it clicked and my mouth fell open, Jowls and Jules had created a shallowing! Animals nestled in burrows and hollows flung themselves out of the flaming trees. Hitting the ground they ran in panicked circles as their limbs and bodies rapidly burned away. Yet the flames themselves carried on, scampering about and tunneling beneath the moon-pale sand that had become the forest floor.

"Ooooh, so pretty," Rudy whispered as nearly every tree within eyesight blossomed into orange flame. "Sounds lovely." His claws scrabbled up the length of my neck until his wobbling weight rested between my ears.

Everyone, magi and familiars alike, stood with jaws agape.

Jules smiled at the Blackwings. "Any of you care to duel me for this shallowing?"

"What?" Dorothy coughed, covering her mouth with the crook of her elbow. "That cannot be a shallowing!"

"It is a shallowing. The first of several that will be created. Slowly the planes will align over the next few days." Jules smiled in the way a parent explains something to a slow child.

Dorothy stepped forward, jabbing her finger at Jules' chest. "There is no way you could have done this! Who is backing you? Who created this?"

"We all stand on the shoulders of giants, m'lady," Jowls sang from near Jules' feet. "Giants that want to see the emergence of House Technomagi when the new Council is formed."

The hairs on the back of my neck prickled, and I checked on where everyone stood. Nobody had moved but Sandra, who'd stopped fiddling with the console and hefted a silver cylinder across her lap.

Jowls chuckled.

What's he trying to pull? I thought to the trio.

After a moment of internal discussion, they answered, *Diplomacy, we think.*

A bad feeling twisted around in my stomach, as if I'd swallowed a live snake. If it were diplomacy, Jowls wouldn't be looking so smug.

"I see," Dorothy said, her voice edged with caution.

"I understand you need to show something to the Crones for the loss of Neelius." Jules gestured to the shallowing. "This one is yours."

"Ours? You're offering use of one of the largest shallowings that has formed in my lifetime?"

Jules held up a finger. "There are minor catches, of course."

The whites of Dorothy's eyes flashed for a moment as she looked back and forth between the shallowing and Jules. She turned toward Veronica, but the bird gave no notice of her questioning eyes; she hadn't reacted to single word. A look passed between the three human magi.

Dorothy turned back to Jules. "Let's hear them."

"You take this, claim it and do what you wish with it. Then you leave the rest of this county to us."

"If we take your deal, what stops you from unmaking it as easily as you created it? House Morganna won't be beholden to a lesser house for a tass source," Dorothy countered.

Jules looked down at his feet, away from Dorothy's intense gaze. "Those are the terms. Or you can duel me over every single shallowing and transition." He set his shoulders and raised his eyes. "And we both know how that will go."

Rinoa stepped up and whispered urgently to Dorothy, "The black planes."

Dorothy set her jaw. "You're bluffing. Ixey is investigating your cheating at the duel, and now you're attempting to bribe us. She won't allow you to proceed with your duels. Not in any legal fashion. We'll contest you at every shallowing and transition. We will win each share of tass from underneath your electric eyes."

"Tsk tsk," Jowls said. "Jules was so hoping we could come to an agreement."

"Plan B," Jules said. Sandra held up the canister toward the Blackwings and a gout of water four-feet thick blasted from the container. In a motion nearly too fast for my eyes to follow, the water scooped up the magi and their familiars, turned like a snake, and rushed headlong into the burning desert.

All three of the magi glowed with the power of their anchors as Sandra twisted a dial on the control panel with savage glee. The world twisted and the Blackwings, along with the burning forest, disappeared, replaced with a dark void. Whispers of something needled at my ears as sickening feeling of torque gripped my mind forcing my eyes closed. When they reopened, trees, normal trees, once again greeted my vision. I couldn't help but notice they were not the same trees as the ones that had been consumed by the shallowing.

I shook myself and those beside me did the same. Awe and fear rolled out from the trio. Jules turned to us all and made a placating gesture.

"Nobody worry, they'll be fine," Jules said. "We just put the girls and their dogs in a bit of a time out and bought us some time alone."

* * *

After the Blackwings had been pushed out of our reality, Jules and Jowls regaled us with a speech or something. The only thing I heard was the bubbling of my stomach twisting tightly as my moral compass spun in a panic. Trapping the Blackwings like that tasted wrong. But he hadn't killed them either. At least when it came to killing magi, the magical world seemed to have some restraint.

If I'd been alone in my head, I might have gotten up the

gumption to do something about it, but the trio intruded on my internal arguments. Even if I shielded my thoughts from them, I couldn't hide my deepening sense of guilt. Emotions radiate through the bond much easier than thoughts.

They would have done the same to us, you know, Tom said as we returned to the van after the briefing that I hadn't heard.

And I'm pretty sure Dorothy would have done worse to us if given an opportunity, Henry added.

Does that make it right? I asked.

Killing them would have been wrong, Richard said. The other two nodded. *They're not powerless there, Thomas. It's a real risk that they'll find their way home without our help. Six months max. Once Veronica comes out of her funk in a few weeks. It might be much faster depending on how much she knows about planar travel. If Jules is going to use them as a bargaining chip, he's going to have to do it fast. Focus on your own troubles, Thomas. Let the Blackwings worry about theirs.*

What he said made sense. If I really wanted to retain my freedom and operate in the magical world as a mercenary, I was going to have to stop getting the butterflies every time a magus screwed over another magus. This time I hadn't pulled the trigger, but what if a client seriously asked me to do something similar? If I bugged out every time a client hurt another magus, my list of clients wouldn't be very long, would it? The client list was probably already minuscule, trained magi without familiars. Moreover, having sympathy for a group of women that included the one who'd flung me down a hallway in an attempted mugging wouldn't get me anywhere. No closer to the hundred groat of tass I needed to help O'Meara. And beyond that, I looked down at my paws. The Blackwings went from feathered to thumbed in the pace of a second. Surely someone could do the same for me for a bit of tass.

I just had to focus on the work. Think of the money and remember that harvesting tass off a person did no long-term damage. Tass after all was the dew of reality. Nothing like soul collection or anything nefarious like that.

25

By the third day, we had it down. Tom, Dick, Harry and I were the collection team. Jules and Jowls huddled over their map in the morning and figured out where the most lucrative transitions would hit. That's where we would go. Meanwhile, the park had been converted into a construction site. Jules and Jowls built something from machine-produced steel beams as Noise dug out a foundation, joined by a growing number of clanking automatons that weren't rodent-piloted.

As for Rudy, he appeared to be unemployed at the moment. Sandra hadn't forgiven him for losing another elemental to save my tail. He was still a bit shaken up after the whole incident, so he recovered on my shoulders and stirred a bit to make a comment here and there.

On the third day, the rodent's sense of humor had made a full recovery. "Oooh! An ice transition is going to hit the entire supermarket? That'll make Grantsville the town with the largest freezer section in the country! We should sell tickets!"

"No audience. Nobody can see the ice, remember?" I told

him, trying not to roll my eyes as we pulled into the parking lot. The squat brown-roofed building was from the same architectural family as the plaza. The only bit of color on it was a neon-lit sign declaring it to be Grover's! Then in a small cursive font: "Your Family Grocer since 1957." That last bit was new, and the plastic lettering was much less sun bleached than the larger bits.

"Well, we should at least rent ice skates. Particularly if the people in there are going to become ill-tempered ice giants." I felt his small body give a shiver.

"It won't be that bad," I said. "Transitions haven't tried to kill us lately." I squinted at the building. The barest edge of purple crept along the walls. Not long now.

Tom, Dick and Harry were zipping up their winter jackets and internally grumbling about always getting stuck with the grunt work. They'd been getting surly the last few days, as Jules and Jowls never went out to collect tass despite the fact that the trio were the senior magi of the group. Jules had simply countered, "Do you three know anything about the orbit of multiple planes through space-time? We have to keep our gravy train going here. Or would you all prefer our streak to end? It's not a stable thing."

The trio had sputtered, but the fact was that the dimensional control device had been Jules' creation and they really had no idea how the thing worked on anything more than a theoretical level. There were only two familiars, Jowls and me. One of us had to do the gathering, and I was the contractor. It made sense to me. I perched in front of the van door and waited for us to stop moving.

And waited.

After we circled the parking lot, I shot our driver a quizzical look. "You going to park sometime today?"

"Keep your fuzz on," Harry said. "Soon as I find a spot. It's crowded."

"Crowded? It's noon on a Wednesday." I pushed myself up on my hind legs to see through the window. Rudy's low whistle echoed through the van.

A line of cars confronted my vision. There were so many that people had pulled onto the asphalt islands that capped every row of cars. SUVs were parked so close together that the occupants must have exited out rear doors. Glancing back at the supermarket itself, I saw a sight I hadn't ever seen before: a line to get INTO the store. I hadn't seen a store this mobbed since I'd made the mistake of attempting to secure an Elmo for my niece on Christmas Eve a few years back.

"Something tells me that nobody's here because Fruit Loops are having a double coupon day," Rudy said.

"Well, it doesn't concern us. We're just here for the tass," Richard said as he popped the latch on the door, which roared back across the van.

The van jerked to a stop. "Hey!" Harry snapped as we all bounded out.

Just keep circling, Richard thought to Harry as he and Tom flipped out the black tass collection bags.

Harry assented. Minor disappointment flowed from the man, but he held his thoughts to himself, as Rudy, Tom, Richard and myself approached the group of people that waited in front of the store. I fletched as their scent caught my nose, their fear tainting the air around them with bitter-sweet notes and stirring my appetite. A cop stood by the door, his back straightened and his hand drifting to the baton on his belt as we walked up. His mirrored shades prevented me from seeing his eyes, but I felt them rake over the length of my body.

"No dogs allowed." The man coughed. "It's crowded enough today."

I blinked and sat back on my haunches. Nobody had ever challenged my right to go anywhere since O'Meara had gotten me the service dog harness. At least he didn't even seem to see Rudy. Surprise blossomed from Richard as he stepped up beside me.

Richard paused while he cobbled together a response. "Ahhhh, sir, he's my service dog. He goes everywhere I do."

"You don't look blind, you're not in a wheel chair and you heard me. You don't appear to need a dog to function. What's he do? Carry your booze? He's a hazard in there. A Saint Bernard like that will make a puddle of drool that somebody will trip on."

"Hah! I told you ya drooled." Rudy sniggered.

I didn't have time to laugh at my squirrel friend, as Richard's thoughts turned to disabling the cop with a violent spell. *Tom, get contact with Thomas and ready a shock spell. We don't have time for this. We can't miss this transition!*

Right, so we assault the police officer and then get flattened by a store full of people as they run screaming out. Great plan, I thought back. *Why don't you try this first?* I quickly gave him a script to try.

I have to say all of that? Richard groaned not-so-internally.

Unless you guys know any Jedi mind tricks.

That's not our area of expertise.

Then try talking through your problems. It builds character.

Fine. Richard squared his shoulders, looked at the officer and smiled so hard that I think I heard his cheeks crack. "Old George here is my emotional support dog in these tough times, and he's very well trained. He won't be any trouble at all."

I did my best good dog impression to try to back up Richard's rather languid delivery. Attempting to pant and wag one's tail takes a surprising amount of effort. Neither comes naturally to cats.

Richard moved to the second act. "George SIT!"

I was already sitting, so I fixed him with an annoyed look.

"George Down!"

I lay down.

"George roll over!"

I rolled over despite a squeak of protest from Rudy, who abandoned ship to hide behind Richard's legs. I heard the mechanical click of an imitation shutter as I did my best "what a good boy I am" impression. I didn't know what social media Rudy used, but I'm pretty sure that pic would go viral.

The cop didn't look impressed, but he lifted his hand away from his club to cross his arms. "The trick I'm interested in is the one where he heels and doesn't dash across the store after a scrap of food someone dropped on the floor." As the cop spoke, his breath streamed out in a cloud. The temperature was dropping as the transition began.

Richard took out my leash and clipped it to my collar as his thoughts were growing increasingly frantic. I kept feeding him lines and hoping the cop would give. Otherwise we were going to have to try a different tactic, one that probably wouldn't result in anyone getting what they wanted. I stuck close to Richard's side.

The line had filled out behind us and eventually one of the bystanders took pity on the display. "Ah, let him in, Chris. Everybody needs supplies, even the crazy dog people."

The cop turned his head toward an elderly gentleman

carrying several worn cloth bags. He wore a green puffy jacket that looked nearly as old as he was.

The cop muttered something and stepped aside.

I nudged Richard, who started and said, "Thank you so much, sir."

"See that your dog behaves himself," the cop growled as we walked into the supermarket, the doors sliding open with an airy hiss.

The air inside seethed with the scent of people. Frightened, jittery people walking on their last nerve. A few of them had marks of being in previous transitions. I smelled beef, and not the sort behind the meat counter. Large signs had been posted, drawn up with markers on poster boards. Limits per customer, per day and a list of staples. Several items, including milk, were listed as out.

What the hell was going on?

Thomas, stop staring at the signage and look for the tass. It's getting cold in here. Even as the words drifted into my head from Richard's, frost began to spiderweb across the sign like tiny fireworks exploding in slow motion.

Why the hell is Grantsville rationing food? I demanded. *Do you know?*

All I got in return was a mental shrug. *They're mundanes, Thomas. They've always had their own problems. They'll deal with it in their own way.*

I probed his mind for a brief moment, looking for some sign of deception or errant thought that might indicate that he had an ulterior reason for blowing my concerns off, but he literally didn't care. Nor did he have a concept of how bad things had to be for an American town to start rationing foodstuffs. I looked to Rudy, who was engrossed in his phone.

"Rudy, do you have net access?"

He tilted he head to look at me with a single eye. "Yeah! You're going to be famous on the Cats that Thinks They're Dogs subreddit!" He grinned.

No food but power and internet access? Maybe there was a blizzard on the way? I made a mental note to get Rudy to try to pull up a local news blog or something on the way back to the techno-hub.

I huffed out a sigh and studied the way my breath swirled into the rapidly chilling air in front of my nose. Beyond it, the crowd of people had begun to slow, their postures hunched against the growing chill in the air as our reality slipped into a foreign one. There was something about the way the purple rippled through the air that I recognized. It was the same reality that had formed the shallowing at the plaza, or one so similar it wouldn't matter. The ripple pattern was a sort of fingerprint for the reality. I wondered if I could recognize it and find this plane in a different context, perhaps while assisting a magus' spellcraft.

Jagged ice crystals erupted first out of the freezers and then spread into the aisles. The reality seemed to know this would be a temporary stay and didn't aggressively pursue the shivering shoppers. Still, there was no escape for them. The store filled with the sounds of crackling spring ice as the people surrounding us froze solid. Ice crystals stabbed out of a cashier's tear ducts, the telltale white glimmer of tass forming on its tips, as if pushing out toward us in an offering.

I could feel the presence of three minds crowding around my vision.

"It's in the tears!" Richard exclaimed, and he took an aggressive step toward the registers. His foot skidded forward out ahead of him, the smart looking leather shoe offering no traction on the slick ice that held onto every surface in the front of the store. Giving an unwizardly "Yiiii!" while his arms spun out at his side, Richard toppled.

"I believe that's called a technical difficulty?" I glided over to him on my much more stable four paws.

"Well, in hockey, I think they a call that an error," Rudy quipped.

"Just help me up. We don't have much time. Tom, get the tass," Richard grumbled as he hauled himself back on to his feet using my scruff as leverage.

Tom was far more careful than Richard, or at least behaved like someone who'd actually been on a sheet of ice before. He shuffled over to the cashier and plucked out the ice crystals from the corner of her eyes.

Richard and Tom each took one of the long lines at the registers with me and Rudy in between. Each customer possessed a few motes of tass that had formed in ice crystals pushed out of random orifices. Both Richard and Tom skipped a few where the tass wasn't on their faces but in their pants. I declined to comment, but Rudy had no such inclination.

The magi were hobbled by the icy floor but the aisles were worse. Their floors and ceilings covered in lethal ice spikes that had me checking for floating platforms and bottomless chasms. So to avoid going the way of countless Marios we stuck to the front of the store. The transition proved to be a quick one and the magi were only on their second lines as it crested. In order to gather the tass quickly, I dispensed with the caution of waiting for Tom and Richard to fumble around. Where the tass was easily reached, I batted them off the popsicles people with my paws. Richard gave up his own collecting and followed me around with the tass bag, sweeping anything I knocked to the floor up into it.

It wasn't the proper way to do it and didn't treat my magus with dignity, but it was fast and that's what mattered at that point.

It worked all the way to the last of the nine register lines, where I found that same old man who'd intervened on our behalf with the cop. He wasn't standing in line exactly, rather it appeared he had been chatting with a younger woman. Her hands were frozen in a sort of fluttery hand motion, perhaps a dismissal which contrasted with her wide smile that threatened to burst into laughter. The old man had been caught in the act of an open guffaw, his nearly empty gums had been filled with icicle-fangs, packed to tightly his appearance called to mind a piranha. Tass shined in each of those needle like projections.

I should have realized that our time was up when I saw his eyes follow me as I pushed myself up on my hind legs. I snapped the icicles from his mouth with a swipe of my paw.

His mouth worked and a strangled "Ooooooowwww," crept out. "Baaaaaad Kiittttty!" His finger waggled in slow, exaggerated motion.

"Oh, I'm sorry," I said before giving any thought to what this meant. "But you're mistaken. I'm a dog." I turned so he could read the words printed on the side of my blue harness. Any moment now the Veil would kick back in.

The man responded, his words now only slightly slowed. "Hooly shitting bonkers! It's a mountain lion! A talking mountain lion!"

He moved to run, but the thaw of his body hadn't quite caught up with his mouth. His leg lifted, but he didn't get it where it needed to be in time, and he toppled over like an ill-posed mannequin. Eyes fell on me as the nearby shoppers looked at the commotion. I paused, waiting for the icy crawling of the Veil on my spine, waiting for everyone to shrug and dismiss me as a dog as they always did.

Yet as slow, ragged calls of "LION!" erupted around me, I realized the Veil wasn't going to come and save my tawny hide.

What did you do, Thomas? Richard cried into my mind as Officer Chris stumbled in through the doorway to Grover's Grocery, hand on his gun.

Get out of here! I thought back, engaging the muscle drive. My paws scrabbled on the now-wet floor tiles for a brief moment before friction caught on and I dashed between two registers. The shoppers screamed as I squeezed past them. I had to choose between a mother and a granny, so I pushed against the mother, shoving her against the counter. "Sorry ma'am! But I really don't want to get shot today!"

"Get off me!" she screamed, and I took a purse to the ribs.

"Hey, watch it! He's got innocent cargo here!" Rudy said. "You really afraid of one cop?"

"I'm afraid of his gun," I hissed back.

"Nobody move!" the cop shouted. "Where'd all this ice come from?"

Dark thoughts flared from Richard, and I could feel him reaching for a focus that was definitely some sort of weapon and pleaded patience. I peeked around the corner to see the officer, his gun drawn but pointed at the floor. His mirrored shades were gone, his hair damp and clinging to his forehead and his eyes wide and wild. I could run for the exit, but he'd have a clear shot at me if I did, and I doubted Officer Chris graduated from the Stormtrooper school of marksmanship. "What now, officer?" I called. "You want me come out with my paws up?"

"Who's speaking?"

"The cat is!" said the woman I'd pinned to the side of the register. She smelled like spearmint gum.

"This is no time for jokes! Where is it?" the cop bellowed.

"He's right here! Pinning my legs and I don't like the way the squirrel on his back is looking at me, officer!"

"Want me to take him out?" Rudy whispered. "He's just one cop."

One gun between me and the only exit. And then I mentally slapped myself. That wouldn't be the only exit. It was the exit for the customers, but there had to be a dock in the back. I had to get out of here before this guy's buddies arrived and we had to start having a debate as to how to disarm a cougar. *Richard, have Harry meet me around the back.*

Hang tight, Thomas, he's positioning the artillery.

What? From the tone of his mental voice I detected zero irony in the Magus' thoughts.

Cover your ears.

Beyond the wall of the store a glob of yellow lit up in my vision. A kinetic channel brighter than I'd ever seen.

With a sickening crunch and the shattering of glass, sunlight streamed into the front of the store as the wall that had been there lifted clear of the building's foundation. It hovered there for a moment before crashing back to earth with a shockwave I felt pass beneath my paws.

People behind us broke into rippling screams that blended into a single chorus of terror as the front of the supermarket flopped forward. Behind it Harry idled in the driver seat of the van, hands clutching a metal rod tipped with a crystal; a larger version of the device I'd seen Jules wield earlier. He grinned with a wicked joy. "There is no Veil!" he called. "None at all!"

A pop cut through the cacophony and Harry rocked backed in his seat, blood splashing across the windshield.

"HARRY!" Richard screamed.

The cop continued to fire. He never even saw Richard whip out his own wand before the beam of force sent him flying into a nearby wall so hard that I heard multiple bones snap.

"What hell are you doing?" I screamed at Richard.

"Just run! Get to the van!" I could feel the three magi's panic flooding into my own mind, knocking aside any room for argument.

Richard and Tom were beating it as fast as their legs would carry them toward Harry. I looked back at the cop. Already people were swarming toward him crumpled under a battery display. Bloody bubbles blew out of his nose. There was nothing I could do for him. So I ran, catching up with the fleeing magi as they reached the van.

26

I can't say I'd ever seen blood fountain out of a hole in a man before. Distantly, through Richard, I could feel Harry fading. Tom pushed him out of the driver's seat, and Richard desperately attempted to stop the bleeding by pressing his hands over the hole in Harry's shoulder. But the blood continued to creep across the floor as the van screeched out of the parking lot back toward Jules' shop.

Richard and Tom's minds were a litany of blame, panic and curses.

"You all teleported here!" I said. "Can you teleport us now?"

"Not without Harry! Where the hell would we go? Jules has the first aid focus back at his shop. It's only a few blocks away!" Richard shouted back at me.

Rudy had climbed up to the back of the passenger seat. "Yeah, but you're driving toward the police station!" Sirens began to howl, as if reminded by Rudy's statement.

"FUCK!" Tom cried and made a wild turn down a side street, the force flinging me so hard that the carpet ripped beneath my claws. "Do something, Richard! He's dying! I can feel him dying!"

"I'm trying, I'm trying!" Richard said as blood squirted between his fingers.

"We need a circle! Now," I said.

"Does it look like I have a circle in here? That'd be a really good idea, but I don't have time for metalwork!" Richard pulled out a pocketknife and franticly slashed at the sleeves of his suit.

"Put your hands on my head and that will be our circle," I said, trying to keep myself calm in the face of his chaotic thoughts. "O'Meara and I did it all the time!"

"I don't have a plane of healing on speed dial! I've never tried healing anyone before!" he protested.

"Then you're going to have to make a deal. Tom, if we can't get to Jules' shop, then try for O'Meara's. Ixey can deal with flesh wounds easily enough."

Something passed between Tom and Richard, a thought I didn't catch, along with a shudder of dread that cut through even the panic. "Not an option," Richard said. "It's either the shop or the park, and if there's no Veil, the munds will see the construction."

"Well then we better make this work. We've got plenty of tass." Now was not the time to figure out why Ixey wasn't an option.

Richard lifted his blood-covered hands from Harry. The bleeding had stopped and so had his breathing. I caught Rudy shaking his head out of the corner of my eye as Richard upturned a velvet bag. A pile of tass crystals fell onto Harry's chest. His eyes met mine, I nodded and he grabbed hold of the sides of my head.

I closed my eyes.

Shape the tass into a vessel for a spirit, I commanded Richard, pressing the memory of a book on basic summoning and several conversations with Ixey into his mind.

Richard tore through the information, devouring it like a pack of piranhas. *How the hell will this help?* Yet he did as I asked, quickly forming the tass into a hollow fourth-dimensional sphere that could open and close. I took it and folded it within myself, into that strange space the dragon had carved into my being, a sort of transdimensional smuggler's pouch.

I only had one shot of making this work. I rose into my mental space and flew out along the path to my anchor. Since Richard didn't know of a plane that held the concept of healing, I only had one idea. Ixey had many spirits at her beck and call. I'd seen her appeal to them to assist in knitting flesh together before. Yet she knew them all by name, having spent countless hours building a web of relationships with beings from other planes.

I traveled to the very end of my soul thread, and pushed through into a skull that had once been my own. He had my human hands around a stout stick and was prodding the dying embers of a fire. The bones of a recent meal lay scattered around it. *Hello, Bone Whistler,* I thought at him.

As I had been a man, Bone Whistler had been a cougar. Archimagus Archibald had purposely tied our souls together and the energies his death had released momentary merged us into a single being, a transition of a single soul but when the Veil sorted us out, I got the claws and tail, Bonewhistler received the thumbs.

Greetings, he who creeps into my head and covets my hands, he thought at me. *"Here to teach me more of a thousand and one uses for opposable thumbs?*

I have a name.

But it is a meaningless name, little more than a series of sounds on the wind. You should get a new one that suits you.

We always had this argument. Whistler was fond of it since I usually lost, but I had no time for diplomacy. *I'm calling in a favor. I need a healer right now. I have a client who has lost his breath.*

Whistler's face, my old human face, frowned in thought. His world appeared similar to Earth at first glance, but he had been intelligent before the Archmagus exchanged my body for his. Every living thing in his world had a voice. No doubt the previous owner of those bones around his fire had pleaded for its life before Bone Whistler snapped its neck. I rarely came to visit Whistler on purpose, but occasionally, when the full moon shined through O'Meara's window, I spent the night in the back of Whistler's head. I watched his thoughts churn, ideas bubbling up and popping as he rejected them. He settled on a particularly black one. *You need the Weaver, who has a debt of life to me. If I call that debt, you will owe me far more than tricks.*

I didn't have time to negotiate and Whistler knew it. Harry was technically dead. I had seconds before that became a permanent condition. *If the Weaver can perform the task assigned, then I'll be in your debt, brother.* I hoped to remind him that on a cosmological level we were the same person. My soul was also his. If I died, so did he. *Time is of the essence.*

Then we will not waste it. Bone Whistler put his hand to his mouth and bit off a small chunk of skin, his teeth cutting as clean as they had been razors. Had I a body I would have winced. He chuckled at my squeamishness all the same. Squeezing bright red blood from the wound, he held it aloft.

"Come, Great Weaver. I hold the price of your debt. Do not tarry or the quarry will escape into the moonlight."

The wind shifted, a chill from in front of us and in the shadows something danced. A voice, a sinister hiss called out from beyond the brush. "You call my debt so soon, Hunter. I would not have thought you would be so quick to be rid of it, given your new affliction."

"There is no time to chat, Weaver. I pass your debt to another." He licked the blood from his wound.

Movement stirred from the brush and a spider the size of a buffalo carefully stepped out of the vegetation. A weaver of webs, long, polished limbs supported a body with a head the size of my torso, sporting fangs that were daggers in their own right. Its chitin shone black as it stepped into the sunlight and watched us through eight narrowed human eyes. "I see, dear Whistler, that another pulls at your string." It laughed a woman's laugh discordant with its harsh voice, as if it had eaten a singer once and had somehow kept the voice.

"See, this is Weaver. I transfer the life debt she owes me to you, Thomas." As Bone Whistler said it, something pressed against my being and passed into it. The spider shivered, and its gaze shifted slightly. But I knew those eight eyes were no longer focused on Whistler. They were looking directly at me.

"I know of your world," it hissed. "I danced among its branches in times nearly forgotten."

Bone Whistler lent me his lips. "Whistler says you can heal a dead man. I need you do to that."

"I can. If the corpse is yet warm. The wounds can be woven together and the soul returned."

"Let's go then." I pushed the sphere into Bone Whistler's body.

With a hard retch, the sphere dropped from Bone Whistler's mouth and into his waiting hands. Dark green like the leaf of an ancient tree, it opened like a flower, revealing an abyss of darkness within.

Weaver regarded the spell for a moment. "I dislike this part," she said, her torso emitting a whistle that might have been a sigh, and then without any warning she flung herself at us. Her body twisted impossibly in midair and funneled down in to the sphere.

With a quick swallow, Bone Whistler passed the sphere back to me. I cradled it, folding it into myself. I had so many questions I wanted to ask about Weaver and Bone Whistler and his world. Yet there was no time.

Thank you, Whistler.

"Do not thank me, Brother. You will not repay this debt easily," he said to me and whomever might be listening.

I dived into the strand of our soul and hurtled back to my body.

27

"What the hell did you do? Where did you go?" Richard exclaimed as I slammed back into our reality with Weaver inside me.

I ignored my bond. Spirits usually couldn't just exist in our world. They needed to be given a body. It didn't particularly matter what the body was unless you wanted them to stick around for a long time. For the short term, anything would do. Weaver was big enough to possess the entire van if I asked her to, but the van wouldn't provide her much articulation. My gaze fell on the tool chest that lay along the side of the van's wall, which contained several foci. It was probably not a good idea to give Weaver foci, but I saw no other inanimate options.

I vomited the spirit forth like a hairball. The tass egg shattered in my throat, and I felt too many legs tumble over my tongue. The tool chest lit up with the yellow of kinetic energy as it rattled. "So much metal!" Weaver rasped as the drawers and hatches opened and closed spastically.

"Thomas! Whatever you did, it's too late. He's gone." Tom had twisted in the blood-covered driver's seat to look back into the van. His arms were wrapped around the seat back as if it were the only thing that kept him afloat.

The tool chest spoke. "He is not gone." Then it laughed, differently now, as if a woman's voice had passed through an electric pickup. That actually made it less creepy. Various tools flew out of the drawers, the wrenches assembling themselves into eight spindly legs that heaved the toolbox into the air and lurched toward us. "Out of my way, magus."

Richard backed away from the entirely still Harry, eyes wide. "Dear Gods..."

Weaver's head was formed from mashing together a power drill and a circular hand saw, her eight eyes all slightly different sized sockets, her fangs screwdrivers mounted on articulated clamps. She would have been a cool sculpture at an art fair had it not been that she moved with a silent grace that whispered of an unearthly presence. The oil dripping down the screwdrivers was also a nice touch. "I am a singular God. And for him, the only one that matters now." She reared up, holding her front four limbs over Harry. A strand appeared between the pliers that tipped each one, green and purple energy running along it. She didn't weave the strand; she danced, her insectoid limbs moving to a rhythm as they stabbed into the air and Harry's body. Something unseen caught in the strands. The strands began to pull against the rhythm, fighting out of sync with the Weaver. She wove it into a bundle of shimmering webbing, forcing it to dance to her tune. As the unheard music climbed towards a crescendo, she seized the bundle with a gleeful hiss and shoved it down into Harry's chest as if his skin and ribs were a dream. With a final motion, she sank a screwdriver fang into his heart.

Harry screamed blue bloody murder. Then took a breath and did it again.

Weaver shrunk back, laughing at the screams. Richard pounced on Harry as soon as the spider was clear, clutching the dark man to his chest. "Harry! Harry! I'm here. We're all here." Harry clutched back with clumsy fingers, wrapping his arms around the taller man.

Relief flooded from Richard, and I closed the link to give them some privacy.

The Weaver studied the pair, clearly pleased with herself as she rubbed her front legs together as if washing them. Her entire body froze when she noticed Rudy perched on the back of the passenger's seat.

He returned Weaver's examination with a narrowed eye. "Nobody's found a big enough stick to squish you yet, Weaver?"

"Ah, I remember you, squirrel. Good to see my handiwork still holds even after all this time." The spider preened with pride.

A moment of confusion spread over Rudy's face. "I don't know what you're talking about."

"Oh? Don't quite remember where you learned my name?"

I gawped between the bug and rodent. "You know each other?"

The spider laughed again. "You are far from the only lost soul that has been bound to my world, and the passage between them was not always so difficult. Earth is my second home and it is good to be back."

Possibilities whirled in my head. Did she mean that Rudy predated the Veil itself? I wondered again just how old the happy-go-lucky squirrel was.

Weaver turned back to me and gave a little bow. "You will call on my services again, Mr. Thomas. I am eager to see what exchanges we can arrange if you survive your Brother's task. Fare thee well."

Weaver turned and jabbed at the handle on the back door of the van.

"Wait," I said. "Where are you going?"

"Why, I am going to spin a web and see what your world offers. It has been too long since I have sampled the cuisine beyond Pangea. Adieu, fellow hunter." With that the van doors swung open and Weaver leaped out into a wooded area, her toolbox thorax clanging as she lurched into the trees. The thin secondary growth crackled under the weight of her metal body.

My own thoughts ran around in a hamster ball, cursing like a hyperactive mantra. *CrapCrapCrapCrap. I let a giant spider spirit out into the world for a hunting holiday. CrapCrap-CrapCrap.*

"I wouldn't worry too much about her," Rudy said. "It takes her days to digest a person. She'll probably grab a cat or two before the Veil drives her back home."

I glowered at Rudy. "Are you saying that to make me feel better, or are you hoping for a reduction in the feline population?"

"Humans aren't actually the top of the food chain, Thomas. Sometimes they get eaten too. Not your fault. You can't protect everybody. Besides, it's not every day you put a magus in your debt."

"Are you really older than the Veil, Rudy?"

"No, of course not. Don't be silly. That would be totally nuts." He made a head nod toward the magi still in the van. If I wanted a chance at clearer answers, we'd have to ditch the trio.

Mentally, they appeared to have ditched us. Richard still clutched at Harry, their eyes closed. Tom leaned back in his

seat to place a hand on Harry's shoulder. The van hadn't
been moving since I'd gotten back from the beyond, and we
appeared to be surrounded by trees on all sides. Had we
driven off the side of the road? I still had the link closed
tightly, so I let out a loud "Ah-hem!" to get their attention.

Tom opened his eyes first, shaking himself as he took in
his surroundings. "That... That was too bloody close for
comfort. What was that thing?" He stared at the darker spot
of carpet where the tool chest had been anchored to the
floor of the van. "Where— You know what? I don't care.
That was amazing, Richard."

"Dude, that was all Thomas," Rudy said.

Tom gave a start, and I felt a momentary spike of fear.
"You can summon spirits? One that large?"

"Course he can," Rudy cut me off before I could respond.
"Anything Harry can do, Thomas can do better, since he
sees what's going on, magically at least."

"What's that supposed to mean?" I protested.

He just held up a paw toward me and said, "Quiet you.
I'm negotiating here," before continuing to speak to Tom.
"Understand that Thomas is a good soul. He don't ask questions. He just saves his clients. No matter how crazy friggin
stupid they've been." Tom and I blanched at the squirrel's
sudden vehemence, and Richard opened his eyes. "That
trick is going to cost Thomas big time down the line and
don't ya'll forget it. That went way beyond the call of duty."

"Rudy, what the hell you trying to pull on me here?" I
whispered.

Rudy rounded on me. "I'm making sure your clients
know what you did for them before you can be modest
about it. Magi understand two things: tass and favors. If you
don't call a favor a favor, they'll be happy to forget it ever
happened."

Richard didn't look happy about it, but nodded. "Harry's rescue was reckless. We acknowledge the debt."

"Would have worked fine if the Veil had fired up," Harry muttered, not opening his eyes. "Nobody would have seen anything definite then."

"And why didn't it?" I asked. "What did you and Jules do while we were gone?"

All three of the magi's eyes snapped wide open. Fear oozed through the link, not the adrenaline-soaked flight panic that had them in its grip while fleeing the cops, but pure dread. The magi didn't have many laws, but a big one was you do not screw the thing that is protecting all magi from the pitchforks and torches. It was punishable by death, with qualifications. Qualifications that meant an elder magus might weasel out of it. But a technomagus? Probably not.

"That's not possible," Richard said.

"Unless..." Tom said.

The pair stared at each other for a moment. Harry paled. Richard turned back to me. "Thomas, we need to confer with Jules."

Tom took out a cellphone and called a number, turning away from me as he spoke into it. Several terse nods later and the three lapsed into silence as he hung up.

"Well?" I said. "I *am* your bond, you know. You going to tell me what's going on?"

"I don't think that would be a good idea, Thomas. At least not until we get clarification from Jules about what he's done," Richard said.

"You might be better off breaking the bond now," Harry suggested.

Richard shuddered. He liked having access to an actual familiar, that was for sure. "Let's hold off on that."

"What the hell has the skinny man and the fat cat done?" Rudy demanded, his tail shaking.

"He wouldn't say over the phone," Tom said. "Told us to meet him back at the 'Pillar.'"

"So we're just supposed to sit here and wait for you?" I said. "Noise is still at the Pillar."

"Noise has no chance at being sullied by this. She's not a magus or a familiar. If Jules did what we think he did, then you shouldn't get involved any further. We'll fix this." Richard's smile was not entirely reassuring.

"Hell no. You ring me when you want to meet," Rudy said as he hopped down on the floor. He shoved my cut of tass into a bag and scrambled up on my shoulders.

"Or just, you know, open the mental link you're clearly straining to keep closed," I added, prodding the link with my mind. Richard had been keeping it closed fairly often over the last three days. Whatever the technomagi were up to, it had him anxious when he thought too hard about it. I kept telling myself it didn't matter, that I had half of what I needed for O'Meara's treatment in my harness already. Waiting through the waning half-moon would take longer at this rate. Once I made sure Noise got fixed, I could revaluate my positions.

Still, I stepped out of the van with deep misgivings.

Tom had somehow driven the van deep enough into the woodland that I couldn't see the road. He backed out hurriedly, a tree claiming a side-view mirror in his haste. Rudy and I watched it disappear down a hill and presumably back to the road.

I did a bit of grooming while attempted to figure out where we were. The skeletal trees weren't much help on their own.

"There's no GPS signal!" Rudy exclaimed. "I've got signal and even data but no GPS!"

"So you have no idea where we are? I guess we'll have to do this the old fashion way." I listened for a road. Oddly, once the sound of the van's engine had faded, I didn't hear another vehicle. I set off in the same direction as the van. "So, who died and made you my agent, Rudy?" I asked, filling the oddly quiet forest.

"If you wanna be crass about it, Harry did, and you weren't going to charge extra for an emergency resurrection. What'd you promise the Weaver? Or was this a first-time-is-free sort of deal?"

"I didn't promise her anything. A friend called in a favor."

Rudy mulled on that for a microsecond. I'd told him about Bone Whistler a little bit previously. "Well congratulations! You now owe a serial killer a favor."

"He's not a serial killer! He's just a—"

"Cougar, and if the Weaver owed him, he's not a cougar. He's more like THE Cougar. And trust me, cougars are serial killers. They'll stalk prey for days or weeks for fun."

I grunted. "Well, he's not THE Cougar anymore. He's got my old body."

"And this has made him a compassionate individual?" Rudy asked.

Rudy's question triggered a shiver. Having joined Bone Whistler's for an occasional hunt, I couldn't describe him as cruel. While he killed his prey efficiently, compassion beyond that had no place in his world or his mind. On one hunt, a cornered deer got down on her knees to plead for her life. Articulating the songs she'd sing in praise and the fawns she'd name in his honor if he only let her go. To Bone Whistler the words were nothing more than the bleating of a panicked animal. He killed her with a single blow and ate her liver raw. "No it hasn't."

"You ain't gonna like what he wants."

"Like kill someone?"

Rudy laughed. "Ha! No. To a spirit like him, killing somebody is no big deal. Cougars as a rule aren't big on grudges. That's totally a house cat thing. Nah, he's gonna want a new hunting ground. That's what cougars want. More territory. Or maybe he'll want you to kill a bear?"

I huffed. "You really have no clue, do you? You're trying to distract me from asking why the hell the Weaver knew you."

"Flaming hot cashews, Thomas! Leave my age alone, will ya? The damn rodents are bad enough."

We reached the crossroads and I immediately knew where we were. More importantly, I knew the way toward O'Meara's. The trio's refusal to go to the Inquisitor's place for help even while Harry bled out had me worried.

"The rodents?" I asked innocently.

"Oh, don't get me started on the rodents! You know squirrels can live twenty years normally, right? That makes us practically elves to a rat!" Rudy chittered so hard I felt the vibration. Interesting.

I did some mental math and said, "It's closer to a dwarf. They're supposed to live about six times as long as a human. Elves live about fifteen times the average human lifespan, if they die of old age at all. Depends on the particular type of elf."

"I am not a dwarf!" Rudy snapped.

"Replace the beer with cashews and I think there's a pretty good resemblance." My lips peeling back into a grin at my own troll.

"You're the dwarf! Mules have nothing on cougars,

apparently. We should just sit this out, Thomas. Take your tass and go home. Whatever Jules is doing will probably blow up in his face," Rudy chittered.

"What says we're not?" I asked, innocent like.

"Because we're going to O'Meara's to tattle on him."

"I prefer the term 'second opinion,' since the trio slammed the door in our noses. Besides, all my stuff is still at O'Meara's."

28

"That's some serious Harry Potter level shit," I said as I first set foot on what should have been O'Meara's property. Rudy's weight concentrated into two points and I heard his little sniffles as he scented the air.

"This IS the right place. Where's the house?" he said.

I scanned the area. "Where's the yard? Even the mailbox is gone!" The house, the entire property, had disappeared like it'd never been here. The space between the two other homes had narrowed to make up for the sudden loss of landmass. The neighbors were now only a stone's throw away from each other. We crouched in the woods behind them. I wanted to creep forward and look at the road and sidewalks; or follow the faint line of purple that threaded between the houses, but both showed signs of occupancy.

Elizabeth, one of O'Meara's neighbors, stood in her kitchen with another woman I didn't recognize. The house's kitchen opened to a back porch through a large sliding glass door, which allowed us a full view of the inside. Across the way, the lights were on in the other neighbor's house. I decided to take a risk. Keeping my body low, I crept onto the deck and hunkered down against the wall next to the door, put my ear against the wood and concentrated. I could hear their voices, but the house's insulation muffled the sound to mere murmurings. Not good enough.

I risked sticking my head out a few inches and pressing my ear against the glass. I didn't hear screams.

I recognized Elizabeth's voice, creaking with fatigue."-bout you? Holding up?

"Oh, don't know any more, Liz! Least you have Ray home. I can call Josh and we can have a normal conversation, but as soon as I try to tell him what's going on at home the call cuts out."

"It's been two nights. He doesn't think it's weird that he hasn't come home?"

"He thinks he's on a business trip! Says the company is putting him up at a hotel. And I don't know what to do about Alice. She refused to come out of her room this morning! Carrying on about turning into a monster or something! I made her open the door and she looked like Alice to me! She asked me if I could see the horns!"

"I'm so sorry, Mary! You don't think..."

"It not just her! I called the doctor and she said to take a number. She let it slip that Alice isn't the first case!"

The woman lapsed into silence as I pulled back out of view. "You catch that, Rudy?"

"Yeah! Did you see how much sugar she put in her tea? Three spoonfuls! Utter madness!"

I groaned. "You know what they're not doing? Leaving town. Let's check out the border of the town, I've got a hunch." I trotted away from the house and back into the forest.

Rudy followed close behind. "Okay, let's go see. So what

you betting on? Endless wall of blackness? Energy field? Or just trackless wilderness?"

It turned out to be none of the above. I didn't realize we'd passed the border for a good fifteen minutes after we crossed it. There is a general scent of civilization, a medley of car exhaust, human sweat and pavement that increases the closer you get to Main Street. We were about a mile beyond the most far-flung development in Grantsville and we hadn't seen a dramatic end of the world. No cliff for desperate citizens to fling themselves off of.

But that scent, instead of fading as we got deeper into werewolf territory, slowly got stronger. When we found an intersection, I realized we were walking back into town from the opposite side, like the tunnel off the side of the screen in PAC-MAN.

"Man, I was really hoping for a view of something!" Rudy noted as we turned around. He found the border first, a subtle line of purple threading through the ground. Looking carefully, I could see the differences in the dirt on either side. Jules and Jowls had managed to stitch the ends of the roads leading out of town together, but it wasn't that even in other places. Out of sight of the cars, folds in space were visible, bright clumps of crumbled space I didn't want to get near. You probably wouldn't even notice you were stuck in one if you got close. The big trouble with traveling through bent space is that time can bend in them as well. And it's hard to see if the space you're in is bent.

But if Jules had put us all in a bubble, why were all the lights on? How the hell did we still have internet? The roads lined up. That didn't point to a jury-rigged hack of Archibald's dragon containment system. I could understand cutting off the town in a panic to hide from Ixey's threat of Inquisition, but trapping O'Meara's house away along with it? That spoke to planning and expertise that went beyond seizing an opportunity.

"I think it's about time we had a serious talk about honesty and forthrightness with our employers," I said.

"Your employer," Rudy corrected. "They fired me for saving your tail, remember?"

"Twice actually."

"Oh yeah! Crashing the helicopter was to save you too! Uh, why the hell do I save your butt? I could be at home watching the Guvinator blow crap up."

"Because then you'd have to walk everywhere."

"I wouldn't need to walk anywhere!"

"It would be difficult to be my agent if you weren't with me."

A brief pause as the squirrel mulled that over. "Fair point. Let's go."

29

I had completely intended to head straight to the park and suss out just what Jules and Jowls had done to Grantsville. Wouldn't have taken more than an hour tops, and zig zagging across the border of town dancing around the zones of crumpled space would have made the trip even faster. It was just, well...I ran headlong into a nap. There's a tree in the woods near O'Meara's that has this stout branch pretty high up and really comfortable in a solid sort of way. I've been a cat for nearly six months, and sometimes I really can't help it. I had a good snooze. Rudy didn't even give much of a protest. He objected but didn't light me on fire or anything. He was pretty tired too. It'd been a hell of a morning.

Hey Thomas. I woke to Richard's voice, and it took a few blinks before I realized he was in my head and not in the tree with me. *Where are you?*

I'm about twenty feet off the ground, I thought back as I squinted at the sun still high in the sky. I wondered why I could still see the sun. Maybe the space bending only applied a certain height from the ground? Could I hurdle myself over the barrier and back into the real world? Could it be that easy?

Thomas, would you focus? Tell us where you are so we can pick you up. We have a lot of work to do.

Well, the prospect of more work didn't appeal to me at that moment. *More tass harvesting?*

Yeah, lots of it eventually. First we need to get a new vehicle. It's going to be a busy week. Richard projected forceful confidence. It struck me as off, since Richard never gave out that sort of feeling unless he was deep into a project. He'd broadcasted it when the trio were working the aegis for Jules, but I hadn't felt it since. I yawned. Getting lied to made me grumpy.

"Are you awake finally?" Rudy squeaked. I craned my neck around to look at him. He was sitting on the middle of my back, jabbing at his phone with both paws. The screen was angled so I couldn't see the phone's surface. A few more taps and he looked up at me. "My battery's getting low. We gotta get to an outlet." He swiped the screen and tilted it so I could see his twenty-five percent battery indicator.

I wondered who or what the squirrel had been texting. I'd somewhat hoped that Rudy and O'Meara might make a good familiar pairing. They both had certain shared loves. But that would require him letting someone else poke around in that nut-obsessed brain of his, and I suspected there was a lot more in his brain than one would expect in something the size of a quarter.

Two could play at the secret game. My harness had an external battery in it that I wasn't going to tell him about. I know, small potatoes against possible immortality, but I had to start somewhere.

Thomas? Richard's thought called me back to the present.

If you don't have a vehicle, how do you plan on picking me up? I'll come to you at the park.

A surge of anxiety bubbled up through the facade. *We have a backup. Sandra's got a car. It will just be a bit of a tight squeeze for all four of us.*

They didn't want me to see the park. Why?

In the distance I heard the crackle of gunfire. Adrenaline purged the sleep from my limbs, and Rudy cried out in alarm as I surged to my feet. Gunfire toward the center of town. Five shots. Pistol, I thought. I rotated my ears towards the sound. Two more shots fixed the direction. Different gun. A gunfight? Not good. Were the mundanes shooting at each other?

I was on the ground heading toward the shots before I knew what I was doing. *Listen Richard, you tell Jules that he can't keep us in this bubble. He's got to let it go.*

What? No, the inquisitors are out there, Thomas! We'll need much more tass before we're ready for that. That's why we need to get to work on the harvesting. You need the tass too. You're only halfway to healing your friend.

The town knows you exist. The pitchforks would be out soon.

Richard gave a mental wince, momentarily reliving the scene in the supermarket. *We're working on that. Look Thomas, we really need your help here. You're our only other familiar.*

I'll meet you at the park. I have to see what people are shooting at, I thought at him.

The munds are shooting at each other? Thomas, stay away! Are you near O'Meara's?

Maybe.

Stop being difficult! Stay away. I'm going to come and get you. We can't have you get hurt! Then I saw it. The thought behind his frustration slipped through the link. The black plane. The hunger plane was coming through again and this time the people in it had guns. Fuck.

Tho— I slammed the link closed. He didn't give a damn about the people in Grantsville. No, that was unfair. He'd care enough to make little sounds of sympathy toward their plight but never enough to actually do something about it.

Four pinpricks peeled the top of an ear away from my skull. I was angry enough that they'd gone flat. "Thomas!" Rudy shouted. Apparently he'd been attempting to get my attention for a while.

"Yeah?" I answered, my pace not slowing.

"If we're trying to get away from the guns, you're trotting in the exact wrong direction. Did you notice that I'm fresh out of elemental-powered machinery?"

"We're practicing Spiderman 101," I told him, forcing my ears to relax.

"That implies you have great power, which unless one of the magi are going to flashbang to your side ready to throw down, we don't really possess any. Plus, big cats in scared small towns are probably the definition of bullet attractors."

"Tell me something I don't know," I said.

The squirrel lapsed into silence. Then I heard the rip of Velcro. "I have three firecrackers and no bottle rockets."

The black plane had landed squarely on one of Grantsville's newer developments, just old enough that nearly all the three-to-five-bedroom houses were sold and occupied, with that just built smell being replaced with the odors of children and pets.

"Oh bury your peanuts in the ground and roast them

with a nuke," Rudy swore as I crept through the woods about a quarter mile from the development's first row of houses. I could see a diffuse haze of purple ahead, but I wasn't close enough for details. I paused mid-step, my front paw raised. The scent of blood drifted lazily through the air. Sirens wailed in the distance but were coming this way.

"What? I can't see yet," I said.

Rudy climbed up onto my head, leaning forward so the underside of his body blocked out the top of my vision. "Yep, that's no transition. That's a shallowing."

A growl escaped my throat and I continued on, placing my rear paws carefully in the depressions my front paws had made. We emerged in the back yard of a two-story house. Reality here appeared untouched, but the sweet scent of fresh blood rolled over me like a wave and made my stomach rumble. I found myself calculating how long it'd been since I'd eaten as I crept along a backyard fence. My human squeamishness had been one of the first things to go after my change. Before, the sight of blood would induce panicky heart palpitations, but now my body had decidedly different instincts. Unless it smelled of rot or disease, gore was the freshest of meat. The only emotional response I had was the urge to lick my chops. My sense of concern overwhelmed my stomach when a friend was injured, but strangers? The cougar thought they were made of meat for him.

Someone inside the house clearly wasn't as conflicted as I. There were ripping noises and growls combined with the periodic crunch of bone. Rudy hunkered low against my neck. "So much for saving the day," he whispered.

I kept creeping forward, my ears rotating like radar dishes, listening for any hint of something sneaking up on us. I made it into the front yard. The purple haze looked to start one street over, but the carnage had started here. Four figures hunched in front of the house across the way, two adults and two kids engaging in cannibalism as a family bonding activity. Maybe you couldn't call it cannibalism, as the figures had clearly strayed from humanity. Their limbs were too long, their mouths so wide that their jawbones might touch in the back of their necks and they pulled hunks of fat out of the pile of flesh that had been a man with claws three times the size of my own. The four all glowed with that sickly mix of blended realities.

"Rudy, how far can a creature of a shallowing get from it?"

"Once they're made, they have a link to it. They can leave. The more they feed, the more a plane like this will spread. Thomas, we have to close that rift," Rudy said in urgent tones. "The meat's only the start. They're going after what they know is edible, but to them everything is edible. Once they realize that, they'll grow unstoppable as they force wood, rock and reality itself down their maws."

"You've seen this before?" I hunkered low in the grass and prayed the things wouldn't spot us.

"Not like this. Never like this. Occasionally a hungry spirit from one of these planes gets out and sows destruction before the magi kill it. But now the reality itself has gotten a foothold."

"Okay, so how do we close the rift?"

Rudy chittered with frustration. "You call the magi. They generally will thank you and then close it."

I had a suspicious feeling this hunger plane was tangled up with all the rest of them. "Can't you do something? Anything?"

"I'm a squirrel, Thomas! I chuck acorns and explosives at problems, neither of which are going to help."

"Can't we force Jules to untie space? Let the Veil back in?"

"The Veil's idea of a solution for this might involve an 'accidental' nuclear missile strike. We need a team of magi to seal this thing off."

I clicked my teeth together in frustration. The sirens were getting loud enough that I couldn't be sure that I'd hear one of those things creeping up on us. Richard had been right. There was nothing I could do about the black plane. I carefully retraced my steps before breaking into a run toward the sirens. I'd been taking nightly constitutionals around this area for months, following an instinctual drive to know my territory. At first it had been an urge I fought against. During that struggle I paced through the house so frequently my paws wore tracks in the carpet like a zoo animal. Tallow put a stop to that, tossing me bodily out the back door when she caught me roaming the ruts. I thanked entities unknown for her drive to protect the flooring now, as I knew precisely how the cops would get to the development.

I had an idea, and it was a stupid one that would probably get me shot. But it was the only one I had to prevent the entirety of the Grantsville police department from getting eaten.

30

I sat on the orange line sans squirrel. He'd called me nuts and disappeared up into a tree near the road.

My tail curled across the top of my forepaws, hiding fully extended claws that itched to bite into the cracked asphalt. In the distance, but far too close for comfort, I heard sirens, the Weee-Dooo Weee-Dooo of three police cars. I couldn't see Rudy, but he and his firecrackers were off to my left somewhere in the trees, his little brain feverishly dreaming up ways of distracting the cops if this went south, maybe.

The place I'd chosen wasn't ideal. The road curved not 600 feet from my position. I could hear the engines now, roaring beneath the sirens. My stomach twisted into a fourth-dimensional knot and the tip of my tail twitched violently. Every instinct, some cat, some older than that, screamed at me to move, to run, to get out of the fracking way before you get pancaked, you stupid familiar!

Instead I gritted my teeth and dug my claws into the road. I promised my claws a good scratching of some nice furniture if we survived this.

The first car ripped around the corner and I knew I had made a mistake, a horrible mistake. As a citizen of the USA, you know cars, you're comfortable with them. While you're inside one, everything is under your control. You perceive thirty-five miles per hour on a road to be a rather serene pace. Everything changes when you're out of the comfort of the driver's seat and the same car is bearing down on you like the sadistic lovechild of a bear and a bullet. I saw the wide eyes of the officer as he realized far too late that I was in the center of the road. The tires screeched. I don't know what he did, but the emblem of Grantsville on the side door loomed impossibly large in my vision.

I jumped straight up. Had it not been a SUV, I might have cleared it and would have made it over even this one had it not been for the two-foot tall antenna that caught me right on the shoulder.

My first thought was that I had made it, and the second involved wondering why the ground was sky blue. Then my shoulders and back flared with pain and the world went sideways for a moment as more tires screeched. A line of blistering pain ran across my neck and shoulder. The scent of my own blood wafted through my mouth. My own blood doesn't smell nearly as good as other people's blood. It's got its own bitter tang to it. That's how I knew it was mine.

The pop of a car door. "-Christ, Jake! We don't have time to see if the dog's alright! We have an active shooter!"

"We're stopped already. Take thirty seconds to put it out of its misery if it's bad."

"Good news, officer," I said with a bit of a groan. "You didn't hit a dog, you hit a cat. Although I would still appreciate it if you felt bad about it." My vision cleared. I was still on the road but facing away from the median. I had a good view of the forest along the edge, but all the cops and their cars were behind me.

"Who's talking?"

"The cat who you just hit, who'd rather not add getting shot to his list of why he should have just napped through today," I said.

"Okay! That's not funny! We're on important business!"

"Come on, Jake! We gotta go!" the cop on a mission from God called.

I grimaced. "Anyone who responds to that call is dead. It's a trap. Everyone in that development is dead." I almost said, *or worse,* but I didn't really want to add complexity to the situation. "I'm going to get up now."

There wasn't an immediate objection, so slowly I rolled onto my stomach. My right shoulder felt like hell on magma day, a line of fire burning across my skin. Yet the limb held as I lifted myself up and looked at the officer. Youngish, he had his pistol out in both hands but pointed at the ground, his eyes flicking back and forth before resting on me. "Damn, that's a big one," he said.

"One hundred and ninety-nine pounds to be precise. I don't quite hit the record books for male mountain lions, but I'm pretty far up there."

"Christ, you do talk." The cop's brown eyes got big. "Oh my God, Grover's Grocery." Now I could clearly see down the barrel of his gun.

"Jake!" A woman had gotten out of the other side of the SUV. I recognized her leathery, beaten face as one of the several cops that had taken pot shots at me six months ago.

"Hi May!" I said. "Long time no see. Remember that time you thought I was a dog?" The woman stared at me as if I had grown a second head. "Ray made a joke about a cougar party? Doesn't that ring a bell? You told him to shut up. If Ray is here, I want him to know I find that whole cougar slash older woman thing very offensive." Slowly, recognition along with bewilderment crept into her face.

Great, she recognized me now. Although I'd have to say that encounter really wouldn't prove my beneficence. However, she'd stopped calling for everyone to get back in their cars. "Now that I have your attention... The place you're all heading is full of cannibalistic zombies, and if you go there, they will attempt to eat you. If you shoot your way to the source, you'll become a cannibalistic zombie too. The best way to deal with this is containment. Also watch out for a giant spider loose in the area made out of tools." I looked at Officer Jake. "Now could you please lower that gun? Maybe even holster it?"

Jake's mouth had tightened into a thin line of a frown, his eyes squinted. "No. You're under arrest, Mr. Mountain Lion."

"What?" *Of course,* I thought to myself.

"You appear to know what's going on here, and I'm not going to let you out of my sight until you tell us what's happened to our town." The cop's voice was calm, clearly in no hurry to take my suggestion and put the firearm away.

Damn it. This never happens in the fairytales, I thought with a bit of bitterness. The mythical talking animals appear, dispense cryptic advice and then fade into the fog. I didn't want to try to explain everything to them. I'd be stuck in a cell at the police station for days. Then if the techno-magi ever let the Veil back in, all the officers would be wondering why the hell a mountain lion is in their jail cell and shoot me without a trial. At the thought of a cage I felt Mr. Bitey stir in the back of my head. "Nope, not going to happen." I stared back at Jake. "You shoot me and nobody will tell you anything at all. If you put me in a cage, I'm dead and you're dead."

"Because your friends who blew up the grocery store will come for you?"

Officer May cut in. "How do we stop this?"

Now there was a good question. The answer was simple enough. You convince Jules to turn off his machine and hope Rudy was wrong about the Veil stamping Grantsville out of existence. However, sending the cops directly at Jules seemed like a bad first step. Jules wouldn't listen, but Jowls might.

"Well? Stop thinking about how much to tell us and tell us!" Jake's voice cracked, and panic flashed into his eyes for a brief moment before he remastered his stern expression.

"You don't stop this," I said. "You take care of the people in this town the best you can. I have to get ahold of cops who deal with magic. This isn't your jurisdiction." Cops who really wouldn't care about the wiping out of an entire neighborhood. I wanted to tell these people the truth, have them storm the gates of the park in a valorous hail of bullets, but it'd be like tossing hamsters onto an electric fence. Wards would be in place now, wards none of them could see. And if they did get through, Noise would be the biggest target in their sights. Not the magi.

He lowered the gun a fraction of an inch. "You can get a signal out? How?"

"I'm magic." Translation: I'm lying through my teeth. I turned and walked into the forest, waiting for a bullet in my back with every step.

Soon as I was out of the line of sight (and bullet vectors) I opened the link to Richard.

Thomas! Where are you? There's a transition in less than an hour!

I growled. Behind me car doors slammed. *The only thing I want you to be doing in the next hour is sealing off that shallowing. I need to have a chat with Jules.*

31

Rudy hadn't reappeared when Richard drove up in a rusty old pickup truck. I didn't worry too much about it, as he would take care of himself and probably show up at a clutch time to bail me out or blow something up.

Richard on the other hand didn't appear to be a reliable asset. Once the cool, collected frontman of his three-man Borg collective, he'd degenerated into a mass of twitching nerves. Dread rolled out his pores in such quantity that it cut through foulness of the car exhaust. He popped open the passenger side and shrank away from me. "It's not my fault," he muttered defensively.

I held the image of the family of four devouring their neighbor firmly in my head. "What, you thought if I didn't see it that would make it okay?"

He shifted the car back into gear, the standard magus excuses already forming on his tongue.

"Save it," I told him. "Just help me stop it. We have to convince Jules to reconnect us to the real world."

"They're working on getting rid of the hunger plane.

After all, it results in zero tass anyway." He gave me a weak smile.

The park had been turned into a construction project. A steel latticework of beams encased Jules' magic pill, the skeleton of a building that would encapsulate the prize of House Technomagi. Noise waved from the roof of the structure as we pulled into the parking lot. She wore a pair of overalls and a red shirt the trio had woven together a few days ago. After Noise revealed that she knew how to weld, Sandra had rigged her a pair of goggles that fit over her eyes. Assisting her were two clanks about the same size as the one Rudy had piloted. These were automatous but still pretty stupid. Their eyes peered down at us with the greenish light of a summoned spirit.

A large tent had been set up in the parking lot, an army surplus job, long as a shipping trailer and tall enough for Jules to comfortably stand inside.

Pretty far from a dark wizard laughing maniacally in their tower of doom. I suppose if you looked at it sideways, all the power cables snaking in and out of the tent, you might term it a slightly sinister but scrappy tech startup. At least the air had the decency to feel evil. Being this close to the wound in reality made everything uncertain. The outlines of objects seemed tense, as if the lines were holding still for my benefit and were anxiously waiting for me to look away. I had to hope Jules and Jowls, who I'd counted as friends, hadn't become as bad as the monsters currently devouring Grantsville. Surely Jowls at least would see reason.

I got out of the truck and pushed myself through the flap

of the tent. Two rather expensive looking 3D printers whirred on either side of the entrance. Jules sat behind a plastic folding table so new that I could smell the fresh chemicals in the air. Jowls lay curled up in a box near the corner of the table, the shine of his iris visible through the slit of an eye.

Jules sat up as I entered, knitting his fingers together on the table. "I've been hearing that you're a bit upset. Let's talk."

Neither his tone or the neutral expression boded well for this conversation. The table didn't particularly look stable enough to support my weight which ruled out having the discussion with my teeth six inches from his face. As intimidating as it would be to have a 200-pound cat up close on your desk, the effect would be countered if I comically crashed to the ground. So instead I wandered among the machinery in the tent. Various 3D printers, laser cutters and boxes of materials lay scattered about.

"Quite a collection of stuff," I said. "And the steel Noise is using doesn't look summoned. I see you're not as cut off as the citizens of Grantsville."

"My shop's enchantments still work with a bit of effort. My colleagues are willing to donate equipment to the cause but are of course too busy to send actual help."

Screw beating around the bushes. "Because you're doomed?"

"We're not doomed. We just need more tass. Which I would really appreciate you helping to gather, Thomas." Jules' tone was level, reasonable. *Bastard.*

I slid my body around the corner of a laser cutter, a metal box six inches taller than my shoulders. It was the best cover available if things kept sliding towards ugly. "That depends, you actually going to do something about the hunger plane? A hundred people are dead tonight as a down payment and I'd bet my claws that's just the latest. Folks have been dying from the hunger plane all along, haven't they?" I asked, struggling to keep a growl out of my voice.

Jules grimaced. "It is regrettable Thomas. We don't have as much control over the transition as you think we do. Our design is more of a predictive mechanism for the majority of the planes."

The growl building in my throat nearly escaped but I swallowed it back down, "Don't bullshit me. I saw how you stitched up the roads so they'd all lead into each other. That's not easy."

"We have control over this plane, yes. Very fine control," Jules said, that last bit sounding low, threatening. "But the others...they're orbiting like planets."

"Then let the townsfolk out. If they don't die from being trapped in a reality blender, hunger is going to get them and I don't mean the black plane."

"Oh, and invite the damn inquisitors over for tea? That's sure to be absolutely fabulous!" Jowls' voice stabbed into the conversation like a spear between the ears. "They're dead anyway, Thomas. That's the sad fact." Jowls stood, ears plastered to the side of his head. "It's just as much your fault as ours. I suspect whatever you let out of that trap turned it inside out on purpose."

"You're keeping them all here, Jowls. Let them go. Then run away if you have to." I stared at Jowls, and he didn't blink. Not a trace of guilt could be found in his slit eyes. Cold dread crept along my spine, and it took conscious effort to keep my claws sheathed.

"It's not that simple, Thomas," Jules said. "The portion of the Veil we trapped here is dead. We didn't think that would happen nearly as fast as it did, but I think transitions actually physically hurt it. With it dead, these mundanes are no longer in its power. They never will be. If we let the Veil in, along with the Inquisition, a natural disaster will befall the town, culling the survivors down to a few crazies that no one will believe."

So pat, so logical. I didn't believe it. The unfortunate souls. They're dead anyway, so why bother? Both Jules and Jowls looked surprised as a ragged hiss escaped my throat. "Then find a better way! Magic can do anything, given time, knowledge and tass!"

Jowls sighed. "The birth of a House is a bit like making an omelet, Thomas. Mundanes die. They do that without our help. You said you'd help us establish House Techno-magi. This is all part of it. No magus will blame us."

"Except the ones you're so scared of," I snarled, not caring if the pair saw my teeth or not.

"Yes, but they don't care about the mortals. They care that we damaged the Veil and made it angry. So we need enough tass to buy them off. You need this tass as much as we do," Jules said.

"With your crimes, Thomas." Jowls grinned. "The murder of two Archmagi will be considerably more... hrm, lets say the bribe is proportional to the sin."

My stomach lurched as if punched by an unseen fist. "I didn't do anything!"

"Aww! You can't lie to ol Jowls Thomas, you're terrible at it." Jowls' eyes glowed with pride. "Richard allowed me to get a good look at that fancy new chain of yours. We knew Archibald very well, Thomas. That's not his work. I'm certain no magus alive could even replicate the way it's woven into your flesh and soul. Poor thing. That Dragon literally took you apart and put you back together again, didn't it? Not that I blame you. You don't say no to a Dragon when its gotcha by the balls. It dispatched Sabrina and Cornelius handily, no doubt, and what did you care about a couple of old magi anyway. You didn't know them."

Bile rose in my throat. "Archibald and the others had been torturing it for over a century. You're all lucky I convinced it not to destroy Grantsville!"

Jowls' grin turned triumphant. I mentally smacked myself. "A valid choice that I appreciate, Thomas, but the Council will think differently. You can see this from their perspective, can't you?"

"I'm sure in your case the most likely sentence for your crimes will be death by vivisection," Jules said, "to gain knowledge back that you have deprived the Council by killing two of their members."

"Point is, Thomas," Jowls purred, "you have more skin in this game than you think. I love that you're so addicted to being the hero, but you need the protection of House Tech-nomagi even more than we do. With enough tass, those niggly questions about the night Sabrina died will never be asked."

I closed my jaw, which had fallen at some point, and swallowed. I tasted bitterness on my tongue, but it was nothing I'd eaten. Was this how it would always be? Any clients or magi I worked for would be nothing but sociopaths looking to get ahead in the games they played with one another. If I didn't buckle under Jules or some other patron, would I be following Sir Rex's path and die for a principle? I looked to Richard, who stood at the entrance flap. Sweat dotted his brow. He'd closed the link when we entered the tent. I ripped it open. *And what do you think? The murder of an entire town. That's all business as usual?*

His head was a snake pit of fear, his thoughts going in

circles. *Thomas, listen to Jules,* he pleaded. *We have to see this through. It's our only chance at survival!*

"It's not so bad, you know," Jowls said. "Jules always manages to find what you need when you need it." He gave a tiny smile. "We'll fix your thumb deficiency, no trouble at all. A set of robotic arms. How's that sound?"

"Like it's a petty thing to worry about after a hundred people just died," I snapped.

"Power has cost, Thomas. Just as your personal power came at the cost of three lives, House Technomagi will be born from the ashes of Grantsville," Jowls said.

"The deal was six. Sabrina, Cornelius, Medoci, Ghenna, Rasasha and Scrags. I doubt you'll know the names of the people in this town," I spat, tracking the auras of Tom and Harry outside the tent, fumbling with something between them.

"We're getting deep in the weeds here, Thomas. You're no better than the rest of us. I want you to take an Oath of Fealty," Jules said, expression neutral as if his request was as simple as handing him a wrench.

"I'm terminating our agreement," I snarled. I broke my bond with Richard right there, snapped it out of him like a whip. He crumpled to the ground, clutching his head without so much as a squeak. The other two of the trio screamed in pain behind the back flap of the tent where they'd been hiding.

Something heavy hit the ground. Jules's eyes flared, his hand diving into his jacket as I darted behind the biggest machine in the tent. Note to self: the rules of cover change when dealing with magi. A flash of yellow and the machine slammed into my side, staggering me sideways. Another flash and it felt as if something seized my entire back half and pulled, wrenching me off the floor. I screamed as my claws lashed out, latching onto the very machine that had just nearly run me over, and I wrapped my forelegs around the control panel.

"Way to make a mess of things, Thomas!" Jowls said. "There's no way for you to come out of this alive now. We were offering you a pathway. You could've been part of a rising House!"

"Great! Sign me up for Murder Inc. and Quarterly Genocide." Jules didn't seem to be pulling me anywhere now. I'd seen his toy move cars, so he probably could have torn me in two if he wanted to. But I'd be a nice bargaining chip to hand to the inquisitors, so perhaps he didn't want to kill me yet. Coming back had clearly been a dumb idea. I clung to the machine vainly, attempting to muscle it between Jules and myself. Then it moved again.

"You impertinent ignoramus! I'm trying to save you!" Jowls howled indignantly..

"Blackmail is a funny way to save someone," I grunted as I strained against the machine. If I could just tip it over, I could break the path of the beam that held me. Jules wasn't holding me steady anymore. He kept looking at Harry and Tom, who were fussing over the device they'd dropped.

Jowls huffed so hard his entire body jiggled. "If you're so eager for your day before the Council, then fine. Hold still and we'll store you safely until your trial."

Grunting, I pulled the machine up onto to wheels, but Jules simply raised my ass well clear of the machine, preventing it from blocking the beam even as it toppled.

A vision of Cyndi's broken body sailing through the air, the stunned horror of Noise's pack as fell to the earth. She had attempted to control me, as she had enslaved Noise and her family, she had been a monster. I hadn't held back, I murdered her without the trace of guilt. Never even lost sleep over it. A laugh began to bubble up out of my chest as realization came with it. *I kill monsters, no matter the face they wear.* And at the rate this cabal was going I'd have to put them all down because there was no else who would.

The laughter grew like a metastasizing tumor taking control of my entire body. It hurt. Cats aren't made to laugh like that. We chuckle and snort but never a full guffaw. A creeping sensation of dampness grew in the fur around my eyes as a huge knot of emotions untangled as I realized I meant that thought.

All of them, Jowls and the magi stood frozen, staring at me as if I'd gone absolutely bonkers. They were right, the thought of a familiar, even a rather big one, with no magical powers of his own taking on hundreds of sociopathic magi was insane. Fortunately I didn't have to take them all on at once. The laughter subsided.

"Surrender," I rasped, gasping to recover my breath. "That's your choice. Surrender or I'm going to murder you all."

Jules made a disgusted sound and sneered. "He's gone mad."

"A true shame," argeed Jowls.

Jules looked to Tom and Harry, who had a reworked LAPIS device between them and opened his mouth to give an order.

At that moment I twisted myself around, snagged my claws on the canvas ceiling, which Jules had helpfully put in reach when he'd lifted me. With a jerk, I pulled the fabric down between myself and the beam. The beam blocked, I began to fall, but not before hooking the thin metal poles in the ceiling and pulling the entire tent down on top me. A flash of purple and a *foop!* of displaced air emanated from my former position. The portal shone above me for a brief second as I tunneled under the falling fabric.

Difficult to control, my ass, I thought. *Bastards had built themselves a portal gun.* I paused as sunlight met my eyes from the lip of the canvas. I could see Jules' aura struggling with the canvas, but Tom and Harry stood resolute, probably having taken a step out of the tent as it fell. If I stepped out, they'd have a clear shot.

"What the hell's going on?" Noise bellowed. "Get your hands off me!" The pair with the portal gun swung out to the left toward her.

"Noise get off the building!" I cried and dived back under the canvas then beelined it for Jules. One bite would end this whole fiasco.

Voop! Two purple flashes lit up my vision as a spell fired, probably a prepared focus, Jules and Jowl's auras disappeared. In the next instant I caught the same two flashes, further away and to my left, within the structure. I changed course for Harry and Tom, leaping up and slamming my weight down on the portal device, ripping it from their hands and dashing it to the ground. The two men shouted and scrambled away from me. Harry rolled onto his back and pulled a long rod from his jacket, the same one he'd ripped off the front of Grover's Grocery with. One blast from that thing and I'd be the world's first cougarnaut. I pounced and ripped it from his hands, taking a few fingers with it.

The black man screamed, clutching at his hands as he rolled away. Growling, I attempted to break the device in half, but it didn't yield to my jaws. Tom held his empty hands up as he backed away. My instincts screamed for his windpipe. Behind him I finally saw Sandra. She'd climbed onto the bleachers along the baseball diamond and now leveling a black rifle at Noise. The clanks had Noise's full attention. One had wrapped itself around her leg, weighing her down like a leaden toddler, and the other had its arms around her neck in a deadly game of piggyback.

I dropped the stick to shout, "She's got a gun!"

Noise ducked but not quite fast enough. The gun thundered. Blood burst from Noise's left shoulder. In retrospect, probably one of the worst things you can do when facing down a 600-pound were-cow-wolf is *almost* miss. With a bellow of pain, Noise ripped the robot off her neck and hurled it directly at Sandra. The woman dived out of the way, flinging herself from the top of the bleachers.

Maybe Noise and I could battle royale our way out of this with fang and fury? The trio was down. How much harder could the rest of the technomagi be?

There are certain questions you shouldn't even think. At that moment the air within the partially constructed building pulsed with green energy and dark shapes pooled within the structure. I swore, the bastards had summoned a cavalry. Jules and Jowls were no mere technomagus and familiar. They had more tricks in the pocket of that button-down shirt than I had teeth.

Noise crushed the clank's head on her leg with her fist and leapt at Sandra. The magus whipped out her wand as Noise reached the top of her arc. The beam didn't send Noise flying, but it stopped her jump dead in the air. For a moment she hung there like a cartoon character that had walked off a cliff and not realized it yet. Then she fell with a thunderous impact, her hoof-like paws hitting the baseball diamond like a pair of meteors.

I bolted toward her and Sandra. Leaping over the fence and barreling down the hill, the pop and ping of bullets followed me. I didn't stop to see who was shooting now. Someone inside the building, probably. Noise set herself like a linebacker against the beam, the dust streaming around her planted feet.

Bullets whizzed behind me as the sporadic pops changed to the staccato ratchet of full auto. Unlike spells, I couldn't see bullets coming. My run became a zig-zag as I searched for some sort of cover. They'd pulled down the dugouts and the backstop, so the only structures nearby were the bleachers. Behind the bleachers lay a steep slope, an almost straight ninety degrees to another flattened area with a covered picnic shelter; its columns could provide some cover. Beyond that lay several grassy hills that ramped up toward the town pool. Figuring a little bit of cover is oceans better than none, I ran up the hill behind Sandra and flattened myself against the cold, soggy grass. Bullets whined over my head so closely that my whiskers trembled from the displaced air, but the shooters on the ground floor of the building didn't have an angle on me.

Figures, men-like shapes with lumpy rifles and veiny green skin, were climbing into the second story of the half-complete metal structure. Had Jules summoned an infantry unit from another reality to fight for him?

I remembered the force wand clutched in my jaw and spat it out, desperately looking for some way to make it work. The tip was a crystal that pulsed with kinetic energy and the rod itself contained a meshwork of spells. Nubby dials dotted its length and there, just below the crystal, was a friendly red button. I pointed the rod roughly in the direction of the iron scaffolding and slammed my paw down on it.

I missed. Small and nestled right under the fitting that held the crystal, the device hadn't been designed for those of us with manual dexterity issues. A normal, calm me would have carefully extended a claw and depressed the button. However, panicked me just slammed the thing over and over again, shouting, "Fire! Fire! Fire!"

On the tenth shot I found the right angle and the yellow light flicked out in a broad cone. It ripped open the ground in front of me and flung sod at the building in a massive chunk. The green soldiers caught in the beam lost their footing and either sailed backward or grunted in pain as the beam pinned them to the walls they'd been climbing.

The structure itself held. Either it was just that much stronger than Grover's Grocery or one of those knobs had the device dialed way down.

With the chatter of guns quieted I heard a high-pitched tink and Sandra's beam winked out. With a roar, Noise barreled down on Sandra, who tossed her overheated wand away and reached into her back pocket. As Noise reached her, the technoshaman stepped off the bleachers and a golden ward flared to life around her. A panic ward, similar to the one Rinoa had used on my behalf, enclosed Sandra.

Noise swung her fists down like two hammers. Sandra screamed as the ward deformed like a ball of silly putty, bending inward under the force of those massive fists. They came within six inches of Sandra's prone form before the ward surged back to its original shape, flinging Noise into the bleachers.

I caught another pulse of green from Jules and Jowls before a new salvo of automatic gunfire ripped through the air. Noise howled with pain as bullets splashed into her flank. She rolled to the side, taking cover behind Sandra's ward. The bullets made its surface ripple like water as the deadly projectiles collected in its surface.

The wand I held was heating up and the scent of over-taxed electronics filled my nose. More green summoned men were appearing within the safety of the building's lowest floor. Too many to fight. Magic is one thing, but lots of guys with guns are another. "Noise! Come on!" I shouted as I attempted to angle the rod downward. The steel groaned under the force of it. Noise kicked out spitefully at Sandra's ward before dashing up the hill toward me.

"Just keep running!" I shouted and snatched up the rod, dropping in behind her as she passed me by. I didn't run directly after her. Instead I curved around the picnic area. An isolated gunshot rang out as I flung the rod down and smacked the button. The yellow beam blasted the thirty-odd picnic tables out onto the field. The wooden tables shattered against the steel and set it ringing like a gong on the receiving end of a tommy gun salvo. I smiled as the men like things were tossed from the structure and crashed into the earth. Our retreat thus covered, I grabbed the wand and joined the retreat at full speed.

32

We were running so fast that we never saw the web. One moment I was right on Noise's heels. Next I was pressed against Noise's buttocks, swaying back and forth ten feet above the ground, trapped in a net woven of fine chain that stank of motor oil. My only weapon, Harry's rod, lay on the ground below us.

Noise let out a low moo of distress as sweet laughter rained down from above. "Oooh yes, I knew if I was patient I would catch something tasty, but now I have both something tasty and something interesting." The grinning toolbox lowered itself out of the canopy. Precisely how I read the facial expression from eight ratchet eyes and screwdriver fangs I can't be sure, but that eight-legged bitch positively vibrated with amusement.

I played it cool. "Hardy, har, har, har, Weaver. You can put us down now. We're kinda in a hurry." Technically the toolbox that was her thorax contained no digestive system, but I'd seen her catch a soul and put it back into a body, so challenging her ability to eat me might lead to an unpleasant demonstration.

"You're on social terms with giant spider spirits now?" For someone who was the size of two of the world's largest football players put together, Noise's voice reached an impressive octave.

I sighed. "Noise, meet the Weaver, a spider god who's really good at healing. Weaver, meet Noise, my... ex-girl-friend." We hadn't really talked much since she'd attempted to eat me. The technomagi had kept us both busy and separated the last few days, so we hadn't had a chance to sort ourselves out. Not that I was in a hurry to have that conversation.

Crushed against Noise's thigh, I felt her take a deep breath before the muscle rippled beneath me like living steel. "I am a member of the Granite pack and you should not be here, spirit."

The spider spun on the strand of chain that it dangled from, laughing with that marvelous, and I suspected stolen, voice. "Oh, I see the strands between you both now, caught in a web of your own spinning, my dear."

Noise growled. "What's that supposed to mean?"

Weaver swung close, hooking the net with two legs. "Just imagine that Khatt next to you happy, healthy and in love with someone else!"

A two-fingered fist slammed into the Weaver's face with the force of an electromagnetically driven piston. Her head shattered, her eyes scattering in every direction. Screeching, Weaver swung away from us like an awkward tetherball in a schoolyard. She collided with a tree and skittered into its branches, dripping a trail of motor oil in her wake.

Noise reached up and grabbed the chains at the top of the net. Snap! Gravity hit me with a vengeance and I found myself twisting through the air before hitting the ground on all fours. It shook from Noise's impact beside me.

Noise rubbed her fist. "For the record. I hit her because she gave me the opportunity, not because I flew into a jealous rage."

As if I was going to argue with her! "So noted," I said. A motion caught my eye. A socket, one of Weaver's eyes was rolling over the bare forest floor. It moved slowly, weaving around sticks and leaves that lay between it and the tree that Weaver had fled up. A wet patch spread across my back. I looked and found my back soaked with red. Vaguly beefy smelling blood dripped from the dull claws of Noise's injured arm, which hung limp. Wondering how much blood she'd lost, I nosed her knee. "Come on, let's get out of here."

She didn't budge. Instead she called up to the tree the socket was now rolling up. "If you want to deal, then let's deal on even footing."

Weaver inched down from the foliage. She'd reassembled her face, with the now-shattered bits of tools proving more flexible than entire tools. The shape of her head now had a much closer resemblance to the one I'd witnessed with Bone Whistler.

"Your werewolf thing is quite rude," Weaver hissed.

"Sorry but you know werewolves. Impossible to train, even when they're not the size of a small house."

Noise growled. "Watch it. I could still use you as a peace offering to Pa."

Ignoring Noise, I met Weaver's seven eyed gaze, the eighth socket still making its way to her. She made no move from her perch. "Next time you carry me into your world, you will provide me a body of natural materials, none of this noisome metal. My web must have both have the strength and flexibility to bind those within it."

I didn't point out just how flexible the chain of hydrocarbons that made up a portion of her body could be. Noise might have had much more difficulty snapping a net of nylon than chain links. "You think there will be a next time?"

"You snared us because you need something," Noise said. "What is it?"

"Need is such a silly word. I am a God, a weaver of both souls and webs. There is nothing I need from the likes of you, little cowwolf. Yet I do want things, and my time on this plane grows short. You wish to trade a want of mine for your need? Untangling your soul from that meadow would be a trivial thing for one such as I."

"And what would that cost me?" Noise folded her arms and glared at the god.

"Since Thomas cannot, you could build me a proper body of oak and willow, obsidian for my fangs and opal my eyes. Store it in a dry, locked space until you or he have need of me."

"Why would we need you?" I asked, fearing I knew the answer.

Weaver turned her seven eyes to me, smiling slyly. "Why indeed? Why indeed have something that can reverse death itself at your call? Swallow a spider and its web, and travel to Bone Whistler in the presence of a suitable body. I will meet you there."

"The price for your services?"

"Just a small piece of yourself." The weaver chuckled with that soft feminine voice. "Quite a bargain against the end of one's life."

"Deal," Noise grunted.

"Noise!" I protested.

She gave me a sidelong glance as she stepped forward. "There's no harm in building her a statue. I need to get back to normal." She looked up at the spider.

"You will be responsible for keeping it safe," the spider responded.

"If it's destroyed while under my care, I'll rebuild it. If it's destroyed while you're using it or you don't bring it back, that's not my issue," Noise said.

"Agreed." Weaver clambered down the tree, and I took a step back. Noise stood her ground. Even Weaver, as large as she was, only came up to Noise's waist.

I saw something knit together between the two of them, a strand of gold, the color I usually only saw in wards. But this was entirely different. Both stared at each other a bit. Noise's tail remained firmly between her legs, and her big ears were rotated downward as if they wanted to fold back against her head but couldn't quite manage it. Weaver's many eyes scanned her up and down, the spider's posture posed to leap away at a moment's notice.

Noise nodded after a moment and spread her arms. Weaver darted in and plunged four legs not into Noise's chest, but her head, the pliers bending into those invisible angles. The limbs flashed in a series of motions and withdrew. No dramatic flares of energy or spider bites. "It is done," Weaver announced.

Noise appeared unchanged. She looked at her still-two-fingered hands with disappointment.

"The influence of the meadow will fade once you fulfill your end of the bargain. I have healed your injuries as a courtesy," Weaver said. The spirit did a sort of bow to her and then me. With a final "Till we meet again," the tools crashed to the ground in a shower of metal.

33

Noise and I hid ourselves in a patch of tangled space along the border once Weaver had left. Oddly, Jules never sent anyone after us. Probably too busy making anti-cougar wards around the park. If that was his game plan, then creating wards over an area that large would take them at least a night.

With O'Meara gone, the most natural spot to retreat to was Rudy's tree, but thanks to Noise's bulk we had to take a roundabout route that avoided the major roads. Without the Veil, getting spotted would mean police or people shooting at us. Going back to the cops might not be a bad idea, but my thinking was the squirrel, lacking natural weapons, might be our best spokesperson.

Noise disagreed. "You're going to send Rudy to talk to the cops? Don't even suggest that to him. He'll think it's a great idea and promptly blow something up!"

"Well, my run-in with them left a bad taste in everybody's mouth, but I didn't want them bum rushing the technomagi. Harry would have mowed them all down with his force wand." The wand in question lay strapped to my back. Neither Noise nor I had the manual dexterity to use it well.

"So we blockade them. They have to come out to harvest tass, right? And Jowls is the only one who can see it."

"Then we're at a stalemate that's ripping apart the town." Not to mention there were lots of ways for magi to slip past a checkpoint. Invisibility, tunneling, and outright teleportation.

"And you didn't see this coming?"

"Look, Jules and Jowls saved my bacon before. Therefor I assumed we had other things in common like 'killing non-magical people is wrong.'" I stopped and looked at her. "Werewolves don't eat people, do they?"

Noise grunted, "Not habitually, no. But no werewolf is going to be particularly bothered if an annoying neighbor disappeared. We traditionally protect our sheep. Humans provide things and comforts that we like. However veil or not we disappear into the forest every month for two weeks. Human's find that weird and weirdness attracts mobs with torches."

"Wizards have no such constraints."

"Thomas, magi might not even talk to a mundane within a year. They regard werewolves as animals to be caught and trained. Jules is probably perfectly reasonable to other magi and probably thinks of himself as progressive for talking to werewolves. Advocating that he should worry about the mundanes in Grantsville is the same as arguing that a pile of kindling shouldn't be burned on the fire."

My ears drooped as a realization struck me. "Magi... don't face any consequences for their actions at all." I looked up at Noise, "Do they?"

"On mundanes? Not unless they make the Veil work too hard." She paused and knelt in front of me, blocking our progress forward. "Thomas, you'll never be able to save them all. No more than you could save all the mice in the world from all the cats. Simply because you have hands and can talk doesn't make you 'not lunch' for something larger. Humans are still part of a food chain. There are other creatures out there who do prey on humans, in the same manner you kill a deer. They have to; otherwise they'd starve to death. It's what they are. They didn't ask to be predators of humans any more than you asked to be a cougar." A sad smile played at the edge of her muzzle.

"You better not be telling me I can't slay monsters." I said as sternly but couldn't keep the end of the sentence from sounding like a question.

She snorted, "Naw. Any prey animal has a right to defend itself. Humans have society to avenge them. I'm saying you're going to have to let some deaths go. Pick your battles. Otherwise they'll just add you onto the pile." Her hand slid down the back of my neck as she talked, brushing the tips of my raised hackles.

"Magi are human. They need to respect the lives of all humans. This is dark shit, Noise! This is the death of ten thousand people! Individuals! If that's not a good hill to die on, I don't know what is. If Jules and Jowls can't see what they're doing is wrong, then they need to be stopped."

"And if you succeed, what then, Thomas?" She gently pulled me into her arms and I found myself pressing up against her enveloping warmness. "Systematically execute every magus that's killed a mundane? You'll be just as much a butcher as they are by the time you're done."

I buried my face into the thick, bristly fur covering her bicep, "I don't know! People aren't just resources to be mined, Noise," I huffed. My body ached for more touch, to calm the boiling anger in my chest.

Noise hugged me tighter but did nothing further, "Everything in this world can be used for something. You got lucky. You got to be an exception to the system because of that dragon, because Archibald did something to you. Congratulations."

"Things have to change, Noise!" Turning in her arms, to look up at her, I found her staring down at me with one big golden eye. "And it will start here! Maybe! O'Meara only killed in self-defense! It was overkill, granted. But still! She's a decent human being! And so is Ixey! They're not all monsters and predators! Hell, Ixey even respects spirits. You should have seen the glare she gave Sandra once she saw how she keeps those elementals."

"Course they're better." Noise gave a little shake of her head. "They're inquisitors. They have to clean up for the rest of them. They're outliers."

"Do you know that? Do you know any magi outside of this town? Rinoa helped me save you from the hunger plane. She saved me when she didn't have to."

Noise grimaced, "That sounds like you're going to leave."

I let my head fall back and stared at the dead forest surrounding us. "I think I have to. Once this is over. I have to see what the rest of the magic world is like."

"And if you find that the majority of magi ARE monsters in your eyes? What then? Become a serial killer of magi?"

"O'Meara once told me that Archibald had been exiled here because he attempted to destroy the Veil. Maybe he had the right idea!"

"Thomas!" Noise's voice cracked and I found myself dropped onto the earth.

"Do you see what will happen here without the Veil?" I said, rolling back onto my feet. "Folks are figuring out that the magi are responsible and they're taking steps to stop them. Maybe they won't succeed, just like a deer that's spotted me might not get away, but now they can perceive what's happening to them. They won't just walk into the slaughter unaware."

"Thomas! Werewolves can't hide at all without the Veil! The humans would finish off what the magi nearly did!"

She had a point. "Well, it's not a perfect solution, I admit." I let my tail lash with indecision before plowing on with the thought. "But from humanity's viewpoint it'd be a better world! Things would change. Werewolves would have to get better at hiding or convince their neighbors that they really are protectors."

Noise snarled. "I'm a wolf, Thomas."

"Your father's at least half English bulldog and you've got enough Rottweiler that you have the coloration. For packs like yours it would be easy to present yourselves as protectors."

"Like a bunch of guard dogs?" Her hand shot out seized the scruff of my neck and hauled me into the air. Were were my nose to her teeth. "Never! If you ever think about killing the Veil again I'm going to find you and making you eat your own tail! Do you understand me Thomas?"

"Y-yes." I stammered.

"Good." She dropped me. I barely landed on my feet.

Her arms crossed and stared daggers down at me. "Now if you're done being silly, we have a squirrel to find."

34

Rudy didn't appear to be home. His nest, which usually had some movie playing in it at a volume I could just make out, was completely dark and silent. Night had fallen before we arrived and the stars were out in force, which struck me as odd.

"Rudy?" I whispered loudly to the still air. "Where are ya?"

I heard a rustling up in the tree and expected to see Rudy bursting out of the branches. Yet no rodent appeared. The tree essentially had two arm-like branches. One of those branches, pointing deeper into the wood, shook as if in a strong wind, the naked branches flexing. The other remained dead still.

"I think it wants us to go that way," Noise said.

"Guess so."

We set off. I mentally shelved the questions I knew the damn squirrel would never answer. Deeper into the woods proved to be a bit of a misnomer, as the forest was a strip of wood about 500-feet wide with houses running along either side. A precisely measured thickness so you couldn't see a hint of your neighborhood through the trees and a home-owner with a tall fence could pretend that they lived in the wilderness while looking off the back porch. For me, Rudy and most of the wildlife, stretches like this one functioned as a roadway into or away from the center of town.

I picked up Rudy's sign almost immediately, the acrid scent of a firecracker at the base of a birch tree in the dead center of the forest strip. I tasted the air; the expression looks like a snarl, but it's sort of like sticking a finger in your ears and cleaning out the wax. It opens everything wide and scents hit me like a jackhammer when I do it.

Rudy himself doesn't have much of a scent. Natural squirrels' territories aren't larger than what they can see. Rudy had set off firecrackers every thousand feet or so and Noise appeared content to let me do the tracking. The forest, while young, had a tree sprouting from the ground every two feet or so, which made Noise's passage, well, noisy to say the least. With her massive bulk, she had to thread through the dense trees sideways, breaking every single one of the dried up branches up to eight feet off the ground. Between that and the thunder of her footsteps, it sounded like Rudy's tree had uprooted itself and was giving slow chase.

We followed the trail into the wider wood where the path got more difficult. Rudy had cut back and forth across streams and hills. Wherever he'd been going, he'd either gotten lost or interrupted.

"There!" Noise pointed after tracking a total of thirteen fireworks.

I looked in the indicated direction and saw nothing but a rocky outcropping. "Really?"

"On the other side."

I leapt on top of the outcropping and immediately spotted a soft glow in the distance. Damn eight foot tall bipeds! The light proved to be a cellphone propped in a tree, its completely white screen illuminating the end of a hollowed out log.

"Bout time you two showed up!" Rudy scolded from the top of the log, tail lashing like a windsock. "Much longer and I'd have to shove a few firecrackers down your cousin's throat."

"Cousin?"

"There's a bobcat sulking around," Noise said with a smirk. "Didn't you smell him?"

"I was a little busy playing follow the firecracker." I sniffed and changed the subject. "Rudy, what are you doing out here?"

"Hunting wild cashews! What's it look like I'm doing?" He stamped his feet on the log, directing my gaze at it. Shavings littered the ground at the mouth of the hallowed out tree. As I crept closer and my eyes slowly resolved details. The entire opening had been leveled and symbols had been chewed into it. There was the faintest glimmer of magic contained within them. I looked up at the squirrel in wonderment. He'd gnawed the rim entirely flat and chewed a latticework of Greek around the rim. "Do you have any idea how hard it is to find a wooden hole big enough for a cougar to fit through in a forest where the average age of the trees is less than twenty years?"

"Well, it would have been easier if you'd kept in a straight line," Noise said. "Trees get older the farther you get out of town."

"I was heading in a straight line!"

Noise and I shared a glance.

"Oh good, you two are already bonded then? You had to bond to make your dramatic escape from Jules and Jowls, right?"

"Bond! Us?" Noise sounded revolted. "Why on earth would we do that?"

"Neither of us are magi!" I said. "There'd be no point."

Rudy gave us both the how-can-you-both-be-so-stupid stare. "You haven't figured it out yet?"

"Figured out what?" I asked.

"Magi aren't frikken special! You're both magi!"

"I'm not a magus!" Noise snapped, then growled.

Rudy didn't even flinch despite how far she loomed over him. "Yes you are! All werewolves are bound to the same conceptual plane. All you're missing is a familiar and education."

"You're full of bullshit, rodent!"

"I'm not! A magus is taught that they're special through a five-year apprenticeship. Familiars get two weeks of training and then BAM! Bonded. Most familiars never realize they have nearly as much control over magic as their magus does. Remember Oric's teleportation tricks? The bird's a magus and doesn't even know it."

"I thought you wanted to be a familiar, Rudy," I said.

"I want to be many things, but I'm a squirrel, and that's what I'm gonna be."

"A squirrel that apparently knows a crap load more than he lets on. What's this?" I gestured to the log and its intricate carvings.

"This is about four millimeters of very hard work." He smiled and showed me his teeth, which were nearly worn back into the gums.

"And it does?"

"Absolutely nothing unless you two bond and get some magic mojo on."

Noise knelt to examine the carvings. "And then?"

"This here is one end of a druid's gate," Rudy said, his tail erect with pride.

I squinted at it. "Then why's it in Greek?"

"Cause the Greek magi hacked the hell out of the original spell! They used it all the time for getting around Europe. Like the internet but with people and stuff. After a bit, the Veil started attacking it and people didn't always come out. They stopped using it, but the spell is still out there, listening for doorways with the right inscriptions. Got it?"

"Since there's no Veil here, it should be safe. We could use it to get out of here and get the inquisitors!" I exclaimed.

Rudy chittered, "If you were particularly dumb. Sure, you could do that. But it would let the Veil back in."

"Where else do we go then?" I asked, suppressing an urge to snap at Rudy's know it all nose.

Rudy pointed at the cellphone that illuminated his handy work.

I realized with a start it wasn't an iPhone! It was a Samsung Galaxy in a pink and ruby rhinestone case! Rudy wouldn't be caught dead with that phone. The bolt of recognition hit me like a slap. The phone belonged to Rinoa.

"You want us to rescue the Blackwings? Are you nuts?"

The squirrel gave me a stern side eye.

I bumbled onward, "Rudy, that would just be trading one group of ambitious magi for another. How will that fix anything?"

"You can set your own terms," Noise said. "You'll be their only option, or they can sit there like hostages till the technomagi trade them away for favors." She chuckled. "Include a morality waiver."

"Not to mention you're going to need some friends once the Council finishes organizing itself," Rudy said. "House

Morganna doesn't have the clout it boasted twenty years ago, but they're good in a scrap."

This mess was my fault, so I had to fix it. After that... I'd heal O'Meara with my blood money and then run away into the woods. That way I'd never have to deal with a magus ever again. At least that's what I do if I had any intelligence at all.

Still, I could only live with so much misery in my future. Jowls' taunt of death by vivisection echoed through my mind, jumpstarting the self-preservation engine. Even if we ran to the inquisitors, they'd get around to asking about the night I let the dragon out as soon as they could. Jules and Jowls would certainly be screaming about it in the hope of earning leniency for their crimes. House Morganna might just be the protection I needed. And I could do it with a lot less blood on my paws if I played it right.

There were a lot of 'ifs' in this plan. Notably how the hell I was supposed to use Rudy's gate to locate the Blackwings. I looked hard at the phone and there in the case was a faint glimmer of gold, the remnant of the ward she'd used to save my tail from Noise. A thought occurred to me, but I pushed it away, hoping it wasn't true. "What am I supposed to do with the phone? Scent her out between dimensions like an extraplanar bloodhound?"

"Exactamundo! See!" Rudy turned to Noise. "He can be taught! There's hope for the universe." He rubbed his paws together. "Okay, make with the bondage! Those tech-nochumps are gonna come after us as soon as they've got their wards up. If they're smart."

"You sure this will work, Rudy?" I asked.

"Nope! But I don't got a better idea. How bout you, big, tall and snarly?" He looked up at Noise.

Noise crossed her chest and indulged in a brief glower at

the squirrel before turning back to me. "How deep in my head are you going to be?"

"Dunno until we try. Been different every time so far." Richard had been distant while O'Meara and I could become one person in two different bodies if we weren't careful about it. "This will be a new data point," I said, mentally prodding Mr. Bitey to get ready to do his thing.

The snake hissed aggressively in my head, not liking the idea of bonding without terms. It demanded I offer them to limit this bond. Yet, if this was going to work, Noise would need access to all my (very limited) understanding on how magic worked. Despite all she'd done to me, I couldn't help but trust Noise. Even if we couldn't work as a couple on account of the cats vs. dogs thing, I still wanted her in my corner.

I shook myself out from nose to tail and stretched. With great reluctance, Mr. Bitey uncoiled from his fourth dimensional hidey hole. His silver chain-link body snaked out from my neck and sinuously wavered in the space between Noise and me. Noise's eyes, glowing with the light of the cellphone, tracked him, but she didn't move. Only a subtle swallow betrayed her nervousness.

"You ready?" I asked.

"No. But do it anyway."

Mr. Bitey flashed across the gap, spun out around her neck and the world was bathed in a glare of pale silver light.

35

I stood on a plane of nothing, facing her, a pale silver wolf;
the moonlight illuminating her muddled the evidence of
her heritage. She regarded me warily, yellow eyes casting a
light entirely their own, her form still, tail erect but not
moving. I took a step toward her and a pulse beneath my
paws. A wind blew out from her, carrying notes of thought
with it that caught in my mouth and delivered a medley of
emotions: anger, bitterness and fear, all rushing to the back
of my mouth, screaming for attention. But they couldn't
drown out the sweetness of her love for life, of running, of
coding, of working, salted with hope and fortified with the
savor of duty to fulfill. Duty to her family, her pack, and... At
that point my mind stumbled and nearly tripped over itself.
For her thoughts also tasted strongly of something totally
unexpected. Yet another sense of duty.

To me.

We met nose to nose and pressed our foreheads
together, allowing words to flow through us, along with our
history and emotions. Affection passed between us easily as
a river flowed downstream. Yet the path of our lives mixed

turbulently. Her duty and my growing wanderlust took the form of unyielding stones, creating turbulent whorls and eddies that churned our future path into a raging river of snarling foam.

Faced with all of her, beautiful and conflicted, I did the only thing I could do and forgave her. Both for her hand in making me what I am and not becoming the stable anchor I'd built her up to be within my own mind. In turn she forgave me for my own ego and trespasses. We let it all flow out. Our fears mingled with our hopes. Our anger wrestled with our dreams. We watched it all, like two friends slumped together after a hard day. Here we could love each other without the entanglement of biology and culture. No matter where our paths led from here we'd have this moment and we savored this simple communion of laying out who we'd become and accepting the other. We kissed like lovers and pulled back as friends. Perhaps in the future world there'd be room enough for the both of us. But there were battles to be fought before that time.

We opened our eyes to find Rudy impatiently tapping his foot. "Are you guys quite done being nauseating? I think my appetite has run off for Florida to drown itself in guns and religion."

Quickly realizing just what our bodies had been doing while our minds had been occupied, Noise and I separated, my ears putting out so much heat that they probably raised the global temperature a few degrees that night. Noise, however, didn't seem bothered at all and smiled at Rudy with a grin that could have swallowed the squirrel whole.

I groomed myself for a few minutes, waiting for my ears to cool and my focus to return. "Okay, Rudy. Tell me how this is supposed to work."

Rudy frowned. His eyes flicked between the phone and

the gateway. Tail twitching back and forth, he pondered for a moment. "Uh, there's a certain tone associated with the gateway and you've got to match it with the tone on the phone? I dunno. The gate usually connects with another premade gateway. I've never made one without a destination before."

I winced, as that was entirely unhelpful. "We need a circle."

"Now that I can do." He punched the phone and it made a strange warble. He placed it between Noise and I. "Done! One circle of sound."

"Uh, Rudy, that's not how it works, buddy. Noise and I have to be outside the circle. How do we do that with a circle of sound? The border's a little fuzzy."

Rudy opened his mouth to protest and paused, an objecting digit half raised in the air. He wobbled for a moment before deflating with a sigh. "Nevermind." He leaped down to the ground and pulled a Swiss Army knife from under a patch of leaf litter, flicked open the blade and began to scratch a line in the dirt.

"Rudy, the chalk in my harness is going to work much better than a line in the dirt."

"Why didn't you say so?" Rudy threw up his paws and I had to dodge the twirling knife.

After a few minutes of clearing leaves, the three of us constructed a passible magic circle around Rudy's gateway, placing Rinoa's phone on an errant log. I had them pull out all the tass I'd been saving for O'Meara and place it in the circle. All fifty-two groat of it. Rudy whistled when the bag was placed in the center and opened to reveal the purified crystals of tass inside.

Noise kept her mouth shut, but she wasn't so good at keeping her thoughts to herself. *So that's what the bitch needs, huh? Pretty rocks?* Jealousy loomed in her like an angry serpent.

We just shut that door, Noise. Why you gotta be jealous? I scolded her.

Cause you're still mine until I find someone new. I can't help the feeling that O'Meara has beaten me. She's the one that's going to get to keep you.

That's not true. I had plans now. I'd even showed them to Noise a moment ago.

If this works, you're even more entangled with the magi, not less. Waiting around for them to put you on trial. Going to Vegas will make it more likely!

I won't spend the remainder of my life hiding from the Council. Even if that makes the remainder of my life short. It's worth trying.

That doesn't mean I have to like it. We stared at each other, thoughts stewing before we both hrmpfed at each other. "Stubborn mule cat," she said.

"Overprotective cow-wolf," I muttered back.

Together we turned to the work at hand and looked at the spells before us. Noise made a gurgling noise in her throat as I eased her perceptions into directions that should not be. Rudy's gate connected to a lattice of purple threads that shined with the wet light of the deep sea. The web work stretched into the sky, shifting around as we looked at it. There were holes in the weave, patches that pulsed, hungering for something. A destination perhaps? I tried to follow the spell, but it faded out as it exited the circle, beyond our perception.

We tried the phone, staring at the enchantments on it. They were simple spells consisting of a technomagical circuit that had once powered the shattered remains of the ward that'd saved me from the furious hunger of Noise under the influence of the black plane. I scryed as deeply as I could, peeling away layers of enchantment until the barest threads of magical essence remained. There was a thread, faint as a blonde hair resting on a sheet of yellow construction paper. We followed it until it exited our circle and faded in the surrounding ether.

Noise growled. *What are we doing? How do we begin to touch any of this? I see it but...*Noise stuck her massive hand into the circle, trying to grasp at the fragile strand. Yet, her hand remained in our plane and didn't reach into space the magic resided in. *I can't touch any of it.*

I couldn't say I was totally clear what to do either. Both O'Meara and the trio had been able to twist their soul cords into a sort of magical limb and use that to manipulate a spell. It was a trick they all learned during their apprenticeships. A basic lesson that no one had bothered to teach me. The cord itself was a muscle you usually weren't aware of. Richard had built that bowl of tass I'd used to ferry the Weaver back to our reality. Just how had he done that?

Concentrating on my soul thread, I edged my consciousness into it but not so far to lose the sensation of my body. I felt along its length before it penetrated into another world, pushed myself into its surface, and gave it a flick. My body shivered as I sent a wave into it, a twitch of power. When the trio had investigated Noise's entanglement the second time, they'd built a spell that appeared to be a small machine that crawled up her thread and brought our perceptions with it. It'd been fueled by two different planes. If we could build something similar then we'd have a shot at making this work. Yet the runes that made up the spell were not coming into my mind. In this space the runes had interlocked like gears and interacted seamlessly. I got my soul cord to slash into the tass, but nothing more. I didn't have the trick or the strength to pull the tass apart and build something with it. Despite what Rudy had said, I was no magus.

I growled with frustration as I hopelessly flailed at the fragile thread connected to the phone. It snapped. The thread started to float away. *FUCK! Damn it, catch it!* I thought and swore.

And something did. A thin silver chain swooped in from the darkness and caught the thread between its links.

Noise mooed in alarm and fell back from the circle, the magical ether flashing from existence. "What was that?"

"I dunno. Stop looking away so I can see it."

Grumbling, she resumed her rather uncomfortable looking lotus position and looked. The chain still held the thread, wrapped around it as a snake might coil around prey. *Mr. Bitey,* I thought.

"Who?" Noise thought back.

"Our bond. The snake." I looked, not at the chain but inside ourselves, at the tunnel between our minds. It didn't matter how far we were apart in physical space. Our thoughts flowed along the dragon-made chain, so flexible that it slithered through the two worlds with ease. I'd been using the wrong ends of our minds. Mr. Bitey had the flexibility and movement we needed. He could be our hands.

And as I thought it, the chain coiled into a two-fingered hand in front of me. Noise's hand. I sensed a general frown as she concentrated and the two fingers split into four useable digits. I followed suit, producing my own hand. I tried to form a second one, but the first faded as soon as I moved my attention off it.

We had a functional pair of hands between the two of us. The thread seemed to want to slip from our fingers, but we coated them and the thread with tass, giving it girth we could work with. We still didn't know what we were doing and spent several hours attempting to reel in the thread from beyond the circle, but it always snapped, no matter how we strengthened it with tass. Climbing it didn't work either. Our perception ended outside the circle. Whatever trick the trio had used that allowed me to glimpse the space beyond their circle, we didn't know it.

After hours of futility we decided to take a break. We tied the thread to the gateway spell so it didn't float away into the ether.

The gateway pulsed, and I realize we'd done something. The greek carvings lit with power that rivaled a neon sign. Rudy *eeed* with pain, clamping his fists over his ears.

"What the hell did you did do?" he shouted.

"Tied the spell to, uh, Rinoa I think."

"You tied it to a person? Oh man, this is gonna be messy." Rudy leaped onto the rim and began hewing several more letters into the ring. The glow faded to a less intense level. "Okay! Now it probably won't kill her."

"Now what?" I asked.

"You walk through! It's a one-way trip!"

"I can't fit through that!" Noise said. "I can maybe get one arm through that log!"

Rudy shrugged. "This here's the biggest hollow log in this entire forest. You'll have to stay here. Uh, you probably should break your link now. Mental links and time dilations are never a good thing."

I winced, remembering readings on planar travel. If a plane is under stress, time there would speed up. Snagged in the dragon grinder, it would definitely speed up. And for that matter, were we already sped up compared to the real world? Could that be why the Inquisition hadn't broken in?

Noise's ears wilted. "What the hell am I supposed to do? Stand here and wait?"

Rudy crossed his arms. "That'd be silly. We won't come back this way. The Blackwings will need to build something to get back. Should be easy-peasy with this tass!"

The backs of my paws itched for a grooming. There were so many ways this could go terribly wrong. Yet I found myself still resolved to go through with it.

I took a step toward the log and I found myself hoisted into the air like a newborn kitten. Two furry arms quickly crushed me to Noise's chest followed by a wet kiss. *Don't die. You hear me?* Noise bellowed in my head.

I'll do my best with that, I promised and gave her the hint of a purr. *Ready?*

Noise grunted and squeezed me tighter. *Yes, you can get out of my head now.*

I broke the bond as gently as I could and she set me down on the ground.

"Come on! Before the damn thing burns out!" Rudy chittered with impatience and leapt on to my back.

"Wait!" Noise said. "I almost forgot." She reached into the pocket of her overalls and produced several slightly bullet-ridden packets of beef jerky. "The Technomagi never got the concept that I'm a vegetarian at the moment." She tucked the salty meat in my harness. My stomach grumbled in appreciation.

I circled around her legs in thanks then plunged through the log before Rudy blew a gasket. Darkness seized me. A crushing squeezing sensation forced pain to flow through every bone in my body. A sharpness, then I remember nothing more.

36

"We're here to rescue you!" Rudy said, followed by desperate coughing and hacking of somebody else.

"Oh God! Blech! Muaa!" I reluctantly opened one of my eyes to see a haggard Rinoa retching and spitting on the dusty ground. Tack looked between his mistress and me with an expression of utter bewilderment. Rinoa sat back on her heels, coughing and wiping at her mouth. "Tastes like I bit into a fucking fur coat! Bleh!"

"We could have come out the other end if you prefer," Rudy said, but I couldn't see where he was. Wrenching open the other eye didn't help either, so I lifted my head and immediately regretted it. My muscles felt like I'd been through a meat grinder.

I let out a groan of pain. Rudy was near my rump and had a bag slung over his shoulder, a Crown Royal logo on the side. Something weigh it down, but it wasn't full enough for me to see the shapes of the objects within. Rudy laughed. "I bet you feel like a fresh noodle out a nozzle because that's sorta what happened. There are mechanisms keep you safe, but they make sure you don't want to do it again. You'll be fine!" He turned back to Rinoa. "So toots, where's the rest of your peeps?" Rudy climbed up on said rump despite my wincing and spun around, scanning the horizon.

Tack growled, the German Shepard looked worn, his ribs visible through patchy fur. Still he angled his body to provide the maximum amount of protection to Rinoa. The magus gave a sad chuckle and placed a hand on her familiar, who stilled. He looked down at the ground with a sorrowful expression. "I don't know. I haven't seen them in a week."

"What! Why would you leave? Cabals are supposed to stick together! Thick and thin. Like the three musketeers!" Rudy gesticulated wildly.

"I had to leave them," she said, wrapping her arms around Tack's neck. Rinoa had thinned, her face gaunt, her previously fiery blue eyes dulled to smoldering embers.

I sighed. "She killed Neelius."

"What?" Rudy's tail flashed back in forth.

I pushed myself to my feet. My muscles protested all the way as if I were a hundred years old, my joints creaking and popping. "I'd rather hoped you hadn't confessed to them."

"When did you figure this out?" Rudy demanded.

"Soon as you showed me the phone and the blown circuit on it. It was nearly identical to one that detonated below the dueling space. Ixey couldn't track it back to Rinoa because she hadn't realized Rinoa was a technomagus." I looked over to Rinoa. "Right?"

Rinoa blew a wayward bang of out her eyes. "I'm not a technomagus. I dabble in it a little. It's neat."

"And it was you in the trees watching us the night I showed Jules the tainted tass in the grinder. You, or more likely Tack, probably smelled that the tass we were harvesting was corrupted and vulnerable to disruption."

"I thought I was being so clever," she said, her voice muffled by the fur on Tack's neck.

Tack meanwhile still had his ears flat against his head as he watched me, although he'd covered his teeth. "W-Why didn't you open the portal? You on a weird power trip to come here through Rinoa's mouth?"

"Because this is a jailbreak, not a bargaining session," I said. "Jules is screwing everybody now, and if we don't do something about it, everybody in Grantsville is going to be in somebody else's stomach."

Rinoa sucked on her cheek and chewed for a moment before answering in a whisper. "The black plane. It came back, didn't it?"

"Worse. It's a shallowing now," I said.

Rinoa stood abruptly and pointed across the plains, the horizon dotted with flames. "Then you need Veronica. I last saw them that way. Seven days ago."

"Alrighty! Let's go!" Rudy bounded three feet in that direction, then stopped when he realized nobody was following. He turned back to me. "Come on!"

"I'm not going back until Veronica calls for me. I've got karma to pay." Rinoa gave a weak smile. "I'm the reason it's all gone to hell."

"Lot of good you'll do anyone out here." I walked over to Rinoa, telling my muscles to shut up with the protests, and offered the side of my harness. "I've got a few granola bars. Take two."

Pride and hunger warred in her face for a moment but a pleading look from Tack tipped the balance.

"Thomas! Didn't you hear? She killed Neelius! If she's

gonna stay here and do time, let her! We got no time for playing Guilty McGee."

I ignored the squirrel. "Look Rinoa, you believe in karma, right? You pay that off by doing good, not by doing nothing. If we don't find the Blackwings soon, everybody in Grantsville is going to either be dead or mutated beyond recognition."

Tack looked up at her, tail giving a hopeful little wag.

Rinoa breathed in and closed her eyes. Under her breath I heard the wisp of a song. "Broken causes, never gather applauses. As I sit to ponder all, where or when does my witching hour fall." Her voice wasn't magical, it didn't bring life to the endless desert around us, but it had a clear effect on the magus and her familiar. When her eyes reopened, they were resolute. "Fair warning. They won't be happy to see me."

"Dorothy in particular?" I asked.

"How'd you guess?" She smirked with a half breath of laughter.

Rudy's tail flicked back and forth impatiently, "Okay good! We're all properly motivated now. Let's move. We're dealing with at least a two-X time acceleration here. Maybe more. That's good, but the sooner we get going the— " The ground rumbled like a growling stomach beneath us. "What was that?" his voice squeaked.

"Fire worms!" Rinoa shouted, her aura bursting to life. "Everyone scatter! I'll distract it!"

Of course the blasted fire desert had giant worms! That makes perfect sense! I thought as I ran to scoop up Rudy up onto my back. My back had other ideas and exploded in pain as the tender muscles spasmed, jerking my front half from the ground. My front paws clawed at the empty air as the rest of my body toppled to the ground like a poorly balanced teapot. Dust flew up around me as the tremors increased to a cacophony. All I could do was close my eyes and think, *Well, in all the many ways I was likely to die in the coming year, death by sandworm hadn't made it into the top ten.*

"Thomas! Um, ah, you have to stay- Stay absolutely still!" Tack's voice came to my ears.

I ceased trying to stand. I hadn't realized I'd been trying to get up until I stopped. My body is apparently as stubborn as I am. Then I heard the hooves pounding all around me. An unseen stampede encircled me, and my heart crawled up my throat looking for a hug. Yet there was no hooved mass trampling me into the dirt. Instead, pinpricks of yellow exploded all around me and then passed, marks of Rinoa's magic. The rumbling stopped as the sparkles raced away. A bare thousand feet away, like a whale breaching from the sea, a massive head exploded from the red sands. A mouth formed of four separate pieces yawned wide around the area of Rinoa's auditory illusion. The creature could have swallowed a VW Bug in a single bite. Its jaws closed with an ear-splitting snap, and then it submerged.

"Looks like I owe you again," I said.

"Shhh!" Rinoa shushed harsh and desperate.

The worm erupted from the ground again, its four jaws thundering with an angry rumble. It extended itself several stories from the ground before letting loose a high-pitched scream that bent my whiskers out of place. The scream grew as the worm's head swung in a wild arc.

"Aw crud, that's the biggest bat I ever did see," Rudy said. I felt two small paws on my rear. "Come on, Thomas, get up! Time to go. It's echolocating."

I tried to take the suggestion to heart, but my muscles simply refused to obey even as the beast stopped its rotations to draw a bead on us.

"Damn it," Rinoa breathed. She was already on her knees, panting, Tack supporting her. "That worked last time."

"Rudy, do you see Harry's rod behind you?" After the encounter with Weaver, Noise had made a hole in my harness to stow the rod.

"Honey roasted California cashews!" he responded, which I translated to a yes. He grunted as I felt a tug on the harness. "Got it! Wow! There are a lot of buttons on this thing! Where's the trigger?"

The worm reared back in preparation to strike, its four jaws swinging open to display the glow of molten magma within its throat. "The top button!" I shouted as the worm's head zeroed in on our little group.

The yellow beam struck it dead-on as worm head lashed forward. The worm's movement slowed but didn't stop. The great jaws opened and closed in slow motion. A whine filled the air, like the charging of an old-fashioned camera flash.

"Turn it up, Rudy!"

"I'm trying!" The beam narrowed a bit. "Rotten walnuts, would it kill the technomagi to label things?" Rudy swore as the worm picked up speed. "Aha! Other way!" The worm's progress froze all together as the pitch of the whine increased. "That's as far as it goes!" The beast shook as it strained against the kinetic energy field. Its jaws opened and closed, and its body pulsed as the light from its throat grew to a red that threatened to sear my retinas. An acrid scent crept into my nostrils. "Bad worm!" Rudy cried as he swung the beam downward, slamming its head into the ground. The worm screamed fire as the ground shook beneath us.

"No cheating!" Rudy pulled the beam upward, pulling monster from the ground like a titanic earthworm, its writhing body so long that it blocked the burning sun high over our heads.

A loud pop sounded against the high pitched screams, and the bright yellow beam winked out of existence. "Aw nuts." The worm began to fall. "TIIIIMBEEEEEER!"

I struggled up to my feet, trying to ignore my spasming muscles. I got three legs moving while my rear left leg locked into a scream-worthy charley horse. Growling with the effort, I hobbled to the side of the falling worm just before it hit the ground. My world became dust and thunder.

We all found each other through our coughing and sneezing at the dust. The four of us huddled, breathing through Rinoa's sand-caked clothing as we waited for a seeming eternity for it to settle. When it finally did, only the smoothness of the sand greeted our eyes, with no sign that the worm had ever existed.

37

We set off, following Rinoa's lead. Honestly, it just appeared to be a random direction to me. I couldn't see or smell any trace of her passage along our route. I didn't see the focus that allowed the Blackwings to transform into crows among the scant few on her person. Tack sported no foci at all.

The sun never moved, and there was no night. Eventually my bruised muscles gave out entirely and I slept. When opened my eyes opened again, the only evidence of the passage of time could be found in the way Rudy's coat had gone from gray to a dusty red. A breeze kicked up, sending the clouds of dust that erupted from every footstep rolling toward the distant horizon. I grew so bored that I started to see the shapes of faces within the dust stirred up by Rinoa and Tack's feet. A few strips of the jerky helped the growling of my stomach, but I had nothing to deal with my growing thirst.

We set off again without much conversation. The desert wasn't beastly hot as long as we stayed away from the burning bushes that dotted the landscape. I wouldn't call it pleasant with my winter coat, but my tongue didn't hang from my mouth. Unlike say Tack's, which was dry and covered in dust. If he complained about it, he didn't do so to anyone but Rinoa. Initially my muscles had protested the movement but soon settled into the timeless rhythm of walking. I had to hold myself back and not get ahead of Rinoa. With only two legs, her pace over the dust was a crawl.

With no solar movement, I lost track of time. Only when Rinoa literally keeled over did I realize my own endurance had been spent. Tack pulled a water bottle from her bag filled with a green ichor. Rudy assisted with the cap, and Tack poured it into her mouth with surprising dexterity. She coughed and sputtered to life, pushing her familiar away as she sat up. Eventually she took the bottle from his teeth and then nursed it like a cold beer.

"After we left, we walked for three days straight," Tack said as Rinoa drained the last of the ichor. Recovering, Rinoa and Tack showed Rudy and I how they'd been surviving. We went to the nearest flaming bush, a big one, nearly a tree, reaching up past Rinoa's head before the branches burst into forge-hot flame. Tack dug a circle around it, and the pair sat themselves on opposite ends. The tree's flame abruptly went out as the pair weaved a spell onto it. Small, blackened creatures, scrabbled among the branches in aimless panic. One by one their ashy carapaces unfolded marvelously iridescent wings that buzzed until the creatures took an ungainly flight, drunkenly bobbing and weaving until they exited the circle and burst back into flame. Within twenty minutes, two dozen winged fireballs were in-flight away from us, heading for shelter in nearby flaming plant life. The tree itself had sprouted green thorns among its blackened branches. The growth was so fast I could hear the wood groan under the strain. The thorns extended, growing thick and plump, glinting wetly in the sunlight.

With a gesture of Rinoa's hand, the fragile branches shattered with a thunderous boom. The fruit and wood fell to the ground as the few stout branches that had withstood the blast sputtered alight. Rinoa picked up one of the thorns and bit into it. The thing nearly exploded with juice.

I trotted up and sniffed at one of the fruits. "What did you do?" I asked. They smelled vaguely of fermented vegetables.

"Magic." She chuckled, biting the top off one and squeezing the gooey pulp inside into Tack's waiting mouth. "All House Morganna's apprentices are responsible for a garden. You learn a few things about plants."

To watch Tack's tail, the pods contained either pure sugar or ice cream. I crunched one experimentally. It was wet with a gummy skin, like a fruit snack with sugary syrup, but the syrup tasted like kale.

I ate about twelve. Gulped them down as if they'd been fish scattered on a dock. There's simply a point where the taste of one's food becomes irrelevant.

It might have been two days or perhaps two weeks but eventually the fiery vegetation thickened and the ground beneath my pads solidified into soil. Some patches were so large and so hot that we had to go around them to avoid getting our hides cooked. Even Rudy panted from the heat given off by the vegetation and animals, which, excepting the smaller slithering cousins of the big worm that wove among exposed tree roots, all wore flame as if it were fur. Beneath the burning canopy were a bewildering variety of body types, from the horse things that hung out under the huge inferno trees, to tiny fire mites that seemed to enjoy perching on my whiskers until they burnt through them. Rudy served as a fire crew for Tack and I, dashing from one to another and squirting the little buggers with thorn juice wherever they landed. I began to understand why the pair had opted for banishment in the desert. In a forest of flame, you didn't dare sleep.

A caw of alarm followed by the flapping of wings that didn't carry flame was the first indication we were getting close to the Blackwings. The gale force winds allowed me to identify just who'd spotted us. The trees in front of us flared into raging infernos. My poor whiskers withered to black-ened remnants as the temperature climbed far too close to the ignition point of dry fur.

"Well, this is a fine welcome!" Rudy shouted over the howl of the wind.

"She uh, -promised to kill us if she ever saw our faces again." Tack's singed ears looked as if they might melt off his head.

The wind wasn't directed at us, but around us, fueling the flaming vegetation. We were trapped us in the eye of Dorothy's windstorm.

I looked to Rinoa. "How long can she keep this up?"

"Several hours if she needs to!" Rinoa had her hands in the ground, digging out a circle. "She's got an endless supply of hot air with or without magic. Distract her for a few moments!" Tack joined her on the other side of the circle, and the pair closed their eyes.

I turned back to the blaze. With dust pelting my eyes and nose, I could only see outlines and brightness through my nictitating membranes. The flames between two trees parted to admit a figure that shined with the blue of a channeled anchor. It didn't appear that diplomacy was going to be an option. Last time we met, Dorothy had thrown me down a hallway with a stab of her finger, and getting flung into a burning bush was going to hurt a whole hell of a lot worse than smacking into a locker.

"Rudy, do you remember the Dragon Geronimo?"

"What? Oh, hells yeah." I felt him seize hold of the scruff of my neck. "Roger dodger."

I charged straight at her with a snarl of fury, then sprang to the side to evade the massive gusts she hurled at me like invisible dodgeballs. I zigged and zagged around the barrage of wind. Even if I hadn't been able to see the energy propelling the air at me, her flinging arms telegraphed what was coming perfectly well. Rudy and I closed in on her. She tried to anticipate which way I'd duck next, working feints into her kung-fu wind dance. The howl of the storm that trapped us began to fade as I forced her attention onto me.

"Get ready," I growled, and I felt the squirrel set his legs for a jump. I charged for her, and this time she responded with a wide gust of wind sure to catch me no matter which way I dodged. The wave of energy rushed forward, and I leapt straight up, hurling myself fifteen feet into the air.

"Geronimo!" Rudy screeched at the top of my arc. He dashed over my head and flung himself off my nose, limbs outstretched like a skydiver. He sailed. A look of panic spread across Dorothy's face as she desperately tried to shield herself from the oncoming rodent projectile. She had no time to focus and fired her windblast out in every direction, pushing Rudy off-course. Rudy tumbled out of the air, landing on his feet with an aggressive chitter.

Her attention on Rudy, I landed without worry and charged around to her other side. Faced with two targets, her aura flared as the gale flowing out of her redoubled.

Unfocused, it didn't have the strength to knock me down. Rudy just flattened himself against the sand, still crawling toward her exposed ankles.

She emitted a cry of pure frustration that transformed mid note into the rasp of a crow. In a blur of black feathers she took flight. A violent stream of water knocked the bird out of the air and sent her crashing into the branches of a fire tree with a squawk, the bird expanded back into a woman just before the crash of impact.

I turned to find Rinoa and Tack with spookily identical grins. Rinoa clutched what appeared to be a firehose that pulsed the green of a summoned object. The force of the water pinned Dorothy to the trunk of the now-extinguished tree.

"Yield, Dorothy!" Rinoa demanded of her former cabal-mate as she steadily walked closer.

Dorothy could do nothing but shield her face with her arms from the torrent of water. "I yield! I yield!"

"Formally now!" Rinoa scolded, easing up on the water pressure. If the girl was tortured with guilt over Neelius' death, the apparent rivalry between her and Dorothy had utterly suppressed it.

"You traitorous bit- Blurbleburble." Rinoa's water washed the insult right out of Dorothy's mouth. Dorothy blocked the stream with a hand and spat out a mouthful of water. "I, Dorothy Chambers, yield to you, Rinoa. I fucking yield!"

"Good." Rinoa turned her hose on the rest of the trees in our vicinity.

Dorothy fell to her hands and knees and watched us through hooded eyes. "So you're working for them now. All those tears spent were an act to get away and join up with your new techie friends?" She attempted to spit, but it turned into a retch as she vomited up a stream of water.

"Completely wrong," I said.

She fixed me with a glare that if it had been from O'Meara I'd be worried about spontaneously combusting.

"We're defecting to you guys!" Rudy said.

The look of utter confusion on Dorothy's face was well worth my poor whiskers.

38

A crow swooped down. It snarled. even before it transformed into the black lab Fee, her too-large ears plastered
against her head, nearly encasing her entire skull. "You
dare! Come back to finish the job with new friends, eh?"
Her words were so venomous that I would've sidestepped
had they been aimed at me. Instead they whipped past.
Judging from the intensity of the stare, I doubted Fee even
saw me. Rinoa stared levelly at the dog, the firehose
lowered but her hands still on the nozzle. The green aura
was fading; it would slide out of existence in less than a
minute.

I stepped from between Fee and Rinoa. "As previously
explained to your magus. She's here because she doesn't
want you and your cabal to die."

"She's a murderer," Fee growled.

"I hardly think that is uncommon among magi."
Thinking of the several hundred that likely lay dead in
Grantsville already, I was getting tired of explaining the definition of murder and people telling me it was wrong. "And it
is, at this moment, entirely irrelevant to getting everyone out

of here before the planes start smacking into each other. Now tell me where Veronica is. I need to talk to her."

Fee barked at me, white teeth flashing, and it took considerable effort not to return the display in kind. It would have been literally zero effort for Dorothy to pass our intentions onto Fee and my annoyance threatened to turn into rage. Needing to do something other than remove her nose from her muzzle, I directed my teeth elsewhere. A knot of fur that had been pulling every time I moved my left foreleg received a savage gnawing.

A small aura hung in the air in the ring of trees, and the impromptu grooming allowed me a brief glance at a crow that perched in the extinguished branches. That struck me as unwise. The trees didn't appear to be dead, as the tips of the branches glowed red hot and occasionally coughed out sparks in an attempt to reignite the branches. "Naomi, I presume. Care to join us?" I said, or attempted to say as I worked on the knot that wasn't a knot, but a mass of burnt fur that crunched like a Saturday morning breakfast cereal. I didn't see any evidence of Morie. If Naomi had been planning a fight, he'd have been there. A positive sign.

She hopped down and became human. Of the three ladies, her dress was comparatively pristine, a bit of dirt clung to the hem. Had she spent the majority of the time as a bird? More than the others, she looked exhausted, and while both Dorothy and Rinoa had passionate fires that fueled them, the circles under Naomi's eyes threatened to consume her face.

"Can we talk to Veronica now?" Rudy called to her.

"Sure." Naomi gave a mirthless snort of laughter. "You can talk to her all you want. Follow me."

"Naomi!" Dorothy screeched with an indignant whine that became a coughing fit.

"Nothing can hurt her any worse than what's been done," Naomi said, giving Rinoa the fleetest of glances. The sonic magus flinched and averted her eyes. Whatever had been in that look, no tempest Dorothy could summon would hurt the girl more.

"I'll go then. I've done my part," Rinoa said, biting her lip. Naomi nodded.

"Nope," I objected. "Rinoa comes as well. She can't do anyone any good wandering this plane until she gets eaten."

I could feel Dorothy's eyes burning a hole in my back, but I ignored the bully of a woman. Naomi set her hands on her hips, "And what gives you the right to decide that?" Her tone was more exasperated than challenging.

"Is Tack as guilty as Rinoa? Does he deserve to be stuck here as well?"

Tack, who'd sunk into the sand as soon as he'd seen Naomi, whimpered. "I'm sorry, I'm sorry, I'm sooorrrry!" Rinoa immediately grabbed her sobbing familiar and pulled him close, whispering soothing words in his ear.

Naomi reached up to grasp at nothing, frustration rippling through her face at the blubbering pup, before dropping it with a gesture that resembled a backhand. "Fine! I don't care. If Veronica ages her to dust, it will be on her own head. Follow me."

It was several minutes before Rinoa could convince her guilt-ridden companion to stand, so we all spent the time waiting in awkward silence.

Everyone except Rudy. He climbed one of the extinguished trees to prod at a few growths on the blackened branches. One objected by opening its shell to unfurl blazing wings of blue fire. "Well, that's no nut!" was all the comment Rudy made before leading the beetle on a merry chase through the treetops.

39

The Blackwings led us through the burning forest to a clearing where a hut had been roughly constructed from the white trunks of the trees. Morie glanced at us as we approached then turned his attention back to the hut. He sat inches beyond a large circle of ash drawn around the entire clearing, and golden wards pulsing feebly just beyond it. Inside the circle, soil was discolored. Closer to the hut the dusty ground faded from its normal red to ash grey. Inside the hut was an aura of someone I didn't recognize.

I stopped at the edge of the circle. "That's not Veronica," I declared.

"It's what's left of her," Naomi said, turning to glance at Rinoa, who seemed unwilling to come any closer. "Her bond with Neelius was a deep one."

"Too deep," Dorothy spat.

"What happened?" Rudy asked.

"Rinoa confessed to her butchery," Naomi said in a flat voice. "Afterward she stopped trying to hold herself together." She gestured at the hut. "If you want to speak to her, go right ahead. The conversation will be... one sided."

I eyed the gradient of dirt warily. Rudy hopped off my back and shot me a grin. "That's entropy aura in there. Can't risk any more gray hairs here, nope. Way too many already!"

"Rudy, you're a gray squirrel. Your entire body is gray."

"That's what you think!"

I rolled my eyes and entered the circle, half expecting the ground to give way and swallow me whole. The earth beneath my feet proved solid and once I nosed open the crude door, I found Veronica curled up on a bed of sparking grass. She stared into the wall of the hut, irises dilated so they were a thin line of blue surrounding pools of absolute darkness. She stank of waste and bile, her limbs already wasted skeletally thin. My heart tumbled back into my tail and my stomach raced for my throat. I'd expected to find her sad, depressed, like Scrags had been after Archibald's death, but her condition was something out of a horror film hospice. Whatever had motivated Rinoa to confess her crime, the result hadn't been a kindness.

"Stupid," I muttered to myself, at myself. I'd imagined that I'd sashay right in here, bond Veronica and she'd be so grateful that we'd walk out and stomp all over the techno-magi, save Grantsville and then... well, I'd deal with that when the time came. I'd been a fool in thinking it would be that easy. Nothing had been easy since I'd gained my tail and lost my thumbs. I slinked into the hut and pushed the door closed with my butt. "Magus Veronica?"

She didn't stir. It was tough to tell she was even breathing. Further, louder calls gave no further response.

Outside, Dorothy called, "You see? You see what the traitor did to her?"

Mr. Bitey uncoiled from around my neck, and after some gentle encouragement wrapped around the catatonic woman's neck. With a breath I found myself in that place, the negotiation place Mr. Bitey took me before a bond had been formed.

No one stood on the other side of the table, just the tunnel to Veronica's mind. I sought to walk around the table and peer down that tunnel. The attempt earned me a hiss from Mr. Bitey and a force pulled me back to my spot. There would be no bonding a magus without a contract, without consent. He wouldn't be anyone's leash. He didn't think this at me, but the fact of the matter appeared in my own mind, tinged with an acid threat. Both a servant and a watchdog. A superpower that policed itself.

My respect for the dragon went up, but it didn't help me with the problem.

"Hello!" I called with my voice and mind.

"GO AWAY!" a chorus of voices answered, thoughts echoing through the negotiation space.

"I'm here to help!" I called back. "I'm a freelance familiar! I want to bond you. Help you escape this place."

An incoherent screech echoed along with a chorus of "NO!" that hurled me back into my own head so hard that it felt as if I got bounced around inside my skull a few times. I staggered against the hut wall and the entire structure creaked in warning.

Yet when I closed my eyes I found the way open, the bond complete, and a screech of invitation echoing. Someone inside that head had said yes among that chorus of no's and that was all Mr. Bitey wanted. Pushing through the bond, I strode into a violent storm. Memories and thoughts pelted me from every angle, each blow delivering a painful insult, a barb. *You'll never get it right! Useless! You're going to wear THAT?*

I staggered, trying to shrug off the invading thoughts, stumbling until I found shelter under a wing. Neelius stood over me, two disembodied eyes staring, floating in space above a messily severed neck. I nodded thanks to the ghostly eagle, who towered over me like a stone guardian. Those eyes turned from me back to the maelstrom of chaotic thoughts.

I followed his gaze and looked out over the mindscape before me. Storm had been entirely the wrong word. This was a battle. Veronicas of all shapes, sizes and colors fought each other in a brutal brawl. Thousands of battles waged, fears against hopes, habits versus quirks, intuition fighting logic. In the center of it all, two oversized pieces of ego battled it out in an arena flooded with black sludge. A child-like Veronica with giant fists pummeled a frail shadow of adult Veronica in a white cape. The adult Veronica used her billowing cape as a matador would but earned a swift right hook every time she attempted to sweep the cape over her younger self's eyes. The adult faltered under a counter assault, staggering to her knees. Child Veronica seized her throat with those huge hands and slammed her down to the area floor, the entire mindscape rippling with the force of the impact.

I touched Neelius' side with a paw. "What is this? What am I seeing?"

The eagle's burning eyes turned toward me. "Hope and Ambition. Innocence and Experience. Fear," the bird rasped, then turned its eyes back to the battle.

"Thanks for clearing that up," I replied. Innocence would be the young one. Experience the old one. Innocence was doing her level best to kill Experience. But just as it appeared Experience might be defeated, the frail woman struck with a thunderous force, sending Innocence flying across the mindscape. Experience stood, dusted herself off and shook her head sadly as Innocence charged her once again. The cycle repeated itself, neither combatant emerging victorious. It's hard to kill a piece of yourself.

I decided it didn't matter what parts of Veronica these titans represented. I had to stop this fight. I backed out from under Neelius' wing to get a running start and leapt into the mindscape, sailing over and through the smaller fights, aiming for the center of it all. I landed short, belly flopping into an inky wetness that flooded Veronica's mind. The sludge stung like millions of ants chewing at my skin as I thrashed against it, each sting a painful memory.

O'Meara lying there, not moving, my empty bed by her side. Her mind awash in magical puss, dying because of me. Because I'd been so arrogant as to try to change things, to cling to ambitions of my own.

Noise torn apart by her own family because I hadn't fixed her, hadn't pushed hard enough because in the back of my head I figured she'd deserved to know what it felt like to be thrust into an unfamiliar body.

And behind them all were the faces of Grantsville, distorted by the pain of hunger and too many teeth in their mouths. The citizens I'd failed to save. That I'd doomed to die because I hoped to make a quick pile of tass working with the technomagi. The tass I'd harvested from the faces of mutating children that left wounds afterward. I'd believed Richard when he'd said they'd be fine. Even if it's true, what sort of monster goes around making kids bleed?

And it was all going to get so much worse if I didn't get out of here somehow. I paddled up and up until my head broke the surface of the black ocean. Things had to get better. Things were fixable! If I just could get Veronica's attention, we could save Grantsville! I took that hope and threw it in front of me. A glittering raft appeared, floating on the flood of despair. I hooked my claws onto its side and pulled myself aboard, guilt clinging to my skin like oil.

"Ruined! We ruined it all!" Innocence's voice boomed as her blows rained down on Experience's cringing form.

"It's not lost! We can rebuild! A set- Ooof!" A fist screamed through Experience's guard, and in the shock of the blow I saw Neelius' death, the bond ripping apart and the hole of pain it left. Innocence sank another blow into Experience's gut, the sensation of his comforting weight on her shoulder; a sensation she would never again feel.

Experience countered with an elbow filled with a memory tinged with age, a dress, the fabric tattered, fraying even as she sewed the pieces of fabric together, the machine jamming, rusting under her newly entropic touch. The loss of her original craft.

Snapping her head back, Innocence dodged the blow and swung her head to impact Experience's with a sickening crack. The blow knocked another memory loose. Rinoa stands on stage, screaming, singing, her hands a blur on her guitar. Admiration flows from Veronica for her Cabalmate's skill, even as she releases a weave of indifference into the crowd again and again. A montage of images of Rinoa's spiral into a pit of despair as her once promising career shatters against a wall of carefully crafted apathy. The girl finally awakens when the gun she put in her mouth fails to fire.

"And we believed she would love us for that! Do we love our master for doing it to us? Do we?" Innocence screamed.

No, this was not the voice of Innocence, but Regret and Fear of consequences.

Experience fell. "We want to create, to build. We needed a Cabal, so we built one." The tone, hard, matter of fact, the voice of Ambition.

Veronica wouldn't be the one to challenge my "magi

are terrible people" stereotype. She'd allowed her ambition to get the better of her good sense and that had finally cost her. Now I needed to convince her that beating herself up about it wasn't going to help things at the moment.

"HEY!" I shouted.

Ambition turned her head to look at me only to catch a fistful of the terrible things she'd done to Dorothy, which unsurprisingly involved a tornado in Kansas. Regret gave no indication of hearing me. It wasn't the most observant of Veronica's aspects.

In retrospect, there were probably better ways to get Regret's attention than climbing up the skirt of her black goth-Lolita dress and sinking my teeth, fortified with a memory of stepping on a nail, into her earlobe. Yet that scream of sheer shock gave me such satisfaction that I barely felt the counter blow that sent me careening through the mindscape and crashing into something rather soft. I moved to right myself and felt the impossible smoothness of fine silk on fingertips, the scent of perfumed linen, and the taste of green on my tongue. Memories of fabrics, I realized with a laugh.

I didn't have much time to appreciate the depth of Veronica's knowledge of fabrics, as I was rudely yanked upward by the scruff of my neck and hoisted into the air like an errant kitten. I gave Regret the most put upon scowl that I could manage.

"What are you doing here?" she growled. "Get out of my head!"

"Trying to stop you from doing something you'd Regret?"

The cacophony of the fighting stopped. Veronicas paused mid-blow or flight, and the few that didn't pause their hostilities got the dirtiest looks from the others. Apparently noticing an invader in your brain was important enough to focus her shattered mind.

"We have to kill him. He's seen too much." Ambition rose up behind Regret, her face gaunt, a skeleton with a skin thrown over it. "He'll ruin everything."

Regret narrowed her eyes for a brief moment before she backhanded her compatriot. Ambition collapsed like a falling building.

"Nice one!" I said. "Deciding not to kill your familiar is the first step on the road back to not dying." I grinned with all the front desk cheer I could muster.

"My familiar is—"

"Dead. I know, I was there. Which means you need a new one. Fortunately, I'm available, as my former employer and I had a bit of a disagreement."

Veronica teared up. "You cannot replace Neelius! Leave me alone." I felt ground beneath my paws. Well, the wetness of the grief and guilty sea, but I found something solid right below that. My eyes were still level with hers. I'd either gotten bigger or she'd gotten smaller. Hard to tell in minds; sometimes you were larger than giant, other times you were a rodent scurrying between the walls. Regret-Veronica turned away, no longer looking so young, and fell onto her butt and clutched at her knees, her comically large hands knitting together.

"I never said I would replace him! I'm far too snarky for that." I heard a screech of protest in the distance. "Think of me as a temporary grief counselor."

Veronica hunched her shoulders and put her hands over her ears. Cracks formed along her skin as she strained to shut me out.

Yet she was not my only audience. Countless other

pieces heard me speak, and while many had turned their back on me, not all of them had.

"So you've been led to ruin by your Ambition," I said.

Ambition snorted angrily.

"You wanted something so badly that you gave your Ambition free reign. Now you don't want to do anything." I paused. "Because you're afraid. Your Ambitions bit you in the ass and you'd rather lie down and die than find out how everything else is going to blow up in your face."

Veronicas all around me hissed with anger. Diplomacy was clearly not my middle name, at least with this crowd.

Still, a few were listening. I stalked toward one, hoping Veronica's compassion was among them. She had to have compassion; she loved her Cabal members, particularly Rinoa. She wouldn't be having this breakdown otherwise. Entwining myself around a Veronica whose skin had a pinkish tint, I purred my pitch. "Grantsville is getting stran-gled, and there are thousands of people who need help, who need their homes protected. You can do something unre-lentingly good for a change if you help me."

That Veronica pushed me away, but I found myself in the arms of another.

Regret spoke. "They are all doomed anyway. The Veil will reject them now and will probably attempt to kill all the mundanes in town."

"We have to at least stop Jules' machine! Stop the planes from grinding together," I snapped.

The Veronica holding me whispered, "We can do better. With a bit of tass, a pathway to Las Vegas could be opened. There the mundanes could get their bearings and then trickle out slowly. The Veil won't smash anyone."

Fear spouted forth dozens of objections, but I didn't hear

them. The Veronica who held me had started scratching my ear and the sensation made the world go sideways. Each stroke felt more solid than the last, as Veronica's pieces coalesced in a single mind. I drowned out her doubts and fears with the constant purring engine of my vibrating throat.

40

I opened my eyes to find two thin arms wrapped around my neck. Veronica and I shared a tender moment until I made the mistake of breathing in through my nose. Our minds open, we both gagged as one. Horrified, Veronica tried to scramble to her feet and promptly fell over. I broke her fall, but catching isn't something I can do well anymore.

"What's wrong with my legs?" Veronica's voice was a harsh croak.

Oh, they're probably fine. Something to do with not eating for a week, I told her mentally.

A week? Veronica held her hands out in front of her. They resembled little more than a thin covering of skin over bone. Her entire countenance was similar to that of Ambition's, though Ambition had smelled better. She turned her hands over and looked over her body. Her eyes filled with tears as she realized exactly what all the stains on her dress were. Dry heaves racked her body as she frantically stripped out of her clothes. "I can't let them see me like this! I can't let anyone see me like this!" As soon as the clothes were off she started making a circle in the hut's dirt floor. After she finished she dragged herself over to her position at the circle and looked at me expectantly. When I didn't budge, she made a huff of annoyance and gestured opposite to her, the familiar's position at the circle. *Well, get on with it. You are my familiar, are you not? You do know how this works. Right?*

I opened my mouth to try to breathe without smelling anything. It made it worse. *We aren't doing any magic until you get some food in your stomach and hold it down.*

Don't be ridiculous! I need a dress and at least some perfume before I go out there.

I gave her a level look. The woman couldn't even stand without assistance and wanted to do a summoning. I'd been a bit too busy to paw through her memories, but I had more than a hunch that summoning wasn't her strong point. *No,* I told her.

Her jaw dropped. *You are my familiar!*

We're bonded, an agreement I can break at any time. You asked me to help you. I'm helping. It was a little more complicated than that. Technically I couldn't break the bond until she, or at least the part of her that was still Neelius, admitted that I'd helped her. If she stonewalled me, I'd be stuck for a good long while. Course, she'd also accepted my want to save Grantsville, so at least I had that. I padded over and offered her the handle of my harness. *They'll be impressed enough to see you upright. Trust me.*

She commanded me to say, "You flea-bitten litter brain! My mistress will not expose herself to any magi!" Confused, I quirked an eyebrow. Veronica's anger wilted as a fresh wave of grief washed over her. Apparently she had frequently fed her former familiar his snarky lines.

I chuckled without mirth. *Sorry, but I'm not a sock puppet either.*

She grabbed the harness' handle, not to stand but to sob into my side. Thoughts of Neelius tumbled through her mind. The bird had been very different from the front he'd put up and bent himself six ways to Wednesday to make her happy. I let it wash over me and gave her the shoulder she needed. Sometime later, after she forced herself to stop crying, she spoke to me. *What are you? A furry shrink from hell?*

I was a librarian. Although it appears that maybe with this freelance familiar gig I better read a few books on counseling.

She snorted at that, a wet, phlegmy sound. *You're doing it all wrong. I never cried on my therapist.*

Maybe it was the wrong therapy, I said as I nosed her, urging her to stand.

She made another plea to help her summon clothing, which I promised to consider if she stood up. Eagerly, she hauled herself onto her feet.

Great! Now put your game face on! I thought at her, and then batted the door open with a paw.

Veronica's back immediately went rigid. *You are a terrible, awful and no good familiar!* she thought-screamed at me as she fought to put a smile on her wasted face.

Is that why the rest of the Cabal uses canines? You expect them to all roll over for you? I tried hard not to call Neelius a doormat. Veronica's anger and embarrassment were focusing her at the moment. Inducing true rage wouldn't be helpful.

"Veronica?" Dorothy's voice drifted through the doorway as I pulled Veronica through. Dorothy and Naomi stood outside the ashen circle. Dorothy blinked as if she didn't believe her eyes, while Naomi fell to her knees, her hands pressed together in a sort of prayer. She looked to the sky and mouthed the words 'thank you.'

"None of that, Naomi!" Veronica snapped. "This cat has no halo. His help isn't free." She pushed herself up to her full height. Naked, sporting skin so thin that I counted every rib she possessed, Veronica still managed to clothe herself with authority. "However, the price is one we will not object to." The violent images flowing in her mind were hardly ladylike, but I wouldn't argue that Jules needed a swift kick to the groin. "Now, where is Rinoa?"

Both of the Blackwings glanced at each other. A grimace flashed over Naomi, while Dorothy's mouth sported a smirk as she turned back. Naomi spoke first, cutting Dorothy off. "We sent her away."

"Bring her back then. We are not leaving her here. I want to speak to her."

Dorothy's smirk died.

Rudy, who sat in between the two women, flicked his tail as he watched. "I'll get her," he said, and then bounded into the fire-lit wood.

Nobody said anything after I lost sight of the squirrel's bounding tail. Veronica remained standing, although it took all her concentration. *Dramatic much?* I asked as I repositioned myself so she could more easily lean on me. Despite her height, the woman had no weight to her at all. *You guys are as bad as the werewolves.*

I cannot lead if I allow them to mother me to death. I'm going to fall, but damn it, not until I'm good and ready.

I gritted my teeth and siphoned some of the exhaustion that flowed through her mind. The thick blackness of it rolled across my eyelids and weighed them down. Veronica straightened, pushing the sag from her posture as footsteps approached. Rinoa appeared, Rudy on her shoulder, Tack hiding behind her with ears as droopy as his tail. His mistress' shoulders slumped until she saw Veronica. Defiance sparked in her eyes as she scanned her leader's form up and down. Her lips pressed together as she rolled her shoulders and straightened her posture. She walked until she stood within arm's reach of Veronica. Rinoa's aura was sparking, like fiddling with the trigger of her gun.

Rinoa's eyes searched mine for a moment before returning to Veronica's face. "I'm impressed. I'm not sure who deserves the credit though. I felt so bad when I saw you break, when I saw you did feel. But... seeing you stand like that, I'm angry all over again."

Veronica's hand cracked against her cheek. The blow staggered Rinoa, but she caught herself and spun back to Veronica, fists clenched, aura crackling with torrents of energy. A trickle of ruby blood ran down her cheek where the dry skin had split open from the force of the blow.

Veronica's teeth ground together. It appeared to the outside that she was baring her teeth, but in truth the clenching was her last ditch effort to keep her mask of control from cracking. She saw no anger in Rinoa's eyes, but the pure seething hatred cut her down to the core. She hadn't seen it before, blinded to it and it hurt in equal measure to the loss of her best friend. "That was for Neel-ius." She let out a shaky breath through her teeth before sucking back in. "And he deserves far more vengeance than that, but that's all he's going to get."

Confusion glittered in Rinoa's eyes. Both she and Tack cocked their heads, unsure if they'd heard correctly. "That's it?"

"I forgive you," Veronica said quickly, forcing the words out before she lost the courage to say them.

"What?" Dorothy whispered in a tone of disbelief that was just as clear as on Rinoa's face.

Veronica's mask of dignity cracked as a stuttering sob

worked its way from her throat. *Oh gods, not yet. Please not yet. I'm such an ugly crier. Help me please. I have to say more.*

I pressed warmth into her, wrapping her mind in the memories of hugs I'd received. She lacked very many of her own. *Keep going,* I urged.

Veronica wrested control of her vocal chords back from her emotions and looked into Rinoa's eyes. "I forgive you!" She shouted the words, and with them a weight lifted from her entire soul. She smiled. "There will be no inquisition into his death."

Rinoa's jaw dropped. Tack whimpered, pawing nervously into the ground.

Veronica's mind whirled in circles as she groped for words. "Nobody's innocent, Rinoa. You cannot give me Neelius back, and I can't give you back the stage you loved. I can't give anyone back what I destroyed to awaken each of you." Her voice cracked. "I did it..." She groped for reasons. *Because I wanted a cabal,* her ambition supplied. *Because awakening outweighs the pain,* her pride declared. *I needed a family,* whispered her mothering instinct. Each reason seemed as effective as toilet paper in the face of the hurricane of her imagination where she walked in each of the women's shoes.

In Veronica's mind, Rinoa's face echoed into her memory, back in the shack a week ago soon after they'd first been banished into this blasted land. Rinoa and Veronica faced each other in the same way, tears flooded Veronica's vision.

"You don't understand! I grieve every day for the stage, to feel myself in front of a crowd, to taste that energy. No amount of magic ever makes the fact you ruined me ever go away! I think of how it could have been every moment. I wanted revenge for that. I thought making you hurt would make this damn pining go away! And it didn't!"

Veronica had laughed at Rinoa's innocence because Veronica actually did understand, understood perfectly. A magus had done the same to her, and how she had hated her. In that moment she'd finally seen herself and the monstrous things she'd done to all of her Cabal.

In the face of seeing herself clearly, Veronica had shattered into a whirling storm of self-reflection and now threatened to do so again as individual pieces of her tried to break away, to hide from the words burbling up from a part of her that she'd forgotten. In groping for stability, she flung our bond wide. Her mind clung to mine. I wrapped myself around her, squeezing, trying to hold her together. Physically, she wobbled, stepping toward Rinoa, away from my side. "I'm—" She fell.

Rinoa stepped forward and caught her.

Veronica clung to Rinoa with desperate strength as the two women sunk to their knees. "I'm sorry," Veronica whispered before she gave in and sobbed, pressing her face to the younger woman's shoulder. At first Rinoa knelt there, stiff and awkward as Veronica bawled, holding her as if she were a crying stranger in a bar. But as decades of pent-up tears flooded out of Veronica, Rinoa began to sniffle, her eyes blinking back her own tears as her grip tightened around Veronica. Tack let loose a long, mournful howl.

I shut my eyes against my own tears but found the auras of everyone burning bright in the darkness, all rolling with a storm of emotion. All the magi and familiars were connected into a web of silver thread that I'd never seen before.

Beside Dorothy, Fee lay down in the dirt, clapping two

paws over her muzzle. She shook with effort, but as Tack sounded again, Fee threw back her head to echo the howl of mourning. As Morie joined in, all four of the magi wept. The threads flared between them as bursts of emotions flowed through the web. Flashes of memories burst in my mind's eye but were neither mine nor Veronica's. The web pulsed like a heavy bass beat as the dogs' separate howls synched into a song of mourning. Not for Neelius only, the pack mate, the leader when the Blackwings flocked, but the experiences of all four pairs unspooling between them, without words, without images. The notes of each life flowed along the threads. Not of friendship, but of shared experience and loss. Human voices joined the canine one by one. A note of guilt sang out and was echoed by forgiveness and became motes of light that danced among the strands webbing. The howls becoming a stage for them to play upon. The song grew a gravity of its own, and I couldn't resist. My screams tore through the melody. The song rippled and bucked until wings beat through the music. The screech of a black eagle answered us from everywhere within the weavings. The silver threads began to pull away from the women, folding like a spider's origami in on itself. Wings took shape, then a body. It opened its beak to scream with Neelius' voice.

No one sang anymore, but the song continued as the silver Eagle before us gained size and strength even as we felt the pieces of him lodged within Veronica's mind like shattered glass melt away. It bowed to her.

Veronica reached out, but she could no more touch it than you can catch hope in a jar.

It spread its wings and they reached beyond the confines of the reality we resided. This wasn't Neelius. This bird wasn't dead. It'd been born. Through us, through the world we sat in, it took flight and launched itself into the beyond.

Everyone looked at each other with mutual wonder.

The sun on this hellscape had set and a pale moon rose in the sky.

41

I awoke to a harsh tugging at the stubs of my whiskers. My eyes opened to Rudy looming right in front of my nose. He smelled delicious.

"Congratulations! Your singing broke the sun!"

"Uh, hrm... Did it?" I replied, licking my chops. How long had it been since I had actual meat and not the overly salty jerky?

Rudy, eyeing my mouth, moved a bit to the side. "Yeah, it's been like ten hours! And it hasn't come back!" Rudy tapped the phone slung over his back.

Groaning, I forced myself into a sitting position. The only light to see by was cast by the moon. The forest had gone silent and dead. Fragments of the previous night bobbed up into my consciousness, and my muzzy brain began to piece them together. I didn't believe them. It made no sense. The Blackwings, magi and familiars, slept peacefully, the canines curled against their mistresses. I felt a pang of guilt that I'd awoken several feet away from my new client. She lay alone in the chill air, her back against a tree that hadn't been there before. It pushed from the dusty soil between Veronica and Rinoa, its unburnt wood white as bone in the silver moonlight. The trunk extended eight feet into the air before splitting in twain, becoming two thick branches that curved out and back, calling to mind wings in flight. Smaller branches reached out like skeletal pinions, bowing under the weight of green banana-like structures that hung from every single one.

I stared at the tree, then looked to the squirrel. "What the hell happened?"

Rudy shrugged. "You all had a very loud cry? Then you all fell over. Maybe it's a pack thing."

"What about the bird?" I asked. "Did you see the bird?"

Rudy scratched his ear. "Bird?"

"Never mind," I muttered and rose to my feet. I added it to the pile of mysteries accumulating in my head.

Rudy nodded. "You know, if the whole freelance familiar thing doesn't work out, I think you might have a future in group therapy!"

I snorted. "I don't think I had much to do with last night. Something about the nature of this place."

"Well, something's keeping them all sleeping!" Rudy hrmpfed. "And we ran out of cashews days ago!"

I smirked. "I'm not out of meat yet."

"Cats..." he chattered. "Wake them up and let's get us home before your stomach embarks on a murderous rampage!"

I didn't see a problem with that plan. Whatever held the magi in dreamland would be no match for the roughness of my tongue.

As a side note, very dusty, very stressed people taste terrible.

* * *

Magi like to say that magic can do anything, given time, skill and tass. O'Meara generally said you could cludge it together if you had two of those. Turned out she forgot an essential element: health. It took two days for Veronica to recover enough strength to focus on anything and at least two more to construct a spell. Veronica knew how to move the Blackwings within the plane, but creating tunnels between planes wasn't within her experience. The theory had been there within her head, moldering in her many memories of listening to lectures from her own mistress, but the gap between theory and practice proved wide. By the time the four magi finally cracked it, thanks to Naomi, Rudy's magic iPhone batteries had finally given up the ghost.

Everyone cheered as the portal crackled to life outside the hut.

"Now remember the first thing about returning home," Veronica lectured beside the portal. "Food and water. Our bodies will attempt to replace any alien matters as soon as possible. If we can't replace the water quickly, we'll come down with traveler's sickness and it will be impossible to raise a finger against Jules and his cronies." Veronica had gotten far less formal in the preceding days. She stayed mostly naked, a loose bind around her chest and a loin cloth, all formed from strips of Naomi and Dorothy's dresses. None of them were exactly fit for society. Rudy and I weren't much better. Our coats were patchy with burnt fur.

Looking at that portal, though, my world narrowed to only one thing: meat. On the other side of that portal would be something I could sink my teeth into that wasn't a person, nor a tasteless wet banana. There would be deer. I didn't wait for the Blackwings to organize themselves. I charged through.

And straight into the middle of a firefight.

42

Bullets are not food. In fact, they're about the farthest thing from it. As my paws hit the blessedly damp earth, the air exploded in the thunder of automatic weapons fire. The world smelled of gunpowder and tree sap. My vision was a purple haze.

The portal had opened directly into a shallowing. A very contested shallowing. I flung myself onto the ground and tried to make sense of the bright world. An engine roared and coughed, like a sports car that had ripped off its muffler. Gunfire echoed along with the sharp pings of metal striking metal.

Voices.

"It's not working!"

"Keep moving!" a deep voice bellowed: Noise.

"I got a better idea."

My vision clearing, I crept forward to poke my head over a fallen tree, its bark speckled with fiery red blisters that didn't look friendly. I saw the source of the engine, a machine that appeared to be the love child between a VW camper van, a tank and spider. At first I thought it was a product of the shallowing, but it had no mixing of reality in its structure. Within it, Jules and Jowls' auras sat. Sparks flew from a roof-mounted, cannon-like focus as the bullets ricocheted off it, golden flashes of light indicating that a ward, not armor, protected the delicate machinery. Two long, three-jointed limbs extended from the roof, their pinchers ripping chunks of rocky growths of sparkling tass from the trees and depositing them into a hopper on the roof.

I felt Veronica enter reality, the bond flooding with a panic of thoughts.

Get DOWN! I roared at her even as the contraption's arms paused. The cannon jerked in the direction of the portal with an alert vrrrt!

A man burst from a bush 200 feet away clad in green camo. He bowed his goat-horned head and charged.

"COVERING FIRE!" somebody shouted. "AIM FOR THE TURRET!"

The forest lit with the flashes of gunfire. Dirt churned as the van-tank's treads clawed up the earth below it. It lurched backward, the turret wheeling toward the goat-man. Something gray flew from the man's hand. The turret shot out a neon bolt that arced into the runner. He disappeared, but the gray tube flew true, twirling over the turret and thunking onto the roof. I ducked down beneath the log. A pregnant second later, it exploded with the sound of screaming metal. The wards flared, turning the van-tank into a golden egg in my vision, an egg that the arms had been way outside of. When the rain of sizzling woodchips stopped, the van-tank was in full backpedal mode, the engine roar punctuated by the sharp beeps of a backup alarm. I ducked again as a ricochet whistled right by my ear.

This... is not what I was expecting, Veronica noted.

Did I forget to mention the Veil doesn't work here anymore? I thought back.

Peeking through her eyes, I got a literal bird's eye view of myself, and the dozens of individuals in camouflage stalking toward the retreating vehicle. Only one carried no gun. She carried a sledgehammer in a single two-fingered fist.

Friends of yours? Veronica thought.

The gang stopped firing. One of the men lifted a walkie-talkie to his lips. "All yours, road block."

"Roger," the box crackled back.

A distant boom vibrated the ground beneath me.

"Amateurs," Rudy muttered from somewhere overhead before the walkie-talkie crackled back to life.

"Negative, Green One. Fucker plowed right through."

The entire group sagged and several cursed.

"We stopped the harvest and damaged that damn thing," Noise said. "That's enough for today."

Figuring that was as good a cue as any, I stood and said, "You'll do better tomorrow."

The whole damn unit swung around as if they were all synchronized swimmers. Let me tell ya, eleven barrels are a lot of guns to stare down at once. I recognized several of the cops I'd run into on their way to becoming hunger nibbles. Every one of them sported echoes of reality collisions. May's skin had turned green and her eyes seemed to be composed of ice crystals. The guy next to her had only one boot; the other foot ended in a cloven hoof. Noise stood surrounded by the squad of mongrel people, unchanged since she'd shoved me into that log, her amber eyes large and round.

"Thomas!" she bellowed, then she was on me like a two-ton puppy. Gravity went on vacation as I was snatched, tossed in the air and hugged. Then she repeated the cycle again. "I thought you'd gone and offed your stupid self," she finally said as she ended a brutal cow-wolf hug.

Rudy's chittering laugh rained on down.

"You want a round too, Rodent?" Noise grinned up into the tree as I attempted to get my lungs working again.

"Nope! I'm fine with the show! You got any cashews?"

"Did you find them?" Noise asked me.

In answer, Veronica cawed, and the other Blackwings fluttered down from the branches. Veronica informed me that she'd stay feathered until we could get her some proper clothes.

Dorothy sprang into her human form within Noise's personal space. "What the hell is going on? You worked with technomagi before! And where did all these Blended come from?"

Noise gave Dorothy the look of a Great Dane being charged by a teacup Terrier. "It's a war. And nobody's winning."

"We can change that," I said, "but we need food, Noise. Nobody here's had anything substantial for weeks now. It took all we had to get back."

Noise grimaced. "You're welcome to what we have, but it's not much. There's surprisingly little food in Grantsville. I don't know if the technomagi know it, but they're starving us out, and the Cannibal Zone is growing every day."

"Cannibal Zone?" Rudy said, beating me to the punch.

"That's just the start of it. We'll explain later. Follow me. We gotta move." Her companions were starting to look nervously up at the sky.

43

Noise led us out of the warm jungle with the blistering trees and back into a forest with fresh snowfall. I didn't recognize the area, but it was northeast of town, the least developed corner where the evergreens grew. Clustered beneath them was a small camp full of old canvas tents. A few brighter modern tents were there too, but they were all nestled near the trunks of the largest trees. People were there, but I didn't notice them, as my nose detected something warm and meaty drifting through the air. I zeroed in on the source of the scent, a large pot in the center of the camp.

Without a word, a bowl was ladled out of the pot and placed in front of me. Or attempted to be. The bowl made the journey to the ground while the gruel, or stew or as far as I was concerned hot ambrosia with a few chunks of heaven, were inhaled into my stomach faster than the velocity of a laden sparrow. I could have consumed the entire pot myself, but I was driven back by the sheer velocity of three canine tails.

"Oh my! Oh my!" croaked the woman serving up the gruel. "You brought friends. Do they all talk?" I recognized her despite the icicles protruding from her bald head, the same woman I'd pinned to the counter back at Grover's while attempting to avoid being shot.

She had no time for small talk, as four crows became a murder of skeletally thin women among the canines, dressed in scraps of fabric that had once been dresses.

Not a single thought, Veronica warned me when I recalled her desire to find clothing. She forced everyone into an orderly line with herself at the back, all despite the fantasies playing in her head about seizing the pot and plunging her face into it. Her stomach howled for the stew even louder than mine and the bowl had been the barest of appetizers for me. In my starved state I could easily pack away twenty pounds of meat.

The old woman served everyone and brandished a stout wooden spoon at me and anyone else who went for seconds. Tack attempted puppy eyes and SMACK! went the spoon on his nose.

"Told ya." Rinoa chuckled as Tack came back to hid behind her legs, whimpering.

"I assume these are friends of yours?" The old lady directed her gaze behind me.

I found Noise standing there, arms crossed. Rudy sat on her shoulder, his arm shoved into a foil bag of Planters peanuts, which spoke volumes of his own desperation for food. Noise's eyes were on the magi, her head shaking in disbelief as they licked the last bits out of their bowls. "This here is the Cavalry."

The old woman only snorted. Polite, that one was.

Noise gestured to one of the men that had been on the raid, a tall man I didn't recognize, and told him to dig up some clothing. Ill-fitting jeans and overly large t-shirts were quickly distributed to the Blackwings. All but Rinoa looked uncomfortable. Veronica had started devising a spell to transmute the clothes into a dress as soon she had been handed the package but reveled in the feeling of clean underwear.

The camp had at least two to three-hundred staying in the shadow of the evergreen canopy. Almost everyone had some obvious feature that had been gained from transitions. Moof-hood and her band of merry mutants. Nobody tried to make conversation. They just stared like they weren't sure what to make of us. Only Noise offered a smile, which we followed into a meeting tent.

In that tent hung a map of Grantsville, and then I understood. A full third of the map was covered in black outline.

I wasn't the only one either. Rinoa and Veronica stopped and stared at the map, and then Noise. Noise settled herself cross-legged at the head of a long table down in the center of the tent.

"The Black Plane?" Rinoa said as Veronica pawed through my mind about the zombie-cannibal-spewing shallowing.

"We call it Hunger," Noise started. "Given its rate of spread, it will reach this camp in two days."

"Is everyone within it..."

"Mostly evacuated, to what we're calling Moo-town. A shallowing with the... mildest of side effects."

"You put them in a shallowing?" I said.

Veronica studied the map. The center of the town, the most populated areas, had been carved into colored sections. "Are all these outlines shallowings? Moo-Town? Iceville, The Jungle, Melting Pot?" Only the heavily forested and sparsely populated areas near the edges of the map were free of some color. "They really did it then. They've doomed themselves."

"They certainly did something," Noise grumbled. "Hours after Thomas and Rudy left, we lost all internet, power and nearly everyone found themselves a resident of a shallowing. The lucky ones, the ones who already had an echo, changed slowly. The others are part of the shallowings. I gathered up everyone I could find who wasn't screaming or rooted to the ground and brought them here. That was about a week ago."

"And you're trying to prevent them from harvesting tass?" Veronica observed. It made sense. The technomagi only had one familiar now, Jowls. They could probably use the tass they had to crush the townsfolk, but every bit they used was less they had to buy their way out of the Inquisition.

"It's all we can do. They've warded off the park. We can't get near it."

"And both of the town's grocery stores are no longer grocery stores," I said.

Noise nodded. "We're scavenging food from any house we find, but I have three hundred people. Even a well-stocked house doesn't go far, and if the residents are there, they don't always want to share."

"So you're starving each other out," Dorothy said. "That's so stupid! Why don't you just sell them the tass?"

"Because Jules and his cronies are going to get everyone killed!" Rinoa snapped. "Black plane, remember? There is no tass there. It's eating tass!"

"They're not stupid. Not stupid at all." Veronica still stared at the map. "They're maximizing their yield. What's the Melting Pot? Is it navigable?"

"No, everything there is melted into splotches. It's all this lake of shifting multicolored wax," Noise answered.

Veronica stared hard at the Melting Pot. It was the shallowing first in line to be swallowed by the black. The Jungle surrounded Valentine Park. "These shallowings were laid out in order of ease of harvest. A shallowing like Melting Pot will take years of study to figure out a safe way to harvest and forms a temporary barrier to the Hunger. How often do they attempt to harvest? And how long does it take for you to shut them down?"

"We managed to wound a few of them early as they exited the park. Now they just appear. I have scouts with keen ears posted. Takes a good hour after detection to disrupt them. And I still lose people," Noise said.

"They are gathering tass. But they shifted everything to shallowings so they didn't have to be punctual," Veronica thought out loud. "With shallowings, unlike transitions, the tass will grow over time. In fact, it's best to wait till the last minute. We're in a bubble of space."

"If Jules could have cut the Black plane out, he would have," I said.

"But he can't because?" Veronica asked.

"All the planes are tied together, snared on a machine left here by the Archmagus. He used that machine to twist space around the town itself." I showed her what I knew of the machine that Jules had built.

Veronica frowned in thought. "Moving planes like that would take tass."

"They had tass," I said. "A lot of it. Nearly three hundred groat."

"Yet they needed more," she said. "A lot more. So they invested it. They used it to align all the planes to create shallowings."

"But it's all going to get eaten by the black. Can they harvest enough tass to make it worthwhile?" Naomi said.

A dark thought flickered through Veronica's mind. "Not

in the amount of time they have, and not with our friends here harassing them. Unless..." She stopped and stared at the map.

"Unless what?" Noise asked. I winced as Veronica's thoughts crystalized.

"You destroy them," Dorothy cut in. "You rip them apart."

Naomi covered her mouth in shock. "When the grove died..."

Veronica pointed a finger in her direction. "The great trees produced a great bounty of tass as they died. Their wood was laced with it. Nearly everything within a shallowing becomes tass when the realities are forcibly separated."

"You just gather everything within the area! It would be easy to sort out after the fact," Rinoa said.

"What happens to all the people inside them?" I asked.

"They die," Rinoa said. "But Jules won't care, because everything in this entire bubble is going to die because of the Black Plane. It will consume everything without the Veil to stop it."

"So Jules is going to beat it to the punch." My ears wilted. "We have to get everyone out. Can we... pull the people who're part of a shallowing out of it?"

"I'm afraid they're lost, Thomas." Rinoa looked down at her fingers.

Veronica shook her head. "No, because in order for a true shallowing to occur you need the Veil. It knits realities together. No Veil, so they're not real shallowings. They're more like long-term transitions. If you pull someone out, they should revert. At least somewhat."

"Nothing changes if someone leaves one of the shallowings," Noise interjected.

"Because reality here is putty!" Veronica replied. "For

example, that cannon on the top of that tank-van abomination? It's not killing people."

"It's not?" Noise sat bolt-straight.

"It's a space-bending spell, not an energy spell. It probably shuffles the victim sideways out of this plane slightly. Here that's more efficient than blasting them with kinetic or photonic energy."

"You mean all the dozen people that I've seen disappear with that thing could be alive?" Noise asked.

Veronica winced. "I don't know. Unless the designer intended it to be nonlethal, they could have survived the bolt only to suffocate in the void. I'd need to have it in my hands and undamaged. But if that's the case, we might be able to modify it and link it to the grand portal in Las Vegas. We could zap them all out of the shallowings. As I said, space in here is like putty. That's why we had to come back here. We didn't have the tass to pierce a more solid reality."

I inhaled. "So the plan is simple. We break into Valentine Park, possibly beat up the technomagi, steal their tass and use it to evac all the people we can save before this reality pocket consumes itself and implodes."

"Couldn't we just harvest some of the tass for ourselves and get a message to the Matrons?" Naomi asked.

Veronica shook her head. "The technomagi must know we're back. We do anything major and they're likely to figure out where we are. Right now the main thing we need is proper food."

A man barged into the tent, panting as if he'd been running. "Excuse me, ladies! Sorry to interrupt!" He saluted Noise. "Captain, we have a development."

Fear flashed through Noise's amber eyes and her hackles rose. "What is it, Alfred?"

"Robots!"

"Robots?" Rudy spoke first but everyone echoed the word.

"Yes sir. An entire army of them just marched out of the park gate ten minutes ago."

So much for planning.

44

Noise and her crew drove us to the edge of Moo-town, where it bordered Main Street. It'd been a strip mall, but now a sea of grass waved from what had been black pavement. The buildings were now a collection of barns and silos, their stylings from a storybook farm instead of the industrial wheat factories to the south of Grantsville. We climbed to the top of a four-story tall silo that had burst up between barns that read JCPenney and Office Depot in white painted letters above their doors.

Across the street, a winter wasteland howled. Ice glinted in the dull light that streamed through gray clouds where buildings protruded through the snow. Frozen people still stood in line to Grover's Grocery despite the shattered exterior.

Main Street stood untouched as a hundred robots clanked down it. Sandra had been busy. In the middle of the army three dump trucks rolled like floats in a bizarre parade.

"*We are out of time.*" Veronica perched on a rail in front of me with the rest of the Blackwings. *That is definitely a harvest crew.* She directed my attention to the mass of spells contained in the bed of each truck. *Those are probably tass purification foci.*

Behind me, Noise stood, peering through a single side of a pair of binoculars that she held between her thumb and forefinger. Her other finger stuck out as if she held a fancy teacup. "They've all got guns, big ones. Shit. And shovels. I've got a crew mining ahead, but if that doesn't work..."

Dorothy suddenly stood beside me. "Fee and I will stop them." She stepped onto the rail and leaped off the silo, regaining her winged form with a flare of her focus.

Alarm coursed through Veronica and she burst into her human form, human arms now pinwheeling for balance. "Dorothy wait!" I moved forward to stop her from falling, but she stabilized, finding balance on the thin metal railing. Dorothy didn't hear or chose not to hear as they winged out parallel to the road. "Impatient! Always so impatient," Veronica fumed. She hopped off the railing and turned to the rest of us. "We need to gather tass quickly if we're going to get through any wards."

As if in answer, purple flared in the distance so brightly it was as if a purple sun prepared to rise over the horizon. The light reached up into the sky and seemed to latch onto something there. Veronica stilled as I passed the image to her and set her mind bubbling with the possibilities as to what the technomagi were doing. None of the possibilities were good.

"Actually!" Rudy piped up from his perch on Noise's shoulder. "I've got something that might help with wards." He leapt to my back and started rooting around in one of the pockets of my harness before pulling out a quarter stick of dynamite wrapped in gold foil, otherwise known as an M80 firecracker. The squirrel grinned.

"How long has that been in there?" I cried, disturbed by the proximity of an explosive to my kidneys. I imagined just what would have happened if a fire mite had crawled into the pocket.

Rudy waved a paw dismissively. "Just since we went to tree-hell. It was a backup plan for getting back. With the right circle, one of these babies can blow a hole straight through space-time."

"AND you didn't tell me? We could have escaped that prison plane a week earlier!"

"Dude, as fun as that place was, trust me, randomly falling through space and time is a lot less fun. That's how I met the Weaver. Besides, I only got the one left. I was saving it for a special occasion."

"Then there is no reason to delay. Dorothy will serve as a distraction. We fly now," Veronica said and nodded at Naomi and Morie. The younger magus took out a piece of silver string and laid it around me, forming a circle.

I saw Veronica's intention and plan. I couldn't protest. There was no time. Instead I asked Naomi, "How much is this going to hurt? And what about Dorothy?"

As if in answer Veronica gripped the rail behind her.

Naomi said, "Stay as still as possible," then she knelt in front of me, touching her hands to the string. Morie took up position behind me. Her aura flared like a column of propane flame.

I'd known agony when I met the dragon. Nothing compared to the searing torture that it'd been put through. Yet that ultimately had been someone else's pain. As the fire claimed my body, it was as if every single bone I had shattered while my own muscles sought to strangle me. The world went white, to red and finally to black. When I opened my eyes, the world had been split in twain.

"DON'T TRY TO MOVE. YOU'RE IN SHOCK!" a giant over me thundered. The giant flared into blue flame and enormous eagle wings extended from the flame. The eagle screeched and terror lanced down my spine.

HAWK! HAWK! HAWK! Something in my head screamed at me. I found my own voice and croaked in terror. My legs moved, but they moved wrong, the muscles backwards. The world lurched and then I was seized by the talons of that huge bird.

Veronica curled into my mind, pushing away the last vestiges of the pain. *Calm down. It's okay. It's all part of the plan, remember?*

Naomi couldn't turn into a bird big enough to carry a cougar. And they had no time for me to learn how to fly, so with me in her talons and Rudy on her back, Naomi lifted into the air and flew toward the park where Jules and Jowls were getting ready to murder more people.

I shut my eyes against both the sight of the ground and the vertigo of seeing the world through non-binocular eyes. My arms, my wings, spasmed, wanting to stretch open. The way the air tore at my feathers was wrong, so wrong. I needed to face into the wind.

I opened one eye to see the Blackwings behind us. Veronica, Rinoa, Tack and Morie surfed in the wake of the eagle as it tore through the air. My flock. A euphoric feeling of belonging rang through my head like a gong.

Before I could even process that, the ground approached. It was rather hard. I barely had time to get my legs under me before an icepick seemed to split my head open.

"Hold him! Hold him!" Someone said before the pain burst my eardrums and the outside world shattered under the weight of the agony.

I'm sorry. I forgot it hurts so much without the focus, Veronica's thoughts drifted over me as she stroked my side.

I couldn't even manage to grumble at her. The pain disappeared, leaving only exhaustion. Relief coursed through me as Veronica stroked my own fur. A little voice in me protested that thought. *You're human, you big dolt! Don't you remember?* I tossed that voice back into the recesses of my mind. At the moment all I wanted to do was enjoy the warmth of my magus and the feeling of her fingers running through the few patches of fur that weren't singed or tangled.

"Veronica!" a voice spoke. "You don't have time to cuddle. That's why we flew."

"Give him a minute more. Forcing a cat's mind into a crow's head is a bit disorienting."

Veronica scratched my ears as I fought down a purr. After putting me through all that, she didn't deserve a purr. I wasn't some canine who'd instantly forgive any slight. Forgiveness was going to cost her some mighty fine slabs of meat after all this was over. Yes indeed!

I popped open one of my eyes and revised my previous thought. She owed me a pile of prime rib IF we survived this. Jules had been busy! We'd landed in a sheltered area in sight of what had been the front entrance to the park. The gate had been replaced with a ten-foot-high wall of gleaming metal. Golden gems were set into the top of it every ten feet or so, declaring that this area was well protected. Opening the other eye, I found the actual gate by locating the road that seemed to vanish into the wall. Behind the wall loomed a stout tower about four stories high, which by Grantsville standards made it the tallest building in the land. Rectangular in shape, steel panels had been riveted to the skeleton Noise constructed. Four spikes jutted up at the sky from the four corners of the roof, which crackled with purple energy and projected it upwards. Above it the sky itself appeared to be slowly bending.

How had they built this compound within a week? I stood and looked at the wards. They were simple but dangerous. The amount of amperage they would channel through the body of anyone or thing that touched that wall would ruin anyone's day.

Amateur jobs, Veronica commented as she hauled herself to her feet.

Can you get through them without the bomb?

Of course. But if we want to get in there before that tower does whatever it's starting to do, then absolutely not. Veronica fiddled with a bracelet on her wrist. Blackness swelled from within it, engulfing her hand before forming into a long black blade. I'd seen Sabrina summon a similar weapon when she had fought O'Meara. The world dimmed around it. Veronica approved of my dread. *It is not a nice weapon, but it is effective.*

Veronica directed my attention to Rinoa and Naomi, who were sitting a few feet away, kneeling over a tangle of silver thread. Morie, Tack and Rudy circled around them anxiously. "No No no!" Rudy chided them. "It's gotta be lit before you throw it. I've got tass laced through the wick. If it doesn't burn, the main charge won't go off! Then all we'll get is a dent!"

The two magi huffed in annoyance. The dogs ran off into the woods and returned a brief moment later with two branches that could have served as walking sticks. Each magi took one gingerly, careful of the angry red blisters on the wood.

Rinoa looked in our direction. "We're ready."

Veronica bit her cheek so hard I felt the pain. And I... felt numb. This entire month seemed unreal. People I'd trusted, backed and laughed with had killed hundreds of people and were preparing to murder thousands. For what? A place in history? How had this gone so wrong?

Veronica placed her hand on my head. *The technomagi are scared, Thomas. They stumbled into a crime that will be a death sentence to them. They are doing whatever they can to survive.*

Somehow I'd thought you'd be bitterer at them for banishing you and your Cabal into that hell. You're the last person I thought would be sympathetic.

Bitterness is Rinoa's department. If things had gone differently, you would be storming my stronghold with them at your side. Had Rinoa not taught me that ambition has its own costs, I would have let the munds die, although I think Rinoa would have tried to stop me and maybe Naomi. That is my hindsight hope. She twirled the sword in her hand. *I do not want to kill Jules and his friends. I want to save them.*

"Do it," Veronica said out loud to the others. Hoisting the thread into the air on two sticks, the string unfurled into a web with the tass-laden firecracker in the middle. Rinoa and Naomi charged across the road, each with a stick in-hand, and drove them into the ground a foot from the wall. Naomi's form blurred into that of a bird as soon as her stick stabbed into the ground, but Rinoa stayed, struggling to light the fuse with an uncooperative Zippo.

"Rotten Peanuts!" Rudy charged across the road as a klaxon sounded. Glowing eyes peered over the wall by the time Rudy had made it to the webbing.

It begins! Help me, Thomas! Veronica gripped either side of my head as the circuit between us formed. She flung her consciousness down her thread as I braced her in mine. She slammed back into her body a second later full of energy as the bots on the wall were leveling large caliber weapons at Rinoa. The fuse caught as Veronica flung a small metal disk infused with black energy into the air. Shots rang out. Rinoa dived into her bird form and they missed by a miracle. The disk, the lid of some canned good, landed on the road on its edge, three bullet sized holes in it. The fuse disappeared into the firecracker and it glowed with a piercing white light.

"TAKE—"

BOOOOM! The firecracker exploded in a horizontal column of white flame. It roared both into the wall and back into the forest. I blinked against the brightness and it was gone.

"...Cover," Rudy finished, looking at the lopsided hole that had been burnt through the wall. The ward that protected it had popped in a spray of golden sparks.

"Right girls! We're going to shut down that tower! Follow me," Veronica ordered. Activating another focus on a chain around her left wrist that cast a shell of thin black light around her, Veronica walked unhurriedly toward the opening in the wall. I trotted next to her, and we passed through the wall together.

There were a lot of robots. They weren't all armed. Most looked at us fairly quizzically, their arms full of bundles of construction materials. Still, there were an impressive number of guns pointed at us. I stopped counting at twenty. Sandra stood on a balcony about one story up, her arms enmeshed in a control panel of some type. Her head was shaved and she wore a cap bursting with electronics. She glared down at me with a feral curl to her lips. "STOP RIGHT THERE OR I WILL SHOOT YOU DEAD!" she called out, her voice echoed out from speakers that hung from the corners of the building.

"Fire a single shot and I will cleave your skull in twain from here," Veronica replied.

"YOU WOULDN'T DARE!"

"You're not a magus, dearie. Why don't you and your friends power this down and we discuss the terms of your surrender to the Inquisition?" Veronica asked in a sweet voice.

Sandra smiled, wide and mad. "THERE IS NO SURRENDER TO THE INQUISITION!"

I groaned. "Is this the part when you fling cows at us and then threaten to taunt us again?"

The world flickered as the air surrounding us came alive with bullets. Then in the distance, in the shadow of the building, I caught sight of a purple flare. *Incoming!* I thought at Veronica.

See it. The black sword spun out and parried the purple lance of a displacement spell.

The trio were huddled at the corners of the building, Tom on the left, with Richard and Harry to the right. Two more dots of energy appeared, but Veronica's blade ate the spells as if they were nothing, as easy as a Jedi parrying storm trooper fire. Indeed, the blade seemed to draw in the beams.

"This is useless!" Veronica called out. Yet the technomagi were undeterred and fired beam after beam at us amid the chatter of the rifle fire. Veronica didn't have to move the sword far to parry the blasts, but their mere existence began to sap her limited strength. We'd rested some and gotten food, but all of the Blackwings were still half-starved, a fact that Richard, Harry and Tom angled to take advantage of.

This would usually be the point where Rudy came and saved our butts.

I think your squirrel friend is out of tricks, but Naomi is not!

Abruptly the gunfire stopped, the blackness surrounding us fading to something I could see through. And I saw Sandra above with a face full of bird: a crow and a falcon. Sandra's arms flailed, but Naomi's form shifted to a shape something akin to a dinosaur and tore the electro-studded cap from her head.

One down! Stay close. Charge the one on the left. Veronica crowed through our link.

We charged forward, jumping over the mound of bullets that had piled up around us. Well, she charged. Veronica's sprint wasn't much more than a trot for me. I could have closed the distance in a third of the time, but staying within the bullet shield seemed prudent. Jules' creepy summoned soldiers could still be around.

A flash of blue behind us heralded Rinoa's entrance to the fight. A chorus of ear-shattering blasts stopped the other two technomagi from firing their displacement spells. Veronica's sprint faded into a triumphant march toward Tom as he continued to fire at us in vain, each shot sucked into Veronica's sword like a noodle.

"Give it up, Tom!" I called. I didn't really expect him to. Tom had struck me as the least moral of the trio.

Yet when he nodded, put the displacement cannon on the ground and raised his hands over his head, I found myself reevaluating.

"Alright! You got me!" he said. "This has gone terribly pear-shaped, you know."

Veronica breathed a sigh of relief. "At least one of you is sensible. Really, this was over as soon as we breeched your wards. Turn around and put your hands behind your back. Thomas, if he channels, bite off his balls."

There were devices that could prevent a magus from channeling. Unfortunately, we didn't have any of those.

Veronica pulled out a pair of zip ties instead. *This isn't the one that can shock me?* Veronica thought as her sword dissipated back into her wrist jewelry.

No, he can't. He channels circuit concepts.

Veronica snorted. *No worries there then.* She knelt to secure the ties. "Tell your famil- bond-mates to surrender."

"They're down already." He flared, twisting slightly as he grabbed Veronica's hand. I sunk my teeth into his thigh as Veronica's black sword burst through his belly.

But too late.

Alien diagrams came flooding into my mind. *Resistant to the ampers, serial capacity;* nonsensical words and jumbled engineering terms spiraling up to fill me. I closed the link, but Veronica slumped to the side, eyes wide with shock.

"Gotcha," Tom coughed. "And they all called my anchor useless." Then he fell over like he lacked a bone in his body.

"Why the fuck did you do that?" I shouted at him, but the technomagus was gone. So was the bullet shield.

The world went purple and the sky disappeared.

45

Jowls' voice echoed out over the loud speaker. "You can all cease the hostilities. House Technomagi has won a fabulous victory!"

Yeah, fabulous, I thought to myself, looking at the blood pooling around Tom. Veronica had pulled a knife from her pocket and was scrawling mathematical nonsense in the dirt with it.

I stared up at the sky. There were no stars, no moon, no sun, simply blackness. The only points of illumination were several spotlights anchored to and around the building to aid with all-hours construction. Within the tower a harsh purple light blossomed. Staring into the dark of my eyelids, I saw Jules on the third floor of his tower, bent over a criss-cross of magical circuitry. Surrounding him were the green outlines of his summoned soldiers.

That's where the soldiers had gone. He'd pulled them back to protect his own ass. I needed to get the drop on him.

"RINOA!" I roared. "BLOW ALL THE LIGHTS."

No answer.

In a moment of horror, I realized I couldn't see her. Had they gotten everybody else?

"Rinoa," Jowls' voice crackled out of the loud speakers. "That's the chick with the colored hair, right? I don't see her aura, kitten. No wait, I see her. She's been shifted sideways by the trio's little toys. Would you like her back, Thomas? Perhaps a little medical attention for Veronica there? It is over."

A squad of three soldiers broke off from the group upstairs. Rinoa was gone, but I could still see Naomi on the other side of the building. Her outline was larger than it had been, glowing with the power of her anchor. Jowls could probably see her as well as I could. Had they bothered with actual cameras? I looked back at Veronica, a magus probably more powerful than Jules, reduced to desperately scratching symbols in the dirt. I opened the link a crack, but her brain was like a progressive metal concert composed of mad math.

My best chance was going to be taking out those soldiers before they shot Naomi. They looked to be traveling down in a circular pattern, a spiral staircase perhaps. I crept around the far corner of the building as Naomi rounded the other side with Morie and Tack at her feet. She'd taken the form of a wingless harpy, her taloned hands cradling one of the trio's displacement cannons. Our eyes met and we nodded. I had no idea what we were nodding about, other than a vague "hey, I see you."

I gently unhooked myself from Veronica's mind. Understanding the circumstances, Mr. Bitey didn't materialize and immediately touched himself to Naomi's consciousness with an offer. *Temporary binding for this operation.* Naomi's eyes widened and Morie's ears went back for a moment, but they nodded.

Three soldiers burst through the back door of the building. The first disappeared in a flash of purple from the muzzle of Naomi's weapon, and I pounced on the second. The third fired a shot before disappearing in a second purple blast.

An inarticulate howl of pain blasted through my mind. I looked up from the sack of meat I was standing on to find Naomi clutching a bloody shoulder. *It's okay. I can heal it. They got Rinoa with a lucky shot beforehand. Almost got me too, but I think the black guy missed on purpose. Tack says he can still feel her, but she's in a black void. She can breathe at least. How bad is Veronica?*

Veronica's down, unless you know how to reboot her?

"Aww, looks like the last Blackwing has an owie." The speakers crackled as Jowls cackled. "OH, it feels so good to have a microphone that works! That can hear me! This is fun! Yes, yes, Jules, I'll focus on negotiations. You realize this is going to be a monologue, right?"

Naomi grabbed Morie with both hands and closed her eyes. Both of their auras flared.

"GOTCHA!" Jowls crowed as the air around them erupted into a purple glow.

Naomi! DODGE! I mentally screamed.

Had they not been attempting to do a spell, they would've had plenty of time, but she pulled back from the spell just in time to watch the world around her go black. She and Morie disappeared from my view with a pop, taking a sphere of everything around them, including a small portion of the building.

Tack looked at the shallow bowl in the dirt with an expression of profound despair.

Naomi's thoughts were considerably less demure than

her mouth. The curses that streamed through the link would have challenged O'Meara's best.

Are you okay? I thought at her.

I stopped the bleeding, but now we're in the dark somewhere, Naomi thought.

It'll be fine. I'm here with her, Thomas. We can still make a spell. We can make it back. Morie's thoughts sounded like they'd been shouted through a tube.

I've never bent space on my own! Naomi responded.

We all helped with the portal from the burning place. We just have to do that again. This time we have Thomas' thread to guide us. Morie's thoughts were calm, soothing.

How much time will you need? I asked. I could feel Naomi's fingers questing for her spool of thread.

I really have no idea! As much as you can buy us. We'll work as fast as we can! Morie assured me.

"Now let's just put Veronica in a safe place as well," Jowls called.

I turned to watch the identical effect happen to where I had left Veronica. My heart dropped into my gullet. Tack pushed up against me and whispered, "T-that's it then? We're doomed?"

"And that will take care of all the magi. Just two familiars left, I believe. You'll notice we used nonlethal means of subduing everyone. Unlike you and your avian-themed thugs. Sandra up here's nearly dead from blood loss and I watched Tom wink out. You're going to answer for them too," Jowls taunted.

Tack wilted further. I nudged him and pointed my muzzle at the hole in the side of the building. "What's Rinoa telling you?" I whispered.

"That if we hadn't killed Neelius, all of this never would

have happened. It's all gone so wrong. She's... not doing well in the dark."

"Then have her focus on your eyes," I said.

"And it's all kittens and puppies on this side," he whined.

"There's some light here, even now," I urged.

He swallowed but nodded. "What do we do?"

"Follow me," I said with as much conviction as I could muster, but I really had no idea what the hell I was planning.

Above us, Jowls had continued to talk, explaining that essentially they had put the entirety of Grantsville in the dragon grinder and if I didn't surrender this instant they wouldn't fish out Noise and Dorothy before they turned the thing on. I loved Noise despite this cat/dog romance impediment, but I'm pretty sure she'd punch my skull in if I traded her life for ten thousand others. I didn't want Dorothy to die either, even if she was a bag of hot air. Really, I'm in favor of nobody dying. But if I gotta choose, then it's bastards who think that I'd ignore the lives of helpless folk who die first.

Tack and I slipped through the hole in the corner of the building, hugging the wall. A central pillar dominated the interior, an apparent improvement and refinement on the pill that Jules had first deployed into the dragon grinder. The pillar pulsed with magic, shifting colors flowing through its bulbous components. I understood why Jules had built the building. This device was the opposite of a stone monolith, more a stack of devices haphazardly cobbled together. A rectangular scaffolding had been constructed around it and various bits had been clamped to it. Really, I could probably kick the thing and throw it out of whack. Course, throwing a device out of whack that currently contained an entire town might result in some seriously bad consequences, so I put it on the bottom of my short list of options. About two stories up stood a floor that was little more than a grate. On it, all the soldiers stood. The staircase occupied the far corner of the building and appeared to be the only way up. Beyond that floor I could see Jules' outline, on a third floor or so.

"Aw come on, Thomas. You're making me go full-on Mr. Bigglesworth here. Admit it, you lost!"

Actually, if he turns that thing on, nobody gets a damn thing. The hunger plane will eat everything. You have to stall them, Naomi thought, surfacing momentarily from a deep concentration.

How long do I have to stall him? I thought back.

Five minutes, at least.

That was a long time in any situation involving gunfire. The soldiers hadn't noticed Tack and I yet; the corners of the tower weren't particularly well lit. But if I spoke up, they'd find us in a jiffy. The two on the stairway had their guns trained on the door.

"How about you, dog?" Jowls crowed, "Tack, right? I bet Rinoa's having a grand ole time in limbo. Just hanging out in the void. Is she cold? You know she's in the bag too."

Tack growled. I nudged him to silence.

I crept along the wall. If I could just get the pillar between myself and the guards... A quiet creak from the stairway was all the warning I had before gunfire exploded. I leapt for the pillar. It almost worked, but a stabbing pain cut through my hind leg as I landed. The leg crumpled underneath me and I fell. I dragged myself behind the pillar. Bullets pinged into the far side of the pillar and the world around me flickered.

"STOP! STOP FIRING RIGHT NOW!" Jowls howled, his voice producing an ear-splitting feedback. "OW!"

A bullet had gone clean through my thigh and blown a

sizable hole out the other side. It didn't hurt all that much, which a logistical part of my brain knew was a bad sign. *Hey Naomi, I think I'm going to need the cavalry a little sooner. I'm shot.* "Hey Jowls! Just how delicate is this thing?" I swatted the scaffolding. The pillar responded with an ominous whine.

Try not to bleed to death before we get this working, Naomi's mind sang with the focus of her concentration.

"You Fools! Get him! It's just one cat!"

Above, a few of the green men were trying to poke their guns through the grated floor to shoot me. Something seemed to convince them that was bad idea and all seven of them started marching down the stairs.

BOOM! A reverberation shook through the tower as the front door blasted off its hinges, revealing a single clank, fist outstretched and standing in the doorway. On its shoulder stood Rudy, his paws on the sticks of a radio controller lashed to the robot's head.

"Hey Lardbutt! I think you forgot about somebody important! ME!" Rudy pushed forward on the stick and the robot broke into a run, hitting the first grunt head on with the outstretched fist. The grunt's head lost in that collision, messily. The second nearly got his gun pointed in the right direction before catching a robot uppercut. The impact set his gun arcing through the air and clattering to the ground right in front of me. "Who wants a piece?" Rudy hollered in a high pitched battle cry.

Turned out the rest of the summoned soldiers did. Rudy barely got the robot's arms up to protect his perch before a hail of gunfire rained down on him. Jowls howled incoherently over the loud speaker. I looked at Tack, who still stood in the corner, ears flat and worried, looking at me. Well, not right at me. His eyes were on the rather large pool of blood that surrounded me. How had that gotten so big?

Tack visibly swallowed. "S-Stay here. I'm going to t-take care of this. Karma and all." Then the German Shepherd was a crow and took flight.

I looked down at all the blood and called out to the bird magus. *Naomi, I really hate to be a bother, but there is a lot of blood here. MY blood. Tack's about to do something really brave and stupid, and Rudy's getting shot at.* Rudy's bot was taking the steps one at a time, but he kept being driven to the back of the bot and away from his controls by gunfire from above.

I need more time, Thomas!

If I die, then what you're doing won't work either!

Where's the wound? I showed her where and she hissed mentally. *Brace yourself.*

I made sure my tongue was safely contained within my teeth. But it didn't matter. I screamed as the bones in my leg shattered and reshaped, feathers replacing the fur on my thigh and scales covering my leg. A bird's leg was now awkwardly attached to my hip, a foot, and three fingers with a long thumb protruding from the back. Fingers. My head flopped to the ground as the transformation finished, my gaze falling on the gun. A weapon operated with fingers. *Do that again. Do it to my front paws.*

That's way harder. Your front paws will want to be wings. I'm losing my grip on the gate spell.

A shiver of excitement gripped me as the soldiers repositioned themselves to get a better angle on Rudy. *Just do it! Unless something changes, nobody on this side is going to make it another five minutes!*

In response, the bones of my front paws seemed to burst into flame. On the other side of the link, Naomi groaned with effort as the digits of my paws stretched into taloned fingers, my dewclaws once again becoming thumbs.

Despite the pain, I gave a breathless laugh. I'd become a cat with thumbs. I'd become doom and ruination, if not for all humanity, then hopefully for Jules. I picked up the gun. It was lumpy in weird places, but it had a trigger and a pointy end. It would do. I gripped it in my teeth and started to climb the scaffolding. The sheer joy of closing my fingers around something again made the tip of my tail twitch as I clambered up and squeezed onto the second floor.

Purple flared in my vision from Rudy's direction. I set down the gun in front of me and carefully grabbed the stock. The soldiers had stopped firing, and I heard Rudy curse, but the soldiers didn't turn around. The gun didn't fit my taloned hand. My fingers were too long for the grip, but I made do. Lacking a big boney shoulder, I braced the stock against my chest and carefully lined up a talon on the trigger. I pointed the barrel at the back of the closest soldier and depressed the trigger. The gun hammered into my ribcage and green blood splashed out of the creature's body. A wave of shock seemed to go through the soldiers as their fellow fell forward into them.

I pressed the trigger and wrenched the gun side-to-side until it refused to fire anymore. The soldiers either lay on the grated floor or limply leaned on the railing to the stairway, their arms tangled in the metalwork.

"AGH!" Jules screamed from above me. "LEAVE ME ALONE!"

A focus flashed, and I heard a squawk of pain followed by a definite growl. I glanced around. No sign of Rudy or the mech. Another one for the void. Along the wall was another stairway and next to it was a door to the balcony that Sandra had been controlling the robots from, the console still sparking. I started for the stairway but thought better of charging headlong into whatever nastiness Jules had up there.

So I snagged a new gun in my teeth and announced my arrival with a burst of rounds sent up ahead.

Jowls yowled as I went up the stairs clutching the gun in one hand and using the other three limbs to climb. I had no defense against Jules' force wand, so I did my best to keep my head down. Fortunately, I could see his outline perfectly. He held an active force wand pointed away from me, probably pinning Tack to the far wall.

"Stop it!" Jules called down to me. "Every step you take is degrading the harvest percentages! We're so close! Don't you see it? I can cut out the black plane! I can save all the tass!"

I reached the top of the stairs and peeked into the room, firing the gun in Jules' general direction every couple seconds. The room was circular with steel walls, and the central pillar of the device terminated in a dome about five feet tall and wide. Thick tubes a foot in diameter ran out of the dome along the floor at right angles to each other, each pulsing with purple energy. Judging from the angles, they powered the curved horns on the top of the tower that had somehow pulled all of Grantsville inside the dragon trap. The dome had several open panels and spare parts littered the floor around it.

Jules crouched behind the dome. But I didn't see Jowls, just felt his teeth as they sunk into my wrist. My hand opened and the gun fell out of my grasp as I jerked away from the pain. Jowls twisted away from my fangs and raked his claws across my nose.

"NOW! HIT HIM NOW!" Jowls cried as Jules stepped out from behind the dome and flung Tack at me.

I took Tack to my broadside. I heard the snap of bones,

not sure whose, and the force of the blow knocked me sideways.

I hit the metal wall of the chamber so hard it rang like a gong.

Jules stood in front of me, one hand holding the force wand. The other was pressed over his right eye, blood dripping down from under his fingers. His nose was blowing bloody bubbles. Jowls stood at his feet, looking at me with his remaining eye and shaking his head. Tack lay on his side a few feet in front of me, his breath rattling in his throat.

"So this is how you repay all our kindness, eh Thomas?" Jowls sniffed as he curled around Jules' legs. "We saved you and your inquisitor friend. And you've gone and betrayed us, trying to shatter our dream!" Jowls' lower jaw trembled as if he were about to cry.

I had two questions in my head. Why hadn't he just killed me? Bleeding like that, I doubted he was thinking straight, but I'd seen that wand move a car. It could crush me to pulp. Unless the wall he had to pin me against was more fragile than it looked. I checked behind me. Yes, that was it. Beneath the sheet metal lay some sort of ward, a mix of gold and purple. I thought to Naomi, *Now would be a real good time to show up!*

Almost there. I'm working on it! Just a few more moments.

Jules pulled his left hand from his ruined eye and awkwardly fumbled for a gun at his right hip.

I hissed, "Well, I hate to be the wet blanket, Jowls, but dreams of mass murder really shouldn't come true."

He growled, "You killed Tom. You killed Cyndi, Sabrina, Cornelius and who knows who else is going to die because you let out a dragon. Now every moment we have to focus on you we're losing more tass to that black plane. You're the bad guy, Thomas. I should have known too. I always fall for the bad boys. You don't keep your word and you stab your friends in the back! So we will fish out all the Blackwings because we're *not* murderers like you! But you can live a few seconds more imagining what it will be like for Rudy and Noise as we set this thing to puree."

Jules flicked his thumb, peeling me off the wall. I floated toward the pair. He pulled his gun from the holster and it slipped from his blood-soaked fingers. The magus swore. I stopped moving and hung in midair. My limbs felt as if they were encased in steel, bouncing up and down as he struggled to keep the beam focused on me and retrieve the weapon.

"No," I said. "That's not okay. You need to spare Rudy and Noise."

"So they can try to kill us?" Jowls tsked as Jules got a grip on the weapon. So much for stalling.

Naomi! I thought desperately as the barrel of the gun swung toward me. *Whelp,* I thought to myself, *I gave it my best shot.*

A gun coughed.

I crashed onto the ground, my feet catching me on the bare metal floor. No pain.

"My jelly JULES! No!"

I opened my eyes to see Jules slumped against the dome, red spreading from a hole in his shoulder. Jowls scrabbled over his legs and slapped his paws over the wound. Jules' stared straight ahead, eyes wide with shock.

"Please no!" Jowls pleaded. "I'm too young to go back to the TAU! Don't die. You're not allowed to die!"

Tack lay sprawled on the ground a few feet away, the misshapen rifle between his paws. He flashed me a grin, tail wagging limply.

GOT IT! And with that thought, purple light erupted

beside me. A round portal formed, allowing Naomi and Morie to step through. *What a mess.*

Jowls ran to her. "Oh sweet, merciful angel! Please don't let my magus die! Please!"

Naomi didn't move. Morie sniffed, and I felt the pang of an alert from him. He dashed forward, grabbed the fat cat by the scruff of the neck and flung him into the portal they'd just stepped through.

Jowls screamed as the portal snapped closed behind him.

I blinked. *Was that necessary?*

We're not taking any chances on this bastard, she thought back. *Try to find some tass while I stop everyone from bleeding to death.* She started walking to Jules but abruptly shifted her path toward Tack and knelt before him. "How you doing, soldier?"

"B-been better. Busted leg. A rib too," he wheezed.

"You did good, Tack." She scratched his ear as she took out her silver thread.

As she and Morie healed Tack's injuries, I watch Jules' aura fade away to nothingness. Veronica's words echoed in my head. *I don't want to kill them. I want to save them.* Then I recalled the family of four devouring their neighbor and realized I didn't agree. If he had lived, no magi court would make him pay for that crime.

Jowls, when or if we fished him out of the void, would go back to the TAU for either reassignment or retirement.

I laughed as a realization struck me. Depending on how deep the bond had been between Jules and Jowls, the shattering of their bond could do significant damage to the mind of the surviving partner. Veronica knew how Neelius had died because of what her Cabal had told her. There was no trace of the duel itself in her mind. That meant, despite being the driving force behind the founding of a House, Jowls might emerge from this completely ignorant of the evil he'd attempted. Is that why Tom had forced Veronica to kill him? The bonds between the trio had been deep. Would that act wipe the memories from Harry and Richard?

It might. Naomi's intrusion into my thoughts surprised me. *They're both alive. Rinoa stunned Richard at the same time he got her. I stole Harry's portal gun out of his hands and shot them both with it.* Naomi pushed deeper into my thoughts. *Come on, let's get you walking and then we'll see about setting things right.*

46

Two days later, the six of us, O'Meara, Ixey, Garn, Rudy, Veronica and I, all stood on O'Meara's front porch.

"O'Meara!" I shouted as I plunged my head into her stomach, enjoying the small oof it drew from her. Her hands flowed down my neck and thumped my shoulder. The air echoed with her laughter.

"Should have known. Should have known you'd come out alright," she said with a sniff.

"Yeah, you should have! Shouldn't have worried at all! He was with me!" Rudy leapt up on the armrest of the wheel chair and was swiftly snagged by O'Meara's meaty arm and hugged. He didn't protest too much, a single "ACK!"

"Sorry, but I'm afraid I didn't get you that tass yet," I said. "I had half of it, but we had to use it all." I tilted my head to offer her a better angle on my ears.

O'Meara stopped petting me and picked up my muzzle to look into my eyes. "You got your paws on fifty groat?" she squeaked. "What did you use fifty groat for?"

Rudy used her bewilderment to make his escape and hopped onto my back.

"He used it to save the Blackwings," Veronica cut in. Mentally, she cringed at the inefficiency of that, but she expertly kept it out of her face.

With a slight sigh I pulled away from O'Meara and circled back around to Veronica to sit beside my current client. "Noise and I aren't the most efficient portal makers." I looked over to where Tallow and Noise were embracing. The cow had finally started to fade, but Noise still dwarfed her sister-in-law. Their tails wagged, and the cubs bounded around their feet. Howls echoed in the distance; the whole pack was on their way now.

"Oh, don't worry about them," Ixey said. "Tallow and Eagle, while not really reconciled, are talking. It was hard for them to avoid each other after Grantsville disappeared." Ixey smiled, but dark circles around her eyes spoke to the strain she felt. "Is the town going to come back?"

A poorly kept front lawn hosted the rest of the Blackwings and the growing werewolf reunion. Beyond that stood a national forest. Jules had taken the entire town, minus O'Meara's domicile, into the dragon's crucible to hide his deed from the Inquisition. Veronica and I both tumbled words back and forth, debating the best way to respond to Ixey's question.

I decided to be blunt. "It's not coming back, Ixey. Grantsville is gone. We managed to evacuate about ninety percent of the people out to Las Vegas, where hopefully their mutations will fade enough for them to be accepted by the Veil. The rest..."

"The rest have been consumed by the Black Plane. Along with the artifact that caused all this trouble," Veronica finished.

Ixey looked down at the ground. "Then... I failed utterly. Our... my protectorate is gone." Ixey still wore the Inquisitor's sword over her back. "I spent a week trying to find the town..."

O'Meara placed a steadying hand on her apprentice's shoulder and squeezed.

Now would probably be a bad time to mention that she got Neelius' murder wrong too, I thought to Veronica before I could stop myself.

That is a mystery that will go unsolved except within the Blackwings and House Morganna. She and Tack will do their penance according the will of the Matrons. They will be lenient.

Fair, I conceded.

Rinoa sat on the grass, Tack's head in her lap, apart from Dorothy and Naomi, who were watching the werewolf reunion. Rinoa had worked harder than anyone else pulling the citizens of Grantsville out of the shallowings and then sang to them in the evenings while we attempted to explain the frightening new world they found themselves a part of.

"So what now, Thomas?" O'Meara said, changing the subject.

"Well, I've promised Veronica to stay on until the TAU find a replacement, or a year, whichever comes first. That plus services rendered should be enough to convince Lady Cavell to fix your link, O'Meara."

O'Meara blinked.

"Most of that time we'll be in Vegas, helping the arrivals get settled. And although we didn't get much tass out of the deal, more than a few of the citizens are showing promising channeling talents, and others might be joining the TAU. If they stick, then I think the population of the magi in North America just doubled," I explained, trying not to imagine the place we had left the refugees, in the tunnels beneath Las Vegas.

O'Meara groaned. "That means the familiar shortage is going to get worse."

I smiled. "It's going to be a great time to be a freelancer." And in the back of my head I remembered what Rudy had said back in the woods: "Magi aren't so frikken special!"

The End

KEEP THE ADVENTURE GOING...

Buy Book 3, High Steaks

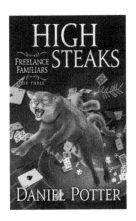

or

Join My Mailing List for Free Stories & News

ACKNOWLEDGMENTS

First I have to thank Amanda Potter for the huge amount of effort she's put into helping me create this book. She is my alpha reader, my idea bouncer off-er, my reality checker, my last pass editor, website designer, book designer and emotional support.

Thank you to my fans who have embraced *Freelance Familiars* and turned the first book into a success. In particular, a huge thanks to my Beta readers, Jennifer, Mary, Dusty, Dave Mac, and Lisa who all helped make this installment a lot less confusing. Thank you to my editor, Garret Marco who punched my prose into something readable.

Shout out to the Living Room Luminaries, my writer's group, and a hug to my friends in the Lightbourne channel for always being supportive.

A huge thank-you to everyone who has shared *Off Leash* and talked about Thomas' adventures to friends and family. I hope *Marking Territory* gives you even more to talk about.

ALSO BY DANIEL POTTER

Freelance Familiars Book 1: Off Leash

Freelance Familiars Book 2: Marking Territory

Freelance Familiars Book 3: High Steaks

Freelance Familiars Book 4: Aggressive Behavior

Rudy & the Warren Warriors (a Freelance Familiars short story)

Rise of the Horned Serpent Book 1: Dragon's Price

Rise of the Horned Serpent Book 2: Dragon's Cage

Rise of the Horned Serpent Book 3: Dragon's Run

Rise of the Horned Serpent Book 4: Dragon's Siege